KILLER SMILE

ALLAN EVANS

IMMORTAL WORKS
SALT LAKE CITY

Immortal Works LLC
1505 Glenrose Drive
Salt Lake City, Utah 84104
Tel: (385) 202-0116

Cover Art by Ashley Literski
strangedevotion.wixsite.com/strangedesigns

ISBN 978-1-953491-62-6 (Paperback)
ASIN B0CFJ7DKHJ (Kindle Edition)

This book is dedicated to my family. Without you, this wouldn't have been possible.

And to Jen, who wonders why any collection of things I buy at Home Depot always looks like I'm about to take hostages.

CHAPTER 1

Wednesday

It was September in Minnesota. The humidity had subsided, while the warm weather lingered. The mosquitos had gone to wherever mosquitos go when they're not biting. Kids were back in school. Life was good, yet Cade's nagging feeling lingered.

Something was in the air.

In his line of work, those feelings could be the difference between life and death. Sure, the tingle on the back of his neck could be nothing more than nerves, or likely, too much coffee, but they also could mean survival.

He supposed the feeling had something to do with the mysterious meeting he'd been summoned to join at the University of Minnesota. Mysterious only because he didn't know the people he was meeting, or why they'd asked for him. Curiosity, as much as anything, brought him to the massive campus this autumn evening. Cade dropped his truck behind the Walter Library, tossing a State Patrol official vehicle card onto the dashboard. No point in risking a tow on the parking-challenged university campus.

The sun had gone down over an hour ago and the breeze had picked up, rippling Cade's windbreaker. He passed a group of students locked into a passionate debate. One of them argued that all first-year students should be taught meditation to reduce stress on campus. The other earnestly countered that that's what beer was for.

As he moved over to give them room on the sidewalk, Cade got a nod from the beer guy and a look of panic from one of the girls who noticed his weapon. "It's alright," he said, as he pulled his jacket back over his holster. "I'm a cop."

Working for the Minnesota State Patrol, Cade Dawkins was one of two full-time plain-clothes investigators out of the east metro division in the Twin Cities. The thirty-one-year-old had already spent nine years in law enforcement and was a recent transplant, having previously been with the Minnesota Bureau of Criminal Apprehension—better known statewide as the BCA. At the Patrol, he'd made his reputation with a once-in-a-lifetime case.

"He doesn't look like any cop I've seen," one of the young women behind him whispered loud enough for him to hear. "He looks like he should be working at Starbucks, if you ask me."

"Amber, you're so bad. Baristas don't carry guns."

"They should. I'd tip them better if they did."

Cade turned around at this and caught the young woman glancing back and couldn't help but smile.

The library's entrance was just ahead, and he checked his watch: On time. He stopped on the front steps. He'd been instructed to wait at the door as the building was secured by keycard. Though it had been renovated, Cade guessed the library was one of the oldest buildings on campus. He'd visited the U of M a few times over the years, but didn't know the campus well. Cade's college days were spent across the river at Hamline University, where he focused on law enforcement, playing soccer, and parties. Possibly not in that order.

A student swiped his keycard to open the door and Cade briefly thought about following him inside, but an older man stepped out and glanced at him. "Are you Cade Dawkins? You must be." He laughed. It was the sort of laugh that encouraged other people to join him. "No one else would wait outside. C'mon in," he said with a wave.

Inside, the two men shook hands. "I'm Darius Crocker, professor of computer science. I appreciate you coming."

Cade studied the man. Early forties Black man, looked to be in good shape once, but had gone soft in the middle. Maybe a former tackle or lineman, based on his build. For someone used to the dark arts of football, he had kind eyes.

"To tell you the truth, I'm not sure why I'm here." Cade shrugged. "Yet, here I am."

"I appreciate that. Let's head down to the lab where we can talk. I'll explain everything." Crocker led the way to an elevator. After the doors opened and both men stepped inside, the doors groaned shut. Crocker pushed the button for the basement and the ancient elevator shuddered and lowered. Neither man said anything for an awkward moment while they rode. The piped-in music was the only sound beyond the creak of the descending elevator. Cade listened to the music and cringed. There ought to be a law.

The doors opened again, and both men stepped out into what looked to be an unused sub-basement. He followed Crocker down the dimly lit hallway that closed in on them as the sideline debris of boxes and dusty furniture grew by the step. This was where discarded university furnishings came to die.

"Is there where you bring all your victims?" Cade asked, genuinely curious.

Crocker looked as if he was going to say something, but then pointed at him and grinned. They stopped outside a metal door where a new-looking, dust-free security box was mounted on the adjacent wall.

"You take your security seriously," Cade said as Crocker punched a code into the keypad.

"You have no idea," Crocker said. "This box uses a patented algorithm on its keypad. This technology randomly reshuffles the numbers into displays on the four-button keys after each use, making it impossible for others to access your code no matter how many times they watched you enter it."

Cade looked around. "I'm thinking you don't get many people down here spying, but you never know."

Crocker chuckled as he made a show of looking over his shoulder. "True. You never know."

"It's been my experience that what usually happens is the access code is given to the wrong people."

Crocker paused for a moment before pushing the door open. He looked to Cade for a reaction. And wasn't disappointed.

"Holy shit. Would you look at this place?"

The room was larger than expected and filled with state-of-the-art computer gear. Racks of computers and networking equipment lined the walls. The cables were entirely maroon and gold. LED lights blinked and computers hummed. A dozen workstations with multiple monitors were set up around the space, and a lone man sat at a wooden table in the middle of the room. He looked like he was born in the same decade as Crocker.

"That was my reaction as well," the man said as he leaned back and smiled.

"This looks like something NASA should be using for their next shuttle launch. Yet, you're hiding this command center in the sub-basement of one of the oldest campus buildings?" Cade asked.

Crocker nodded. "I wanted a place off the beaten path. When I asked around with the facilities people, they'd mentioned this place. It was perfect. Over the summer, I cleaned it up, hauled out a shit-ton of junk. I personally ran the data lines here—I wanted it done right. Brought down the equipment piece by piece. Firewalls, intrusion detection, mass storage systems, and of course, an advanced AI/machine learning system that actually detects interesting things. And as you saw, I secured the entrance with state-of-the-art security. It's my sanctuary."

Crocker gestured to the man at the table. "This is Professor Clement Tubbs, chair of the Psychology department. An old friend." Tubbs, like his colleague, was a forty-something Black man with a touch of gray in his hair. His eyes lit up as he smiled.

"I'm not that old," Tubbs said in what Cade guessed was a regular refrain between the two colleagues. There was an ease about them that spoke of friendship and shared laughter.

The professor's grip was firm when they shook.

"Wait, you two are Crocker and Tubbs? Like in Miami Vice?" Cade laughed.

Crocker smiled and said, "It was Crockett and Tubbs, but yeah, we've heard it before."

"That didn't stop us from being friends, though. Or from working together on this." Crocker looked at his friend, his expression turning serious. "Maybe I should tell you what this is."

Curiosity getting the better of him, Cade leaned forward and nodded. "Maybe you should."

Crocker sat across from Cade, taking the chair next to Tubbs. There was an awkward pause before he spoke. Cade waited patiently.

Crocker cleared his throat. "I'm the chair of the computer science department here at the university. With so many hackers out there looking to cause trouble, computer security has become vital. From individuals to nation-states, hackers are responsible for service disruptions, data and identity theft, trade secret poaching and stolen secrets that compromise leaders. Many of those hacked secrets end up in one place, where they are sold and traded."

"The dark web," Cade said. He'd heard of it, but so far had no experience with it. The dark web was something from the CSI shows and thriller movies.

"You got it," Crocker said. "The dark web is the place to distribute and sell malware, and since computer security is vital to what we teach here, understanding what threats are out there makes a huge difference."

Tubbs held up a hand. "Maybe you should explain to our detective friend what the dark web is. I had no idea when you brought me into this."

"Good idea. I'm used to being around computer-obsessed people and forget that not everyone knows this stuff." Crocker leaned forward, his eyes alive. This was clearly his area of passion. "The internet has three main parts: surface, deep and dark web. The surface web is what we deal with daily. It's the sites that Google finds for you. But that's only ten percent of the internet. The deep web is vastly larger. It houses many password-protected things like emails, databases, medical records and bank accounts. Much of the deep web is transitory and created on the fly."

Crocker paused to take a sip from his water bottle with a golden gopher on it. "And then there's the dark web. The dark web is a decentralized network of internet sites designed to make users as anonymous as possible. Communications are routed through multiple servers and encrypted at every step. The dark web is anything not accessible by standard browsers. Any information can reside on the dark web. It's only considered dark because of its more limited accessibility."

Cade nodded, wondering if there was a point coming soon.

Crocker continued. "But most of the dark web's sites are of the criminal variety. There are online markets where you purchase darn near anything. You can find falsified documents, pot, prescription drugs and heroin. And it gets worse from there. If you want to arrange for a murder for hire or get a rocket launcher, it's probably there. If you want something illegal, you can find it on the dark web."

"This is interesting," Cade said, "but I'm guessing there's a connection to the dark web that prompted you to call me." He let his words hang there as he watched the two university professors.

There was an exchange of glances and Cade had that feeling again. Something was in the air.

Crocker leaned forward. "Yes, and we appreciate your patience while we got you up to speed." He took another sip and set the bottle back on the table, running his finger along the side. Opening a folder, Crocker slid a piece of paper across the table. "But first, I need you to sign this NDA." He held out a pen.

"What do you think I'm going to disclose?"

Crocker laughed. "Good try, but I can't tell you what you could disclose until you sign the paper."

Cade grabbed the pen. "Fine, I'm too curious to not sign it." He scribbled something that even he couldn't decipher when he looked at it.

Crocker slipped the document into the folder without glancing at it. "Thank you. In my research, I came upon a dark website called Orbiting Cortex." He hesitated as he looked to Cade for a reaction, but continued when he didn't get one. "At first, I didn't realize that the name meant something; it felt kind of esoteric to me."

Tubbs spoke up. "Since this is my area, I'll explain. The name is a nod to the orbital cortex, the area believed to be involved with ethical behavior, moral decision-making and impulse control. People with low activity in the orbital cortex are either free-wheeling types or sociopaths," he said. "Without the orbital cortex doing its job, you have unchecked rage, violence, eating, sex and drinking. Serial killers have been found to have little to no orbital cortex activity."

Cade leaned forward. The conversation suddenly became a lot more interesting.

Crocker continued. "Orbiting Cortex is a site for serial killers. Made up of serial killers."

"Really?"

Crocker nodded. "Really. I thought it was odd too, as the typical serial killer is more of a lone wolf. You never hear of them working together. That's why I went to visit my friend here, Clement. But he set me straight."

Tubbs nodded. "While serial killers typically don't work together, they're often quite social. That's why they're able to blend into society so seamlessly and can hide in plain sight. Look at the notorious BTK killer, Dennis Rader, who killed ten victims around Wichita, Kansas. He was married with two children and was president of his church. Most serial killers aren't monsters who act strangely. They could be right in front of you, and you'd never know."

When Cade glanced at Crocker—sitting in front of him—the

professor held up his hands. "Not me. I'm way too sweet. Ask my wife." He let out a loud belly laugh, and Cade decided he liked the man.

"Anyway," Crocker continued, "I found the site and brought in my colleague here. The problem was getting into the message boards section. As you might suspect, it was password protected, and it required us to turn on a video camera so they could see who was typing in the password."

"Damn." Cade rubbed his chin. "What did you do?"

"That's where he showed his genius," Tubbs said, hooking a thumb toward Crocker. "Usually, he hides it remarkably well." Both professors laughed.

"So, how did you get in?" Cade asked, moving to the front of his chair. "I'm guessing you got in if you called me."

Crocker leaned back in his seat, crossing his arms. "Yes, we got in. Remember the deep web I mentioned? I figured the site would have stored video clips of previous password entries. Using my considerable talent, I accessed their records and looked for a user who'd been on the site only once or twice and hadn't been back. I found one with *nevermore27*."

"Why didn't you hack into the site if you already could get into the records?" Cade asked.

"Remember, this is the *dark* web. The access point is barricaded stronger than Fort Knox. I got *nevermore27*'s password from the video clip, but I needed him, too. They needed to see *him* enter the password. So, we used that 4K monitor to project the clip," he said, pointing to a large screen, "Then we aimed the webcam at it and we were in business."

"Brilliant," Cade said, nodding. "What did you find?"

Crocker took a slow, deep breath and shook his head. "It was disturbing. Seriously disturbing. The users shared exploits, bragged, and even challenged one another. It was disgusting stuff, the stuff of nightmares. There's something seriously wrong with these people."

"Well, yeah," Tubbs said. "But what do I know? I'm just the chair of the largest psychology program north of Chicago."

"This is why we contacted you," Crocker said. "We're guessing that since you stopped the Blonde Killer a few months back, you may have some practical knowledge about catching these killers."

A vision of a blade slicing through the air. Blood. Lots of it. Not something Cade wanted to face again.

The Blonde Killer had been a serial killer preying on nearly identical blonde women in the Twin Cities. Cade worked the case as an investigator with the Minnesota State Patrol when several dead women were found as one-car fatalities. When it became clear it was the work of a serial murderer, the case was handed over to the state's BCA, the Bureau of Criminal Apprehension, for jurisdictional reasons. That decision hadn't sat well with the killer, because he carved "fraud" onto the chest of the new BCA lead investigator. The governor put Cade back on the case and his work led to the discovery that the killer was on the governor's own staff. It came down to a bloody conclusion, made worse by not all the blood being from the killer.

"I've caught just the one. That doesn't put me into the expert category by any stretch of the imagination." Cade paused as he studied both men. Neither said anything. "Are you wanting me to travel around the country looking for these killers? That feels more like a federal case, to be honest. As interesting as this is, I don't think it involves me." He stood up, already thinking about the long drive back home to Stillwater.

Glances were exchanged between the university professors. There was clearly more to the story than they'd let on so far. Cade's frustration threatened to overcome his good manners, but he held it in check.

"It doesn't involve me, does it?" But there was that feeling again.

Crocker cleared his throat. "Actually, it does. After you caught the Blonde Killer, there was significant discussion on the Orbiting Cortex site. They were incredibly intrigued by the cat-and-mouse game that went on between you and the killer. Though there was a consensus that the Blonde Killer wasn't as intelligent as he thought he was, they considered you a worthy opponent."

A chill ran down Cade's back. He didn't think it was from the air conditioning.

Tubbs leaned forward, concern written on his face. "Remember we said the killers challenged each other on the site?"

Cade nodded. Goosebumps joined the shivers, and he sat back down.

"A new challenge was issued," Tubbs said. "A challenge that poked the beehive and got them all buzzing."

He paused.

"Damn it, Tubbs, what was the challenge?"

Staring directly into Cade's eyes, Tubbs said, "The challenge was to come to Minnesota, kill here, and outsmart the man who caught the Blonde Killer. We don't know if it means a single killer or several, but we knew we had to warn you."

"But it might be none, too. However, if they do come," Crocker said evenly. "They're coming for you."

CHAPTER 2

Two Weeks Later

Jarn smiled and shivered. It was that thrilling first-time-riding-a-bike, first kiss—hell, first-orgasm—kind of delicious moment as her hope went to wherever hope goes when it's forever lost. The woman was blonde and beautiful, exactly the type he'd hoped for. It was only fitting, after all. She would be a warning shot across the detective's bow.

He'd known right away when he spotted the stunning blonde at the ultra-swank RH Rooftop Restaurant. Like a jungle predator, Jarn had ascended the two flights of the grand staircase, his eyes sweeping ahead for prey as he entered the light-filled dining room encased in a glass roof that should be the norm for Minnesotan restaurants. Flanking the room were two wine terraces with balconies. A bubbling fountain provided light acoustic ambiance, and giant chandeliers—many, many chandeliers—sparkled above the diners. It felt part Napa Valley, part Real Housewives of Beverly Hills. It was, in a word, opulent.

The blonde had long legs, wore nude high heels and a dark berry-colored dress. She sat at a table with three other women, but Jarn didn't consider them. He'd found his prey. This one was dressed to impress and had succeeded far beyond the others in the room. Her flowing blonde hair was worn long with light curls. Her nose crinkled when she smiled and, in her eyes, he saw something more beautiful than the stars.

He would have her soon enough.

Jarn was a meticulous planner. Murder was a dangerous calling and the more contingencies you planned for, the more opportunities you had to kill again. Every detail was meticulously considered for when he acquired his victim. It was far too important to be left to chance. His serial killer brethren were known for their stalking, as their need to kill built up until they had to strike. Jarn, on the other hand, waited until the need was near-consuming and then he'd go to a target-rich environment. He preferred the spontaneity of selecting his prey in their natural habitat. Sometimes, it would be a fancy nightclub or an upscale grocery store. Today, it was an expensive restaurant. Here in her affluent setting, Jarn's thousand-dollar suit gave him both cover and respectability. Like usual, he'd rely on his wits, cunning, and charm to separate her from the herd before he struck.

As luck would have it, when the group said their goodbyes and left, the blonde had stayed behind to use the restroom. While she was making use of the facilities, he'd positioned himself in the doorway outside the men's room. There was psychology that said male strangers were perceived as less of a threat when they walked ahead of a woman.

When the moment came, Jarn took a few steps and then paused mid-step to check his pockets. Jarn turned to her, gave her his practiced smile and said, "I was worried that I left my keys back at the table. The food was so good, I'd planned on returning, but not that soon."

She returned his smile. People often did, not realizing what lay behind it. "It was good, wasn't it? What did you have?"

"The lobster roll, which was a little slice of heaven." He gestured for her to go first as they reached the staircase. "How about you?" He knew what she had, but the conversation had to be had. He took in her exquisite legs as she made her way down.

On the landing, she answered. "I had the salmon. It was so yummy. Even though the lobster roll looked decadently rich, I'm willing to chance it next time. It didn't appear to hurt you any." She touched his arm. *That was a good sign.*

Holding the door for her, they stepped outside into the twilight evening. There was no moon tonight, which was good, as he preferred to work under the cover of darkness.

Their conversation continued as they moved across the lot. His heart quickened when they passed Jarn's rental car. She was so close, but they moved on until they reached an expensive white SUV. "This is me," she said.

"I never caught your name," he asked. His hand slid into his pocket, feeling for the comfort of the knife handle.

"It's Kimberly," she said with another of her dazzling smiles. "What's yours?"

"Mr. Jarn, at least that's my byline for my reviews. I'm a freelance restaurant critic for Twin Cities Magazine." There wasn't actually a Twin Cities Magazine, but it had a familiar ring. "You can call me Nathan, though."

Her look was one of delight. "Oh, I love that magazine. I wonder if I've read any of your pieces."

"I hope so," he said. "In the latest issue, I reviewed that new restaurant on Seventh. The food rivaled the ambiance, which was out of this world. It felt like a jungle in the private dining area. I felt right at home." He gave her a smile, which she returned.

"That place is on my list. I'd love to read your review," she said.

"I have a dozen copies of the new issue in my car," he said, dangling his bait. He hooked a thumb toward his nearby car. "C'mon, I'll happily give you a copy."

His eyes swept the lot as they walked. There was no one close, other than a couple headed inside.

Jarn walked to the rear passenger side and opened the door. His breathing was slow and steady, and he was sure his pulse hadn't moved over 60 beats per minute. Calm and cool until the moment he took her. Reaching into the car, he pulled the syringe from the box on the floor, hiding it under the magazine he'd purchased at Target.

Jarn turned and smiled.

His prey didn't see what was coming as she took the offered magazine. Pouncing, Jarn latched onto her wrist with a vise-like grip and pulled her in. Wrapping her up, he plunged the needle into Kimberly's neck. The sound of her panicked alarm echoed across the parking lot. She struggled momentarily before collapsing in his arms. Jarn guided her onto the rear seat and pushed the door shut. His predator eyes coolly scanned the lot, but no one was there to look in their direction. He took a deep breath, enjoying the cool evening air.

Leisurely slipping off his suit coat, Jarn draped it across the passenger seat and climbed inside. He reached back and brushed the woman's hair from her face.

She reminded him of someone from his past, also achingly beautiful.

Jarn buckled, started the engine and checked his smartwatch. 60 beats per minute. Still in control. He put the vehicle into drive and eased out of the lot.

Taking the Crosstown freeway east, he merged onto 35W toward downtown Minneapolis. The highway was only moderately busy, and his GPS app said he'd be at his destination in thirteen minutes. He expected the woman to be out for the duration of the trip, but if she awakened early, he'd be ready. A second syringe sat next to him on the seat. One of the tools of the trade.

As Jarn approached the looming buildings of downtown Minneapolis, he took the first exit and turned west. This was the off-campus housing area of the University of Minnesota, and the sidewalks were filled with young people. His GPS took him through a retail and restaurant-filled area that led to a bridge over the Mississippi to the downtown area. Minneapolis was a beautiful city. He was happy he'd decided to come, not just because he'd been concerned about wearing out his welcome back home.

Too much killing, he guessed.

In fact, a quick peek at the GPS told him he'd be killing again soon—Jarn was almost to his killing spot. Picking the right location was part of the fun. You want to strike the perfect balance between safety and making a statement. Jarn liked his statements to be loud and bordering on the spectacular. Go big or go home.

Nicollet Island was an island across the Mississippi from downtown Minneapolis. It was a peaceful historic retreat in the middle of the busy city. With beautiful skyline views and brick-paved streets in the housing part of the island, it felt like you'd been transported back in time. While that appealed to Jarn, he was interested in the other part of the island. The quiet part.

The woman was beginning to stir as Jarn pulled his vehicle to a stop on the island's northern tip. The area was deserted, and he had no qualms about muscling her out. She nearly collapsed against the car as she got her feet underneath her. Jarn noticed she'd lost a shoe. "Stay put," he growled. He reached into the back, grabbing his bag and her shoe. He handed her the shoe and pushed her forward on her wobbly legs.

"What's going on?" Kimberly asked, starting to get her bearings. "How did I get here? Did you do something to me?" She didn't seem angry or afraid, just confused. He could work with that.

"You fell. We're going to get you some help."

She didn't look convinced, but it was all good as long as she walked where he pointed. Following a path, they plodded along with an occasional stumble from the woman until they reached the entrance. Jarn grabbed her arm, and she turned on him.

"I'm not going to get help, am I?" Kimberly looked resigned. Sometimes they fight, sometimes they don't.

Jarn shook his head. "I'm afraid not." The knife was in his hand now. He showed it to her.

"Will it hurt?" Her reaction was beyond the pale. No panic or tears, just curiosity. He studied her, wondering what was going on inside that unusual mind of hers.

"I suppose it may, but only for a moment." Jarn took a step toward her and brushed her blonde hair back. Curiously, she didn't flinch. "I don't like to drag these things out."

Her gaze never wavered, and he felt a bond as he looked into her eyes. She was an odd one, but it was refreshing. "Why do you do these things? Do you enjoy killing people?"

He shrugged; not sure he knew the answer himself. "You couldn't possibly begin to understand. Why does a jaguar kill? Because it needs to kill to live. It's a damn jaguar. That's how I'm wired. I need to kill to live. But I realize it's also a choice, and I choose to kill."

He looked at the woman in front of him. Blonde, curvaceous, desirable, sumptuous. Killable.

He pounced.

CHAPTER 3

The strobe of the emergency lights lit up the Yukon in front of Cade Dawkins' squad. The driver slowed and pulled onto the shoulder on Interstate 94, the 3M headquarters building looming over the scene. The moment both vehicles came to a stop, Cade bolted and crossed between the two vehicles for a shoulder approach. Traffic stops were inherently dangerous and law enforcement studies showed that three simple things can increase the officer's survival odds. The first was getting to the vehicle as quickly as possible to reduce the occupants' opportunity to create problems. The second was tugging on the trunk to see if anyone was hiding inside that may pose a threat. The third was to approach from the passenger side to improve sightlines into the vehicle and to the driver.

Adjusting his equipment belt for the umpteenth time, Cade was happy he didn't have to do this every day. God love the troopers for what they do to keep the roads safe, but he much preferred the comfort of the street clothes he wore as a plainclothes investigator. Between the heavy belt, the vest, and the trooper hat—Cade was not a hat guy—he was totally uncomfortable. At least his being in uniform was only for a short time. Investigators were required to work periodic shifts to stay current on trooper skills and equipment.

That didn't mean he had to enjoy the experience.

Cade knew he was a little on edge—hangry was a very real concept for him—but he didn't want to be doing this. Especially dealing with a potential DWI that could keep him wrapped up for hours.

Cade came up to the passenger window and rapped on the glass.

The man showed surprise to see him at the passenger window, but he rolled it down right away. Cade shined his flashlight around the interior. The man was in his upper fifties with the sandy blondish gray hair many older men often transitioned to. He was wearing an expensive suit jacket, which likely meant he was coming from work or happy hour. Cade decided to get to the point right away.

"Sir, your eyes are pretty red. Have you been drinking tonight?"

Without skipping a beat, the man replied, "Officer, your eyes are pretty glazed. Have you been eating donuts?"

The reply caught him by surprise, and Cade couldn't even feign anger. He simply dropped his head and laughed. There was nothing else he could do. He knew he'd lost control of the situation, but it honestly didn't matter. Cade decided long ago that laughter was the best response to life's absurdities. And as anyone familiar with law enforcement knew, cops used humor as a defense mechanism to keep from going insane from the pressures and emotional trauma of the job.

As he walked back to his vehicle with the man's license and insurance paper, he waved at the second patrol vehicle that had tucked in behind his. It wasn't uncommon to have another squad join the "fun" on slow evenings, either out of support or boredom or both. Cade didn't mind, he welcomed the company. As soon as he slid behind the wheel, his cell buzzed. When he checked the number, it was the governor's office. That could only mean one thing: something big had happened.

With Trooper Swanson taking over the DWI stop, Cade raced toward the governor's residence in St. Paul. The call with Ritter had been typically brief: "Get over here now, something's come up."

Everyone knows someone who exudes the sort of warmth that makes you feel appreciated and special. Governor Winston Ritter would never be that person. If you weren't part of the media or standing in front of said media, Ritter was not the one to give you the warm fuzzies. But turn the cameras on and Ritter could charm the pants off an eighty-year-old catholic nun. Though, Cade wasn't sure if nuns actually wore pants.

Something's come up. It made his heart race.

The governor's residence sat on the most prestigious part of the prestigious Summit Avenue in St. Paul. An assistant impatiently waved Cade down the hall and into the governor's office. A well-fed man with eyes set a little too close—think ferret—Governor Ritter sat behind his massive desk. The cherry wood piece of furniture dominated the room, clearly designed to shout that a powerful man sat here doing important things. The desktop was clear except for a few framed photographs and a silver laptop that held the governor's attention. Ritter's eyes lifted from the screen and he motioned for Cade to sit.

After a few moments of waiting while the politician kept his nose in his computer, Cade picked up the framed photograph and studied the woman captured in black and white. She had dark hair and a severe expression. She hadn't been looking at the camera when the picture was taken.

"That's Eleanor, my wife," Ritter said, without looking away from his screen.

"Nice frame," Cade said, setting the picture back.

Ritter closed his laptop and adjusted the angle of the frame ever-so-slightly. An annoyed look colored his face. "Why are you wearing a uniform? I would have been informed if you'd been demoted."

Cade shrugged at Ritter's snark. "Minnesota requires its Patrol investigators to work the occasional trooper shift to stay current on the job and equipment."

"I wouldn't think either would change any too frequently. Feels like a waste of time."

"I'd have to agree with you. It's not the favorite part of my job." Truth be told, it was one of his least favorite parts. In fact, the only part he disliked more was the political part. The irony wasn't lost on him that he was sitting across from the state's leading politician.

"So, you called this meeting..." The small talk felt like it drained his soul away. "Something happened, you said."

"Earlier today, a body was found in Minneapolis." The governor paused.

"Sadly, that's not uncommon these days."

"But what made this death significant was that the victim was a woman." Ritter paused. "A blonde woman who was well-dressed and beautiful."

Cade felt his face flush.

"How did she die?"

"It sounded like she was stabbed."

Cade let a breath out. Okay, that was different from the Blonde Killer method. He never used a knife. There was always the fear of a copycat killing with high-profile serial murders.

"It sounds like a different M.O. than the Blonde Killer used. I'm sure Minneapolis can handle it. They don't need me."

Ritter shook his head. "You don't know everything yet. It was more than a simple homicide. Her body was found on Nicollet Island near Satan's Cave." Cade's eyebrows rose. "And there was a note that mentioned you specifically."

Cade blinked. "Me?"

Ritter looked irritated. "Yes, you."

His conversation with Crocker and Tubbs came back to him. He hadn't done anything about the serial killer site's challenge because there was nothing he could do. There were no details, no timeline and no crime had been committed. The university professors had promised to be in touch if they discovered any new information, but Cade hadn't heard anything. "What did the note say?"

Ritter handed him a printout. The quality wasn't good, like it'd been photographed in low light by someone after three cups of coffee. He was expecting a ransom note with cut-out letters and words, but this note was painstakingly hand lettered. The elaborate writing looked like something a monk on LSD might churn out in a dimly lit monastery. Unfamiliar symbols bordered the words in the middle. The actual message chilled Cade to the bone.

The weaver of the web kills. But we inflict, we maim, we slay.
Scores will cry out and bleed. Their blood is on you.
You're out of your league, mortal Dawkins.
Death has arrived.

"Holy shit," Cade said slowly, as chill bumps ran up his arms.

"I know," Ritter said. "That's why I'm activating the major crimes task force that you will lead."

After the debacle of the Blonde Killer, where there was a jurisdictional fight for who owned the case, changes were made. While the serial killer had terrorized the state in general and blonde women specifically, the case had been pulled from Cade and the Patrol and given to the state's BCA—the Bureau of Criminal Apprehension. That was until the new chief investigator, Freddie Goodwin, had been brutally carved with a knife by the killer. From what he'd heard, Goodwin was now selling timeshares in Brainerd. Governor Ritter, a political weasel if there ever was one, dumped the hot potato case back into Cade's lap and made things clear: catch the killer or lose his job. Cade had stopped the killer, Marlin Sweetwater, who turned out to be on the governor's own protection detail. To avoid further political fallout, the Commissioner for the Department of Public Safety—who oversaw the State Patrol, as well as the Bureau of Criminal Apprehension and Homeland Security and Emergency Management—created a major crimes task force to be activated for high-profile cases. The task force was designed to be immune to jurisdictional issues and political maneuvering. Cade was picked to lead this new task force, though lead may be an exaggeration as he was the only member.

"Dawkins, this is an effing big deal. We can't let our state become a killing field for this crazy. You're officially granted authority to pull in whoever you need to solve this case."

Cade nodded. "Okay. So, what do we know about the woman? What has Minneapolis found so far?"

Ritter had returned to his screen. "You'll need to talk to Minneapolis P.D. They're not going to be happy you're taking over their case, but c'est la vie. Find a way to work with them."

"Will do. But you know the media will be all over this, too. They love this serial killer shit."

Ritter looked up. "Don't get in a pissing match with them. We don't need any publicity. Just put this one to bed quickly and quietly."

"Understood." Cade stood up and moved toward the door. Something about being close to Ritter made him feel like showering.

"One more word."

He'd been so close, one foot in the hall, but no. Cade sighed and stepped back in.

Ritter held Cade's gaze. "I felt somewhat...coerced...to form this task force of yours. But at the end of the day, it is what it is. And to be honest, I see some benefit in having a task force that answers to me. Do a good job and you'll have more crime-fighting opportunities in the big leagues. But know that if you fail, your career could be negatively impacted. Am I clear?"

Ritter waited for his acquiescence. Cade felt his anger rising but decided to get it over with so he could get out of there. "Clear as can be."

"Good. And change out of that uniform. You look like a barista on Halloween."

Valiantly trying to suppress his smile, it was no use. "So, I've heard. If there's nothing else..."

He was almost entirely out in the hallway and then, "There is one more thing you should know. The victim's body was elaborately posed. No one even somewhat close to sanity would have done what was done to her."

AFTER CHANGING out of the uniform and getting on the road, Cade called his supervisor with the Patrol. Capt. Leah Rejene had transferred to the East Metro District office as the killer blonde case began. She'd been feisty and supportive—always having Cade's back—and let him run his investigation while she ran political interference. Cade both liked and respected her.

She answered with, "I heard."

Cade laughed. "Yeah, I figured you might have. Chain of command and all that happy horseshit." He took Highway 36 toward Minneapolis and merged in behind a Target semi. "Are you okay with me pulling in Rob?"

"Officially, I can't say no. But could you use him sparingly? I'm already down an investigator with you gone."

"No worries, I'll try to use him mainly as a sounding board. He helps keep my roguish instincts in check."

"Roguish is a good word for you." Laughing, Rejene added, "I take it you're on the way to Minneapolis?"

"Yeah, the crime scene is at Nicollet Island. Going to meet up with Minneapolis P.D."

"They won't be happy with you walking onto their scene and taking over." She always looked at the political considerations.

"They'll get over it." Cade knew he didn't think about politics enough. It could be his undoing someday.

"A word of advice. Make nice. You need their cooperation." She paused. "Maybe you put someone from Minneapolis on the task force. That way, with one of their own on the task force, it won't be so much of you versus them."

"That's a great idea. But I have no idea who to conscript. Any ideas?"

There was a pause. "I don't. Most of my career has been in the Rochester area, so I don't know who to grab from their department.

But I'd be happy to make a call to the Minneapolis chief of police. I'm sure he'd be happy to make a recommendation."

"Appreciate your help." After ending the call, Cade looped onto 35W with the Minneapolis skyline looming ahead. He shook his head. Rejene had just solved her potential investigator shortage by suggesting Minneapolis give up one of theirs instead. That was sneaky-good maneuvering on her part. He couldn't help but smile.

Rob also answered with, "I heard."

Rob Zink was Cade's investigative partner in the east metro division of the Minnesota State Patrol. A former St. Paul patrol officer in the capital city's west side, Rob had transferred agencies several years ago. Switching between law enforcement agencies wasn't uncommon. Sometimes you simply needed a change of scenery to keep your career alive—and your sanity intact. That's why Cade had made the switch from the BCA to the Patrol. He'd been ready to quit law enforcement altogether until his transfer gave him a fresh perspective.

They had a unique office arrangement, with both investigators sitting on opposite sides of the same desk—much as they had opposite shifts. Each had their own cases but assisted the other as needed. They overlapped three days each week, giving the two investigators time together. Like many partners in law enforcement, they'd become close.

"How did you find out so quickly? Capt. Rejene?" Cade pulled around a black SUV. Easily 90 percent of all SUVs in Minnesota were black for some reason.

"Yep. I was in her office when she got the call from the Governor's office. Are you at the crime scene yet?"

"I'm still a few minutes out. I'll let you know what I find." He hesitated. "But I will use you more as an advisor than an active participant. Officially Rejene can't say no if I request that you join the task force, but it would leave her without an investigator. So, I'll loop you in as I can."

"No worries. Have you given the task force a name yet?" Rob asked. Cade knew him well enough to hear a smile in his voice.

Cade chuckled. "It doesn't need a name. It's just a task force." He was fast approaching a cluster of cars and sized up his best strategy to get around them.

Rob laughed. "All those branding people are going to hate you. You're undercutting their livelihood. Imagine if McDonald's was named simply Hamburger Drive-In?"

Grinning, Cade cut to the inside lane on 35W before moving back to the outside lane. "Yeah, but isn't the purpose of branding to differentiate yourself from the competition? Last I checked, there wasn't another major crime task force in Minnesota. Hey, I'll be in touch." Cade ended the call, took the exit, and sped down the avenue.

CHAPTER 4

Nicollet Island sat tucked away mid-river below the Hennepin Avenue bridge. Not a likely location for a murder, yet here he was. Cade left his FJ Cruiser near the cluster of official vehicles and jogged toward the crime scene.

Flashing his badge, he was allowed to join the uniformed officers and suits on the other side of the crime scene tape. Cade wore jeans, hiking boots and a flannel shirt with a dark peacoat. His dirty blond hair was worn longer than most of his fellow law enforcement officers. He didn't look like a cop, which explained why a uniformed Minneapolis officer headed him off.

"Hey, we said you crime bloggers need to stay out of here. This is a crime scene, dammit." The man was shorter than Cade but outweighed him by a good seventy pounds. The man had no neck and made up for it with his side-of-beef arms. The officer didn't allow Cade the opportunity to identify himself and lunged for him. When the officer went to grab him, Cade simply pushed the man's arm away.

This appeared to make the man angry, judging by the guttural snarl he unleashed.

"Rogers," said a woman behind him, an air of authority in her voice.

The man froze in mid-swing.

"Stand down. He's one of us." The woman was dressed in her blues, her brown hair pulled back severely, and a gold shield shone on her uniform. She smiled and stuck out her hand. "I know who you are. I'm Kallianne Mogler. Call me Kal. This is my precinct. What brings you my way?" She had the sort of wariness a third-grader had when a fifth grader complimented their lunch.

"Cade Dawkins. State Patrol, but I'm not here in that capacity." He paused and smiled. Mogler didn't return his smile. "Sorry, I'm new to this. Governor Ritter activated the major crimes task force and put me on this case."

Her eyes narrowed. "Wait, you're stealing our case?"

"Stealing is a strong word. It's more of a work alongside each other kind of thing. In fact, one of Minneapolis' finest will be joining the task force. So, we should be able to play nice." Cade tried to give her his best smile.

Mogler stared at him. She wasn't happy about giving up her school lunch.

"I haven't heard anything about this. Who's joining the task force?"

Cade hesitated as he didn't have the name yet as his boss was contacting the Minneapolis chief. There were clear chains of command to be followed, which was one of the things that annoyed him most about the law enforcement bureaucracy. But what could he do? It was like expecting all the slow drivers to move out of the left lane. Some things you had to live with.

"Let me check," he said, pulling out his cell as they walked across the grounds. "I don't recall the person's name, but from what I heard, they're a rising star in the Minneapolis Police department. Possibly the greatest living cop in any police force, anywhere." There was a hint of a grin on Cade's face as he read a text from Capt. Rejene. "Here, we go. His name is Terrance Rooker."

"Wait, did you say Terrance Rooker?" *The name did sound familiar.*

It took a moment before he noticed Mogler was no longer walking alongside. Cade glanced back to find her stopped in her tracks. He wasn't inclined to answer her question—he didn't like where this was going.

"You're using Rook?" she said and burst out laughing.

Cade shook his head. There were times in life when someone laughed, and you couldn't help but join in. This wasn't one of those times.

"What?" Cade asked, but he wasn't sure he wanted to know the answer.

"Rook works with the Violent Crimes Investigations Division. If you've seen his track record, you'd know he can be—."

"Yo, Mog. Have you seen Dawkins? We're supposed to be meeting up. For the task force."

The man standing there was a little under Cade's height but had an extra 15 pounds of muscle that he didn't. His head was shaved, and he had a close-cropped beard. Wearing white athletic shoes, jeans, and a leather varsity jacket, he looked back and forth between Mogler and Cade.

"You him?"

"I am him." Cade stuck out his hand. "Cade Dawkins from the governor's task force."

"Hey. Terrance Rooker. Though most people call me Rook." They shook hands. "You sure you want a brother for your sidekick?"

Mogler coughed and turned away.

"It doesn't matter to me as long as you do your job. Okay?" Cade held his eyes until the man broke out into a grin.

"Just messin' with you. No problem. Don't take life so seriously."

Cade was inclined to mention that maybe they should be serious as they were at a homicide scene, but instead opted for, "Let's go find out what happened here." Cade headed for a cluster of people hanging around the taped-in area. Yellow markers were strewn across the ground and a man was on his stomach with a camera. A dozen other people in uniform stood around doing nothing. A typical crime scene, in other words.

Rook hurried to catch up. "Hey man, wait. What's the name of our task force?"

"It doesn't have a name."

Rook stopped. "Wait, what? Everything needs a name. It would be complete anarchy without names. Do you want to be responsible for the total breakdown of society?"

Cade paused to think of a suitable reply, but Rook didn't wait.

"Think about it. People running around willy-nilly calling things by whatever name pops into their head."

"Willy-nilly?" Cade didn't have a comment for that.

"Exactly. Willy-nilly. It's a technical term for chaos you're probably not familiar with. I went to college." Rook said this with such smugness that Cade had no idea if he was being teased.

"C'mon. A task force needs a name. Everyone knows what Five-o is. It wouldn't be nearly as charismatic without—"

"Charismatic? You did go to college."

Rook grinned. "See? I know what I'm talking about. I'm just saying our task force wouldn't be nearly as impressive and likely to scare the criminal element without a name."

Cade broke into a laugh. "Okay, you have me convinced. Can't be having the criminal element running around willy-nilly and unafraid. So, what do you have in mind?" They moved toward the yellow tape again.

Rook stopped. "Wait, you want me to come up with the name? That's above my pay grade, isn't it?"

Not even close to being able to hold back his grin, Cade put a hand on Rook's shoulder and smiled. "It's exactly your pay grade. Come up with a name and let's get this investigation started."

"This is a lot of pressure for my first day."

Cade laughed. "You got this. Just make it catchy and Minnesota style."

"Five-o," Rook began. "Five-o."

"That's been taken."

Rook gave him a look not dissimilar to the one you might give when someone says, "Why yes, it is raining."

"Wait. I got it," Rook said with complete delight. "Five Below. There's nothing more Minnesotan than that."

"Five Below," Cade said, trying it out. He didn't hate it and honestly, he really didn't care what they called the task force. Rook looked at him with the anxious expression of a teenager who'd suggested a band name for the group practicing in his parent's basement.

"Okay, it works. Get the business cards printed up. Can we get going on the actual case?"

"Wait, business cards?" Then he saw the look on Cade's face. "I see you're messing with me. You can't go messing with a man's business card. That cuts right to his identity." Cade smiled and broke up.

"Man, that's just wrong." Rook shook his head.

They approached the group at the crime scene, where a man knelt by the victim, holding a stethoscope to her chest. It seemed pointless as the knife sticking out of her abdomen made it more than obvious she was dead. But that was how the coroner worked. They needed to pronounce the death before the body could be released.

Rook typed into his phone while Cade stood back and waited.

The man rose to a freakishly tall height and approached Mogler. He pushed up his glasses and said, "She's been pronounced and her body is released. One fatal stab to the abdomen. You have an economical killer. Good luck."

The victim was a blonde woman approaching thirty—before the rest of her life was taken away. She had a similar look to the victims the Blonde Killer had targeted: long blonde hair, stylish and stunning. She had on a dress the color of dark berries that looked appropriate for going out. Nude-colored high heels with red soles dangled from her delicate feet.

Her body had been posed.

She was draped over a boulder on her back. Without the rock, her arched pose would be likely found in the advanced yoga class. Cade walked around her in a circular motion with Rook by his side. The woman's head hung down, and her eyes were open. Something protruded from her mouth, and he was sure it was the woman's panties based on the lace. An open umbrella stood over her, the handle wedged in her armpit. The note Ritter had told him about was taped to the handle. The victim's dress rode up on her legs, exposing more than a PG-13 audience would be comfortable seeing. There was writing on her right thigh and Cade moved into position to see what it was. "1st" was all it said. It looked like it was written in black sharpie.

It was then that Cade noticed the No Dumping sign that stood behind the victim.

"Holy shit," he said. "I hate this guy already."

"This is messed up," Rook said. "No one deserves this."

They took a few steps back and stood silently as they took in the scene.

After a few moments, Cade turned to his new partner. "Thoughts? Observations?"

Rook ran a hand over his shaved head before shoving his hands in his coat pockets. "He's a sick one."

"Anything more specific?"

"The writing suggests that there will be more victims to follow, and this is most likely the work of a serial murderer. The note is either a threat, a warning or a taunt. Or all of the above. The panties in her mouth makes me suspect she was sexually assaulted. The umbrella was possibly used to preserve the note and crime scene, meaning he's not worried about evidence leading to him. Dumping the body right in front of a no dumping sign suggests perverse humor at our expense." Rook shook his head.

Cade nodded but didn't say anything.

"Hey, man. How did I do?" Rook looked curious.

"This wasn't a test, just wondering if you saw anything that I missed," Cade said. "The crime scene feels like we're dealing with an organized killer. Are you familiar with the organized/disorganized serial killer concept?"

"No, man. But I've seen The Silence of the Lambs four times."

Cade couldn't help but smile. "I can work with that. Hannibal Lecter would be considered an organized killer. Some organized attributes include above-average intelligence, social competence, skilled profession, sexually competent, mobile, a planner, inconsistent childhood discipline and controlled mood during the crime."

"Sexually competent. That doesn't raise the bar much."

Cade ignored him, thinking that might be the best strategy going forward with his new partner. "Buffalo Bill from the same movie would be an example of a disorganized killer. The attacks are typically unplanned, and they're violent killings, with no moving of the body afterward. Perpetrators usually have lower intelligence, poor social skills, and aren't mobile which means killings are often close to home. The perpetrators are likely from an unstable or dysfunctional family."

"Got it," Rook said.

Cade put a hand on Rook's shoulder. "I believe this was the work of an organized killer. A meticulous planner, with above-average intelligence and under complete control."

"This guy won't be easy to catch," his new partner said. "Not at all."

"Who discovered the body?" Cade asked Mogler. She gestured to a herd of people standing by the police mobile command van. Nearly a dozen waited there, some in running clothes, some in hiking gear. A group of Minneapolis cops stood watch while plainclothes detectives interviewed several people.

"Help yourself." She waved a hand toward the group.

Cade studied the group and his gaze ultimately latched onto a nervous young woman sitting alone. She sat with her legs tucked underneath while she nibbled her nails. She looked to be around twenty with dark hair pulled back into a ponytail. Cade walked up to her and waited until she looked up. He hooked the "c'mere" finger gesture.

"Why are you bothering me? I'm just trying to get through my day." She looked put-out and a little uneasy.

"We need a little of your time." Rook said. "Talk to us and we can get you out of this shit show."

She frowned. "I won't have to stay and talk with the regular cops?"

Cade laughed. "Nope, just us irregular ones."

The woman perked up. "Good. Those cops are thumpers."

Cade glanced over to Rook, who gave a slight shake of his head. *Leave it alone.*

Pointing to a bench away from the others, he had her sit. Looking between the two investigators, the woman waited. Cade let her wait.

Rook eventually cleared his throat. "We're from the Five Below major crimes task force."

The woman snorted. "Since when does a discount chain retailer care about major crimes?"

Cade almost snorted himself. Rook shook his head. "No, it's like Five-o. Only it's here, not in Hawaii."

She shook her head. "That's lame."

"Maybe you need to rethink the name," Cade suggested.

"I can't, man. I already ordered the business cards."

"Really?" Cade had no idea if Rook was messing with him or not.

Pulling out a notebook, Cade turned to the woman and asked, "What's your name?"

She looked down at her nails. "Ella," she offered quietly.

"Do you have a last name?" Rook asked. "Most people do."

"Then I'm like most people," she said agreeably. "I do have a last name."

Rook stared at her, his eyes narrowing. "Witness is uncooperative," he said as he typed into his phone.

"Wait, what? I'm cooperating." Ella had a concerned look.

Cade shook his head. "Rook, you didn't actually ask her what her last name was, you only asked if she had one. She answered your question."

"No, man. The question was implied. If I'm asking if you know where the train station is, I want you to tell me where it is, not to find out if you know where it is. You don't always have to hit someone over the head with something to establish a connection and learn what they know. The English language is at its most beautiful when you employ subtlety."

Ella leaned forward. "I'm only a college student, but I would think you'd be better at your job if you didn't beat around the bush so much. Do hardened criminals usually respond to your beautiful subtleties?"

Cade turned away as he coughed.

Rook made a scoffing sound. "Like you're a hardened criminal." Rook wasn't going to give up.

"Not that you know of," Ella said. After a brief pause, she continued. "My last name is Steblay," and she spelled it out.

"Well, thank you so much," Rook said as he typed into his phone. "Steb. Lay. Witness cooperates after being shown the proper way to interpret questions."

It was Ella's turn to cough.

"Okay, Miss Steblay, tell us what you saw," Cade said. "Walk us through the events."

"We were coming to the caves."

Rook interrupted. "What caves?"

"There's a series of caves under the north part of the island," Cade answered.

"Actually, while my favorite caves are here in the northern tip, there are also more in the southern part of the island. Anyway," Ella said, "Me and my friends like to explore the caves."

"Can you tell me what you saw?" Cade asked. "When you first saw the body."

Ella gestured toward the crime scene. "We'd just parked, and I went on ahead. There was a guy headed for the parking area. When I'd passed him, I thought it was strange that he was in such a hurry that he almost knocked me over."

"Well, you are on the small side," Rook said. Ella rolled her eyes.

"What did the man look like? Tall? Short? Average?" Cade asked as he jotted in his notebook.

Ella thought about it. "The guy was average. Not tall, not short. He looked like a dad. Nothing remarkable. I would never have noticed him if it hadn't been for the collision."

"What was he wearing?"

"A Minnesota United sweatshirt. And jeans."

"Soccer? He's a terrorist for sure, then. Or he likes his sports to be boring," Rook said.

"Hey," Cade and Ella said in near unison.

"I play soccer," Cade said.

"Me too," Ella added.

"You are both crazy then," Rook said. "Studies have shown a strong correlation between watching soccer and being overcome by boredom."

"Really?"

"I forget who did the study, but they said there were far better sources of entertainment than soccer. Like watching hockey or baseball, or even staring at the inside of a Pringle's can." Rook folded his arms and smiled a rather smug smile.

"Can we get back to the man?" Cade asked, beginning to get irritated. "How old was he?"

Ella shrugged.

"How much do you think he weighed?"

Ella shrugged.

"Any facial hair?"

Ella shrugged again.

"So, you're saying he didn't look out of the ordinary?" Cade asked as he looked up from his notepad.

"No, just a dad. The kind you see pushing a lawnmower or cheering on the sidelines of a soccer game."

"Okay, tell me what happened after that."

Ella leaned forward and clasped her hands. "I kept going, figured

I'd wait up at the entrance for my friends. But when I saw the woman..." She paused, a faraway look in her eyes.

Rook looked over at Cade, who looked back with raised eyebrows.

"It looked obscene to see her that way. I knew she was dead right away." Ella shivered.

"What happened next?" Cade asked.

"My friends came, and then everyone was screaming. We ran back to the car. We called 911 and waited for the cops."

Cade asked a few more questions but didn't learn anything new. They walked her to her car and thanked her for her time.

"What do you think?" Cade asked his partner.

"I'm not convinced the man she encountered was the killer. He may have seen the victim and ran away, just like your soccer girl did."

"Agreed. We should check to see if there are any cameras nearby, but I have my doubts. This is the rustic part of the island. He's probably a dead end, anyway. We may never find anything on him. Toss the sweatshirt and no one could pick him out of a lineup."

They headed back to the crime scene and found Mogler. "Have you found out who she is—who she was?" Cade asked.

Mogler shook her head. She watched as the crime scene crew carefully lifted the woman's body off the boulder. Two of them supported her torso, while a third lifted her legs. A fourth was there to keep her head from hitting the rock. They shuffled her over to a waiting gurney.

"We haven't found any ID or purse at the scene. We've taken fingerprints and we'll see if she's in the system.

"Good," Cade said. His eyes drifted to the boulder. There was something there, and he moved closer. There was writing on the rock. "Hang on," he said, waving Rook and Mogler to join him.

The writing wasn't words; it was more of a symbol. If he had to guess, it was written with the same sharpie marker used on the woman. Inside a circle was the number five.

Mogler waved over the crime scene tech to take pictures to

document the finding. The three huddled together. "What do you suppose it means?" she asked.

Rook shrugged. "We can't say for certain it wasn't here before the body was placed. Odds are it will match the writing on the victim."

Cade pulled out his cell phone and brought up a picture. He held it out for the others to see. It was a promo photo of a beautiful blonde woman—not dissimilar from the dead one—with a television station logo of a circled number five. "It looks scarily close to the Five News logo."

"Oh," Mogler said. "They are similar." Cade wasn't sure if she meant the logos or the blonde women. Either way, both looked eerily similar. "I don't know what it means."

"I hope it doesn't mean he's going after my girlfriend."

Rook's eyes widened. "*You're* going out with *the* Reynolds Devries? From the Five? Dude, she's a ten." Rook looked him up and down for a moment. "You must have a lot of money."

But Cade had stepped away and was already on the phone. He paced back and forth anxious for her to pick up. Reynolds' phone maddeningly went to voice mail and Cade spoke urgently. "It's me. Something's happened and I need you to not be alone. I'm coming to the station. Be wary of anyone you don't know." He ended the call and waved for Rook to follow.

"We're going to see Reynolds. I'll drive." And they ran for Cade's truck.

When they got back to the parking lot, it was clear word had spread. News vehicles had arrived from all the major Twin Cities' stations to cover the day's big story. If the killings continued, it wouldn't be long before the national media joined them.

So much for the Governor's request to keep things quiet.

CHAPTER 5

Cade's FJ Cruiser flew down University Avenue. With the emergency lights activated, he pushed his speed as Rook called out potential obstacles. While most vehicles moved over as they approached, not all of them did. Some were oblivious to the lights and siren as Cade came rocketing up behind them.

"How can they not see or hear us coming?" Rook asked, shaking his head. "We're bright and we're loud."

"Some people couldn't find their ass using two hands," Cade said as he steered around a Jetta. The driver had his mouth open as they shot around and headed east on University Avenue toward Reynold's station.

Cade had met Reynolds Devries when she was working on the Blonde Killer story. After she'd received a tip, Reynolds used a false pretense to surprise him with a live camera. After that rocky beginning, they'd run into each other at a Stillwater restaurant, and something inexplicable and unexpected sparked between them. They were brought together several times as the investigation continued and found themselves growing closer. It turned out the earlier tip had come from the killer himself, and eventually he'd grabbed Reynolds to use as bait. Cade and Reynolds were sleeping together by this time, and Cade was thoroughly smitten. When he got the killer's call, there was no way he couldn't go after Reynolds. The resulting showdown between cop and killer was bloody and violent, but he'd saved her in the end.

No way was he going to put her at risk again. Cade sped up.

Rook continued to call out obstacles completely unfazed like this was something he did every day. The man was focused and cool under pressure. Cade's opinion of him ticked up a notch.

At the station, which was a sprawling complex that had grown over the decades, Cade left the truck on the curb by the main entrance. Both men ran for the door and stepped into the lobby where they were met by the receptionist. "Hey, Thomas, is Reynolds here?" Cade asked. He'd been to the station enough that he remembered the young man's name.

"Yessir, Mr. Dawkins. She should be almost out of her production meeting. I'll message her assistant. Can I get you gentlemen an expresso? I make it myself."

"No, thank you. If I get any more wired, I'm going to shoot someone."

"I'll have his," Rook said. "I have a high tolerance for caffeine. Comes from years of stakeout coffee."

"That's more like battery acid than coffee. That stuff kills more law enforcement personnel than all the bullets and donuts combined."

Cade paced while they waited, something he often did. He looked up as the elevator dinged, and Reynolds stepped out. His breath caught in his throat.

Wearing a white and gold patterned sheer top that was translucent enough to hint at what was underneath, shiny black leather leggings and black pumps with pointed toes, Reynolds Devries was a vision. Her blonde hair was worn long, and her smile lit up the room.

"Hey, honey," she said as she wrapped Cade up in a hug. "I wasn't expecting you today."

She must have read his body language because she pulled back and looked him in the eyes. "You're tense. What's wrong?"

Cade brushed back her hair. "Can we talk somewhere? It's a little sensitive." It wasn't lost on him that he was telling this to arguably the most high-profile news media journalist in the Twin Cities. Reynolds led them to a conference room and shut the door.

"Who's your friend?" she asked as she sized up Rook. "You look familiar, though."

Holding out a hand, Rook introduced himself. "Terrance Rooker, but call me Rook. I'm with Minneapolis P.D."

"Reynolds Devries. Nice to meet you." She looked back to Cade. There was something unspoken in her gaze. "This feels like an official visit. It is, isn't it?"

Cade sat back in the chair and looked at Reynolds. "This needs to stay in this room," he began as he caught her look of annoyance. "At least for now. This is a breaking story, so you'll be talking about it soon enough. But there's part of it we need to keep to ourselves. In cases like these, details are often kept from the public to verify information from tips or to establish a pattern. If the killer finds out we're aware of a pattern, they may change it, making it more difficult to identify them from future crimes."

Eyes narrowing, Reynolds said, "Cases like this? Pattern? Future crimes? Doesn't sound good."

"It's not," Rook said, shaking his head. "Not good at all."

There was a light rap on the door and Thomas came in to hand a small cup to Rook. "Your expresso, sir." He backed out and pulled the door closed.

Seeing the other two looking at him, he held up a hand. "What? A man can't have a little luxury?" He took a slow and deliberate sip that wasn't quiet.

Cade looked to Reynolds. "There was a murder today on Nicollet Island, which you probably already heard about. Your station's remote truck was on the scene." She nodded. "The victim matches the Blonde Killer victim's profile exactly. She was stabbed, and a note was left that mentioned my name specifically. It looks like the opening salvo of a new killer here in town."

"Damn." Reynolds let out a long breath. "Why us? What would bring another killer here?"

Cade knew the answer, but this wasn't the time or place to bring that up, especially with a signed NDA.

"There was a symbol found underneath her body." He pulled up the picture of the circled number 5.

Reynolds' eyes widened and her jaw dropped. "That looks like our station logo." She looked back and forth between the two men. "I see why you're here." She shivered.

Cade nodded. "Having you in danger once was enough."

Reynolds paused, clearly deep in thought. When she looked back to Cade, there was determination in her eyes. "This story needs to get out."

"Reynolds..."

"You can sit on the station logo part, but people need to know about the kind of murderer that's here." She leaned forward. "Are you prepared to make an official statement? I want you on camera. Today." She held his gaze.

"I suppose," he said after a moment. "This investigation is being run under the new major crimes task force, with assistance from Minneapolis. Rook here is my task force teammate." He nodded to his partner.

"We're the Five Below major crimes task force. Don't leave that part out." Rook shot a glance to Cade, who simply shrugged.

"Five Below? Like the discount store?" Reynolds asked, the hint of a grin at the corners of her mouth.

"Yes, dammit. Just like that," Rook said. "But badder and bolder."

"Badder?" Cade grinned.

"Yeah, badder. I can't say more bad, so it's badder. Are you the grammar police too, man?"

"Nah, I've got too much on my plate as it is. You're good." Cade held up a fist which Rook promptly bumped.

"Back to the story," Reynolds said, all business now. "We have a news crew out at Nicollet Island, but we'll shoot your segment right here. It'll be brief and we'll edit it into the location shots. Let me get this moving." She stood up.

"Reynolds."

She paused and turned back to Cade.

"You need to take this potential threat seriously. All strangers are threats. Don't put yourself into a one-on-one situation with someone you don't know. Don't go anywhere alone when you're out of the station bubble."

"Okay, okay," she replied. Reynolds took a step back, anxious to get the reporting going.

"For me," Cade said. "Do it for me."

Reynolds stepped back in and kissed him. "I will. Promise." And then she was gone.

There was a moment of silence before Rook let out a long whistle. "I don't know how you do it. You're batting way out of your league, man."

Cade leveled a look at his partner. "You think?"

"Most definitely."

"I'm okay with it," Cade said with a grin. "And I don't have lots of money."

Rook glanced up. "Oh, you heard that. I didn't think you were listening."

"I hear everything." Cade laughed. "Watch yourself."

"I'm not exactly known for being careful, truth be told." Rook said quietly.

Reynolds returned. "Crew is on their way. Come with me; my producer has things set up for us." The men followed her across the lobby.

"That was fast," Rook commented.

"This is television news. If you're not fast, you're last." She gestured for them to get in the elevator. "We'll do the interview in our studio C. America will get you mic'd up. The whole thing should take under five minutes."

Where the media was concerned, Cade realized they were useful. He could use them to not only get his information out but talk directly to the killer. Some serial killers were voracious consumers of the news, especially when following their own stories. These were the organized killers, the ones who were more socially adept, the ones with egos that could be played to. There was nothing wrong with using all the tools available to you.

Studio C was a cozy space with two overstuffed leather chairs facing each other. The walls were for show as they were mounted on wheels and placed for a backdrop behind the chairs. A dozen or so lights hung from the ceiling, and a large camera was set up nearby. A control board sat behind the camera.

"I'm America," a young brunette said. "I'm here to get you ready for the camera."

She clipped the microphone to his collar. Cade stood uncomfortably while she ran the wire inside his shirt. She plugged it into a small box. "Say something," she prompted him.

"Something."

The guy with headphones sitting at the control board gave a thumbs up. America clipped the box to his belt.

"Can you do something about his hair?" Rook asked. "He looks like he should be making fancy non-fat soy coffee drinks for young urban professionals."

America studied his hair, which didn't help Cade's comfort level. "I don't think there's any taming of this beast," she said. "It'll help him stand out."

"No doubt about that." Rook grinned.

"I'm happy you two are having fun," Cade said. Truth be told, he didn't mind a little good-natured teasing. That had always been the character of the law enforcement community. It was only when they stopped teasing that you had a problem.

"We are, actually," America said with a smile. "You have to enjoy life."

Reynolds swept into the room, closely followed by another blonde woman. "This is Ronnie, my producer."

Ronnie pointed to a chair and said, "Cade, this is where you sit. The format is a simple question and answer. Reynolds will ask you a question and then you'll answer when you're ready. If need a second to compose your answer, say something like, 'good question' or 'I'm glad you asked.' It buys you a moment. The main camera is there," she gestured to the large camera which was being operated by a thirty-something woman. Her sleeves were rolled up, showing off intricate tattoos. "We'll also use a secondary camera to shoot over your shoulder to give a different perspective. But I don't want you to pay attention to either of the cameras. You shouldn't ever look at the camera. You're simply having a conversation with Reynolds and we're watching. The main point is to be relaxed, so you come across natural."

Cade nodded. "I can do that."

Reynolds sat across from Cade. "It helps if you keep your answers short, maybe a sentence or three. We want to keep the dialog going back and forth, which makes for a more interesting program for our viewers."

Cade nodded again.

"Okay, everyone. Let's get this started," Ronnie said. "Places."

America tugged on Rook's sleeve. "We can watch from back here." She ushered him to a spot behind the control board. Ronnie perched herself on a stool next to the board.

"Three, two," Ronnie counted off while gesturing with her hand. Instead of saying one, she simply pointed.

Looking directly into the camera, her expression one of concern, Reynolds said, "I'm Reynolds Devries with the Five. I'm joined by Cade Dawkins, head of the..." She paused and glanced up.

Rook pointed at her, mouthing the words, "Five Below."

Reynolds continued, "Five Below major crimes task force." Cade winced but quickly regained his composure. "Viewers are likely familiar with Detective Dawkins after he famously put a very violent and very permanent end to the Blonde Killer, Marlin Sweetwater. Thank you for being with us today, detective."

"No problem." Cade kept his eyes on Reynolds, even though he wanted to look at the camera. Tell someone not to do something and that's all they wanted to do—it was human nature.

"Can you tell me what was found today? At Nicollet Island?"

Cade took a deep breath. "The body of a woman was found posed on a large boulder on Nicollet Island. She had been killed with a knife, which was left inserted into her abdomen."

Reynolds nodded, her expression serious. "Were there any similarities to your famous—or perhaps I should say infamous—case of the Blonde Killer?"

"Although Sweetwater never used a knife to kill his victims, this particular woman fit his profile." Cade hesitated.

"Meaning?"

"She was an attractive blonde."

"I see," Reynolds said. "Do you believe this to be the work of a serial murderer?"

Cade leaned forward as he held Reynolds' gaze. "This is early in our investigation. As you might suspect, an in-depth forensic investigation of the crime scene will shed further light on what happened and who was responsible. We'll keep you informed of developments as the investigation proceeds."

Reynolds had that look that Cade knew well. She was stubborn and wouldn't accept a brush-off easily. Here it comes.

"Was the blonde woman murdered by a serial killer?" She held his gaze.

"There was something written at the scene that would lead me to believe that, yes, she was." He held up his palm. "But it wouldn't be prudent for me to offer details at this time."

Reynolds nodded. "I understand completely. One final question. Are you going to catch this killer like you did the Blonde Killer?"

Cade stroked his chin before nodding. "That's why we have the major crimes task force, bringing together the best and brightest in law enforcement. Yes, we will catch the killer."

Cade turned to the camera.

"I know you're out there, watching this, thinking you got away with it. But you're not as smart as you think you are. I stopped Sweetwater, and I'll stop you too. Count on it."

There, that should create some attention.

CHAPTER 6

"Damn, you have some big ones," Rook said when they were back in the truck. They'd left the studio right after the interview. Reynolds had promised again to be vigilant and not take chances.

"It's not that, as much as I wanted to establish that I'm calling the shots, not him. I'm not above using the media. They don't seem to mind using me."

"I don't want to hear about what you and your girlfriend do in your private time."

Cade snorted and laughed.

"Just messing with ya." Rook laughed.

"No worries." Cade got Mogler on the phone and put it on speaker.

"Hey, any developments?" Cade headed back down University Avenue.

"Yes, the victim has been identified from her prints. She's Kimberly Ann Albright of Edina. She was 33 years old, single, and worked as a financial planner. That's how her prints were in the system. She was fingerprinted as part of the certification process." Mogler sighed. "But we haven't located her vehicle yet. It's a new white Infiniti QX80, which should be easy to spot. I've put out a BOLO for it."

"Thanks, that's good work," Cade said. "When we find her car, we'll probably find where she was taken from." Cade ran a hand through his blond hair. "One favor. The killer's note should be sent over to the BCA to the attention of Grace Fox. I've worked with her before, and I trust her instincts."

Grace worked at the BCA, the Bureau of Criminal Apprehension, basically Minnesota's version of CSI. The bureau provided expert forensic science and criminal investigation services throughout the state. The BCA was the first crime laboratory in the nation to identify a suspect based solely on DNA. And Grace had been instrumental in solving the Blonde Killer case.

"Will do," Mogler said. "So, speaking of working together, what do you think of Rook? He can be a real piece of work." Mogler paused, waiting for Cade's reply. He let her wait.

Cade glanced over at Rook, who placed a hand over his heart dramatically before thrusting his middle finger toward the phone.

"I like him. He's brilliant and sweet." Cade winked at Rook. "I'll be on scene shortly." Cade ended the call.

"Sweet? Even my momma never called me sweet." Rook shook his head.

"I wanted to give her something she wasn't expecting. Sounded like I succeeded."

They drove past the U of M's athletic facilities, Huntington Bank Stadium, Williams Arena and Mariucci Arena. The road swerved to the right and became Fourth Street, and they continued heading west through the Dinkytown neighborhood.

Cade glanced over at his partner. "I want to ask you something, but let me give some background first. About two weeks ago, I'd been summoned to a meeting at the U where I met with several professors. They had me sign an NDA before they would tell me anything."

"And you're going to tell me anyway, aren't you?"

"Yeah, this is too important not to discuss with you. Legalities be damned."

"Spoken like a true cop." Rook laughed. "What did these professors tell you?"

"They said in their studies of the dark web, they'd come across a site for serial killers." Rook turned toward Cade, clearly intrigued.

"On this site, the killers shared exploits, bragged and even offered challenges to each other. Apparently, I was the subject of many a conversation after I killed Sweetwater."

"Really?"

"Really," Cade nodded as they crossed over the interstate. "But this is where it gets interesting. The professors said a new challenge was issued to the killers on the site. To come to Minnesota and kill here. To get the best of me."

"Damn," Rook said slowly. "What did you do?"

Cade shrugged. "There wasn't anything I could do. No crime had been committed, no names were attached to the posts, and no timelines were offered. So, I put it in my back pocket, so to speak."

"Time to pull it out then. Maybe the dark web professors can shed some light on who accepted the challenge, 'cause clearly, someone came here." Rook shook his head. "Most people like the internet, but I'm not convinced. Facebook can go away for good, and no one will be the worse for it."

"But then where am I going to post pictures of what I ate?" Cade grinned. "People need to know."

"The world revolves around your meal choices. As it should."

When they arrived back at Nicollet Island, the quiet island had become anything but. All the local media stations were present with their various mobile broadcast trucks. The onlookers on the outside of the crime scene tape had grown. Scanning the crowd, Cade picked out the crime-beat reporters for the StarTribune and Pioneer Press newspapers. This was today's big story.

Flashing badges, Cade and Rook entered the scene. They followed the wooded path back to where the body was found. Mogler spotted them and came over.

"Hey." She didn't look at Rook.

"Hey." He gestured to the boulder where the victim had been posed. "Anything?"

Mogler shook her head. "Nothing. Albright's body has gone to the medical examiner, who'll give her a complete workup. It's been made their number one priority. I also sent an officer to run the note over to the BCA. Looks like we need to let the lab do their thing now."

Cade nodded, thinking.

An officer approached Mogler. "Kal, the victim's car has been found. It's in Edina at the Restoration Hardware. There's a restaurant there."

"I've seen it, but it's too pricy for my cop budget. I'm more of a dive bar kind of girl." She thanked him and addressed Cade. "Next steps?"

"We'll head to Edina to scout the scene. Keep me updated on the lab findings. I appreciate your diligence here."

They headed back up the path to the parking lot as a rumble of thunder shook the sky. "Rook, why don't you head out to Edina and see what you can discover. Chances are that's where she was grabbed."

"Will do," he said. "What about you?"

"I'm going to the U. See if they can shed some light on the dark web."

"Okay, later." Rook climbed into his blacked-out Charger and started it up with a roar. Cade gave him a thumbs up and climbed into his truck and then waited. Once Rook was out of sight, he climbed down. He headed back to the crime scene.

Finding Mogler talking with a group of Minneapolis cops, he waved her over. She held up a finger and then joined him shortly.

"What's up?" she asked.

"I wanted to talk to you about Rook," he began. Mogler held up a hand.

"I know what you're going to say." She shook her head as the first drops of rain came pattering down. "It was only a matter of time before his reputation caught up with him. I can see about getting you a better replacement."

This time it was Cade that held up his hand. "I'm afraid there's been a misunderstanding. I don't want a replacement for Rook. In fact, I'd prefer that you keep your opinions to yourself regarding him. I can make my own determination."

She looked like she had something to say but stopped.

"Let's keep this professional," he said calmly.

That seemed to ignite something in her. "Professional? I watched your interview with your girlfriend from the Five. Don't even."

She turned to leave, but Cade stopped her. She glared at his hand on her sleeve.

The rain picked up in intensity. Another rumble of thunder.

"I don't have a problem with you. All I'm asking is for you not to disrespect my task force teammate. He's my guy now."

With a shake of her wet hair, Mogler looked him in the eye. "Fine. You two deserve each other, anyway."

Cade shook his head. So much for good relations with the Minneapolis P.D. The rain was coming down in buckets now. Some days offered more challenges than others.

CROCKER WAS at the door of the Walter Library when Cade arrived. "I wasn't sure if I'd see you again," he said as they shook hands. Crocker led him to the elevator.

"To be honest, the dark website felt so theoretical. You know how it is on the web, there are so many big talkers. But so few actual doers. I figured there was nothing I could do until something happened." He paused.

"And now something's happened, I heard." Crocker again led the way down the dusty and cluttered hallway of the sub-basement. "I caught your interview on the Five. Interesting strategy."

Crocker entered a code into the security box and opened the door. Tubbs was seated at the table sipping a coffee. "Hey," he said as he stood and shook hands. "Good to see you again."

"You too, but as they say, I wish it was under better

circumstances." Cade took the same chair as when last he met with the professors. Crocker also grabbed his same seat across from him.

"Let me bring you up to speed," Cade said. "A 33-year-old Edina woman, Kimberly Ann Albright, was found dead earlier today. Death resulted from a single stab wound. Her body was posed on a large boulder. She was found on her back with her dress riding high and her panties in her mouth."

He pulled out his phone and brought up his pictures. "These you need to see." The first picture was a close-up of the writing on her thigh. He handed the phone to Tubbs.

"First," Tubbs read the message out loud. "That likely means he intends for there to be a second. And he wanted that particular grisly fact understood." He gave the phone to Crocker, who looked at it briefly before handing it back to Cade.

"Yup," Cade said as he pulled up the picture of the note.

Again, Tubbs read it aloud. "We hurt, we maim, we kill. Their blood is on you. You think you're so smart, but you're out of your league. Their deaths are on you. Scores will cry out and bleed. Dawkins, death is here."

"Holy..." Crocker ran a hand over his head. "If there was any doubt that the killer wasn't part of the Orbiting Cortex site, that note kicked it to the curb. He called you out by name, son."

"Yup," Cade said as he pulled up the picture of the circled five. "And this was written directly on the boulder in what looked like the same marker. It was found underneath the body."

He handed the phone to Tubbs. "Five?" He passed the phone to Crocker.

"Five. Is he saying there's going to be five victims?" Crocker looked perplexed.

"Go to the next picture," Cade suggested.

The picture was a promo picture of Reynolds with the television station logo of a circled number 5 in the background. "That's my girlfriend, Reynolds Devries."

"Oh," Tubbs said.

"Holy..." Crocker exclaimed. "That's not good."

"Not good at all," Cade said. "But the station will keep a security officer with her at all times. And I'll pick her up and stay with her after that."

"Way to take one for the team," Tubbs said with a hint of a grin.

"I'm all about making sacrifices," Cade said.

He looked around the space, taking in the large room and the computer gear. Plenty of space for a task force command center. The idea came to him, and it felt right. He looked back to Crocker and Tubbs.

"What are you thinking?" Crocker asked.

"How would you like to help me catch this guy?" Cade asked. "So far, I've got a task force of two, a budget for whatever I need, but no space or personnel. I need researchers and people with insight into both the psychology of the deviant mind and the inner workings of the dark web. I have to believe the Orbiting Cortex site is a goldmine of information that will help catch this killer."

Cade glanced at the two men who looked back with interest.

"If *we*," he paused after emphasizing the "we" part, "can figure out which of the site's killers are here—and where he's from—our odds of finding him and stopping any further killings will greatly increase."

Tubbs nodded. "There certainly should be some clues in his previous posts. We'd need to figure out which ones are his, though."

Crocker leaned forward, his eyes bright and focused. "We could put out word to the graduate students, assemble a team of volunteers and get them working through the posts, cataloging them."

"Yes," Tubbs said with passion. "My psychology grad students would also love to dig into this. The Behavioral Analysis Unit at Quantico has resources we could use that can help differentiate characteristics of the individual killers posting on the site."

Cade liked where this was going. He leaned back and took in the exchange between the professors. It was like watching a tennis match as they went back and forth.

"We could offer extra credit."

"The grad students will eat that up."

"Think of the thesis papers this could inspire."

"Wait, *we* could publish."

"Yes, *we* could."

"This could be legacy-worthy."

"Yes, it could."

Together, the two colleagues turned to Cade. They looked like kids who were promised a trip to Disneyland. Eagar, excited, even a little breathless.

"We're in," Crocker said. "We can have a skeleton crew in place by tomorrow to get things rolling. Recruiting will speed up with people in place. They can recommend additional volunteers. I'd expect to be fully staffed by the end of the week."

The two men were positively beaming.

Cade smiled and shook their hands. "It looks like Crocker and Tubbs are back in the crime-fighting business."

Both men groaned but never lost their smiles.

This could work.

The killer had the television on, looking for coverage of the woman's death. It never failed to help him relieve the moments when the TV people spoke of the poor victim. Taken savagely in the prime of their life. A knife left buried in the victim.

Some killers strangled, some used ropes, some even used chainsaws if the movies were to be believed. He preferred to keep it simple. The tools of his trade came down to his favorite knife.

His trade. He'd taken to it a tender age.

When Jarn was seven—back when he was still Jeffrey—he scared his mom. He knew it, and she knew that he knew it. He'd heard her on the phone talking to one of her friends. His own mom said she was frightened by his dead stare. She said he was manipulative, and a pathological liar, already on the path to becoming a killer. At seven, he had to look up manipulative and pathological to see what they meant. He couldn't disagree with what he read. He wanted what he wanted and just because she was his mother, she shouldn't stand in his way.

A single mom, she'd raised him in a strict religious way, but it had never felt genuine to him. It was more like the rules were there to keep him in his place rather than to offer a lesson or benefit. Even though the rules never sat right, he instinctively knew he could better bend and break those rules if he understood them. So, as he grew and matured, he stayed in the church. Even though he was active and involved in their small church, it wasn't as a believer. It was as a non-believing manipulator.

His mind drifted again.

Of course, his mom had been right. He was going to be a killer. It was when he was fourteen—the age kids were dealing with issues like puberty, the opposite sex, and awkward middle school dances—that the idea came to him. He'd often find himself dwelling on more substantive things than the average teenager. Sex, death, and the relationship between the two. Both brought a feeling of excitement and power. But at fourteen, he'd yet to experience either. Late one night, the realization came to him—as these things often do—that it was on him to change that.

There was a woman at his church that he couldn't stop thinking about. She ushered with her family twice a month, the second and fourth Sunday mornings. Always dressed in a conservative matching skirt and blouse, there was something about the heels she wore. Even though they matched her outfit—in color anyway, there was something that didn't quite match. Her heels, always taller than the other women's, spoke about a different side of her. A side that she must save for her bedroom. Every second and fourth Sunday at church, he got hard watching her.

It wasn't difficult to get his mom to make the introduction. By fourteen, he'd become adept at using his mom when he needed something. She looked at him with fear and wariness, but she long ago gave up trying to rein him in. Now, she rolled over when he made a request of her. The introduction went well, as he showed a different side of himself. Smiling and saying nice things about her outfit, she warmed to him quickly. He discovered that a little charm could go a long way.

The woman's name was Ashley Conway, and she lived a half-mile away from Jeffrey and his mother. He'd worked his way into mowing her yard each week and doing the occasional odd job for her. Even at her home, she was better dressed than the other church women. She had the legs of an athlete and almost always wore some kind of heels. Young Jeffrey ached for her.

Then, one Saturday evening, things changed. Forever.

It was late summer, and he'd been over to mow her lawn. He always took care to be meticulous so she would keep him coming back. After an hour in the hot sun, she'd brought him water and the usual twenty-dollar bill. He'd have done it for free. As they chatted as they often did when he finished, she mentioned that her husband planned on bringing the kids to the drive-in that evening to see the latest Disney movie. Ashley planned to stay behind to repaint the main level bathroom. She laughed when he offered to come back to help, putting a hand on his sweaty shoulder and said that she had it. It was a small bathroom.

He couldn't get it out of his head that his Ashley would be home alone. It was like a bug bite that itched incessantly. No matter how often he tried to think of something else—anything else—his thoughts kept going back to her. All alone. Just a half-mile away.

He made his choice.

As soon as it was dark, he climbed out his bedroom window and rode his bike to the Conway house. It was a quiet neighborhood, with no one outside. The upstairs lights were off, and her garage was open, with a single vehicle remaining. He slipped into the garage and eased the door open into her house. He heard faint music past the kitchen, where the bathroom was.

He slipped his shoes off and padded through the kitchen. The room was clean, with dinner dishes washed and drying in the dish rack.

The music got louder as he moved closer. It wasn't the staid, reserved church music he'd expected. She had on the local hits station and was singing along. He found himself standing around the corner listening to her beautiful voice. However, the lure of Ashley Conway was too much, and he peered around the corner. The bathroom door wide open, he had a clear view. Ashley stood on a step stool wearing jean shorts and a tank top and young Jeffrey was riveted as she reached her brush up toward the high spots. Her toned calves were to die for, and he found himself stepping out from the safety of the corner.

This was what he'd wanted all along, and he was thankful his plan worked. Desires grow like weeds, and his did too. Emboldened, he took another step toward the object of his fantasy. He couldn't have stopped then if he'd been tied to his front porch; he'd have found a way here. But that was as far as his plan went, he wanted to get close to Ashley.

That's when his lack of planning failed him.

She'd sensed he was there and spun around, her face showing surprise. It wasn't her family returning early from the drive-in. Her wide eyes weren't showing the grateful look he'd hoped for. She dropped the paint roller, lavender paint on her white tile.

"Mrs. Conway, Ashley," he began as he took a step forward. She took a matching step back, retreating into the bathroom. There weren't many steps left for her to take. "I thought maybe you could use some help."

That didn't explain the knife in his hand, the kitchen paring blade comfortable in his sweaty grip. He knew it and he knew she knew it too. He briefly wondered if she recognized the knife from her kitchen.

"Maybe you should leave, Jeffrey. Before something happens

you'll regret," Ashley said with a waver in her voice. She was holding it together, just barely.

A sideways glance toward the door, Ashley was sizing up her chance of closing it before he could stop her. He made a split-second decision that changed both their lives forever.

Jeffrey pounced.

He was all over her, the small knife coming up. The blade entered Ashley Conway in her abdomen, slightly below her navel. It slid in as easy as it would a grapefruit, perhaps even easier. They were face to face like lovers, as he pinned her against the sink. Jeffery held her gaze as she trembled. He lost track of time as her life slipped away. It may have been a minute, it may have been ten. He'd been hard the entire time.

Those heady minutes were defining for young Jeffrey. When it was clear that Ashley had taken her last breath, he'd moved her body to the toilet. Not sure why, but he wanted to pose her body for maximum effect when her family returned from the drive-in. Frustratingly, he couldn't keep her head up, so he let it fall back as if she were staring up to the heavens. He gazed at her with affection for a long moment, then picked up the can of paint and dumped it on her.

On the ride home, a wave of sadness washed over him because never again would he be around her. But killing was power, a power that once experienced, wasn't one you could walk back from.

He'd gotten a taste for it.

CHAPTER 7

Terrance Rooker steered the Charger into the Restoration Hardware lot and spotted the black and white patrol car. Several spots down, he backed into a space, and headed over to the officer. The lot was filled with expensive vehicles looking as pristine as they were on the showroom floor. This was Edina, the wealthy first-ring suburb of Minneapolis. There's a long-standing joke that Edina residents were cake eaters, meaning the pretentious citizens can have their cake and eat it too. Basically, Edina is where old money goes to die.

The Edina officer was taller and thinner than Rook and had close-cut blond hair with a thin mustache. His uniform looked freshly pressed, and his shoes were shined enough to impress even the strictest army drill sergeant. The officer looked at Rook with a wary expression as he approached. The officer's right hand slid down and touched the grip of his service weapon, and this irked Rook more than he would've guessed.

"Hey, man," Rook said, reaching for his badge. Of course, the man tensed. Rook shook his head. "Look, I'm Minneapolis P.D., so you can relax. I know you don't get many brothers out here in the suburbs." He held up his badge case. "I'm following up on Kimberly Ann Albright's vehicle."

P. Brewer, as his gold nameplate read, looked irritated, but lowered his hand. "This is her vehicle. It's locked."

Rook didn't roll his eyes. "Good police work, Brewer. Have you talked to anyone inside the restaurant?"

"No, I was told to stay with the vehicle."

"Again, good job." Rook peered inside, looking for the victim's purse or for anything of interest. He didn't find either. The car looked immaculate. "I'm going inside to check the surveillance video. Thanks for finding her vehicle." P. Brewer gave a stoic nod.

Restoration Hardware, or RH as the sign read on the impressive gray building, was three stories of glass and marble. It looked like it would be home to a Maharaja or a crown prince rather than home furnishings. The word opulent came to mind.

Given his police salary, Rook had never shopped there.

The inside was as stunning as the outside. Sweeping views and museum-worthy pieces were a treat to Rook's eyes that were used to shopping at Target. Several people wandered the uber-expensive furnishing displays, but the floors were mostly empty. He was greeted right away by a stylishly dressed woman, asking if she could help him with anything.

Rook shook his head in mock annoyance. "Yeah, I was wondering if your delivery policy had changed." Rook could see he had her curious as she took a half step and cocked her head. "You see, last time I was here, I had a hundred-thousand-dollar order to outfit my pad, but the salesman said there was no way you'd deliver to the hood."

The woman's eyes went wide, and she didn't appear to know what to say.

Rook broke out laughing. "I'm just messing with you." He held up his badge. "I'm with the Five Below major crimes task force."

The woman, whose nameplate read Anya, looked like she was going to say something about the task force name. Rook waved a finger at her before she could and continued. "A woman has been murdered and the victim's car was found in your lot. I'd like to have a look at the security footage."

"Let's find my manager. She can help with your request." She led Rook through the showroom to an office area tucked behind a display room. A fifty-something woman with auburn hair, wearing a black cashmere sweater with a pineapple brooch, looked up over her glasses as they approached. There was something in her expression that gave him pause.

"I know I'm a little scruffier than most of the clientele you get in here," Rook said apologetically, running a hand over the two-day whiskers he'd been cultivating for the last three days. "But—"

The woman held up a hand. "Please. In this dot-com economy, money doesn't look the same. Rather than a Harris tweed from Brooks Brothers, the wealthy may show up in shorts and flip-flops. I'm never one to pre-judge." She looked earnest. "So, how can I help?"

Rook held up his badge. "I'm investigating the murder of a woman whose car is in your lot."

"He's with Five Below," the saleswoman interjected.

"Wait, what? The discount chain?" The manager looked confused.

Rook took a calming breath.

"I'm a Minneapolis detective assigned to the Five Below major crimes task force. We're not well known. Our branding campaign hasn't started yet."

The woman rolled with it. "I'm guessing you'd like a look at our security camera video. I can pull it up right here," she said and turned her laptop so Rook could see the screen.

Rook read her name tag. "Thank you, Pressley. Can you pull up the parking lot first?" Rook leaned in as she made the parking lot feed full screen. The display was in color, and the resolution looked considerably better than average. Win-win.

"What timeframe do you want?" she said, looking back over her shoulder. "Today? Yesterday?"

"That's anyone's guess. But start with yesterday's lunch crowd. We're looking for when this white SUV showed up," Rook said as he pointed at Albright's Infiniti. The Edina officer was still with the vehicle.

The manager entered yesterday's date and selected 11:00 a.m., saying that's when the first of the lunch crowd might arrive. She fast-forwarded as vehicles arrived and left. A couple of moments came when he thought maybe, but then it wasn't the right vehicle. The timestamp counted up into the dinner hour, and it wasn't until 7:29 p.m. that the Infiniti arrived.

"There," he said. "That's her. Can you pause and zoom in?" The woman had come around her car and walked toward the building. Pressley paused the video mid-step as the woman—Kimberly Ann Albright—looked up toward the camera. Rook shook his head. He'd seen the victim in death but now seeing her alive had him angry. It helped ignite the fire detectives needed to see a case through the ups and downs that were to follow. The image of the woman remained clear as the store manager zoomed in. Albright had been beautiful. Her long full blonde hair cascaded around her shoulders. She wore a wine-colored dress that showed off her long legs.

"She's beautiful," Pressley said. "Should I keep the video rolling?"

Rook pulled out his phone. "No, let me snap a picture first." He leaned in and took a picture with his phone. "Okay, go ahead."

"I can print from here," Pressley said and hit a button on the keyboard that got a nearby printer humming. "Whenever you want an image, just say so."

The video continued, as the woman walked toward the camera until she moved out of frame. Rook hadn't seen anyone suspicious in the footage but had her run it again to confirm. Nothing out of the ordinary. No one lingered.

"Can you pick her up inside?" he asked.

"I'm already on it." Pressley was back to the screen with the various feeds. She selected one and made it full screen. The scene was of the main floor showroom. She took the video back to 7:29 p.m. the day before and hit play. A minute later, the dead woman came into view. She briefly met with a salesperson who gestured toward the stairs. Albright walked through the frame and ascended out of sight.

There was something decidedly odd about watching someone

you knew would be murdered in a short time. Would there be something different about them, something that gave the tiniest hint they were a short-timer? Rook had yet to discover it if it was the case.

"She must be going to our rooftop restaurant. It's the trendy place to be seen," Pressley said. "I'll pull up that camera next. She went back to the feed screen and selected the rooftop feed. Once it was full screen, she returned to the right time. The screen showed a large bright room with a greenhouse-style glass roof. Decorative green trees were strategically placed and many crystal chandeliers hung overhead. A circular fountain sat in the middle of the crowded room. Business was booming, there wasn't an empty table in the place. Albright came into view and a group of women waved. She crossed the room and joined the women at their table.

Rook leaned in, peering at the screen. "Zoom in on that table. Please."

The screen zoomed in on the four women. Two of them faced the camera while Albright and another woman sat with their backs to the camera.

"Print that image, please. And can you get me any information on the table? A name for the reservation? Credit card receipts?" He could interview the other women if needed.

Pressley picked up her desk phone and asked for someone to come to her office. She turned to Rook. "Bruno is our restaurant manager. He's coming down. Bruno will identify the table and the server. From there, he should be able to pull names from the dinner charge receipts. Unless they paid in cash, but no one does anymore."

"I don't even think twice about pulling out my card for a pack of gum or a donut." He looked at her and then broke out laughing. "I don't eat donuts, actually. I'm the only one on the force who doesn't. They almost put me on probation when they found out."

Pressley offered a polite smile.

While they waited, Rook had her scan the room, looking for men in the restaurant. "Most killers of this type are men. I'm going with the odds here."

"There was a female serial killer on Criminal Minds."

"That's television; hardly ever based on reality. And I never said he was a serial killer." He studied the screen.

"It was the way you referred to him as a killer of this type. Made me think of serial killers. I watch a lot of crime shows." She zoomed in on the different men in the room. Maybe a dozen men were there, some with women, some seated with other men. Several servers were men—he couldn't rule them out as possibilities. But there was one man who appeared to be by himself. Seated off to the side, he had a clear view of the victim. Like Albright, he also faced away from the camera. Rook pointed at the man. "Him. How can I see more of him?"

Pressley zoomed in and Rook leaned forward to study the man. The man wore his hair long enough that some of it went over the collar of his suit jacket. An open book sat on the table in front of him. But that was the extent of what he could glean from the angle.

"Hello, boss. What's up?"

"Hey, Bruno. This is a detective," Pressley said to the man who wore a dress shirt and flowered tie. "Bruno is our restaurant manager," she said as an aside to Rook. "Bruno, can you pull receipts on this table here? Get us names. A guest was found murdered."

"That's horrible. But certainly. That was table six at 7:30 last night. Easy to do." He turned to leave, but Rook waved a hand.

"Yo, Bruno," Rook said. "Can you do the same for this table here?" He pointed to the man. "I have a feeling about him."

"Can do. I'll call down with the information." And Bruno was gone.

Rook pointed at the screen. "Look at the angle of his head. Like he's watching table six instead of his book."

"I think you're right, classic serial killer move," Pressley said and winked at him.

"I never said he was a serial killer."

"Okay, I'm going to advance the footage." She started the feed playing in real-time. The women ordered and started with drinks. Nothing unusual.

"Go back to fast forward. They could be there for hours. I've seen women when they get together." Rook stopped talking after receiving a look from Pressley.

With the video on fast forward, the time flew by as people came and went. Servers moved around the room. However, the solitary man never moved from his spot. At one point, two of the women got up from Albright's table and walked out of view.

"That's the restrooms over there," Pressley said, pointing to where the women disappeared. Soon after the pair returned to the table, another woman from Albright's table stood and headed in the same direction. The man never moved. He didn't appear to be interested in anyone other than Albright.

At 9:32 p.m., all four women stood, and Pressley slowed the footage back to real-time. The group moved toward the stairs, still talking. There was a round of hugs. Three of the women descended out of the picture, but not Albright. She went the other way.

"She must have stayed behind to use the restroom," Pressley said. "Her friends left without her."

"Which effectively isolated her," Rook said, shaking his head. "There," Rook pointed to the man as he got up. The man kept his head down and turned away from the camera. Right before he went out of view, he moved to cover his face with his book. "He knows where the camera is. Look how he's shielding his face."

"He's headed for the restrooms, too."

It was a tense few minutes waiting for Albright and the mysterious man. Rook bounced his leg as he fidgeted. Sitting still was never one of his strengths, just ask pretty much any teacher he'd ever had. But then the man came into view, closely followed by Albright and descended the stairs one after the other. At the moment before they went out of sight, her head turned.

"Can you go back a second or two?" Rook asked. "I'd swear she turned as she went out of view."

Pressley reversed the footage and slowed it to half speed. Albright's head did appear to turn as she looked over her left shoulder before going out of the camera's view. "It's difficult to say for sure, but I think she did," Pressley said. "I'll pick her up from the showroom camera."

She pulled up the showroom feed and advanced it to the right time with practiced hands. Rook was stunned to see Albright and the man walking side by side as they stepped off the stairs. They were clearly having a conversation.

"Pause it for a second. See how he's on her right side, so he's turned away from the camera? If he'd been on her other side, we'd have a clear view of his face," Rook said, shaking his head. "He knew what he was doing."

"Did she know the man?" Pressley asked as she pointed. "See how she's smiling. And look at her hand. It looks like she's reaching for his arm." She started the video again. Albright's hand continued, and she did indeed touch his arm in what looked like a friendly gesture.

Rook shook his head. "I don't think they knew each other. I mean, they were seated near each other, but there was never any interaction."

"Well then, he's one smooth operator," Pressley said. "He must have laid on the charm on the way down."

"I guess so," Rook said. "But, man, that's some fast work." The man held open the door and followed her out into the night.

"I'm switching back to the parking lot camera." When she had it at the right time, they watched Albright walk out with the man. They appeared to be in a conversation the entire time. The pair headed across the lot to Albright's Infiniti. After a moment's hesitation, they walked back to a silver sedan parked nearby.

"What the..." Rook's stomach tightened as the scene unfolded. Pressley slowed the video to half speed and zoomed the picture. With the man leading the way, the pair walked to the rear door on the passenger side. He opened the door and leaned into the vehicle, like he was reaching for something either on the floor or under the seat. When he reappeared, he moved rapidly as he pulled Albright into him, and after a moment, he pushed her into the vehicle. Rook guessed the killer had drugged her given how the woman had so quickly collapsed.

The man scanned the parking lot, a hand raised over his eyes. And then unexpectantly, he lifted his hand as he looked up to the camera. He was holding up his middle finger. Unfortunately, the man's hand obscured his face as he made the gesture.

"Bastard," Rook said as the man climbed into his car and drove off into the night with the unconscious woman stowed in the back seat. The entire time, the man knew where the cameras were and made sure his face was obscured. The middle finger gesture was made knowing that law enforcement would see the video. He was taunting them. And, knowing what happened next to the woman, Rook hated the man even more for it.

"Let me see what I can get on the car," Pressley said after a moment. She reversed the video and paused as the silver sedan backed up, right before it turned and left the parking lot. The picture tightened as she zoomed in. "We use 4K security cameras exclusively because they deliver the sharpest details, and their large image sensors allow for higher quality digital zooms. We upgraded after a rash of catalytic converter thefts from our lots. They were so brazen, even doing it in broad daylight."

As the image got tighter, details came into focus. The make of the sedan was a Chevy Cruze. Rook's pulse quickened as the license plate became clear. "Got it," Pressley gushed. "That must be at the far reaches of the camera's capabilities, but there it is. Printing now."

Rook grabbed the stack of printouts and looked at the license plate. Clear as if he was standing thirty feet away. He got on the phone and called in the plate. The Minneapolis police admin said it would be a second as she pulled up the registration information. Pressley's phone rang, and she jotted down notes soon after. She said, "Thanks, Bruno," and hung up.

She handed over the note. It had four women's names, one of which was Kimberly Albright. Below that was a single word.

Cash.

Bastard must have paid his bill in cash. Who carried cash anymore? There must be something seriously wrong with him if he carried money. Either that, or he didn't want to leave a digital trail.

The police admin was back on the line. "Yes, detective. The plates are registered to Alamo Car Rental. But they're not for a silver Chevy Cruze, they're for a Nissan Altima. A red one."

The killer switched the plates. Clearly, the guy was a planner, and a careful one at that. His ability to stay away from surveillance cameras, using cash, and then the license plate switch, this killer would be challenging to track down—to say the least. And he'd learned nothing here that would help catch him.

Rook dropped his head. Today was not going well. Not at all.

CHAPTER 8

It was always bittersweet going back to a former workplace. There were parts of the job you liked—usually the people—and parts you didn't. Ironically enough, the disliked parts were often the people as well.

Cade found himself parking in his old spot at the Bureau of Criminal Apprehension. The BCA fit into a unique niche, providing investigative and specialized law enforcement services to prevent and solve crimes in partnership with the Minnesota law enforcement community. Statewide, the BCA had more than 300 agents, analysts, scientists, and support staff between field offices and the St. Paul lab and headquarters. Cade had been one of those agents before joining the State Patrol as an investigator.

Grace Fox was Cade's favorite person in his time with the BCA. An accomplished crime scene technician, they'd crossed paths frequently. He found her to be intelligent, insightful and irreverent. And frankly, anyone who didn't take authority—or themselves, for that matter—too seriously was someone Cade could relate to. Grace had consulted on the Blonde Killer case and her insights into the deviant mind of serial killers had been invaluable.

Grace been with him when the killer, Sweetwater, had called to say he'd taken Reynolds. She'd insisted on coming along, knowing it would be a trap for Cade. She said she could create a needed diversion. Smuggling a weapon into the killer's compound, Grace paid a heavy price via Sweetwater's blade. But Grace survived and returned to the job she loved following weeks of recovery.

Cade signed in and went back to the crime lab where Grace

spent most of her days. He knew she was often there seven days a week, but he also suspected she had a wild streak when she wasn't working. Everyone needed a release, and Cade wasn't going to ask too many questions. Safer that way.

"Hey ya, Grace. How's your day going?" Cade asked as he entered Grace's domain. The killer's note was up on the large screen that dominated one wall. A face looked up from a mop of brunette hair, and Cade recognized her loopy grin. She let out a squeal and ran over to wrap him up in a hug.

After a moment, they released as people do after hugging. He gazed into her eyes. "How are you doing?" Cade asked.

With mock annoyance, Grace pushed him away. "People are always asking me that. Like I've been damaged somehow and everyone's afraid around me."

Cade nodded. "Well, in my defense, you were sliced open by a serial killer. That doesn't happen very often. It might leave a scar or so."

Grace held open her lab coat so Cade could see. A white line ran from her knee up to the hem of her skirt. At the time, Cade worried she wasn't going to make it, but she'd survived. At least physically, anyway.

"I can't believe you're wearing a skirt. Most people would want to hide the..." Cade's words trailed off, worried he might have said the wrong thing and hurt her. Instead, she punched him in the chest.

"Are you kidding me? We went toe to toe with an actual serial killer and I have this as proof." She gestured emphatically at her thigh. "Damn right, I'm going to show it off. I wear nothing but skirts now." She looked insanely proud as she stood there with her hands on her hips. "When I'm out at the club and someone finds out how I got this, they think I'm so badass."

"You go clubbing a lot?" Cade asked with the slightest hint of skepticism in his voice.

Grace pointed her finger at him. "Hey, we had a deal. You don't ask me about my personal life, and I don't give you a hard time about you having a media star as a girlfriend."

Cade laughed and grabbed a stool. "Forget I ever said a thing."

Grace gave him a smug little smile, and they both turned to look at the killer's note on the screen.

The weaver of the web kills. But we inflict, we maim, we slay.
Scores will cry out and bleed. Their blood is on you.
You're out of your league, mortal Dawkins.
Death has arrived.

"Yeah, that," Grace said as she joined him on a stool. She tucked her long brunette hair behind an ear and nodded. "It doesn't look good."

"Not in the least. Thoughts?"

Grace put her hands and fingers together, drawing them up to her lips. She sighed and leaned back. "There's so much to unpack. Obviously, the note is a challenge to you. But it's also an announcement of intent. This killing won't be the only one, more will surely follow. Meaning this is a serial killer." She looked over to Cade. "The writer sounds particularly affronted by you for some reason. Since you recently put down another serial killer, this feels like retribution. Like the killer is here to slay, as it was put, and there's nothing you can do. It's definitely challenging in tone."

She paused, and Cade gave her time to process.

"I find it interesting," she began, "that the writer never uses the singular. It's not *I* slay, but *we* slay. There's often an egocentric component to a serial killer message. Jack the Ripper bragged and savagely taunted the police in letters. They were of the *you're shit and I'm smarter than you and you'll never catch me* variety. Serial killers typically are extraordinarily 'me' focused. Inclusive is not in their vocabulary. But instead of saying that I've arrived, we get that death has arrived. It's quite unusual."

Cade cleared his throat. "There's something you don't know about."

Grace's eyes flashed at him, and she tented her fingers. "Please share."

"Several weeks ago, I was invited to a meeting at the University of Minnesota. A professor of computer science doing research on the dark web came across a site for serial killers. On the website, killers share their exploits, brag and even challenge one another. He thought the site was unusual and brought in a psychology professor colleague. When I asked the reason why they called me in particular, they said something surprising. The killers were so intrigued when I shot Sweetwater, the site buzzed with comments for weeks. And then a new challenge was issued. Go to Minnesota and kill, get the best of me."

Grace shook her head, alarm coloring her face. "Not good."

"Nope, but I didn't do anything with the information because there wasn't anything I could do. There were no specific threats, no names, no timeline. It felt so theoretical." Cade shook his head. "Maybe I could have said something, should have done something, and maybe Kimberly Ann Albright would still be alive."

Putting a hand on his, Grace shook his head. "This isn't on you. You didn't kill her; this whack job did," she said, gesturing to the projected note. "There's nothing law enforcement could have done to prevent her death. Do they stop everyone entering our state and ask if they're a serial killer? Of course not. That's not how law enforcement works. You know that. We catch the perpetrator after the fact—hopefully before they kill again."

Cade looked up from his hands. "Thank you for that. I needed to hear that."

"Of course. Don't worry about stupid things." She grinned. "I should have that put on a t-shirt. I bet there are millions of people who need to hear that. Not just you." Grace turned back to the note. "The website explains why the killer wrote the note the way he did. It's an announcement of arrival. But it also raises a hell of a question."

"Like?"

She paused and looked at Cade. "Like, how many other killers are coming?"

They looked at each other for a long moment. It was the loudest silence he could remember.

"There's no way to know," Cade said as he shrugged. "But I reached back to the professors who first told me about the serial killer site. They're putting together a team of graduate students to dig into the site to see what they can discover. Maybe they can see if there are more coming. And maybe they can find out something about the killer that we can use to find him."

"I haven't heard about any other deaths that could point to a killer like this," Grace said. "Unless the body hasn't been discovered yet." She visibly shivered.

Cade got to his feet. "I don't think so. The killer wrote something on the victim's thigh in sharpie marker. It said first."

"First implies there will be a second." Grace folded her arms.

"Exactly," Cade said. "But it also means there weren't prior killings."

"It begs the question though, if there's more than one killer, are they communicating with each other?"

Cade paced in front of the screen. "I think that's what the Orbiting Cortex site is for. It's how they communicate."

"Orbiting Cortex? That's sublime. Totally a play off the orbital cortex, which controls aggression, concentration and regulates impulse control. Brain scans of serial killers have shown deficiencies in that area of the brain." Grace got up and headed to a small refrigerator. "Water?"

"Sure, thanks." She tossed the bottle to Cade.

Grace sat while she studied the screen. She opened the bottle and took a sip. "There's symbolism in the killer's note. The writer begins with 'The weaver of the web kills.' That's meant to be symbolic of the spider. Notice that some of the intricate drawings on the note's edges are webs and spiders. I have no idea what the other symbols are or what they mean."

Grace touched her lips with her index finger. "Spiders are the perfect symbols for dualism in the physical realm because they show us the power of creativity and manifestation that is balanced by destruction." She paused with a single finger to her lips. "Have you heard of arachnids? My grade school teacher would tell us it's simply a fancy name for a spider. Arachnids are in a group that includes spiders, daddy longlegs, scorpions, mites and ticks. The name's derivation is from Arachne, a Greek mythology protagonist. The tale recounted how the talented mortal Arachne challenged Athena, goddess of wisdom and crafts, to a weaving contest. When Athena could find no flaws in the tapestry Arachne had woven for the contest, the goddess became enraged and beat the girl with her shuttle, the wooden tool for holding the weaving wool. The tale went on to say that after Arachne hung herself out of shame, Athena transformed into a spider. The myth provided an origin myth of the spiders' web-spinning abilities but was also a cautionary tale warning mortals not to place themselves on an equal level with the gods."

Cade paused his pacing. "That would explain why the note referred to me as 'Mortal Dawkins.'"

"See? The note is consistent with the egocentric nature of serial killers, especially the organized ones. They see themselves on a higher plane than the rest of us." Grace chugged her water and followed it with a small burp.

"Nice," Cade said with a grin. His expression turned serious. "Based on the crime scene, it feels like we're dealing with an organized killer. I'm assuming they're the more difficult one of the two to catch."

"Both types are equally dangerous," Grace said. "But the organized killer is meticulous, has contingency plans, and cleans up after himself. He often transports the body from the crime scene, as well."

Cade nodded. "I think they get off outsmarting everyone, especially the police."

"Ted Bundy spoke about the paranoia and superiority that drove him," Grace said. "How he experienced euphoria when he knew he'd successfully cloaked himself in a mantle of invisibility so he could stand near a crime scene in the presence of the police without fear of detection."

"Superiority, I understand. But paranoia?"

"They will do anything to avoid getting caught." Grace traced her finger around the bottle's opening. "Many will stay under the radar, targeting total strangers, avoiding anyone with any possible connection, traveling hundreds of miles to target random victims at secluded parks and other remote locations."

"I've heard they can blend in surprisingly well," Cade said.

Grace leaned back, crossing her legs, the scar evident. "It's often the case. The murderer blends in entirely with the community he's preying on, and moves right through police surveillance without being spotted, killing with impunity. During an investigation, detectives often say there's the feeling that the killer is right there, only they can't see him."

"I've felt that," Cade said. "With the Blonde Killer case."

"Serial killers can remain undetected for large expanses of time due to a mixture of diligence on their part, a carefully constructed façade, the types of victims that they select, and lucky breaks," Grace said. "They'll do whatever they can do to avoid getting caught so they can keep killing."

"So you're saying they might be hard to catch?"

Grace nodded. "Exactly. They can be chameleons, changing personalities and identities. They may look like us, but not on the inside. They're often emotionally unattached and can fake the human emotion necessary to get you to like them. That's likely your killer, too. A true psychopath, he's extremely dangerous because he seems normal at first glance. You'll never see him coming."

"You kept referring to the killer as a he," Cade said. "Are there no women serial killers?"

Grace shook her head. "There are women serial killers, but stats show that roughly 85 percent of known serial killers have been men. I'm going with the percentages."

"Known serial killers? Maybe women are simply better at not getting caught." Cade took a drink of his water.

"There is that possibility," Grace acknowledged. "Outside of our governor, the most devious people I know have been women."

"Amen," Cade said. She may have been kidding, but there was a grain of truth there. The Minnesota governor was a piece of work. "So, where does all this leave us?"

Grace got to her feet and faced Cade. "This killer will kill again. There's no doubt about it. Being organized, he is a creature of routine. Look at how he selected his victim, and assume that's how he'll go about it in the future." She held out her hand, palm facing him. "But. There's the very real possibility the killer will anticipate you catching onto his routine and purposely vary it to throw you off."

"So, you're saying it's like playing chess against a master?"

She nodded. "I hope you're a strategic thinker. You have to figure out what his moves are and get out in front of him."

"I can do that." Cade's father taught him chess at a young age, and he passionately took to the game. Matches against his father and even some of his father's friends were highlights for him. He remembered feeling bad when he started beating the adults. But not too bad.

"Thanks for everything, Grace. I truly appreciate you," he said as he hugged Grace. The memory of nearly losing her swept through him again. Cade wiped a tear before releasing her, not wanting to embarrass himself. But based on her expression, she knew.

They always knew.

CHAPTER 9

Saturday Morning

"Hey, man," Rook said as he climbed into Cade's FJ Cruiser. Buckling up, he glanced around, noting the discarded coffee cups and wrappers. "Don't you ever clean up in here? A man's ride should reflect him." He ran a finger along the dash, leaving a trail in the dust.

"I've been living in here, driving back and forth from Stillwater. If it makes you feel better, I'll get it detailed when the case is over." Cade pulled out onto the street in the North Loop area of Minneapolis. "Nice neighborhood."

"Yeah, man, I like it. Forbes magazine called the North Loop one of America's best hipster neighborhoods."

Cade guffawed as he glanced over. "Hipster? That's your selling point?"

Rook shrugged. "What can I say? I'm not as vanilla as you think. I'm cultured."

"If you say so," Cade said with a chuckle. "I liked your place, though. Fancy brick townhouse."

"Much better than the straw house I looked at first."

Cade smiled, and they rode in a semi-comfortable silence for a while. When they drove onto the university campus, Cade spoke up.

"So, tell me what you saw yesterday. I know the license plate was a dead end."

Rook shook his head. "The killer switched the plates, so yeah."

"I was talking to my friend, Grace, at the BCA. She said the killer will have his routines, and he'll follow them through his victim selection process, as well." Cade signaled and took a turn. "Did you get a sense for his routine?"

Rook shrugged and turned in his seat. "It was almost organic. Let me walk you through what I saw on the video. The killer was already seated when Albright arrived and joined her three friends at their table. The dude was seated with a clear sightline to her table. He had an open book in front of him, but he was more about scouting than reading. He never turned a page. When Albright and her friends left, she stayed behind to use the restroom. The man got up quickly and headed for the restrooms, too. There's no camera covering that area, but a minute later when the unsub got back into the frame, Albright was right behind him. At the stairs, he gestures for her to go first. And right before they went out of sight, it looked like she turned toward him."

"He must have said something." Cade drove past the Walter Library building and headed for his usual loading dock parking spot.

"He must have said a lot of things, because when they get to the first floor, they're shoulder to shoulder, and she's touching his arm. Like this." Rook reached over and put a hand on Cade's forearm.

"If you do that again, I'm going to shoot you," Cade said as he shut off the truck.

"Fine, it didn't do anything for me anyway," Rook said, grinning. He unbuckled and paused with a hand on the door. "Albright and the unsub were still side by side all the way out to her vehicle. After a moment's pause, they walked back to his sedan, and he opened the rear passenger door. It looked like he jabbed her with something and shoved her into the back seat."

"Bastard."

"Yep."

Getting out, they walked in silence to the library's entrance. The morning air was crisp, and the sidewalks were full of students with backpacks, maroon and gold sweatshirts, still half-asleep faces, even with the omnipresent coffee cups and energy drinks. Ahh, college life. Cade remembered it fondly.

At the front door, Crocker wasn't waiting this time, so they followed a pair of students inside. They stood in the lobby area and tried not to be overly conspicuous.

Cade glanced around before turning back to his partner. "It sounds like our unsub was caught on camera a fair amount. Did you get a good face shot so we can run it through facial recognition?"

Rook shook his head. "The dude had it figured out. I was flabbergasted. Not once did he offer a decent view of his face. He'd either be looking away, covering his face, or positioning himself out of the camera's view. And then, just to prove he knew the camera was there, he flipped off the one in the parking lot before driving off." Rook held up the screenshot of the man holding up his middle finger for Cade. "Notice how he uses his hand to cover his face."

"Let me see those," Cade said, gesturing to the printouts in Rook's hand. He flipped through the pages, pausing to look at the parking lot closeup of Albright. His stomach tensed as he studied her. "The killer picked a victim that perfectly matched Sweetwater's victims. Every one of them blonde and stunningly attractive, the kind that turn heads when they enter a room."

"Why do you suppose this killer chose that type?" Rook said.

Cade shook his head. "If I had to guess, I'd say he wanted to catch my attention. That's why he called me out in the note, and left Reynold's station logo at the murder scene."

"Makes sense." Rook looked up as Crocker joined them and stuck out his hand. "Terrance Rooker, Minneapolis P.D."

"Darius Crocker, professor of computer science. Nice to meet you."

Cade filled him in while they made the trek to the basement, Crocker asking the occasional question as they went. They stopped outside the door to the lab as the professor keyed in the code.

"The cleaning crew doesn't get down here any too often, do

they?" Rook said as he looked around. "It doesn't look like anyone gets down here, to be honest."

Crocker laughed as he pushed open the door. "That's the way we want it."

Cade couldn't help but smile at Rook's wide eyes at the state-of-the-art computer equipment beyond the door. He wandered around the room, taking it all in. Tubbs was in his usual chair but was joined at the table by three older students, two women and a man.

Crocker introduced the detectives and Tubbs. He nodded to the students. "These are our graduate students." All three looked nervous as they looked up at the investigators, but only one spoke up.

"I'm Jackie," the blonde-haired woman said. "I'm the lead graduate assistant. If you need anything, come to me." From the looks on the other two's faces, this was the first they'd heard about their lower status. The other grad students were introduced as Denver and Courtney, both in the computer science program. Jackie was in Professor Tubbs' psychology program.

Crocker nodded to Cade, giving him his speaking cue.

"Thanks everyone. We're happy to have your support," Cade said as he took a seat. Rook sat next to him, hands stuffed in his jacket pockets. "I'm sure you've all been filled in, but let me make sure we're on the same page. Your professors have discovered a dark website for serial killers called Orbiting Cortex. Because of the recent high-profile killing of Marlin Sweetwater, the Blonde Killer, a challenge was issued to its members to come here and kill. We've had one murder so far that is most definitely related to the Orbiting Cortex site. We believe this site can be an invaluable tool to help identify the killer and help gain insights into his thought process. Serial killers tend to work alone, so sharing of exploits is typically post-mortem—after they've been caught. With your help, we can catch this killer before he kills again."

Cade looked around at the eager faces in front of him. "Any questions?"

Denver, the computer science grad assistant, waved a hand. He looked to be mid-twenties, in shape, and Latino. "I'm new to the whole serial killer thing. Is this killer moving here permanently? Or is it more of a murder vacation?"

The other two grad students grinned. One said, "Murder vacation: band name."

Cade smiled and nodded. "You raise a good question. We have no way of knowing which it is. If I had to venture a guess, I would say he's here short term. Long enough to meet his objectives, whatever they may be. But you never know."

Courtney held up a hand. "Are we in any danger helping to catch him?"

Cade shook his head.

"It's okay if we are," Courtney said. "I like a little risk and danger. It makes me feel alive." She said this with the passion of someone having just survived jumping out of a plane.

The other two grad students turned and stared at her.

Rook leaned forward.

"It's the dopamine," Jackie explained. "Certain people tend to live life on the edge—it involves the neurotransmitter dopamine, the brain's feel-good chemical. Studies suggest that facing risk and danger increases dopamine release in the brain, possibly enhancing the expectation of reward. Thrills in this case. Our little thrill-seeker," she said, giving Courtney a nudge.

Cade wondered what he'd gotten himself into. "No, you shouldn't be in any real danger. You're isolated down here from pretty much the entire planet, let alone from the killer. There's no way he could ever know that you're helping the major crimes task force."

"The Five Below major crimes task force," Rook added. "Trademark pending."

"Dude, I think someone's beat you to it," Denver said with a laugh.

Cade rolled his eyes, but he was also grinning. "I think this is going to work out just fine," he said. "But we need to get going on this ASAP."

Crocker nodded. "My thought was to catalog the posts. Figure out how many users there are on the site and work up a profile on each one. Maybe we can identify characteristics of each and find out what area of the country they are based out of. From there, you can reach out to the local law enforcement agencies and see what they have as far as modus operandi," he said. "Hopefully, you'll end up with actionable information that will help catch the killer."

Cade glanced to Tubbs, who was on his tablet. The man had been silent for much of the discussion. For the next half hour, the team worked out specific roles, and discussed recruiting a few more grad students to spread out the workload. Denver and Jackie both said they knew people they could ask. Courtney said she would try to come up with someone as well. When everyone agreed on how to proceed, Cade stood up.

"Thanks, everyone. You're all pioneers in this endeavor. Your work here will save lives."

Crocker said he'd walk the detectives back to the upstairs lobby. As Rook followed him out, Tubbs spoke up. "Dawkins, a word."

Something in his tone told Cade it was important. He told Rook and Crocker he'd meet them upstairs and stayed behind to talk with the professor. Tubbs waved him over to a desk away from the grad students huddled around a monitor. "I thought your partner's name sounded familiar, so I looked him up. Seems he has a reputation."

Sighing, Cade put a hand on Tubb's arm. "Let me stop you there. I won't be vetting your grad students, and I'd appreciate it if you'd offer me the same professional courtesy." He held the older man's gaze.

After a moment, Cade broke into a grin. "Still friends?" he asked, holding out a hand.

"Of course," Tubbs said with a smile. "I'm a grown-ass man. We're allowed to have disagreements. That's part of life." He stood up and said, "Now go catch the killer. You have more important things to be doing than humoring an old man."

Rook waited for him in the busy lobby. Neither said anything until they got outside, and then Rook shot Cade a sideways glance.

"So, what did he have to say about me?" Rook walked alongside Cade as they headed toward the loading dock.

"You picked up on that, huh?" Cade said.

"It wasn't difficult. The way he'd look at me while he was busy on his tablet. Then, after a moment, his eyes went wide, and he was eyeballing me again." Rook shook his head. "You have one bad day..."

Arriving at the truck, Cade gestured for Rook to follow him around to the vehicle's rear. He swung open the cargo door and lifted the lid off a cooler. Cade handed Rook a water and opened one of his own. After taking a long pull, he leaned back on the edge of the cargo area.

"It doesn't matter to me what reputation you come with, but since you brought it up, you have me curious about your one bad day," Cade said as he glanced at his partner, "Would you care to share? This is a judgment-free zone."

Rook ran a hand over the stubble that was his hair. "You have anything stronger in that cooler?"

Cade laughed. "Of course, we're not some aloof major crimes task force. I have Blue Moon if you want a beer."

Rook handed his untouched water bottle back to Cade.

After taking a long pull on the beer, Rook turned to Cade. "Here's the story. I was working robbery homicide. Last year, a series of ultra-violent liquor store robberies happened around south Minneapolis. I don't know if you remember them, but there were these two guys, brazen as hell, that came in guns blazing. They'd fire at anything; people, windows and especially bottles. They'd shoot the bottles off the shelves like it was some carnival sideshow. The liquor store would be a frickin' disaster after they'd left. They never made any attempt to cover up or hide their faces. We had them on multiple cameras clear as day, but they were so average looking, no one could say they recognized them." Rook glanced at his partner. "I mean, you people do look alike."

"Us people?" Cade asked, shaking his head.

"Yeah, you white dudes with your facial hair and plaid shirts. Y'all want to be lumberjacks or something?" Rook grinned at him and winked.

Cade grinned back. "You're the one living in the hipster neighborhood."

"Fair point," Rook said. "Anyway, since their faces didn't give away anything, I studied the videos looking for something else and noticed one of the dudes had a slight hitch in his walk. His right foot turned slightly inward as he stepped forward. I watched the surveillance videos thousands of times, studying his walk and I noticed that his foot wobbled a bit as well." Rook demonstrated the perp's walk for Cade.

"As luck would have it, I was in Uptown having breakfast at Spyhouse coffee. I was chatting with the barista, and something about a customer caught my eye. Something raised that red flag we get, know what I mean?" He looked at Cade.

With a nod, Cade said, "I do get you. We all have that intuition when something isn't quite right."

"Yeah, I had that. Anyway, I watched him in line as he went up to the counter. But it wasn't until he picked up his coffee and walked out that I recognized his peculiar gait. It was the dude from the hold-ups. So, I asked Muffy—"

"Muffy?"

"Yeah, Muffy, the barista. Pay attention. I asked Muffy to watch my laptop and stuff, and I followed him out. He had two cups and was drinking from one of them as he walked. The dude was absolutely slamming his coffee. I've never seen anyone drink coffee like a shot of fireball before. Mainlining his caffeine, I guess."

"I guess," Cade agreed.

Rook took another drink and continued. "Down the block, he meets up with another lumberjack-looking dude and gives him the other cup. They were hanging there, gulping their coffees and gazing across the parking lot of the strip center. I looked that way, and across the parking lot was a liquor store. They're casing the place I figured. But when they tossed their coffees to the ground and marched across the lot, I knew they were going to hit the place."

Nodding, Cade said, "That would've been my guess as well."

"I pulled out my pistol and reached for my phone, but I'd left my phone at the table back at Spyhouse." Rook held up his palms. "There was nothing else I could do, so I ran over to a woman standing nearby. She looked petrified seeing me run toward her with a gun. I told her it might look confusing, but I was a cop and needed her to call the police."

He paused while he took another drink. "Right as she nodded and pulled out her phone, there was a crack of a gun firing, followed by easily a dozen more in several seconds. Both men must have completely unloaded when they got into the store. I turned and ran for the liquor store."

Rook looked off into the distance before continuing.

"They were coming out as I got there. I identified myself and told them to drop their weapons. The one with the odd gait hustled off, and the other drew on me and opened up. I dove for the protection of a car while he peppered it with bullets. A lot of civilians were in the area, and I was worried they'd be hit. I holstered my weapon and ran down the length of the row of cars before doubling back on the other side. When I got to the end of the row, he was right there. His gun was still pointed at the vehicle I'd used as cover. I tackled him harder than a Vikings' defensive lineman spotting the Packer's quarterback looking the other way. He went down hard, his head hitting the pavement. The impact left him dazed, and I had him cuffed in a moment. His odd-gait partner climbed into a beater Mustang that was parked on Hennepin Avenue, and he pulled out squealing tires."

Rook turned to Cade and looking him in the eyes. "I couldn't let him get away. It was a complete stroke of luck that I'd spotted him. What are the odds I'd ever see him again?"

"Slim to none," Cade said matter-of-factly.

"Yeah, exactly. But when I reached into my pocket, it was empty. My car keys were also back at the coffee shop. I remember calling out in frustration that I needed a car. A man nearby held up his keys and said I could take his. He was standing next to a blue Volkswagen Beetle."

Rook ran a hand over his head.

"You know in life, there are those moments where you reach a crossroads, and you hope you take the correct road." Rook paused. "I did not."

"Really?"

"Really. You see, right next to the Volkswagen, a woman climbed out of a Mercedes. A beautiful cardinal red Mercedes that had to have a powerful engine. I looked back at the Beetle and said, "f that," and went for the woman's vehicle. I told the platinum-haired woman I needed her Mercedes and suggested she get out of the way. She wasn't exactly happy with my choice, but the bad guy was getting away. I climbed in and took off down Hennepin Avenue. The Mercedes had a lot under the hood, and I caught up with him by 27th. He'd taken a left and soon I was right on his bumper. He blew through a stop as he turned on Lyndale and headed north. The interstate was less than a mile down the road."

Rook's eyes lit up as he relived the chase.

"The dude weaved through traffic like a pro, and it was all I could do to avoid the other cars. I wanted to return the woman's cardinal red Mercedes in the same pristine condition as when I borrowed it."

"Borrowed is one way to describe it," Cade commented.

"It's as good as any other word." Rook said. "At the intersection before the freeway entrance, the dude runs the red, sideswiping a car turning into the lane. It spins and I end up clipping it as well. We hit the ramp, and now we're rocketing past other cars onto 94 near downtown. Without a phone, there was no way to alert backup of my location. I couldn't lose him."

Rook finished the last of his beer. "When I pulled alongside, he swerved right at me. With the Mercedes no longer in pristine condition, I swerved back, and we were grinding up against each other like two high schoolers at prom. He's looking over at me and I'm looking back. No way this dude was getting away."

Cade was getting a feeling where the story might be going.

Rook handed his empty to Cade as he continued. "As our speed climbed past ninety, we approached 35 where the never-ending road construction was going on, and the lanes shifted down to three and then to two. He's yelling at me, and I held up a finger, just so he knew I understood."

"Communication is so important in our line of work," Cade said, as he grabbed several more beers from the cooler. He opened his and took a drink.

Rook accepted the offered Blue Moon and flipped the top into the cooler. Taking a long drink, he sighed. "This was another of those crossroads where I could have chosen another path. In retrospect, I should have simply slowed and tucked in behind him. There wasn't any way he was going to outrun me; I would have followed until I could flag down a State Patrol trooper or one of us ran out of gas. But no, I stayed right up against him, jockeying for position and advantage, as sparks flew from our car duel. At one point, I considered rolling down the window and taking a shot at him. But then, when we got down to two lanes, he nudged me onto the gravel shoulder, and I lost traction. And not a little, either. The Mercedes went into a crazy spin, and I was launched into the air."

Rook turned to Cade. "You know how when they are redoing the roads, they push all the dirt and gravel into a huge mountain so they can use it later? Well, the Mercedes ended up in that mountain a good twenty feet off the ground, the nose completely buried in the heap. I had to climb out the back seat to exit the vehicle."

Rook shook his head. "Worst of all, the dude was gone. I'd lost him."

Cade had a feeling and looked at his partner. "I'm guessing that actually wasn't the worst part."

Rook had a grim look on his face and shook his head. "No, the worst part was finding out the platinum-haired woman Mercedes owner was the mayor's wife. When word spread that I turned down the other guy's offered vehicle to take her vehicle, the shit hit the fan."

Cade shook his head as he let out a long whistle. "I can imagine."

"Man, you have no idea." Rook took another drink. "The mayor came down so hard on the department everyone was afraid for their job, and then we lost a significant chunk of our operating budget. After that, my lieutenant, as well as my fellow officers, had it in for me. I was transferred out of the prestigious robbery homicide and left to wither and die working nights in the violent crimes division. That was, until you happened along with a lifeline."

Rook studied his partner for a long minute. "Only if you still want me. I wouldn't blame you for cutting me loose after hearing about that shitshow."

Cade didn't say anything as he polished off the last of his beer. He tossed the empty bottle into the cooler. He held out a hand for Rook's bottle. Cade added it to the cooler and closed it.

He turned to Rook. "We wouldn't be Five Below without you. We're teammates, and we're not going to let some bad luck in your past change that." He shook Rook's hand firmly as he held the man's gaze. "Don't worry, you're not going anywhere. We have us a killer to catch."

CHAPTER 10

Michael Pavich stepped off the bus. The ride had been long, but comfortable. Having his own power outlet to recharge his laptop, phone, and Nintendo Switch had kept him sane. And the bus wi-fi had been a huge bonus. The journey to Minneapolis had taken over seven hours, and yet, his piece of work mother had claimed the bus was better than flying. At least she'd paid for his ticket. But he knew she bought his ticket to get him out of her basement for a while.

He had little reason to leave it normally. He'd picked up a website development gig, using the WordPress platform to build out clients' websites. His boss never had to see him, and he never had to see her. They communicated through email, which was best as he stumbled through any conversation with any female. They all made him uncomfortable and nervous.

He blamed his mother.

His mom would never win a parenting award. She berated him and denounced his manhood at every opportunity. But she was all he had; he'd never known his dad. Mother said his dad left the day he was born. She left little doubt that she thought it was his fault.

But if you didn't want me, why'd you conceive me in the first place?

The basement was his refuge. It was a refuge from his screaming mother. His refuge from his weeping mother. His refuge from his drunk mother. But also, his refuge from real life.

Over the last few years, he'd found a reason to leave his refuge. At first, he'd slip out after his mother had passed out just to go looking. He was intensely curious about the opposite sex and wanted to watch them. They'd lived in the rundown section near downtown, where industrial met the poor people's homes. He'd discovered that there was a particular type of woman that didn't mind hanging out in the littered sidewalks, talking to the men who drove on the pothole-filled streets. The women often went for short rides with these men.

It eluded him what men could say that would entice a woman like that to get into their cars. It had been painful in school to blubber out a few words and have the girl turn away and laugh. He stopped trying after seeing the schoolgirls point at him while they whispered who knows what. He could never say anything that would entice a woman. So, he simply watched from a safe distance.

These women on the sidewalk all had a look to them. They dressed utterly different from his mother. With their big hair, tight clothes and sauntering walks, these women caught his attention. He would lay awake remembering the women he saw, developing fantasies about talking to them. Enticing them. Being near them. Touching them.

These fantasies intruded on his work, and he began making stupid mistakes. But even worse, they came during his gaming quests, causing his slide down the points board. It was then he knew he had to do something.

Pavich had been watching the women from his den—that's what he called the hiding place that gave him a clear and protected view from their disappointed looks—and learned their routines. The curly redhead with the obscenely large chest would always go into the alley after coming back from her car rides. The orange-haired one usually wandered off from the herd as she talked on her cell phone. The dirty blonde waited until the others left before she was picked up by the same green and white taxi every night. These behaviors were ingrained into the women just as sure as when his mother screwed off the Smirnoff's cap that she'd be face down on the couch two hours later.

After prodding his snoring mother with his foot, he'd slipped out the back door, careful not to let Mr. Gizmo get out. There was a distant rumble of thunder, and he briefly wondered if this was the best night for boldness. But with HeavyHitter74 overtaking him because he'd missed the troll again, he knew he had to do something. Pavich quickened his pace. His den was two blocks over and one down, and he slid into place as the thunder grew closer. It was nearly 2 a.m.

He watched and waited. The traffic was light tonight with the approaching storm, but there was always traffic. The men never stopped coming. When the curly redhead climbed into the van, he knew it was time. He lifted the cardboard away from the hedge and slid out, looking carefully to check if anyone was nearby. Coast clear, he hunkered his large frame down and ran for the alley. Like most alleys, this one had strewn garbage, chairs sitting outside the back doors of the businesses, and large green dumpsters that were perfect for hiding behind. He knelt behind the furthest one and waited.

The smell was terrible. Warm summer nights with near-tropical humidity brought out the festering garbage odors. He switched to breathing through his mouth to survive his wait, and it helped a little. Another rumble of thunder. He waved away the mosquitos buzzing his ear, but they were undeterred and attacked on multiple fronts, biting in quick succession on his neck, forearm and cheek. He felt his frustration and anger grow.

Pavich peered out from behind the dumpster when he heard a shoe scrape. It was the curly redhead, back from her car ride. She was never gone long, so she must not travel too far. She walked in the glow of the overhead lights to the chairs behind the check cashing place. Dropping into a folding chair, she cleared her throat. The sound of her spitting was drowned out by the thunder's rumble. She opened her bag and pulled something out that looked to be pencil sized. She held it up in the light and he recognized it. It was a syringe.

Enthralled by this unexpected development, he stepped around the side of the dumpster, happy to move away from whatever was burning his nostrils. He took a step closer to the woman. And then another.

Putting her foot on the other folding chair, she leaned down with the syringe. Her shoes were the open-toed, strappy kind with a tall platform and taller heels. Pushing her toes apart, she stuck the needle between the big toe and the second one and plunged the syringe. She gasped. Dropping the used syringe into her bag, she leaned back as her head rolled to the side.

Pavich couldn't help himself and took even more steps to get closer. The woman's shirt lay open and one of her breasts had popped out. This was something new and exciting, something he'd always thought about. It was like one of the women in his game quests. Moving closer, he was well out in the open now. If someone came into the alley, it would be obvious what he was doing. But like a wild animal smelling blood, his lust drove him forward. Consequences were not on his mind, and nothing could have stopped him now.

His immense shadow dwarfed the woman. With her head rolled back, she wasn't yet aware of his presence. Not knowing what to do, he simply stood there. He'd fantasized about stepping out of the shadows and having the woman shrink back in fear. She would tremble as she took in his manliness, but ultimately swoon in awe. The thought that real life may be different from games and fantasies poked at him, but he hadn't paid it any attention.

The rumbling of thunder gave way a crack of thunder as the storm arrived. Fat drops of rain dropped. The woman raised her head and opened her eyes.

"Oh, shit, who are you?" Confusion on her face. Her eyes regained their focus as she looked at him. "You're that guy. The lurker."

She didn't look at him in fear. Or even tremble. She certainly didn't swoon.

If you could picture the reaction someone would have after drinking sour milk, with their look of disgust and anger, you'd be close. Too close.

The blood coursed through his veins as he looked down on her. His hands clenched into fists as the muscles in his jaw tightened.

That was the day he became a killer. As the rain came down in sheets and the sky was alive with cracks of thunder and brilliant flashes, he took her. No one could hear her shrieks as he bit and bled her. No one came to her rescue. No one saved her.

THE KILLER GRABBED his suitcase from the Megabus' luggage area. The bus man looked at Pavich as if he expected something in return just for pulling out his battered suitcase that his mom had rescued from the Goodwill. The killer ignored the man and grabbed his suitcase, easily lifting it over the heads of the other waiting passengers. He pulled the bag behind him as he walked out of the depot, wanting to separate himself. People made him uneasy.

He walked for a mile or more, past the baseball stadium, past the trendy restaurants and shops, past all the apartment buildings. As he walked farther north, the trendy gave way to industrial and run down. He knew he was in the right area when he came upon BJ's Liquor Lounge. Even though it looked closed, seeing a working man's strip club made him feel like he was in his element. Small manufacturing businesses and delivery trucks were common, as was the graffiti and trash. And virtually no ornamental touches that were in the better areas of town. This was the part of a city that felt like home.

As he stepped around a stained mattress leaning against a utility pole, the killer spotted a woman getting off a city bus. She looked in her mid-twenties and was dressed in a navy skirt and matching jacket. She had dark hair and cinnamon-colored skin. She glanced in his direction but paid him no mind as she moved down the sidewalk. She never looked around, keeping her head down.

Pavich followed her.

The killer took in a full breath of air, savoring the moment. He was happy to be hunting again. Over the last several years, he'd taken a half-dozen women from his neighborhood. With each new victim, he'd let himself indulge in the experience of it and let his instincts take over. Oddly enough, it left him with little conscious memory of how it happened. With his brain out of the equation, the resulting ferocity had surprised him. And delighted him.

The killer, his savagery complete, lingered as he took in all the little details. The way her eyes looked when the light had gone out of them. The feel of her body as he tenderly traced rivulets of blood across the bite marks. The scent of her throat...and the other areas. These impressions and memories were imprinted in his mind and carried him until the next time. Until the next kill.

When he was done with his examination, he'd simply leave her, discarding her as so much waste. His mind would be cloudy and completely satiated from the experience as he returned home. He'd taken to using the garden hose, turning the frigid water on himself, before entering his house. There was simply too much blood that could get on everything if he didn't wash it off. Even his hopeless mother would have noticed the blood trail to the basement.

The best thing about his mother was her complete self-absorption. She wasn't worried about what he was up to. And really, having someone interested in his activities wouldn't go well. What if she watched him go out at night? What if she followed him while he stalked? Worse, what if she noticed his condition when he returned home? Or what if she went through his room and discovered his mementos? He'd always taken something from each woman before he left. It helped when he wanted to revisit the experience later.

When Pavich brought up the idea of coming here, of him going to the convention, she was all for it. She'd even paid for his ticket. It hadn't been a tearful goodbye as his loving mother watched him walk away. If it wasn't for the rent she got from him each month, he suspected she didn't want him to come back. He honestly didn't know if he should go home. His work could be done from anywhere, and he certainly could hunt anywhere. Sometimes it's good to broaden the killing grounds before he was found and stopped.

Consequences were never his thing. Or the future, really. He was more of a day-to-day kind of thinker. Other than minimizing his chances of being caught or discovered, he didn't much think about anything beyond today. Getting caught meant no more hunting, and that would be bad. But being locked in a cage would be worse.

For now, he was happy to be on the trail of the woman. A stream of consciousness ran through his head as he walked behind her.

She's mine. Looking down is the prey indicator. I wonder how she smells. She's mine. I'm going to take her. I need a safe place to have her. I'm going to take my time and enjoy every inch. Every single inch.

Thoughts and ideas came lightning fast. He didn't know if everyone was wired the way he was, sometimes he thought everyone was, but then at times he thought he was the most extraordinary person the planet had birthed. Pavich wiped the spittle from the corner of his mouth and ran his tongue over his canine teeth. The killer liked the way the sharp teeth felt against his tongue. When he studied himself in the bathroom mirror, it looked like his canines were more prominent than they should be. He supposed it meant something, but he wasn't sure what that would be.

The killer sized up the surroundings as he continued his pursuit. Not yet. It wasn't time.

The woman led him down a side street of fenced front yards and barred windows. This was not unlike his own neighborhood. People stayed safely shut in from the dangers outside. They weren't at their windows because they didn't want to see anything. Or witness anything.

He knew he needed to take her soon. Once she was inside, he may not be able to get at her. The doors would be fortified in this neighborhood.

The woman paused and turned up a sidewalk, opening the gate and continuing up the walk. At the steps of the porch, she dug into the mailbox. She came back out with several envelopes and was opening one of them as she unlocked the front door.

Now.

Tossing his suitcase over, the killer effortlessly jumped the fence and ran the woman down. He caught her as she opened the door, and he knocked her to the floor. The door slammed closed, shutting out the world behind them. With the guttural snarl of a wild animal, the killer was all over her.

Smelling her.

Tasting her.

Biting her.

Killing her.

CHAPTER 11

Sunday Morning

Cade's head felt like concrete after a long night of drinking. His condition came not from socializing and alcohol but from too much coffee and too little sleep. He'd been going over the information gathered so far—which was not enough by a long shot.

A killer had arrived in his state. A killer was there because of him. Displaying signs of being an organized serial killer, this killer looked to be a planner—yet signs of disorganization were present too. The killer had not carefully stalked his victim, instead he'd relied on his wits and charm to draw her in. She had not been afraid of him at all. In fact, she'd looked attracted to him, judging on her flirtatious touches in the video footage. The ability to blend in and actively acquire his victim on the fly was unusual.

It also made him extremely dangerous.

While the traditional disorganized killer would savagely attack his victim with little regard for his surroundings, this killer was completely aware. Based on his avoidance of the restaurant's surveillance cameras and the switching license plates that added another layer of protection.

Cade sat up, putting his feet on the floor.

The switching plates part had him thinking of questions that needed answering. Was the Alamo rental car the plates were switched from ever found? Did it have the plates for the killer's Chevy Cruze? That might tell them where the killer was earlier. Depending on where it happened, there may have been a camera to catch the killer removing the Altima's plates. But he doubted the killer would've let his face be seen after the restaurant footage. Same for getting fingerprints from the Altima. He was too careful and too prepared to leave behind prints.

With a massive yawn, Cade stood and stretched. He was looking forward to a leisurely morning shower.

And then his phone rang.

TWENTY-FIVE MINUTES LATER, he climbed out of his truck in north Minneapolis, still unshowered. He'd alerted Rook and wasn't surprised to see his Charger already here. The crime scene was a few miles from Rook's home. Minneapolis squads blocked off the street at either end, keeping bystanders and media far away. Several media trucks were on scene, including the local Fox affiliate and Five News. The others would be here soon enough.

The house was a forties-era clapboard that was kept up better than the surrounding homes. The small front yard was fenced in, as all yards were in the neighborhood. Hennepin County sheriffs were on scene as well as Minneapolis officers. Rook stood on the front step and waved him over.

"You look like shit. Maybe a little sleep and a shower would be a good thing," Rook said, eying up Cade's unruly hair.

Patting down his hair, Cade shrugged. "I was on my way into the shower when the call came in." He looked into the house. "What do we have?"

"Better you see it for yourself," Rook said.

"Okay," Cade replied, noting the look in his partner's eyes.

A Minneapolis officer blocked the door. "You're going to have to go around to the back. Can't have you messing with the scene."

Rook followed Cade around the side of the house. There wasn't much space between the houses, and he wondered if the neighbors heard anything. The narrow walk led to the back, where a small but well-kept yard filled with shrubs and flowers. Another officer stood post in the backyard. Holding his badge case, Cade entered the house into the kitchen. A family room was off to his left. He pushed through the swinging door into the small dining room, where he found the open front door.

"I'll wait here," Rook said. "Seeing it once was more than enough."

An officer stepped aside, and Cade stopped at the entrance to the porch. A woman's body lay face up, her eyes remaining open, though she clearly had died. Blood covered much of her body, the surrounding floor, walls, and even ceiling. The coppery smell of blood was strong, but notes of urine and feces hung in the air as well. The woman's clothes had been torn away from her body, though her undergarments remained. Her blouse was ripped open, and she wore the shreds of it still. Something was odd about her skin, and Cade leaned closer to see what it was. Realization dawned on him, and he staggered back into the house.

He and Rook shared a look.

"Those were bite marks. They were everywhere," Cade said and shuddered. The woman's flesh had been bitten and torn on most exposed areas. He'd never seen anything like it. "There have to be a million ways to die, and all of them are better than this."

Rook nodded, his eyes looking watery and haunted at the same time.

"I need to go back in and look."

Beginning with the surroundings, Cade studied the scene. The woman's purse had been dumped; the contents spread out. Some of the papers were on top of the pooled blood, which meant the killer had gone through her purse post-mortem. Her billfold was out and open. Cade knelt over it and poked at it with a pen. Even though there was no money, robbery was not the motivation here. He flipped it over and read the woman's name on her license. Victoria Rae Garcia. 27 years old. A life cut short.

Garcia's body was sprawled between the porch door and the door to the house. Her feet were closest to the porch door and her head was nearest the other door. It looked as if the animal caught her as she stepped into the enclosed porch area, tackled, and ravaged her right there.

Some part of the victim's outfit was near Cade's feet, and he was careful not to disturb it. The navy fabric was torn in multiple places and looked like it might've been a skirt once. A sense of savagery showed in the ripped material. The killer hadn't asked her to remove her clothing; he'd torn it off her. And then he bit chunks of her flesh. Bite marks everywhere.

"Crime scene is here," a patrolman called in.

Cade pulled out his phone, brought up the camera, and took several pictures of the victim before switching to video. He shot twenty seconds as he moved around the scene, wanting to document everything as best he could. Even though the crime scene techs would photograph everything, he wanted his own record that he could study right away. While his anger was fresh.

Rejoining Rook, Cade shook his head. "This guy is not evenly remotely human. Only an animal could have done that."

"An animal that needs to be put down," Rook said through clenched teeth. "But I don't think he's going to be easy to catch."

"We need to start with the basics here," Cade said. "While the crime scene people do their thing, we need to do ours. Someone must have seen something. Let's check with the neighbors."

Moving outside, they found the supervising officer, a veteran with salt and pepper hair who introduced himself as Mahoney.

"Who found the victim?" he asked.

Mahoney took his time answering. He studied Cade, after first giving Rook a sideways glance. Unfazed, Cade simply waited for his response.

"Are you sure you're law enforcement? You look like the fella who handed me my latte this morning." Mahoney squinted at him, while Rook stifled his laugh.

"I hope you enjoyed it." Cade leaned in conspiratorially. "You see, this law enforcement thing is my side hustle. Coffee is my life."

Behind him, Rook sounded like he'd swallowed a bug.

Mahoney stared at him for a moment before breaking out in laughter. "Okay, you had me going there for a bit." After composing himself, he spoke seriously. "One of the neighbor kids found her. He was selling candy bars for a school sports fundraiser."

"I'd like to speak to him."

Mahoney nodded. "He's right over there," pointing across the street where several officers stood near two boys and a woman who was likely their mother.

Cade stuck out a hand. "Thanks, Sgt. Mahoney. By the way, have you started canvassing the neighborhood yet for possible witnesses?"

He shook his head. "We've been securing the area."

Cade nodded. "As long as we're over there talking to the boy, we'll take that side. Talk to the neighbors. Can you have your officers check this side of the block?"

They arranged to meet up afterward to compare notes on the canvassing and shook hands. The earlier tension was gone, and Mahoney seemed like someone that could be counted on. In law enforcement, like life, those were good people to have in your corner. Too often, people were guided by self-interest instead of the greater good.

Rook and Cade badged the two Minneapolis officers posted by the boy's house. Rook took the lead and approached the woman first.

"Hello, Ma'am. We'd like to talk to your son about what he discovered."

The woman nodded and put a hand on the boy's shoulder in front of her. "This is Darrell."

Rook squatted to get face to face with the boy. "Hi, Darrell. I'm Terrance Rooker, but my friends call me Rook. Would you like to see my badge?"

The boy nodded.

Rook handed him his badge, as the boy's eyes lit up. "How old are you, Darrell?"

"I'm twelve, almost thirteen." He traced the eagle on the top of the badge.

"You were visiting the Garcia house for your school fundraiser?" Rook asked.

The boy nodded, still transfixed with Rook's badge.

"Use your words, Darrell." His mother shot him a look while she held onto the other boy, who looked several years younger than Darrell. They were clearly brothers, though. They had the same exact eyes.

"Um, yeah. I'm supposed to sell my candy bars to friends, family, and neighbors."

"What are you raising the money for, Darrell?" Rook asked.

"For my football team," he said.

"Not soccer?" Cade interjected.

Darrell shook his head while making a face. "No way. Soccer is for wusses."

Cade put a hand over his heart while Rook broke up.

"Darrell, I play soccer. Do I look like a wuss?" Immediately after asking, Cade thought better of it when he saw Darrell's face.

"Don't answer that, Darrell," his mother said. "I told you not to disrespect people."

Cade turned to his partner, who looked to be enjoying himself. "I'm sure you must have more questions for the young man," he prompted.

"Darrell, will you tell us what you saw when you went over to the Garcia house?" Rook held the young boy's gaze while the boy turned over the badge case in his tiny hands.

"I knew Miss Vickie gets home from work around six, so I waited until six-thirty before going over. I didn't want to wait because mom doesn't want me going out after dark. I went up to her door and heard something. It was like the snarl in Beauty and the Beast when the king attacked. I glanced inside and ran home." The boy's voice trembled.

"What did you see when you looked inside?" Rook asked.

"There was a giant on top of Miss Vickie. He was..." Darrell's voice trailed off.

Rook touched the boy's shoulder. "I know it was scary, but it will help if you can describe what you saw."

Darrell's mom put a hand around her son's shoulder. He looked up at her, and she nodded.

"It looked like the man was taking bites out of her. She was thrashing like you do when you want to get someone off of you."

"Did you see his face?" Rook asked.

Darrell shook his head. "The man had his back toward me."

Cade stepped closer. "Darrell, how did you know it was a man?"

Shivering, Darrell looked at Cade. "The man turned his head to spit something. I saw the side of his head then, and it looked like his face was wet. That's when I ran. I didn't want him to see me."

Rook nodded. "I understand. I would have run, too."

"He was huge," Darrell added.

Cade glanced at his watch. It was 9:15 a.m. "Darrell, you went over to see Miss Vickie after she got home from work. What did you do after you ran home?"

Darrell glanced at his mother. She nodded.

"I...I went to my room and got under the covers." He looked nervous as he fidgeted.

"Did you tell your mom what you saw?" Rook asked with a glance to Cade. Clearly, he didn't right away.

The boy shook his head. "I told her my tummy hurt and stayed in bed. But when I got up this morning, I went to her and told her I was scared for Miss Vickie."

Darrell's mother picked up the story. "When he told me, I asked why. There was something in his expression. I told him it was okay and to tell me what made him scared. He was crying as he told me the story, and I knew he was telling the truth. That's when I called the police."

"That was very brave of you, Darrell. I'm glad you told her what you saw." Rook rubbed the boy's head. "You did the right thing."

"Will Miss Vickie be okay?" he asked. His eyes welled with giant tears.

Rook shook his head. "But we will catch the man who did this," he said. "So, no one else gets hurt."

Darrell's mother hugged him tight as the tears fell. The boy trembled in her arms.

They turned to leave, and Cade stopped. "Hey, Darrell. Do you have any candy bars left to sell?"

Darrell nodded, his lip quivering still.

"I like chocolate. How much are they?"

His voice cracking, Darrell answered. "Three dollars. Or four bars for ten dollars."

"Three dollars? They used to be only a dollar."

"And comic books used to be a quarter," Rook said. "Pay the boy."

"I guess I get four of them." Cade opened his wallet and pulled out a twenty. "That's all I got."

"Not a problem." Plucking the bill from Cade's hand, the kid headed for the house. "Be right back with your chocolate bars," he said over his shoulder.

"And my change," Cade called out, but if Darrell heard him, he didn't let on.

A moment later, Darrell was back and diligently counted out the eight chocolate bars that Cade apparently had agreed to purchase. "Thanks for supporting my team," he said. "When I turn pro, I'll have my publicist send you an autographed 8 x 10."

Cade was still shaking his head as they headed up the walk. They briefly discussed the canvassing strategy and Cade went right while Rook went left. Time to knock on doors.

THE CANVASSING WAS A DEAD END. No one heard or saw a thing. Not a single thing.

"How could it be that absolutely no one witnessed anything? It strains the credibility." Cade shook his head.

"I don't think anyone is covering up anything for someone else." Rook gestured at the homes that lined the street. "You don't understand the neighborhood. This isn't the suburbs. People here go into their homes and shut out the world. They don't want to know or be seen looking. So, they live their lives inside where they're protected from the outside dangers."

"But it has to be different for the kids." Cade looked at his partner. "They still play outside, right?"

Rook nodded. "They do, but they're under careful supervision. And it's often in backyards." He pointed across the street where several Minneapolis cops stood on the front steps of the house second to the corner. "There's a swing set in the backyard of the corner house. Maybe someone was outside."

"Maybe," Cade said. "Let's take the corner house." They crossed the street, and Cade gestured to the officers that they'd take the next house. An officer gave the thumbs-up sign before turning back to the older couple standing at the open door.

They rang the bell and waited. "I got this," Rook said.

The door tentatively opened, and a small face peered up at them.

"Hi there," Rook said. "We're police officers." He smiled at the young girl.

The girl pushed the door shut.

Rook turned to Cade, who burst out laughing. He gestured for his partner to try again.

Rook rapped on the door.

After a moment, the door opened again. The same young face looked up at Rook. He knelt to get eye level with the young girl. "Hi, my name is Terrance Rooker, but my friends call me—"

The door closed.

"I guess she didn't want to be your friend," Cade said with a grin. "Let me try this time. I've always been good with kids."

"Whatever, man." Rook stepped back and Cade leaned in and gently knocked on the door.

"Watch this."

Once again, the same young face peered out when the door opened.

"Do you like candy?" Cade asked as he tried to smile broadly.

The door slammed shut. "Momma," a young voice shouted. "There's a pre-vert on our porch." The girl drew out the two syllables like it was the worst thing in the world, let alone having one on one's porch.

Rook turned to Cade. "Really? Candy?"

Laughter behind them had Cade and Rook turning around. The pair of officers canvassing next door were doubled over with laughter. "Looks like we may have to arrest this pre-vert," one of the officers said.

"I'll look for evidence in his white van," the other said.

"Get me a chocolate bar," the first officer said. "Pre-verts in white vans have the best candy." He was laughing so hard he had difficulty getting his words out.

Cade tossed him a three-dollar chocolate bar. "It's on me."

The officer looked surprised and turned to his partner. Both were wide-eyed.

"It's a long story," Cade said.

Officer K. Pleasant, as his name badge read, opened the bar, and took a bite. "This is good candy. The internet memes don't lie."

He stepped up onto the porch between Cade and Rook, rapping sharply on the door. "Maize, it's Officer Pleasant. Go get your momma." He turned to Cade and made a show of taking another bite.

The door opened widely. The woman took in the four men, while her daughter clung to her leg. She brightened when she saw Officer Pleasant.

"Officer Kevin, it's nice to see you again." She was giving him a bashful smile. The kind of smile you offer when you're an infatuated teenager.

"Miss Sophie, there's been some trouble at the Garcia home. I was wondering if you'd seen or heard anything? It would have been yesterday evening after five." He looked at her intently.

Brows furrowed, she shook her head. "I don't think so. I don't remember anything out of the ordinary. I was making dinner, then watching Netflix. Nothing special."

"Well, if you think of something..." Officer Pleasant began.

"Maize, how about you? Were you outside? Playing in your backyard?" Cade asked.

Maize looked at Cade but offered nothing.

Officer Pleasant knelt and broke off a piece of the chocolate bar. He looked up at her mom, who nodded. Maize accepted the offered candy.

"Maize, were you outside playing after dinner last night?" he asked.

She nodded as she nibbled on the candy. It looked huge in her tiny hand.

"Did you see anyone you didn't know?" Officer Pleasant lived up to his name as he smiled broadly and handed her another piece of Darrell's three-dollar candy bar.

Maize nodded.

"Tell Officer Kevin what you saw. It's okay." Miss Sophie put a comforting hand on the girl's shoulder.

"A big man was on the road. He was walking his suitcase."

Cade looked at Rook.

Still kneeling, Officer Pleasant calmly asked, "Did you see what the man looked like?"

Maize nodded.

"Was his skin color more like this man's," he pointed to Cade, "or more like his?" He pointed to Rook.

Maize pointed to Cade.

"Was his hair lighter or darker?"

"It was dark," Maize said. Her voice was soft as she drew out the words.

"Long hair or short hair?" Pleasant asked.

Maize's face screwed up. She hesitated.

"It wasn't long or short. Just a lot of it. And it was on his face too." Maize nodded to herself.

"That's good, Maize. Now, let's talk about his suitcase. You said the man was walking his suitcase." Pleasant gave her another piece of the bar. "I'm not sure what you mean."

"You know," Maize said. She looked at Pleasant like he should know.

"I'm not sure I do."

"When you walk your dog. The puppy follows you on a leash." She shrugged. "It was like that. His suitcase followed him."

Cade spoke up. "So, you're saying he was pulling his suitcase behind him? It was rolling on wheels?"

Maize nodded.

"Thank you so much, Miss Maize. You've been wonderful." Officer Pleasant smiled at her.

Cade handed her mother a candy bar. "Thank you."

On the sidewalk, Cade shook Pleasant's hand. "I appreciate you stepping in. You made a big difference."

"Not a problem. Do you have another candy bar?" Pleasant asked. "I gave mine away."

"Do you suppose the killer took the suitcase from the Garcia house? Was it a burglary too?" Rook looked perplexed.

"I know serial killers like to take souvenirs, but an entire suitcase? That doesn't feel right." Cade shook his head.

They walked back to the Garcia house. Rook rubbed his head. "Then that means the killer brought it with him. But why?"

"That's the mystery. It's not like he brought along his knife collection or ropes. He didn't need either." Cade pointed to the back of the house. He scrolled through the pictures he'd taken of the crime scene. "I want to see the body again. I had a thought."

As both detectives knelt near the body, Cade pointed to the woman's neck, which looked like it had been savaged by a wild animal. "See that by her neck. It looks like a lanyard." A pale blue cloth wound around her neck. White letters spelled out a major hotel chain on the lanyard. "It must be her work ID card. Can you ease out the end of it?"

Rook, who was closer, used a pen to gently push the lanyard out from her tattered blouse. The clip was there, but no name badge.

Cade nodded. "Unless it's underneath her, I'd bet the killer took it as a souvenir."

"You mentioned that earlier. That's a thing?" Rook stood and joined Cade in the kitchen.

"The killers like to take out their souvenirs and look at them to relive the crime and the satisfaction they gained from it, including sexual gratification."

"Gross."

"I know. But it gets a whole lot grosser. But it's not only name badges, jewelry, underwear, or shoes. Serial killers have been known to take body parts as their trophies."

"Really?" Rook's eyes were wide.

"Really. Think foot, genitalia, or even a head."

Rook shook his head. "That's seriously disturbing."

Cade led them back outside. "These are seriously disturbed individuals. And clearly, looking at how the woman was killed, there's more than one killer in town."

"I was thinking the same thing," Rook said.

"Just look at the crime scenes. Kimberly Albright's murder was efficient and clean. Her killer was controlled like he wanted her dead and done. Garcia's killer was ferocious and took his time on her." The images of her body would stay with him, haunting his quiet moments eternally.

"Agreed." Rook said. "And that ferociousness rules out this being anywhere close to an ordinary homicide. Looks like another serial killer from the site has come to town."

Cade flashed Rook a look as he thought the worst. It was Rook who said it out loud. "Holy shit. What if there are even more coming?"

CHAPTER 12

The governor called.

There are people who offer kind words and support when life throws situations at you. You look forward to hearing from them. And then there are the ones who enjoy it when you're on the hot seat. In fact, they take pleasure in stoking the fire. Ritter usually took it a step farther than that. Always one to pour gasoline on the fire, the governor's call didn't do anything to help Cade's day.

When he saw who was calling, Cade showed it to Rook, who promptly stuck out his tongue. Cade answered the call on speaker.

"Hello, Governor." He tried not to let his irritation show.

"There's another killing? Seriously? Can't you stop this guy?" Governor Ritter was never one for small talk. That was unless you were media or someone he was trying to impress. Cade was clearly neither.

"Governor, this wasn't the same killer. It was a completely different method of killing. This one was vicious, animal-like. There are bite marks over much of her body. Nothing like the stalking and cunning of the last one," Cade said. And for good measure, he added, "Not at all the same."

"There wasn't a note?" Ritter sounded exasperated.

"Nope, no note. Not even sure this guy could write if I'm being honest." Rook caught Cade's eye and nodded in agreement.

"Well, damn it all to hell in a handbasket." Rook mouthed the word handbasket and shrugged.

"Governor, I need some clarification on the scope of our task force. You activated me and the task force to catch the killer who killed Kimberly Albright. Since this is a different killer, does this new killer fall under our jurisdiction?" Cade held Rook's gaze, waiting for Ritter's response.

A deep breath came through the speaker. "This was not an ordinary murder. Let me ask you this. Do you believe it to be the work of another serial killer?"

"Yes, sir, I do. He has killed before and most certainly will kill again." Cade waited, crossing his fingers. He did not want this case going to anyone else.

"Then you are on the case."

Cade relaxed his shoulders.

"I have another question," Ritter said. "If this killer has killed before, and his killings are so grisly, why haven't we read about it? I know I wouldn't have forgotten about such a death."

"We believe the killer is new to Minnesota. In fact, he was seen pulling a suitcase."

A loud bang sounded, suspiciously like Ritter had slapped his desk. "Why the F would he come to Minnesota to kill? Couldn't he have stayed home and done his dirty work there?" Cade stayed silent and let the Governor continue. He wasn't ready to divulge the existence of the Orbiting Cortex site. "This is bad," Ritter continued. "And you know why? Reelection is next year. And now we have two serial killers operating in my state? People will remember this and say I couldn't keep them safe. There's no way I could win. And I can't go back to being a lawyer again. Corporate law is a major snooze fest."

"Can't have that." Cade shook his head while Rook showed surprise at Ritter's rantings.

Ritter's voice was almost pleading. "Dawkins, you need to get out in front of this. Talk to the media, let the people know you're on it."

"Are you sure? I don't exactly like talking to them. Wouldn't my results speak louder?" Cade asked.

"Really? Have you had any results that I don't know about?"

Taking a breath, Cade decided not to respond. "Let us catch these guys first. Then I can talk to the TV people."

"No, I want you to find the first media person you can and go on air with them. That's a direct order. Tell them you're responsible for catching these guys. That'll take the pressure off me for the moment."

Cade was not surprised that Ritter was saying this out loud. The governor was a political weasel through and through. Based on the look on his partner's face, Rook was surprised, though. He shook his head.

"Will do, boss."

"Don't wait. Talk to the media. I shouldn't have to say this, but I will. Your law enforcement career is riding on this." Ritter disconnected the call without so much as a goodbye or good luck.

"Governor Ritter is such a sweet and supportive man," Rook said, shaking his head. "Not many people could make these two tragic murders all about them."

Cade laughed out of frustration. "The deaths are bad only because of his upcoming reelection? What about the victims and their families?"

They continued grumbling as they walked around the front of the Garcia house, headed toward their cars. Beyond the cordoned-off area, the crowd had grown considerably, and all the television stations were there. Cameras were pointed in their direction, and reporters stood ready to shout questions. It looked as if the Five News team had gotten there first and were set up in front. Fortunately, most were at the far end. Cade didn't want to get consumed in an ad hoc press conference.

He looked at Rook. "We need to get with the University part of our task force. See if they came up with anything from the Orbiting Cortex site. We have to get a handle on exactly who we have here. Then we can get some background on what they've done previously." Cade ran his hand through his hair, wishing he'd had time for a shower. "I suppose we should talk to the media, or Ritter will blow a gasket."

"The man can't have many gaskets left." Rook grinned. "He lost several in that last call alone."

"Welcome to Minnesota politics," Cade said. "Where it's kill or be killed."

They walked toward the closest television truck, the one from Five News. A young guy pointed a camera at them while a salt and peppered forty-something reporter spoke into a microphone. Cade waved him over.

"We have something to tell you. On air."

"Cool," said a woman holding a clipboard who'd been standing behind the camera operator. "Let me grab her." As she headed to the back of the station truck, Cade recognized Ronnie as one of the station's production assistants.

"Her?" Rook asked. Cade shrugged.

The clipboard woman came around the corner and pointed in their direction. Reynolds walked into view, looking resplendent in her green blouse and black skirt.

"Damn," Rook said quietly. Cade gave him a quick nudge before turning toward Reynolds.

"Hi," he said to Reynolds as she approached. "The governor wants us to make a statement."

"We're happy to be of assistance," Reynolds said. "As long as I can ask a couple of follow-up questions."

Cade nodded. "Sure, that's fine."

The production assistant, Ronnie, set up Cade and Rook in front of the camera, making sure the Garcia home was in the background. She said they wouldn't be fitted with microphones as Reynolds would hold the single microphone. Cade knew Reynolds preferred the single microphone as it gave her control of the interview.

"Okay, on three, two," Ronnie said, holding up a single finger before pointing to Reynolds. The lights on the camera lit up.

"This is Reynolds Devries, with Five News. We're joined by members of the Five Below major crimes task force, Cade Dawkins and Terrance Rooker." Cade felt Rook's foot tap him at the mention of Five Below. He ignored him while Reynolds continued. "Behind us, an active crime scene is in full swing. The body of a woman was discovered earlier here this morning. Could you tell us what happened?"

She looked at Cade, waiting for his response.

"We are investigating the murder of Victoria Garcia. She was found on her front porch this morning. The killing looks to be the work of a serial killer, but not the work of the Kimberly Albright killer."

Reynolds pulled the microphone away before Cade could continue.

"So, you're saying there is a second serial killer at work in the cities?" Reynolds used shorthand for the Twin Cities, Minneapolis and St. Paul.

Cade nodded solemnly.

"This is unprecedented, isn't it?" Reynolds asked. She didn't wait for an answer before continuing. "There's more than one killer active here, in the Twin Cities?"

Rook leaned forward and Reynolds moved the microphone to him. "Yes, the evidence shows a clear distinction between the crime scenes, as well as methods of killing and victim acquisition," Rook said. "Descriptions of the killers are also vastly different."

"Can you tell us what they look like?" Cade shook his head.

"Do you have any leads?"

Rook glanced toward Cade, who nodded. "Yes, we have footage of the Albright killer, and a witness who described Garcia's killer. There's a reason Governor Ritter put us on the case. Our task force is streamlined and designed to catch killers like these. My esteemed colleague, Terrance Rooker, and I will continue to gather evidence, and we hope to announce tangible progress in the near future." Rook nudged his foot again, mouthing the word esteemed.

Cade ignored him.

Reynolds pulled the microphone back and looked into the camera. Her eyes had something that simply pulled you in and made you happy to be there with her. "As our viewers know, Cade Dawkins famously stopped the Blonde Killer, Marlin Sweetwater. I can't think of anyone more qualified than him to lead this new investigation."

The camera lights went out and someone announced that they were clear. The operator lowered his camera and headed toward the truck. Reynolds turned to Cade. "Thanks for that."

Cade nodded. "But honestly, I didn't know you were here. I was pleasantly surprised when you walked around the truck."

She held his gaze and her eyes sparkled as she spoke quietly. "Good. You should always be pleasantly surprised to see me."

Rook tapped his foot again. Cade ignored him again.

"No worries there. But we need to get rolling. Time is critical now." It was awkward, but he shook her hand. If it was uncomfortable for Reynolds, she didn't let on. She covered his hand with her own.

"Good luck." She turned and got into a conversation with her production assistant. The detectives headed for Cade's truck. When they were inside, Cade turned to Rook.

"I'm concerned about our workload now that we know we have two killers. We need to get someone—or several someones—to run down some of the routine things," Cade said. "We can't do everything ourselves."

"See that guy?" Rook said as he gestured to the rope line. A man was waving insistently.

"Oh, shit. That's Barry Weiss, the Fox reporter. He's a pushy poser."

Weiss was a tall man with perfectly coiffed dark hair who wore vests no matter the weather. Cade figured Weiss once saw a war correspondent wearing one, and it had influenced his fashion choices ever since. The reporter had a confident manner bordering on arrogance and often belittled his interviewees. It could be the vests or Weiss' personality, but Cade never liked the man on general principles.

"You better talk to him." Rook gestured toward Weiss.

"Why don't you?" Cade asked. "Ritter said I needed to talk to one media person, and I've done that."

"Nope. You're the boss. At least go tell him you can't talk to him," Rook said.

"Fine, but don't expect me to be patient with him." He climbed out of the FJ Cruiser and walked to the rope line.

"I see you've given your girlfriend another interview, but no one else." Weiss didn't look particularly pleased.

"I didn't even know she was here," Cade began, but stopped when he saw Weiss' expression. It looked as skeptical as a used car buyer listening to the salesman talking about the Corvette's previous owner's calm driving habits.

"Look, we can talk a different time, but I need to get going." Cade held out a hand, but Weiss ignored it.

"This is Barry town." Weiss puffed up his chest. "Believe me, you'll regret not talking to me."

Cade tried to fight back a grin. "I believe you. I already regret talking to you."

He turned and walked back to the truck, leaving behind one furious media guy. It didn't bother Cade in the least.

He called the St. Paul police administration on the way to the university. After a brief explanation, some transferring and needless hold music, Cade had one Marley Coutts on the line. He explained who he was and what he needed. At first, it looked like he would have to force her hand with the task force mandate. But oddly enough, Coutts was agreeable when she realized it wasn't coming from her budget.

"Of course, I can get you some investigative help. I have two brand spanking new detectives who recently passed their exams and haven't been assigned yet. Sort of in limbo until all the paperwork gets signed and pushed through. These things never go fast." She sounded distracted, and the sound of rustling paper came through loud and clear.

"That's great. You can text their info to my number. What are their names?"

"Kristen Bednarek and Lorie Thao. They're tougher than their names sound."

"Great. I owe you."

Coutts laughed. "Not as long as you're picking up their salary, you don't."

THE SUBTERRANEAN COMPUTER lab hummed with activity. Both Crocker and Tubbs were there, working with a growing group of graduate students. He recognized Denver, Courtney, and Jackie, and the two new faces were introduced as Miguel and Kenzie. Miguel was from Tubb's psychology program, while Kenzie was in the computer science program. Both were recruited by other grad students and looked eager to be on board.

Cade took a moment to bring the group up to speed on the most recent killing. Speaking candidly, he didn't hold anything back as he described the state of the victim's body. He stared at the far wall as he recalled the horrific scene.

When Cade finished, Crocker stood and walked to the whiteboard. A series of rectangles filled the board, looking much like a flow diagram used by software designers. "This is what we've come up with so far. We've identified 12 users by their usernames. Some are more active than others, some don't post much, or at all. They had to post something for them to show up, though. Some are active every day. Take *Iceyhell*, for instance. This is the one that offered the challenge that started this entire operation," he said with a wave around the room. "He or she is posting most days."

"Posting what?" Cade asked.

Denver spoke up after raising his hand. "I can answer that.

Iceyhell usually responds to other posts, but he posts a lot about ideal victims—he seems to have a thing for sex workers. He's an instigator, pushing the others on the site to do more outrageous things."

"Great, sounds like an upstanding citizen right there." Rook shook his head.

"With that username, *Iceyhell* could be from Minnesota," Jackie offered.

"It's really not that bad here," Courtney said with a smile.

"Yes, it is. What other state can say that penguins visit their birdfeeders?" Jackie replied, with a grin. "Minnesota gets so frigid cold."

"Why are you living here then?" Courtney asked.

"Because the summers are magnificent—and the winter cold keeps the riffraff out," Jackie explained. Pretty much everyone in the room nodded to that.

"*Iceyhell* talks a good game, but that's all it might be. There's no way of knowing." Denver shrugged.

Cade studied the names on the board. It was a weird and creepy assortment of usernames. None of which would do well on a dating site.

BadKarma,
BBF
nevermore27
Tinfoilhat
Gorephic99
Scareology
Slxttycuts
Ghostface
rotbrood_333
chokehalo
jumpscrred
Iceyhell

Cade paused before turning to Crocker. "Could you pull up the stored video clips, like you did for nevermore27? So, we know what these people look like. Maybe we could match them to the restaurant video and to the boy's description."

Crocker shook his head. "I thought of that too, but the archive of clips was empty when I went back. I'm guessing our initial intrusion was noticed. Or maybe they cleaned house. Either way, they're not where they were before. And I haven't been able to get far enough in to find them. We'll keep trying."

AFTER THAT, they wrapped things up, with both groups promising to keep the other updated as discoveries were made. Cade and Rook walked in silence down the musty corridor. Neither said anything during the elevator ride, either.

"Did you notice their faces when you described the crime scene?" Rook asked as they walked toward the truck. Cade shook his head. It was all he could do to talk about it. "Interesting reactions. Some looked scared, like they imagined that happening to them. Some looked squeamish, while others looked totally fascinated."

"Those are the ones that slow down to gawk at car accidents." Cade shook his head.

"True dat."

"All three reactions have to be common," Cade said. "People tend to react in different ways."

"There was a fourth reaction." Cade looked intrigued and Rook continued. "Imagine how you may look when someone described the steps to replace your alternator belt. Assuming you wanted to know how to replace it. You'd be leaning forward, not wanting to miss a single word. Your face would show no emotion other than rapt attention. Maybe a slight nod as you make a mental note of each step so you can replicate it later. Like that."

"Interesting."

"My thought too."

"You might be reading too much into someone's expression," Cade said. "Those people are there because they want to stop the killer. Of course they're going to be hanging on every word."

"It's like true crime in real time." Rook grinned.

REYNOLDS WAS ENGROSSED in her laptop as she was many evenings. Competitive research, she called it. Her producers recorded the other newscasts in their market and sent over the links so Reynolds could see how and what they had covered. She usually zipped through the recordings and stopped only to make notes or watch something unusual.

Cade looked up from his Vince Flynn novel at the mention of his name. "Cade. Have you seen the Barry Weiss Report on Fox?"

"Why would I want to watch that arrogant blowhard?" Cade said. "I'd rather get sterilized by a nearsighted chimpanzee with a seizure disorder."

Reynolds laughed, a sound that never failed to warm his heart. "You know, those aren't your only two options. You could watch The Five at Ten broadcast."

"I never miss it. The news anchor has the most amazing legs." He wiggled his eyebrows at her.

"These legs?" she asked as she stretched out.

"Uh, huh," he said, setting down his novel and moved in Reynolds' direction. They were nice legs.

"You should watch this first," she said and put the sound on the laptop's speaker.

"Barry Weiss is not my idea of an aphrodisiac, but okay," Cade said.

On screen, the Barry Weiss Report graphic came up. Weiss was—not surprisingly—wearing a vest. It was a Lands' End down vest worn over his plaid shirt. He stood in front of the Garcia house. His hair was tousled to perfection yet didn't look likely to move in the breeze. Barry Weiss turned his serious eyes to the camera.

"As a hard-charging journalist, I've built my reputation on telling the hard truths, speaking for the downtrodden and disadvantaged. In this metropolitan arena of corporate news, I'm often the lone voice for the common person, unafraid of repercussions from the man. The rogue reporter, if you will."

"Good lord, this guy is so full of himself," Cade spat.

"Shhh, listen," Reynolds said.

"In this home," Weiss said, gesturing, "a woman was murdered. Victoria Garcia was a hard-working woman who had arrived home after a long shift at the Minneapolis hotel where she's worked for the last seven years. No doubt, looking forward to rest and relaxation when she got home."

"I suppose she was tired after working for seven years."

"Shhh," Reynolds said.

"Instead, Miss Garcia was savagely attacked and murdered. But Garcia wasn't the only woman murdered this week. The body of Kimberly Ann Albright was found on Nicollet Island. Exclusive Barry Weiss Report sources believe this to be the work of two killers. Two different serial killers."

Weiss looked into the camera, pausing for effect.

"Governor Ritter has unleashed the brand-new and inexperienced major crimes task force, Five Below, to stop these killings. Beyond the quite frankly juvenile name, this task force is led by Cade Dawkins. Viewers will remember Dawkins as the Minnesota State Patrol investigator who killed Marlin Sweetwater, the Blonde Killer. Whether by luck or happenstance, Dawkins was in the right place to stop Sweetwater. But do we really want a glorified traffic cop to protect the women of the Twin Cities?"

Weiss' expression made his opinion obvious on the question.

"Speaking of Twin Cities' women," Weiss said as the screen showed a long-range shot of a group of people. The camera zoomed in to show Reynolds and Cade, tightening to the pair holding hands.

"It's an open secret that fellow journalist Reynolds Devries has Dawkins in her pocket."

"I was shaking your hand." Cade fumed.

"One has to wonder if she is orchestrating his so-called investigation to grow her ratings. While a speedy resolution to the investigation is vital to the terrified women of our state, that might not be best for her and her ratings."

The image on the screen showed a tight, pixelated shot of their intertwined hands.

"Perhaps, a more impartial investigator can put a faster end to these killings." Weiss was back on the screen. "This is Barry Weiss, watchdog for the women of our fair state."

"Hound dog of Minnesota women is more accurate," Reynolds said, and closed the laptop. "He's got a bad reputation with his production staff. It's a small community, and word travels between stations."

"I've never heard a newsperson go after another like he did there with you. That can't be business as usual." Cade took Reynolds' hand and pulled her to her feet.

She shook her head. "It's not professional in the least. He's trying to make me part of the story."

"I'm sorry about that. After our interview this morning, Weiss waved me over, but I told him I didn't have time to talk to him then. He wasn't happy with me."

Cade switched off the light as he led Reynolds to the stairs. "The only reason I even went on camera then was because Ritter gave me a direct order to talk to the first media person I saw."

"Surely, that wasn't the *only* reason you wanted to talk to me," she said as she put her arms around his neck and leaned in close.

"No, it wasn't," Cade said. "And stop calling me Shirley," he murmured before kissing her. The kiss was long, slow, and deep.

Later, when they both needed rest, Cade handed Reynolds a water. After draining half, she propped herself up on a pillow and asked an innocent-sounding question.

"So, you're working with the BCA lab on this?" She held his gaze waiting for his reply.

Oblivious, Cade answered. "Yeah, they have the resources and experience to help with this. And after working there previously, I'm familiar with how they do things."

"So, you're working with Grace?"

"Well, yeah. We have history."

The grizzly bear is an alpha predator who goes through life in complete control of his environment. Men fear him, while other animals show him a healthy respect. The grizzly isn't threatened by much and grows in confidence from the day he's born. But all that goes out the window when he steps into the bear trap.

"So, you have history?" Reynolds asked in an even tone, her eyes narrowing.

Cade was getting a feeling in the pit of his stomach. It wasn't a good feeling. Like when the morning orange juice hits your stomach after a night of drinking. There's a moment when you're headed for the bathroom, knowing this isn't going to end well.

"I mean, we've worked together for a while." Cade tried smiling.

"I see how she looks at you. Can't you see it?" Reynolds wasn't smiling.

"Well, we're friends. I don't see her as anything beyond that."

She studied him as she weighed his answer. "Okay, but know I'm sleeping with both eyes open."

"That's creepy. I hope I never wake up to see that." He grinned, which broke the tension.

"You never talk about your time with the Bureau of Criminal Apprehension."

The ceiling fan lazily spun in its slightly off-kilter circle. Finally, Cade took a deep breath and looked at Reynolds.

"I worked as a special investigator. We worked a lot of violent crimes and a whole lot of drug cases." Cade didn't usually dwell on his BCA days. The wound was too raw still.

"I was there for almost seven years," he added.

Cade felt her eyes on him, studying him as her eyes locked with his. It was like she saw right into him. "Tell me what happened." She didn't need to say anything further.

"We—my team with the BCA, that is—were working a drug case in Northern Minnesota, investigating a high-level drug trafficking operation. They were bringing cocaine and pills down from Canada. The pipeline from Canada isn't nearly as constricted or under federal scrutiny like it is down south. We worked jointly with the DEA and US Customs, who apparently had the dealers under observation for some time. Working alongside the other agents, observing the systematic flow of drugs coming into the state, I started to see patterns that didn't feel right. The drug organization had to be getting help from law enforcement—or at least cooperation—for their system to be working as well as it did.

"My gut said if this organization was so successful, they were getting help. And that help had to be coming from someone senior. So I picked one guy to watch. He was a senior customs investigator. It was an educated guess; he didn't act suspiciously or drive a Mercedes. I didn't have anything I could point to at the time.

"I parked myself on his tail, but far enough away as not to raise his suspicions. Whether he was guilty or not, it would've been bad if it got out I was following a fellow law enforcement officer."

"I'd imagine," Reynolds said. "So, you were careful." A woman of few words.

"I was. I've had enough experience tailing suspects. Maybe not too surprisingly, people are creatures of habit. People have routines with remarkably little variation, and they stick to it. Do you drive to the studio the same way every day?"

Reynolds paused, "Except for the occasional stop for coffee or to pick up my dry cleaning, yeah, it's the same route."

Cade nodded. "Exactly. You can follow someone for a few days, and you get a sense of what they're about. You learn their routine. I could go back three months later, and I'll know where to find them if I need them."

Pausing to take a sip of his water, Cade said, "So, I followed this senior investigator. Nothing too interesting—at first. However, after I thought he was down for the night on the third day, he turned off his lights and slipped out. I almost missed it; I was getting ready to call it a night and leave.

"I had to be extremely cautious, so I hung back to give him space. It's quite a bit more difficult to follow someone when it's quiet out, especially after dark. If it's busy, the lights from the other cars can cover you some. But when it's quiet, the flash of your headlights can raise a flag quicker than a cat covering something up."

Reynolds choked on her water. "Say, what? A cat covering something up?" She was laughing.

"Faster than a hobo on a ham sandwich?" Cade was laughing now too. "Oh man, now I've become my dad. My dad always had these crazy expressions. They didn't always fit the situation, but they sure were funny." He paused. "Oddly enough, he couldn't really tell a joke. He'd go on these long rambling sojourns, and by the time he got to the punch line, there was nothing. Literally nothing. My brothers and I would look at each other, wondering if the other had gotten the joke. My dad sure was laughing, though."

Reynolds leaned forward. "I'd love to hear one, if you remember."

Cade grinned. "Okay, but don't forget, you asked for it." He paused, clearly enjoying the moment.

"There was this rich man who decided to build a red brick barbecue in his back yard. He called up the Red Brick Barbecue Company and ordered 1,000 red barbecue bricks. After they were delivered, he decides he'd better count them because they were so expensive. He counts the entire pile and only comes up with 999 bricks. He gets angry and calls up the brick company. 'Look, I ordered 1,000 red barbecue bricks, and I only received 999.' The man says, 'Well, one must have been lost along the way.'"

Cade stopped and waited.

Reynolds looked confused. "That's it? I don't get it. Really, that's all?"

"You see what we went through all the time? No wonder I went into law enforcement. I needed to bring structure to my life." Cade laughed and Reynolds joined in.

"Is that actually why you chose law enforcement?"

"Nah, I looked into economics first, but the idea of wearing a suit and tie every day chased that one away. Could you see me as a banker?"

Reynolds looked him over with a straight face for a long moment, then she lost it. "No, not ever," she said between laughs. "You know what you look like you should be?"

Cade got a hunch where this was going but waited for her answer.

"You look like you should be a barista," she said with a giggle. "Has anyone ever told you that?"

Wondering what he may have done to piss off God, Cade shook his head. "I might have heard that before."

This got Reynolds laughing again. After a moment, she settled down and looked at Cade and said, "Tell me more about the BCA drug thing."

Cade took a deep breath and returned to his initial story. "Well, after he snuck out, I followed the customs investigator to a motel on the outside of town, the Morningside. He pulled around the building, parking on the end. Several cars along with a semi-truck from a Canadian shipping firm were parked in the lot.

"I ditched my car on the opposite side of the motel and walked around the back. I got near enough to see the customs officer, talking with a group of men. I moved alongside a ridge of spruce trees to get closer. From my new vantage point, I recognized the drug dealers we'd watched on that first day in Grand Marais. When I shifted to get a clearer view of the other two men, I couldn't believe it. It was two of the DEA agents from our investigation."

Reynolds had been looking straight ahead as she listened intently during his recollection. She glanced over, concern playing on her face. "What did you do?"

"I had to play it carefully. I got out of there and talked it over with my two BCA teammates. Maybe the DEA agents were undercover and hadn't wanted to share that information with the BCA—a competing agency. However, protocol on an active investigation is full disclosure of all undercover personnel with cooperating agencies. You never want your people in harm's way from the other good guys. We decided it best to contact the DEA regional office in Minneapolis.

"Minneapolis had no idea what I was talking about. I spoke with the senior agent in charge, who emphatically stated they had no one in a deep cover situation—especially during a cooperative investigation. That's what I thought as well. Before he hung up, he said he would look into it.

"A few days passed with no further word from Minneapolis. We had intel a shipment was coming in that night. But after my modest surveillance operation, I thought it best not to share the info with the local DEA or Customs. Instead, my team was going to take the truck ourselves. We followed the trucker as he drove through Grand Marais and south into a rest area outside of Lutsen. Just as we were staging our raid, a delivery van met up with the truck. The Customs investigator and the two DEA agents from our task force stepped out. Obviously acquainted with the driver, they received a duffel bag from him.

"Our only option was to take the corrupt law enforcement officers down as well. However, that's when a pair of black SUVs arrive on the scene. We held back to see what was going to happen. Several people armed with M16 rifles stepped out. They had windbreakers with bold writing on the back."

Cade paused, "This is the bad part."

Reynolds leaned forward, riveted. Cade continued. "There was no arrest, no warnings given. They had no chance to defend themselves. All three agents and the driver were executed. My two partners broke for the killing scene, weapons drawn, calling for the shooters to stand down. As I was on the far side of the semi, I was a good twenty yards farther away than they were. Before I could announce my BCA status, the M16s were turned on my partners. I was horrified to see these two men I shared everything with shot in cold blood. I slipped and dropped to my knees. The last thing I remember is looking up as the butt of an M16 came down."

Reynolds' jaw dropped. "What happened?"

"When I came to, the Cook County sheriff's department was on the scene. My partners were found dead along with the other victims. Agents from the DEA were just arriving—oddly enough, in black SUVs. The funny thing is they had on the same windbreakers as the shooters."

Cade sighed.

"I guess the feds take care of their own. In the aftermath, I was accused of screwing up a simple drug bust. The most intelligent course of action was to accept the blame. I didn't want to tarnish the slain officer's reputations—they all had families who needed their pensions. Besides, who'd believe some sort of federal death squad was involved? So, I resigned from the BCA. I wanted out after that, anyway. So now, I'm on the highways, keeping them safe, while I fight for truth, justice and the American way."

Reynolds' eyes narrowed. "They can't do that to you, can they? Will they come after you?"

"The feds can do pretty much whatever they want. As for me, there's no percentage in it for them to hurt me. I haven't said anything, and I won't, either. I'm not naïve enough to believe if I came forward, anyone of importance would either believe me or act on the information."

Reynolds paused, working through the impossible situation Cade had endured. She obviously had difficulty with his acceptance of it. "So...you're going to let it go? I'm not judging, I just don't know how I could live with it, the knowledge there are people like that out there, people who work for our government."

Cade glanced up. "Think of it as a cooling-off period. I haven't forgotten what happened—and I won't ever forget seeing my partners lying on the ground, lifeless. However, these men crossed a major line when they took out my partners. There will come a time where I will be in the right place, and I will see those guys again. Then, they'll remember me and what they did to two outstanding law enforcement officers."

Cade shook his head. "I sound like that guy from the Princess Bride movie." He spoke with an awful Spanish accent, "My name is Inigo Montoya. You killed my father. Prepare to die." Maybe it was the tension, but he broke out laughing. Reynolds picked up on it and joined in.

"I see you inherited your father's sense of humor," she said, clearly enjoying the moment. "I love me a funny man." She leaned in for a kiss. Cade plucked her water from her hand and set it on the bedside table. He kissed her hard.

LATER, Reynolds walked him to the door and kissed him on the cheek. "Thanks for a fun evening."

He held her tight for a moment, enjoying the sensation. He stepped onto the porch, the cool autumn air feeling good. Cade paused before turning back.

"You know, my dad had another joke."

Reynolds's eyes twinkled. "Go on."

"There was this little old lady who was waiting for a bus. She had her little dog with her. When she got on the bus, it was so crowded, only one seat was left. It was next to an old, cranky-looking man. After taking her seat, the man pulled out a cigar and started unwrapping it. The old lady said, 'Excuse me, sir, I'm allergic to smoke. Could you not smoke your cigar now?'

"He said, 'Look, I paid $20 for this cigar and I'm going to smoke it.' The poor woman was intimidated and so she sat there as he lit the cigar. When he turned and blew his smoke at her, she said, 'Look, if you don't put out your cigar, I'm going to throw it out the window.'

"He said, 'If you throw my cigar out the window, I'm going to throw your dog out the window.' The woman grew quiet, and the man kept smoking.

"But soon, the smoke was getting so thick, even her poor dog was coughing. The woman lost it. She reached over and plucked the cigar out of his mouth and threw it out the window. He grabbed her dog and threw it the window. When they pulled up to the next bus stop, there was her dog. Do you know what it had in its mouth?" he asked with a twinkle in his eye.

"The cigar?" she ventured.

"Nope. A red barbecue brick." It took a moment for her to make the connection, and then she broke out in laughter. Cade smiled as he hopped off the porch and headed to his truck.

CHAPTER 13

Jarn had the TV on.

The killer stared at the television screen, surprised by the news reporter's harsh words about Dawkins. He'd thought the detective was the state's golden boy.

"Perhaps, a more impartial investigator can put a faster end to these killings." The reporter looked at the camera, his face grave as he nodded solemnly. The effect was partially undone by the vest he was wearing. No one wore vests anymore. "This is Barry Weiss, watchdog for the women of our fair state."

So, Cade Dawkins, the state's media darling, was having his effectiveness questioned by said media. Even though it was surprising, Jarn was okay with it. He intended to ramp up the pressure as much as he could. Pressure was part of the game, after all. And the game was to outplay this investigator who achieved such notoriety for stopping Sweetwater.

Jarn stretched on the comfortable bed and changed the channel. The blonde newscaster talked about an upcoming comic book convention, but he tuned out her words as he studied her. This was the lawman's woman, and she would bear watching. He stretched as he took in her appearance, mannerisms, and form. It was the hunter studying its prey. He switched the channel to a third station on the commercial break.

The weather report was on, and he watched the forecast with interest. The temperature was much cooler here than back home. When it was hot enough to melt your tires, maybe that was too hot. He was happy that he had come to Minnesota; the people seemed nice enough, and he was making a difference here. He changed the station to HBO and turned up the volume. Didn't want anyone to hear the noise.

Jarn set down the remote and turned to the woman. She was a brunette with long hair who looked to be mid-twenties. She had an athletic build he liked. Her eyes darted around frantically, looking for a way out. But being gagged and tied to the bed, both knew there wouldn't be an escape for her. Her small pocketbook was next to her phone, and he picked it up, turning it over in his uncalloused hands. Sparkly and featuring a cat, it looked like something a junior high girl would carry. He opened the zipper and dumped out the contents. There were wadded-up bills amounting to less than $30. A couple of receipts. There was also lip gloss and a three-pack of condoms. And a driver's license with the unlikely name of Veronica Rae Valley.

"Veronica Valley? Is that your real name?"

The woman's eyes widened, and she nodded. She was too terrified to lie.

"Okay, Veronica. It sounded like one of those made-up names, like how you get your porn star name by combining the name of your first pet with your mother's maiden name." Jarn picked up her phone and studied it. After unlocking the phone with her index finger of her bound hands, he started with her photos. Paging through the waste of digital space, he shook his head. This woman did not know how to take a picture. No focal point, no rule of thirds, poor lighting, and the most heinous infraction: nothing interesting in the frame. He pulled up her messages next.

Veronica squirmed against her bonds.

Glancing up from the messages, Jarn fixed her with a look. Her struggles subsided.

"I know you're wondering. My porn star name is Tally Pumper. It couldn't be any more perfect, could it?" Veronica didn't offer a response.

Back to the messages, it looked like she used her phone primarily to order food, chat with a friend named Cyndee, her mom, and a boyfriend, Linc. "You and Linc like to share pictures, I see. Brave man sharing pics of something so modest, but to each their own."

Jarn snapped a couple of pictures of the tied-up woman. "I'm sure he'll like these, too." He attached the pics and hit send.

Valley didn't look happy with that. As they say, if looks could kill... But they wouldn't. He would.

Jarn pulled out his knife.

Veronica no longer looked angry with him.

It wasn't the largest or the fiercest looking as far as knives went. But it was remarkably effective. He'd used precisely this sort of knife on many victims.

Starting with her shabby chic blouse, Jarn sliced the material open. He took his time, enjoying the expression on Veronica's face. He pulled the two sides back when he got to the bottom, exposing her stomach. Her lean abs were taught as she strained against her bonds. "This part won't hurt a bit," he said, setting the knife on the bed and pulling out a marker from his kit.

Just below her belly button, he wrote as neatly as he could. Seeing her puzzled expression, Jarn explained. "It says number two. You may be wondering why, but I started a numbering sequence for Minnesota. It gives the authorities notice that this is part of a series. It's a public service, if you will."

Veronica Valley looked less than impressed with Jarn's public service efforts.

Unfazed, he continued. "I think it's time for our feature presentation." He picked up the knife but then set it down again. Instead, he grabbed her phone. "Our feature deserves an audience. Perhaps someone with a vested interest. Do you know of anyone?"

The woman shook her head.

Jarn scrolled through her contacts.

"Linc might like to be involved. Men are watchers, you know. That's why we leave the lights on. But then there's your gal pal, Cyndee. I'm sure she would want to know what you're up to. This would give her a front-row seat."

Veronica shook her head, getting more agitated.

"No? You don't want her involved either?"

More head shaking.

"Okay, then. Mom, it is." Veronica was frantic, head whipping side to side, arms and legs fighting the ropes.

Jarn, unbothered, used the phone's video chat to call the woman's mother.

"Hey, Veronica," the woman's voice said. She sounded older.

"No, this isn't Veronica. She's all tied up and can't come to the phone right now."

Jarn placed the phone on the nightstand so the camera wouldn't miss the action.

"But Mom, there's something you should see." He picked up the knife and held it in front of the camera. There was an audible gasp.

"I see you got the point of this call. Now, let's get started."

CADE'S PHONE lit up shortly after 11 p.m.

It was Russ Horstead, the 911 call center's watch supervisor. They'd worked together on the Blonde Killer case and Cade appreciated what the man brought to the table. And as a Brit, Russ always loved talking soccer.

No soccer this time. "We received a call from a St. Paul woman. She said she got a FaceTime video call from her daughter's phone. But it was a man's voice on the call, and the phone's camera was aimed at her daughter. And Cade, her daughter was tied to a bed."

Cade was on his feet. "How old is her daughter? Do we know?"

"Yes," Russ said. "Veronica Rae Valley was 23 years old."

Cade paused. "Was?"

"Sorry, buddy. The mother said she witnessed her daughter's murder. When the killer was done, he left the knife sticking out of her neck."

"Oh shit. Just like with Albright." He could picture the crime scene, the woman displayed with the knife left behind.

Cade grabbed his jacket and headed for the door. "Do we know where Valley is? Where the murder scene is?"

"Not yet," Russ said, "We're working on it. Her mother said her daughter also lives in St. Paul."

"Okay, text me her mother's address. I'm going to talk to her." Cade started up the truck and put it in gear.

"Will do. Be careful out there, buddy." Russ was gone.

Cade called Rook and got him moving toward St. Paul. He said he'd forward the address as soon as he had it. Russ was prompt, and Cade forwarded the address on to his partner. He got onto Interstate 94 at Cretin Avenue and raced east toward downtown St. Paul. Traffic was light and Cade easily navigated around the few vehicles as he pushed the truck's speed. He took the Mounds Boulevard exit and shot around a slow-moving Honda. Within a few moments, he was moving east on Third Street.

It was a working-class neighborhood of closely built homes. Across from a construction site, Cade pulled in behind a St. Paul black and white. The officer looked up as he exited his vehicle.

"That was quick," the officer said. "Break any speed limits?"

"None that I'm willing to admit to." Cade glanced up at the white clapboard house with a large front porch. A woman pushed the front door open and came down the steps to meet them on the sidewalk. She was heavyset and looked to be approaching fifty. Tears ran down her cheeks and her eyes were red.

"Did you find my baby?" she asked.

"Not yet," Cade said. "But you can help us." He gestured to the front steps. "Please sit and walk us through what happened."

She sat hard on the concrete step and looked at Cade with eyes that knew pain. He felt for her but knew nothing he could do would make it better for her. He needed to stop the killer from taking away someone else's daughter.

"Tell us what happened when you called your daughter."

The woman shook her head. "No, I didn't call her. I answered the FaceTime call from my daughter's phone. When I said hi to her, it was a man's voice that told me she was all tied up. He held a knife in front of the camera and laughed, saying I got the point."

Cade shook his head.

Rook's Charger roared in and pulled behind Cade's FJ Cruiser. He nodded to Cade as he joined them.

"This is my partner, Terrance Rooker." Rook nodded.

"Did you see the man at all?" Cade asked her.

She shook her head. "Before showing the knife, the camera was pointed at the ceiling."

"How about after the knife?"

Another shake of her head. "He must have set the phone down because it was pointed at Veronica and didn't move after that. She was," The woman's voice cracked, and she stopped. It took a moment before she tried again. "She was." This time when her voice cracked, the woman broke down and cried.

Cade sat next to her. "I know this is difficult for you. We need to hear what you saw so we can stop this man. I don't want anyone else hurt."

"Sometimes it's easier to describe what you saw on the screen like it was a television show. Think of the people as actors, not as anyone you know," Rook added. "It can help you get through this."

Taking a ragged breath, the woman continued. "I saw a woman that was tied up. She had a cloth gag in her mouth. Her hands were over her head, and her legs looked to be tied to each corner of the bed."

"Was the bed made?" Cade asked.

Pausing, she thought for a moment. "Yes, it was made. I saw the bedspread pattern around her. It looked like one of those hotel beds, with the obnoxiously loud pattern."

Cade nodded. "That's helpful. What happened next?"

With her gaze fixed on the distant skies, she spoke quietly. "Her blouse was open, like it had been cut. There was something written on her skin, below her belly button. It looked like a hashtag, with a two or five written below that. I couldn't be sure." Cade shared a look with Rook.

She continued, her voice monotone. "The man used the blade of the knife like an artist using a pallet knife on canvas. He swept it over her skin in slow, easy movements. Like he wanted to cover the entire surface with paint. Only there wasn't any paint, just her sweat."

"No blood?" Rook asked.

"No, he never cut her. But you could tell he liked teasing her with it." She stopped and her eyes lost focus.

Cade touched her arm, and she jumped. "Was he talking at all during this part? Did he say anything to her, or you, for that matter?"

She shook her head. "He never said anything. Like he was concentrating so hard, he wasn't going to lose focus by speaking."

"How long did this go on, this teasing?"

Looking at the two detectives, she shrugged. "I don't know. It could have been ten minutes. It could have been thirty seconds. Time had no place there."

Cade nodded. "I get that. And then what happened?"

"He sort of knelt over her and stared down for a while. He held the point of the blade against her skin and leaned forward as he stared into her eyes. It looked like he was going to kiss her, but then he suddenly sat up, rigid. It took a moment before I noticed the knife. I saw the handle, but the blade was completely buried...in my daughter."

She broke down in heaving sobs.

Cade gave her time to settle, gently touching her on the back. Then, "How did the video chat end?"

She took a moment. "I heard him say, 'That's enough,' before he reached over and ended the call." Turning to Cade, she looked at him with worried eyes. "Can you find my daughter? She's out there with that maniac."

"We will find her. It's only a matter of time. Maybe you can help speed the process up. Your daughter, did she work in St. Paul?"

The woman nodded.

"What did she do for work?"

Her eyes slid down. "She had various jobs." There was a slight hesitation before she used the word various.

Rook and Cade exchanged glances. The woman wasn't being completely forthright.

"Ms. Valley," Rook began. "We are here to help. There is no judgment here."

Looking at her hands, the woman hesitated. "Veronica was a sex worker. She liked the money she made. I was worried about her, but she would always tell me that I shouldn't worry. That she was the one in control." She raised her gaze. "But not this time. Not this time."

CHAPTER 14

The smaller half of the Twin Cities, St. Paul had never received the respect Minneapolis had. Former Governor Jesse Ventura famously pronounced on the Letterman show that its confusing streets were designed by drunken Irishmen. The city was initially called "Pig's Eye," a name coined after one of the initial settlers, Pierre "Pig's Eye" Parrant. However, the city was renamed after Lucien Galtier, a Catholic father who later established St. Paul's chapel. It has been said that St. Paul is the largest small town in America, while Minneapolis is the smallest big city.

With Rook following, Cade led the way into downtown St. Paul. He'd contacted St. Paul on the way in to get officers canvassing hotels for Veronica Valley. They stopped on the street in front of the Dark Horse Cafe to wait for word. They leaned against Cade's truck. Neither spoke for a moment.

"This was the first killer again," Cade said. He looked at his feet before raising his gaze. "He may not have the savagery of the other killer, but he's cruel."

"That's for sure. What sort of animal wants someone to witness their own daughter's murder?" He shook his head. "That shit ain't right."

"No, sir, it's not. We need to put this animal down." Cade ran his hand through his hair. "The trick is finding him. Often when you figure out how a killer selects their victims, you can find them. But look at his two victims so far. The first, he picked her out at a restaurant and grabbed her there. The second was a sex worker who likely met him at a hotel. Neither method of selection gives away anything about his identity."

"Or his geographic area. One was from a Minneapolis suburb with the body found in Minneapolis, while the other came from St. Paul. There's no pattern." Rook looked angry. "There's nothing to go on. Even if we found his fingerprints, which we haven't, there's no way to find him. It's not like he lives here."

Cade turned slightly toward his partner. "That's not entirely true. He's staying here somewhere. A hotel maybe, could be an Airbnb or some sort of rental. We need to look for recent arrivals."

"There's probably thousands."

"So what?" Cade shook his head. "We work with what we have, narrowing it down. If the registration is female, it's not our guy. A couple or a family, not our guy, either. But the thing is, we're coming up with a list. A list that can be narrowed down. We might not find our killer because of the list, but we may well confirm him because of the list."

Rook shrugged. "Okay, I'll drink your Kool-Aid. But that's a lot of man-hours spent compiling."

Cade grinned and nodded toward two people walking in their direction. Both were women, one Asian, the other Caucasian. Both were shorter in stature but looked like someone you didn't want to mess with. There was something about the way they carried themselves. An attitude. Yes, they were both cops.

"Here's our help," he told Rook. "Meet the two newest members of our major crimes task force, Kristen Bednarek and Lorie Thao."

"The *Five Below* major crimes task force." Rook stuck out his hand. "Terrence Rooker, nice to meet you both."

Bednarek was around five feet in height with glasses and a pleasant smile. Thao had several inches on her St. Paul colleague and shook Rook's hand with a firm grip. She looked at Rook and said tentatively, "Five Below? I bought my flip-flops there. They lasted a month."

Cade grinned and lightly elbowed his partner. "No relation to the said retailer. We're very much an independent task force."

Bednarek laughed and Cade liked her right away. Anyone with such an infectious laugh was meant to be a friend.

He took a few moments to bring the officers up to speed on the three killings, the team at the University, and their discovery of the dark website. "Based on the Orbiting Cortex site, both killers are new to the Twin Cities. This is where you two come in. Starting back a week, begin compiling a list of hotel check-ins, as well as Airbnb-type rentals. You're looking for men that are traveling alone. They don't make the list if they have a wife or family registered."

Both nodded as Bednarek took notes. She glanced up. "We're assuming that the two aren't sharing a room?"

"Good question," Cade said. "Even though there's been cross-pollination of ideas on the site, there's not going to be sharing of rooms. These two killers are at opposite ends of the spectrum. Killer number one appears to exhibit organized killer tendencies that include advanced social skills and intellect, while killer number two likely has disorganized killer tendencies that include primitive social skills and lower intellect." He glanced between the St. Paul officers. "Ever hear about the intelligence test for dogs where you place a towel over their head and see how long it takes for them to get free? Border Collies and Golden Retrievers are remarkably adept at it, while it might take a chihuahua or an Afghan Hound a lot longer. Killer number two would still be under the blanket wondering why it's been dark all day."

They all laughed, but Cade held up a hand. "Limited intelligence or not, both killers are remarkably dangerous. Don't underestimate them."

"Noted," Bednarek said as she jotted her notes.

"A thought," Rook said as he glanced at Cade. "Killer number one drove a car with switched license plates. Those plates came from the Alamo Car Rental at the airport. See who rented a car that day and add them to your list. Start with Alamo but look at the other rental agencies as well. Use the same dates as your hotel search.

"Also," Cade said. "Did the killer just arrive on a flight? Check all incoming flights."

Thao looked at Bednarek. "Looks like we'll be busy. You know what that means?"

"Overtime," Bednarek said with a laugh. "I'm going to get that puppy after all."

After the two officers left, Cade turned to Rook. "It feels like all our efforts are geared toward killer number one." He waved at Rook to follow. "C'mon, let's walk and talk."

They walked up Seventh past Barrel Theory, another bar and restaurant. "Let's give some thought to killer number two. As a disorganized killer, he's likely to have a lower-paying job and unreliable transportation—if any."

"He was seen pulling a suitcase when he left the crime scene," Rook recalled.

"That he was. So, let's assume he recently arrived. But it feels unlikely he got off a plane at the airport and then headed to a random neighborhood to take a victim. Garcia's home is far out of the way from the airport."

Rook held up a finger. "But the train does connect downtown Minneapolis with the airport."

Cade shook his head. "It still doesn't feel right. And I can't picture our burly animal squished into the middle seat on the flight."

"Neither can I," Rook agreed.

"What other ways are there to get to our fair state if not by plane?" They took a left at the corner onto Wacouta Street. "Planes, trains and automobiles," he said after a moment.

"I love that movie," Rook said. "But there's another way into town. Our killer could have taken the bus. The bus terminal in Minneapolis is a straight shot south of the Garcia home."

"The bus? That's genius." Cade stopped and turned to Rook. "I never would have thought of that. I haven't ridden a bus since middle school."

"Hey, it's not like I take it all the time, either. But they are good for the environment."

"Like your fuel-efficient Charger," Cade said with a grin. "Not that my truck gets much for gas mileage."

"I suppose not," Rook said. "But let's be real. No one buys a badass truck for the gas mileage."

"You really think it's badass?" Ever since he first saw the Toyota FJ Cruiser, it spoke to him, and Cade had to have it. The fact that they weren't made anymore was a testament to the short-sightedness of the automobile industry.

"Of course. But you were saying," Rook prompted.

"We need to check the Minneapolis bus terminal for arrivals, see if our killer was caught on video. We should take the task. Bednarek and Thao will already be plenty busy."

Cade's phone buzzed. He answered and listened for a moment. "We're on our way," he said and turned to Rook. "They found her. At a motel in Midway. Let's roll."

"Okay, but I'm driving this time," Rook said. "I've seen you drive."

"Wait, what? Because I drive like..."

"Like an old lady."

"Dude." But Cade climbed into the passenger seat, anyway. "Like a younger, cougar-aged lady?"

Rook shook his head as he accelerated toward the 94 entrance ramp. "Think mothball-smelling, dozen great-grandchildren and 37 cats, kind of old woman."

"Whatever, just get us there. In one piece." Cade cinched his seatbelt as Rook roared down the ramp onto the freeway. For the most part, the vehicles yielded to the lights and sirens, but not always. Some sat like they owned the left lane and squatted until they were granted title. Rook zipped around them like they were standing still.

After passing Allianz Field, the new soccer stadium, Rook took the Snelling Avenue exit and headed north.

The motel was nothing to write home about. If the St. Paul Hotel was five-star, this was a half-star—if the person doing the rating felt generous. A one-level building in an L shape, it looked to have started its decline in the seventies and never looked back. It was not a place that was cared for. Several St. Paul squads were in the lot outside the end unit, with officers standing around the open door.

One of the most critical aspects of securing a crime scene was preservation. From day one, law enforcement officers were taught to safeguard the scene, minimizing possible contamination and disturbance of physical evidence until the investigators arrived. Because every person entering or exiting added or subtracted material from the crime scene, it was crucial to quickly secure the area. Yet there wasn't an inch of crime scene tape in place.

Cade had a bad feeling.

As Cade and Rook approached, the St. Paul officers backed away. They barely seemed to take in the offered badges, the officers standing mutely as the investigators slipped on cloth booties over their shoes. Cade stepped to the motel room entrance. His breath caught in his throat as he took in the scene before him. The very wrongness of it assaulted his senses. The two queen-sized beds were pulled away from the wall, stacked and shoved in the center of the room. The rectangular writing desk was sitting on top of the beds. A naked woman lay perpendicular across the desk, her back arched with head and legs hanging off the sides. A knife protruded from her throat. Blood ran down her porcelain skin.

"What the..." Cade couldn't finish.

"Oh, hells no." Rook shook his head like he was trying to make the scene disappear from his sight.

Intricate symbols covered nearly every inch of her exposed flesh. These were the same unfamiliar symbols from the note found at the Kimberly Albright crime scene. But unlike Albright, this woman wasn't blonde. She had sandy brown hair and her open eyes stared at the back wall.

"Her body has the same arched backward pose as Albright's on that boulder," Cade said. "It looks like an acrobat or contortionist pose."

"The knife looks identical, too. The killer must have bought a matching set. Maybe we can get a lead on that somehow." Rook paused and took a breath. "God willing."

Cade took careful steps as he circled the displayed body. The only mark, besides the odd hieroglyphics and the #2 written on her abdomen, was the entry wound from the knife. Just the handle remained visible. Pausing, Cade walked back to her head and followed the dead woman's gaze to the back wall. A note was taped to the wall. It was upside down.

"Look at this," Cade said, moving toward the wall. "There's another note. He's taped it upside down, giving it the same orientation as the victim. Who I'm assuming is Veronica Valley."

Cade pulled out his phone and took a picture, not wanting to disturb the paper. Rotating the image, Cade zoomed in on the message. As before, intricate symbols framed the handwritten words.

Unstoppable, the web weavers sow death.
Pain and terror, blood and fear, light our way.
Dawkins, stumbling in the dark.
You had your day. Now it's ours.

"This is crazy. He's openly challenging you. What a prick."

"At the very least."

"I'm just going to say it. We need a little luck here—and soon." Rook ran a hand over his close-shaved head.

Cade nodded and tucked away his phone. "I tell you, the only way we're going to catch this guy is to engage him. Get him ramped up and push him in a certain direction."

"Go on," Rook prompted.

"It's a commonality among organized killers that they watch their media coverage closely. It won't surprise me if one hires a PR firm someday. Dennis Rader, the BTK killer, which stood for Bind, Torture Kill, loved his media attention. He'd regularly contact the local media in Kansas, sending taunting letters, postcards, poems and packages that included his victim's jewelry and driver's licenses." Cade leaned down to study the markings on the woman. It looked like some sort of calligraphic pen had been used.

"The victim's belongings were to prove his bona fides," Rook said. "Real subtle that one."

"Subtlety rarely enters into it. Rader was caught because he sent a letter on a computer disk to a television station. Investigators traced the disk back to his church computer. And get this, BTK was the church council president."

"No way."

"Way. That's why these killers can be so difficult to find. They hide in plain sight." Cade stood up, his knees complaining. "Which is why we need to use the media to our advantage, not his."

Rook stepped back, clearly not wanting to be near the body. "So, you're thinking a two-pronged approach. Get him engaged with our media and maybe he'll make a BTK-like mistake that incriminates him. And we also push him, manipulate him, into a trap."

"Very good, college boy." Cade grinned.

Rook laughed. "You had to have gone to college, too."

"Yeah, but I don't still talk about it. That was almost a decade ago." Truth be told, there wasn't much to talk about. It was four years of average grades and average extracurricular activities.

There was a distinct eye roll from Rook, which made Cade smile.

"Okay, let's focus on our crime scene. We know the victim was a sex worker. How did the killer find her? How did he contact her?" Cade's eyes swept the scene as he circled the makeshift altar. "We know he used the victim's phone to live-stream her murder, but it's not here. Maybe the crime scene techs will find it, but I don't know. That feels like something he might hang onto."

"Most sex workers carry two phones. One for business and one for work. Neither of which appear to be here," Rook said. "And she's probably a freelancer. There are almost no streetwalkers anymore. Everything is done through smartphones and the internet. There'd be a handler or driver hanging nearby if she was trafficked. No way the killer would have had that long alone with her."

"So, we need to find her phone."

"We could trace it. There's a chance it's still on." Rook looked around. "But what about the room itself? Hotels and motels require names, IDs and a credit card when you check in."

"I can help there," a St. Paul officer said. His nameplate read Klonecki. "The room was registered to a Veronica Rae Valley. This motel takes cash, not surprisingly. But she paid with a card." He handed over a photocopy of her license and debit card. The license picture matched the dead woman. Same sandy brown hair, same button nose. Cade returned the photocopy. "Good work."

It didn't make him feel any better to confirm her identity.

"Crime scene is here," another officer called into the room.

They stepped out onto the sidewalk and slipped off their booties, relieved to be outside. Several more squads had arrived, including the Ramsey County Sheriff. Crime scene techs pushed an equipment cart across the parking lot and yellow crime scene tape was finally going up at the entrance.

"Let's give them the room. We can talk to the front desk clerk." He gestured for Rook to lead the way. The motel office was in the armpit of the building's L shape. The landscaping along the sidewalk was dominated by weeds and a hearty crop of dandelions. Cracked glass sat in the door, and Cade pushed it open carefully. The carpet inside was threadbare, and an unpleasant odor that reminded Cade of cabbage tickled his nose. He sniffed loudly.

A woman in her late twenties perched on a stool behind the counter. Her heavily tattooed arms held a Michael Connolly paperback. She ignored their entrance.

Cade cleared his throat.

The woman turned a page and didn't bother to look up.

Cade exchanged glances with Rook before putting his hands on the counter. "We're—"

The woman held up a hand. "Is there a smell in here you don't care for?" she asked.

Generally, honesty was Cade's policy. Tell it like it is and let them sort out their feelings. But he thought, in this case, it wouldn't aid his cause in the least.

Rook jumped in on Cade's pause. "My partner has severe allergies, and I made him hold my cat on the way to the vet earlier today."

Lifting her nose from the novel, the woman looked at Cade with naked skepticism. "What kind of cat?"

"A tabby cat," Cade blurted, naming the only one he could think of. "It's true, cats and I don't get along."

She deadpanned him. "I have six cats."

"I'd have seven if I wasn't so gosh darn allergic to the little devils."

Her nose returned to her book after making a *humpf* sound.

Rook stepped up and sat on the edge of her counter. "Did you ever hear of the Twin Cities' comedian, Mitch Hedberg? He talked about meeting an attractive front desk clerk. When he asked for her number, she said it was zero. But he said when he tried calling her from home, someone else answered." He paused, glancing at Cade and made a fingers-crossed sign.

Setting down her book, the clerk laughed. "I hadn't heard that one. I like it." She sized him up for a moment. "What can I do for you?"

Rook gave her his best smile. "I see you have a security camera." He nodded toward the camera mounted on the wall above the clerk.

She leaned forward, gazing into Rook's eyes. "Would you be surprised if I told you it wasn't hooked up at all? The owner is far too cheap to actually purchase a video recorder."

"Hey. I heard that," a voice called out from the open door behind the clerk.

She shook her head. "That's the owner," she said flatly.

"I figured," Rook said. "So, no video footage?"

"Nope." She blinked at Rook.

"Well, then," Rook began, "Veronica Valley checked into room..."

"Room 113. That was her usual room."

"Her usual?"

"Sure, our owner thinks welcoming by-the-hour prostitutes classes up the joint." She rolled her eyes.

"Hey, I'm right back here." He sounded irritated.

"I'm sorry. I meant to say our owner is a strong believer in empowering women and he welcomes their entrepreneurship in whatever form it may take." Another eye roll.

"Thank you," he said. She held a raised middle finger toward the door.

Rook pulled out his notepad and clicked his pen, placing the point on the paper. He was poised to make notes. "Did you see her, um..."

"Client," Cade suggested.

"Perfect. Did you see Veronica's client when she checked in?" Rook asked.

She shook her head. "But that's normal and why she chose the end room. She was always worried about perverts spying on her business."

"Hey," the owner called out again.

The clerk turned to Rook. "Did I say anything about him?"

Rook shook his head, clearly uncomfortable with being in the middle of whatever this was.

"See?" she called toward the owner's office. "Even the cop says I didn't necessarily mention you." She aimed a finger gun at her head.

"It was implied. But, fine. Just watch yourself."

The clerk made a circular motion by her temple, the universal sign for crazy.

Cade couldn't help but grin. Just then, a man with a stocky build pushed through the front door and Cade stepped aside to give him room. He had spiky bleached blond hair and wore a Hawaiian shirt over cargo shorts and yellow rubber rain boots. Even though Cade had yet to see his face, he thought he might know the guy. There was something familiar about him.

"Hey, Stevie, can I get my key?" he asked.

"It's Stella." She slid a key across the counter. "The police may not let you in, though. There's been a murder in the next room."

The man raised a hand. "See? It's the cell towers. They're creating a tribe of hyped-up killers. Radio waves releasing aggression."

Stella, the clerk, looked less than convinced.

"It's true. I read about it in the Smithsonian Journal."

It couldn't be anyone else, and Cade stepped forward. "Gordy?"

Gordy Stensrude had been a colorful witness in the Blonde Killer case. But to call him colorful was a massive understatement along the scale of calling the Grand Canyon a rather large ditch. It went beyond his bright fashion choices; it was more his unique take on life and his willingness to speak whatever was on his mind. And his mind was the Willy Wonka's chocolate factory of minds.

"Hey, cop guy. How're they hangin'?"

Cade grinned. "Gordy Stensrude as I live and breathe. How've you been? This is my partner, Rook."

They shook hands and Gordy turned to Cade. "The force is strong with this one."

Rook beamed.

Gordy continued, still holding Rook's hand. "He's a brooding hunk of burning love."

Rook's smile went away, and he pulled his hand free.

Cade laughed at his partner's discomfort. "That he is. What are you up to these days?"

Gordy held up a finger. "Hang on, I'm getting a call. Microsoft help center. How may I be of assistance?"

Cade and Rook exchanged confused glances. Cade leaned over to see if Gordy actually wore an earpiece. With Gordy, it could go either way. He did indeed have an earpiece, and Cade turned to give Rook a thumbs up.

"A couple of standard questions. How tall are you?" Gordy asked his caller.

Rook's expression suggested he was surprised by Gordy's question. Cade was not.

Gordy paused. "Like I said, it's a standard question. Okie dokie, thanks. Second question, are you watching porn?" Rook's eyes went wide while Gordy continued. "That kind of content taxes the system and you'll need to reboot. Thanks for calling and have a fabulous day."

Gordy noticed Cade's open-mouthed expression. "What? I tell everyone to reboot. That's the answer to all of life's problems. Things not working for you? Start again." He turned to Rook. "Hey, you got a donut?"

Confused by the sudden change of direction, Rook stuttered, "I...I..."

"C'mon, cop guy, work with me here. Sprinkles, chocolate covered, glazed, I like 'em all." Gordy smiled. "I should be in law enforcement."

"Maybe you should," Cade agreed. "What's the worst that can happen?"

Rook looked as if he was going to say something, but Cade jumped in. "Hey, when did you join the herd of Microsoft minions? This is a new gig for you."

Gordy shrugged. "It gives me some walking around money, and I like talking to people. Helping the common man is my calling. Here's my card."

Cade took the card and read:

Gordy Stensrude, life guru

"Gotta jet, boys. See you later, Stevie," Gordy said, headed for the door.

"It's Stella. My name is Stella."

He held up a finger. "Microsoft help center. How can I assist you this fine day?" Gordy stepped out and was gone.

Cade laughed as he turned to his partner, who stood with his mouth open. "Elvis has left the building. That man is one of a kind." He glanced at Gordy's card and tucked it away. You never know.

"Ready to roll?" he asked Rook, who nodded. "See you, Stella."

"It's Stevie," she said with a giggle.

LATER AT DINNER, Reynolds looked across the table at Cade. Her eyes narrowed, her brow furrowed, and she looked perplexed. Cade had been around her enough to know she was analyzing his proposal from all angles. He'd thrown it out there, offering to go on camera with her for an exclusive. Despite his irritation with the media, he knew they could be useful—they were his only way to communicate with the killer.

If he was going to be on camera, he preferred it be with someone he mostly trusted and made the experience comfortable. A longtime media professional, Reynolds was on top of her game. Cade knew she was a step away from being called up to the majors. A talent like hers —and a face like hers—wouldn't stay forever in the Midwest market. Cade had heard rumors since before the two met that Good Morning America would come calling in the near future. He wasn't sure if their relationship could survive her moving to New York, but he was happy to see her while it lasted.

Her eyes flicked up. "And you think this is a good idea why?" She searched his eyes. "I can see why this is good for the station and me. We get access, and I become the focal point of the story. Best of all, I scoop my fellow media contemporaries." There was a relaxed assurance in her eyes.

Cade nodded along while he studied the menu.

"But it's going to royally piss them off. And not just Barry Weiss. All of them," she said. Cade took a sip of water as she continued.

"And speaking of Barry, you think he's upset now, he's going to be madder than the snake that married the garden hose."

Cade choked on his water. "Weiss is a douche canoe," he said when he recovered.

"That may be, but he has a following of meat eaters in this town. And the other media could turn on you as well. Everyone likes to pile on criticism. It's easy."

She stopped as the server came to the table. Lolo's was busy with the dinner crowd, and Cade could see why. The place was comfortable and unpretentious while having plenty to be pretentious about. Stillwater had a raft of good restaurants, but Cade often chose Lolo's.

"Hey, you two. Glad to have you back. Can I bring you a cocktail?" The server was college-aged and had nice cheekbones that shone when she smiled. Her nametag read, "Nan. I love sushi."

Cade shook his head. "We're both going back to work. Alcohol and law enforcement don't mix well."

Reynolds laughed as she lowered her menu. "Alcohol and the newsroom do mix, but I need to be on my A-game. Especially tonight."

Holding up two fingers, Cade said, "A pair of lemonades, Nan."

"Make mine a strawberry lemonade, if you please," Reynolds added.

"Of course, Miss Devries. I love your work, by the way. I'm studying broadcast journalism at the U. I hope to be where you are someday." Nan looked down shyly.

Reynolds leaned forward to catch her eye. "A bit of advice. Broadcasting is a boy's club, so you need to project confidence, work hard and prepare like your career depends on it—it does. You need to be so gloriously magnificent they can't ignore you. And that's just in the small market where you have to start."

Nan nodded as she spun the bracelet on her wrist. "But it's worth it, isn't it? All the hard work?"

"You mean not only the hard work but the deadlines, the

pressure, the relentless focus on your appearance, the in-fighting and the tragic stories that will break your heart?" Reynolds held the young woman's gaze while she waited for her response.

Nan nodded.

"Damn right, it's worth it. There's nothing else like it." Reynolds reached out and gave Nan a fist bump. "Now go and study hard and never settle for anything less than your best."

"Yes, Miss Devries. Thank you." She turned to leave.

"Oh, and Nan. Don't forget mine was a strawberry lemonade."

"Yes, Miss Devries." She was all smiles as she hurried off.

Cade looked at Reynolds until she broke into a grin. "What?" she asked.

"You are amazing. Absolutely amazing."

Reynolds ran her fingers through her long hair. "Keep talking that way, and the cheesecake won't be your only dessert."

Cade swallowed hard and looked around. Where was that lemonade?

CHAPTER 15

No surprise, Cade found Grace in her BCA lab.

Hair pulled back, glasses on, white lab coat on over yesterday's dress, bare feet and bags under her eyes, Grace looked like she hadn't slept. Cade was pretty sure she hadn't left the lab in days.

"Hey," she said when she noticed him. "Yes, I'm still here."

"How's the social life?" he asked, sitting beside her. He got a very Grace-like middle-fingered response.

"How's yours?" She studied his face as Cade tried not to smirk. "Just shut up. I don't even want to hear about it. You can't talk about food in front of a starving person. Your girlfriend can go suck an egg."

"I'm sure she could." Cade kept a straight face.

"You're such a loser," she said with exasperation, but she smiled.

Cade switched gears. "Did you get the new note?"

Grace nodded, hitting a key. The enormous wall-mounted screen blinked on. "Here's the note in all its dubious glory."

Cade looked up at the magnified note, the words chilling him.

Unstoppable, the web weavers sow death.
Pain and terror, blood and fear, light our way.
Dawkins, stumbling in the dark.
You had your day. Now it's ours.

"It doesn't get better with age. Still hard to read," he said. "But clearly written by the same person who wrote the Albright note."

The onscreen image slid to the side, and the original note

appeared next to it. Grace glanced up at the screen. "For reference, here are both notes side by side. And yes, quite obviously, both were created by the same unsub."

In law enforcement and crime television shows, unsub was short for unknown subject, the person of interest in a criminal investigation. Nobody said perp anymore.

"Obviously."

Grace shifted in her seat, tucking a leg underneath. "Same handwriting. Same threatening tone. Same calling you out by name and challenging you," she said as she stuck the end of a stylus against her lips. "One thing I noticed, even though this is clearly a solo killer, the writer intentionally uses the plural." Using the laser pointer end of her stylus, she circled several phrases. "The web *weavers*. And now it's *our* turn."

"He's acknowledging the other killer from the Orbiting Cortex site. Speaking for him." Cade leaned forward. "What about the symbols? Do they mean anything?"

Grace zoomed in on the markings that bordered the note.

"Beyond the obvious spider webs, I haven't been able to source the others yet. At first, I thought they may be Egyptian hieroglyphics, but I haven't found a match with any of the cataloged ones. I'm sure these symbols must mean something. They were painstakingly drawn out, not haphazardly at all." Grace zoomed in even closer on the markings. "See the ink spread here and here?" She used her laser pointer to highlight several areas.

"I do, but I never would have without this magnification."

Grace pushed up her glasses. "That's why I'm here and getting paid the big bucks. To see what others don't. And to offer context."

It wouldn't be surprising if she made a high salary at the state agency. Her skills and insight were legendary, let alone almost dying to help solve the last case. She was a resource unmatched in the department, or even the state.

Grace continued. "The note writer used slow strokes to make

these symbols. Compared to the words themselves, this part must have taken considerably longer to write out."

"But why?" Cade asked. "For what reason? Does it contain a hidden message?"

Leaning back, Grace folded her arms and looked into the distance. Cade knew Grace well enough to know this was when she'd access her astonishingly deep reservoir of knowledge.

"The Zodiac Killer, who was active in the sixties and seventies, sent messages to the media written in code. They were a patchwork of symbols and characters, and some are still unsolved to this day. He wanted to show off his superior intelligence. But after the first one was decoded almost immediately, he sent increasingly complex messages that have baffled the FBI for decades."

Cade nodded. "I'd read that a Zodiac Killer message had been decoded recently."

Grace looked at him with mild surprise. "Good, you're keeping up with the serial killer lore. It'll give us more to talk about over dinner."

Dinner? But Cade didn't interrupt her.

"It was a Virginia software developer working with an Australian applied mathematician who solved it. Some fifty years after it had been sent to the San Francisco Chronicle. The thing was, there was nothing useful in the decoded message. Certainly, nothing that revealed his identity. It was just more bragging and threats."

Cade looked away from the screen. "So, you're saying that even if there's a hidden message, it may not help the investigation?"

"That's exactly what I'm saying." She took a drink from her water bottle. The words, *Work Smarter*, were stenciled on the side. "But I can't rule out anything. But I find it improbable the killer would offer his name, address and social security number written in code for us to decipher."

"It does seem unlikely. Maybe it's the name and room number of his hotel. That symbol in the upper left looks like two trees." Cade kept a straight face.

"Equally as improbable." She lightly punched his shoulder.

Cade handed her a flash drive. "Those symbols are all over the victim's body this time, however."

Grace perked up. "Really?"

Nodding, Cade said, "Check out the crime scene photos."

In a moment, she had the images on screen and cycled through them until she got to the close-ups of the victim's body. She zoomed in on the woman's marked-up skin.

"I don't have to tell you this is unusual, do I?" she asked. Not waiting for a reply, she continued. "I see he's marked this as his second victim. I believe that's where he started writing. From there, he went on to prepare her body with these symbols."

"Prepare?"

"Sorry, I'm back to the Egyptians again." Grace shifted on her chair. "They believed that body preparation set them up for life in the next world. This feels eerily similar."

"Or."

"Or?" Grace looked intrigued.

"Or the killer is all hat and no cattle."

Grace glanced his way. "I'm a city girl. I'm not following."

Cade sat back. "He's style without substance."

Grace stood up and stretched. "I know what that means, but not in your context. Please elaborate."

"Grace, I think he's full of shit," Cade said. "He's playing us. Throwing in random shit to mess with us. Maybe there isn't a deeper meaning or message."

"There's always a deeper meaning."

Cade gestured that he accepted her point. "Perhaps, but you're talking about the underlying motivation that drives him. I'm talking about the symbols. They are BS. He's not preparing the body for the afterlife. He's sending it there with his knife."

Grace took a moment as she contemplated what Cade was suggesting. "Maybe. But let's look at what else the killer has offered us. Maybe it will help us understand better." Grace pulled the pictures beginning with the motel entrance and then led into the motel room. "The stacked beds with the table. It's like an altar. He's displayed the victim's body, supine. Once again, arched backward with the knife left inserted in the victim."

Cade shook his head at the wrongness of it. "It's like he's proud of his kill."

"It's more likely that he posed her body for maximum shock value." Grace zoomed in on the knife handle.

"Great band name: Maximum shock value."

Shaking her head, Grace said. "I see I'm not the only one who's overtired. Stay focused." She sat and again folded her arms as she stared at nothing. "Serial killers have signatures. These signatures serve the psychological or emotional needs of the killer and originate in their damaged psyche. They often reflect fantasies the killer has about their ideal victim. Profile research has shown these fantasies develop over the years, often incorporating the torture of animals, and increase in intensity until they have to be acted on."

"You keep talking about the signature, but the notes weren't signed." He held her gaze.

"You're messing with me," she said after a moment's hesitation.

"Possibly," Cade said.

"Remember that the serial killer's signature is different from the M.O. That's how they go about killing, like using a knife, for example."

"I'm familiar with a criminal's M.O.," Cade said. "Like the burglar that only goes in through second-floor windows. Like that."

"But the serial killer is an entirely different animal. Some killers simply kill, but then there are some who leave a personal stamp on the victim or the crime scene that can reveal fantasy-driven rituals based on needs or compulsions. That's the signature.

"Let me give you an example." Grace leaned forward. "Between 1990 and 1991, three prostitutes were murdered in Texas. At the autopsy, it became clear that their eyes had been skillfully removed. A tip from a woman who'd gotten away from a brutal john led to a

57-year-old man. A hair and fiber analysis from his home and the victims provided circumstantial physical evidence that implicated him. Interviews with friends and family mentioned that he had a fixation on eyes, likely from his background in taxidermy. He was convicted of the murders, and while in prison, he was often found drawing pictures of female eyes."

"Did they ever find the missing eyes?"

"Not that I know of. Maybe we don't want to know what happened to them." Grace gave a noticeable shiver.

Cade stroked his chin. "So, his signature revolved around the victim's eyes. The body posing is our killer's signature, likely inspired by some fantasy he's had."

Grace pointed at him. "Exactly. Maybe at a tender young age, he walked in on his mom lying naked on her bed. Now imagine she let loose on him, screaming at him. He was hurt and scared, yet oddly aroused. That memory lives with him to this day, and he poses each victim as he remembers his mother from that day."

"But, what's the difference between posing and staging the body?" he asked.

Grace leaned back, scratching her neck. "It's in the name. Staging is an attempt to mislead criminal investigators. Posing is all about serving the fantasy needs of the killer."

"I get it."

Grace ran through the crime scene images several times, before stopping on an image. Her forehead wrinkled and she stood up, leaning over the table to get a closer look.

"What is it?" he asked. He stood as well.

"Hold on," she said distractedly, staring at the screen. She zoomed in on the television and magnified the image farther to focus on the black box on top of the set.

"See that?" she asked, pointing at the box.

"The cable box?"

"Exactly that. Notice the glare there on the left?" She used the pointer to highlight the glare.

"I do," Cade said, but not seeing why it was important.

"I'd bet my next two days off that we're seeing a video camera lens," Grace said as she squinted at the screen. "The box looks to be modified to hide a camera."

"Really," Cade said, thinking about the conversation with the motel's front desk clerk. "The clerk at the motel mentioned that Valley was worried about perverts spying on her business. She insinuated it was the motel's owner she was referring to."

"Did he look like a pervert?" Grace asked, wiggling her eyebrows.

Cade shrugged. "I didn't meet him, actually. He never came out of his office when Rook and I interviewed the front desk clerk."

Grace cocked her head. "And you didn't think that was odd why?"

Cade ran a hand through his hair and sighed. "I need more sleep. In retrospect, it was decidedly odd. But at the time, no. I was focused on the killer and knew it wasn't the sleazy motel owner."

Cade stood and put a hand on Grace's shoulder. "As ever, thank you for an enlightening discussion. Great to see you."

"Wait. Where are you off to?" she asked, confused by his sudden movement.

"Back to the motel. I'm guessing either the owner or his spy camera witnessed Valley's murder. Either way, I hope it leads to something actionable."

"Amen to that," Grace said as Cade headed for the door. "And that's coming from an atheist."

CHAPTER 16

Night had come. The squad cars were gone, along with crime scene techs, media, and any of the curious spectators who were drawn to murder scenes. Veronica Valley's lifeless body had left as well, delivered to the morgue for examination, looking for clues to the killer. All that remained at the motel was the yellow crime scene tape and an eerie heaviness that hung in the air. Maybe it was his imagination, but for Cade, it was a palpable and oppressive feeling.

Cade walked to where it happened.

The door to room 113 opened with a drawn-out creak, continuing until it struck the wall beside it. The stacked beds remained, but the writing desk had been taken down. It stood next to the beds as a reminder of the atrocity placed there by the killer. Black fingerprint powder was on all the smooth surfaces from the tech's fingerprint collection efforts. It was everywhere.

Cade went to the television and knelt to examine the cable box. At first glance, it looked like any other cable box, but he couldn't think of the last time he'd even seen a box on a television. Of course, the giant tube TV looked so very nineties. Like it should be wearing a plaid flannel shirt and listening to Nirvana.

The thing was, now that he was here with the box, he didn't see a camera lens. Stepping back, he tried to determine what they noticed that gave off the suspicious glare. Nothing. He shined a light on it, moved to different angles, and even tried squinting.

Still nothing.

Being bone tired and sleep deprived, it took longer than it should have for the realization to hit him. There wasn't any fingerprint dust on the box.

Which meant it wasn't the same box.

Fuming all the way down the cracked sidewalk, he pushed open the lobby door. Stella looked up from behind the counter. "Where is he?" Cade asked as he moved around the counter. She pointed to the closed office door. Not feeling the need to knock, he pushed right in.

A white-haired man sat hunched over a computer. Startled, he jumped and closed the laptop. "Damn it, Stella, I—" But he stopped when he saw it wasn't his clerk and stared warily. Looking to be close to seventy, the wiry man had a full head of bushy white hair and a close-cropped beard of the same color. His shirt was unbuttoned down to the seventies and a gold chain hung around his neck and nestled into the forest that was his chest hair. His eyes darted so much that Cade was reminded of a ferret.

"Where is it?" Cade demanded.

Of course, the man replied with, "Where is what?" Stallers around the world answered questions with another question. Always. Cade noted the man's body position shift as his leg moved in front of the bottom desk drawer.

"You know damn well what I'm talking about. The box from the murder scene."

The man babbled something about a warrant and his lawyer, but Cade was past the point of listening or caring. When he heard, "my constitutional rights," Cade had enough and pulled the owner off his chair. He landed hard and stopped talking.

"Let me ask you again. Where is the effin' box?"

The owner looked up at the glowering detective and said, "Warrant." Though he didn't sound nearly as forceful or determined now.

Cade knelt down besides the motel's owner and sniffed. The man smelled of fear and desperation. "You want a warrant? Fine. I'll get a warrant, but it'll take an hour or three. And I plan on sitting here until then."

Cade took a moment to look around the cluttered office.

"Who knows, I might just discover something the attorney general could use. He is running for reelection." Cade held the man's gaze.

"Hold on, hold on." Getting to his knees, the owner crawled to the desk and opened the bottom drawer. "Maybe you should look in here."

The box was in the drawer, and Cade knew right away. The shiny black fingerprint powder covering the box meant that this was the one he was looking for. Cade jabbed a finger at him. "You're looking at jail time for tampering with a crime scene. Not to mention spying on your guests to get your voyeuristic rocks off."

Remaining silent, the owner nodded. He made no move to get off the floor.

Cade glowered at the motel owner. "Where does the video go from this box? Is it on your laptop?"

He shook his head. "It's self-contained. There's an internal storage drive. All the videos are on there."

Snatching the box from the drawer, Cade said, "I'm taking this. If I hear one word from you or your bloodsucking attorney, I'm going to personally haul your geriatric ass to the lockup." Cade leaned in closer and stared into the man's eyes. "Are we clear?"

Nodding slowly, the owner spoke quietly. "Yes, sir. Crystal clear."

Leaving him on the ground, he turned and walked past an amused Stella. "Veronica Valley was right; your owner is a perv."

"True statement."

"Hey," the owner called out, but Cade was done with them and hurried out. He stopped at room 113 to lock the door. The weight was still in the air, but now hope was there, too. Hope that something would be on the video to help stop this killer.

"Don't you ever go home?" Cade asked as he set the black box in front of Grace.

She shrugged. "Home is overrated. Nothing happens there."

Taking a seat next to her, Cade studied her. "That's the point, really. Home is your sanctuary, where you go to relax and recharge. You need time away from the lab to be effective."

Grace shook her head. "I don't have to go home. That's why God invented bars."

"I know you're being flippant, but you need to practice self-care. Life is not a sprint, Grace. You need to take care of yourself for the long haul." He held her gaze. "Okay? For me?"

"Yes, daddy." But she smiled.

Cade leaned forward, hands on his thighs. "So, the motel owner, in all his ethical glory, was secretly recording his guests. If I'm right, we'll have Veronica Valley's death recorded on this box's hard drive. Can you retrieve the file?"

Pulling out a cloth, Grace wiped the powder off the box. "It's like glitter. The powder gets on everything, and you can't get rid of it."

Cade looked at his hands. The powder was everywhere, on his fingernails, pads and palms. It was on his jacket, on the front and sleeves. He glanced up to Grace, who giggled and tossed over the towel.

"Told you."

She spun the box around in her hands, nodded and went rummaging through a drawer. With the appropriate plug found, she moved to her keyboard. A file directory came up on the screen.

"They're AVI files. A common video type. Renders decent quality with good compression." She looked to Cade. "We've got twelve files here."

"Play the most recent one." Cade held his breath. This was uncharted waters.

Grace crossed herself and hit play.

But it was the St. Paul officers making the discovery and clearing the room.

"Must be the one before it." Grace started the video.

They both stared at the big screen.

There was an eerie silence. The video had no sound. It wasn't apparent if that made it better or worse.

A man and a woman were in view. He had his back to the camera while she was in profile. Hair cut short, he wore a suit jacket over dress pants. Valley pulled off the man's coat and tie, setting them on the bed. She moved onto the bed, effectively disappearing from view as the man blocked the camera. Still, it was clear she continued undressing him as she reached for his shirt cuffs and then stripped off his shirt.

"Woah."

Every inch of the man's back was filled with tattoos. Tattoos that were similar to the symbols on the notes and the woman's body. Black ink interlocked and flowed from his waist all the way up to his collar. Parts of the design had heavier concentrations, while others were more spaced out. The densest parts were down his spine and across his back, connecting his shoulder blades.

"He looks like the drummer from Fall Out Boy," Grace said, "the way his entire back is covered."

"I'm more of a Green Day fan," Cade said as Valley finished undressing the man, who stood rigid and unmoving. Then, everything changed.

Pouncing as quickly as a hungry jungle cat, the man had Valley by the throat and pushed her back on the bed. He was all over her as she fought against him. He moved up her body and looked to be whispering in her ear. Valley's struggles stopped after that.

Using pre-cut lengths of cord, he efficiently tied her to the bed. And then things paused.

He rolled off her and lay next to Valley, ignoring her. He grabbed the remote off the bedside table and pointed it at the television. After several minutes he raised the remote again. Grace and Cade shared a quizzical glance. Not what they were expecting.

"He's watching TV?"

"Looks that way."

"What do you suppose he's watching?"

"It wouldn't surprise me if it was the news." Some serial killers were known to follow their news coverage closely. Some made regular contact with the media to stay in the news cycle between killings.

After a moment, he lifted the remote yet again and then dropped it. He turned to the woman.

Grace reached for Cade's hand. Here it comes.

But it didn't. Instead, he picked up the woman's clutch purse and dumped it on the bed between them. He picked through the contents before grabbing her license. He looked at it, looked at her, and said something. Next, he picked up an older-looking phone before dropping it dismissively. There was a second phone, and he picked that up next. He moved the device over to her bound arm.

"He's using her finger to unlock it."

For the next several minutes, while Valley straining against her bonds, the man looked through her phone, At one point, he aimed it at her while she struggled even more intensely. Afterward, he went back to the phone.

"I think he took a picture of her."

Then, the knife appeared, and the killer cut away her clothing. He took his time, enjoying her squirming underneath him. He reached into a bag and came out with a marker which he used to write on her abdomen. She strained against her bonds when he picked up her phone again. He did something on the screen and propped it on the bedside table.

"This is when he FaceTimed the victim's mother so she could watch."

Grace looked stunned. "That's horrible."

"He's a sick puppy, this one."

Neither spoke as the scene unfolded on the screen. Using the knife the way a baker might use a spatula to artistically spread frosting over an elaborate cake, he ran the blade's edge over her taut skin. This continued for several long minutes until...

"Oh," Grace exclaimed as her hand covered her mouth.

Hands squeezing the armrest, Cade couldn't pull his eyes from the screen as much as he wanted to. The killer had climbed up Valley's body until he was eye to eye with her. An unsuspecting bystander might think they were sharing a tender moment.

They'd be wrong.

The killer drove the knife all the way to the hilt. Valley thrashed for a moment, the knife in her throat, but it wasn't for long.

The killer stared into her eyes the entire time.

"Damn."

The killer worked on her body with the marker for the next several minutes, creating the elaborate markings they found on her exposed skin. After that, he lifted her from the bed and built his makeshift altar. Once Valley's body was placed on the table, the killer moved out of sight. The video stuttered and resumed when he returned.

"Motion-activated camera," Grace commented.

"Yup," Cade said. "All the pervs have them."

The killer stood facing Valley while he dressed. Afterward, he pulled the note from his bag and placed it on the wall. He grabbed her license and both phones and walked out of the frame. Veronica Valley lay on the stacked furniture, unmoving, the knife protruding from her throat.

The video ended seconds later. Neither Cade nor Grace moved, both staring straight ahead. The only sound was the hum of the ventilation system circulating the air.

Cade let out a long breath and turned to Grace. Tears ran down her cheeks, slow streams of her outward pain showing, her trembling lips and jaw hinting at what was below her surface. Cade gave her a moment, not wanting to intrude.

"That poor woman," Grace said after a moment. "She was terrified. There wasn't anything she could do, and she knew it."

Cade nodded.

"That animal," Grace said, gathering steam. "He ran that knife over her for...forever. And to make her mother watch the entire thing...that was ice cold. She was terrified, but knowing her mother was bearing witness, that's psychological murder. Plain and simple. He killed her before the knife even entered her."

Rubbing his eyes, Cade looked up at the screen, now blank. "I thought he brought Valley's mother into it because of a deep-seated maternal hatred. Most serial killers were done wrong by their mothers. But you got me thinking this was more about inflicting psychological pain on the victim."

Grace nodded. "We're going to catch this animal. I don't care what we need to do, we're stopping him before he does this again. And then you're going to kill him."

"Grace."

She held up a hand. "I know what you're going to say. Law enforcement doesn't work that way. We need to bring him to justice. Let the system work the way it's been designed to work." She made a surprisingly passable impression of him.

Putting a hand over hers, Cade gently lowered it and left it there. "Those aren't my words, Grace." He held her gaze, her eyes staring hotly back. "I'm not about murdering criminals, but this is an animal disguised as a human being. He may walk around in thousand-dollar suits, but he's a killer shark, a rabid dog, a man-eating lion. You don't put those into cages." He paused, studying Grace.

"I hear what you're not saying," she said quietly, squeezing his hand. "I know you'll do what needs doing."

"No guarantees, but we have to find him first. Can you pull some stills from the video? Find the ones that show him the most." She nodded.

Cade rubbed his chin. "Did you notice that even though there's no way he could've known about the hidden camera, he was always turned away? We never got more than a glimpse of his profile."

"That's the predator in him. Always aware of potential threats—even subconsciously."

Cade nodded in agreement. "Like the leopard knowing the hunter is there long before the hunter knows he's even close."

"Exactly," Grace said. "But the leopard knows before it can see or hear the hunter. They just know. Their survival instincts are rooted in their subconscious. Serial killers are wired the same. Some of the wariest creatures stalking the earth, they go to extraordinary lengths to avoid discovery."

"So, getting him on video at all is a big deal?" Cade asked.

"It's like getting bigfoot on your doorbell camera. It's never been done."

Cade stood up, releasing her hand. "So, let's make the most of it. Let's release the best stills you can find. See if law enforcement, somewhere, anywhere, has seen this guy before. This can't be his first rodeo."

"Not a chance," Grace said, getting up.

"Send the images to me. I have an idea how to use them to rile him up a bit." He headed for the door.

"You want this guy riled up?" She shook her head. "Be careful what you wish for," she called after him.

CHAPTER 17

Rook climbed out of the Charger with a groan. He was too young to be making old people noises. He was beginning to sound like his dad. Shaking his head at the depressing thought, he glanced at the people streaming out of the bus terminal. They resembled ants venturing out for whatever ants venture out for. A dozen buses sat on the tarmac. Greyhound, Jefferson, and the iconic Mega Bus. Most everyone pulled a suitcase or had a bag slung over their shoulder.

Rook suspected he'd come to the right place.

Ambling over to the ticketing counter, Rook checked along the way for video surveillance, counting three cameras in the busy lobby alone. No doubt there were more where the buses unloaded. People of all types were spread around the cavernous space. Twentysomethings with noses in phones, parents corralling small children, older folks reading newspapers or dozing. It was a slice of life.

"Hey, man. What's up?" Rook said as he flashed his badge to the ticket counter clerk.

The man was in his mid-fifties, was well-fed, and his shirt looked to be a size too small. Fabric strained on either side of his clip-on tie. He frowned at Rook.

"Look, I checked in. Yesterday." He wiped away his forehead sweat on a sleeve.

"No, bro, it's not that," Rook said. "I'm here to look at your surveillance footage from Wednesday. Nothing else."

The man nodded, though he maintained his wary expression.

"Now, where do you keep the video equipment?"

"It's back in our security office. Let me get you in." He picked up a radio and keyed in the transmit button. "Yolanda, can you come to ticketing?"

"Be right there, boss," a woman's voice said over the radio.

"She'll be right here," the clerk said, and turned back to his duties. Rook guessed it was more about getting away from him than actually having something to do. He looked around waiting for Yolanda.

Rook couldn't miss her. The security officer could start on the Viking's defensive line. Wearing a security uniform of black and blue, the woman stood well over six feet. Her eyes locked onto Rook while she crossed the lobby at an assured pace, easily sidestepping both people and obstacles in her path.

Rook badged her when she approached. "I'm here to look at your surveillance footage from Wednesday."

"Sure, boss. Right this way."

Rook followed the security officer to an office near the bathrooms. Using a key from her ring of a dozen keys, she opened the door and gestured for him to enter the small room. The only light came from the six monitors mounted on the wall. Yolanda closed the door and crowded in next to him.

"Can you tell me what buses came in on Wednesday? Only the ones arriving before 5 p.m."

"Sure, boss." Yolanda stepped around Rook, went to a terminal, and pulled up a list of buses. She gestured for Rook to read for himself.

Jefferson, from Duluth. 1:15 pm arrival.
Greyhound, from Rochester. 2:00 pm arrival.
Greyhound, from Des Moines. 2:45 pm arrival.
Mega Bus, from Milwaukee. 3:00 pm arrival.
Mega Bus, from Chicago. 4:10 pm arrival.
Greyhound, from Fargo. 4:15 pm arrival.

"Let's start watching the video from the Duluth arrival." Rook thought it unlikely that their unsub came from Minnesota as his previous killings would be known in local law enforcement circles. But he couldn't discount that the killer took multiple buses to get here. Maybe starting the journey to the Twin Cities from as far away as Canada.

"Here you go, Jefferson, at 1:15," Yolanda said after a moment. The screen showed the door to the bus opening and people stepping off one by one. From there, they congregated by the cargo hold, waiting to grab luggage, except for a few that simply walked off with their carry-ons. Nobody fit the boy's description of a large-bearded man pulling a suitcase.

He shook his head and Yolanda went back to her computer.

"Next is Greyhound at 2." Much like the first, people streamed out with and without luggage. There was a bearded man, but he was thin and followed by a woman. They left holding hands. Not their man.

Rook shook his head.

"Greyhound at 2:45." A dozen weary travelers, but no bearded man.

He again shook his head and crossed it off his list.

"Mega Bus at 3 p.m." Rook stopped breathing when the third passenger stepped onto the tarmac. Wearing a gray t-shirt with a circular US flag symbol, the huge man dwarfed the passengers in front of him. He had a bushy dark beard with a full head of hair and a pair of headphones hung around his neck. Picking up a suitcase set out with the others, he shuffled off, pulling it behind him.

"You look kinda excited," Yolanda said. "I take it you found who you're looking for."

Rook nodded as he made notes on his pad. "The bearded man there fits the witness description in a murder case. But let's run through the other arrivals just in case. Doing my due diligence."

But there wasn't anyone else even close to matching the boy's description.

"Officer Yolanda, can you get a passenger list for the 3 p.m. Mega Bus? Do you know when it left Milwaukee?"

"Sure, boss. It departed Milwaukee at 6 a.m. the same day." She pointed to the only chair in the room, a metal folding chair. "Have a seat, boss, and I'll pull the manifest." She swept past and out into the lobby. The door clicked shut behind her, the lobby noise silenced.

Rook pulled up information on the Mega Bus company on his phone. He'd seen the colorful double-decker buses advertising a $1 low fare on the interstate from time to time. He guessed not everyone got the $1 fare if they were still in business. The company ran buses between cities all over the US and into Canada. Minneapolis had buses running to and from Chicago, Madison, and Milwaukee.

Yolanda returned with a printout and handed over the sheet of names.

"Seventeen names. I glanced at the list, and you can strike out the women," Yolanda offered. "That leaves you eleven. There's two men with the same last names as two women, so most likely they're married. If you exclude them, that brings the list to a manageable nine names."

Rook nodded as he studied the names. Odds are the killer was one of these men, and his heart raced. There was something about the hunt that got his motor revving.

"So, what's your next step?" Yolanda asked as she moved into Rook's space. She smelled of vanilla.

"Why do you want to know?" he asked, looking up from the names.

"Thinking of getting into law enforcement. I want to see how things work." She held his gaze. "And I can't stay here forever. I'll go insane."

"Fair enough. But do you really want a job where they make you drive fast cars and carry powerful handguns?" Rook asked with a grin.

Yolanda flashed her own grin. "Hell yes. Who wouldn't?"

"You'd be surprised. Some people like spending their days in the cube farms." He shook his head. "Not me, though. Anyway, I'll start by querying the database for these names, get license info along with a picture. That should give me enough to track him down."

Sill holding Rook's gaze, she said, "I like me a man who's not afraid to fight for truth, justice and the American way."

Rook swallowed hard.

"Well, thank you," he said. "Say, can I get the video clip of our suspect?"

"Sure, boss. That's easy." And two minutes later, Rook had the video clip on a flash drive along with Yolanda's totally unsolicited phone number, "just in case you wanted to hang with me later."

THE ST. PAUL police department headquarters was in a newer brick building on the edge of downtown near interstate's 35E and 94. The word POLICE was helpfully placed on the building's exterior in massive block letters. Rook dropped the Charger on the street down the block, leaving a police card on the dash. He headed inside and met up with Bednarek on the second floor.

"Yo, man, how's the detective work coming?" Rook asked. "You solve the case yet?"

Bednarek shook her head. "No one told me how glamorous the work can be," she said. "I feel like a grad assistant doing all the professor's research." She pushed up her glasses and smiled. "But it's better than riding around in the squad all day. It made my panties creep."

She kept a straight face while he studied her, so Rook decided nodding was his best response. Kristin Bednarek looked to be all of five feet tall, with light brown hair and plenty of curves. When she smiled, it brightened up the room. Rook decided he liked her.

"How can I help?" she asked as she eyed the paper in his hand.

"I have a lead on the second killer. Witnesses saw him pulling a suitcase. I found a video of a man matching his description getting off a bus several hours earlier and he was pulling a suitcase. And get this, the crime scene was a mile due north of the bus terminal."

Bednarek shrugged. "I don't know. It feels kinda weak."

Rook put a hand over his heart, now unsure if he liked the detective. "Weak, you say?"

Nodding, Bednarek continued. "What was the witnesses' description of the killer?"

"Bushy beard and hair, a huge guy. Wearing t-shirt and shorts."

"And the bus guy looked similar?" she asked.

Rook nodded. "Not just similar, but exactly that."

"Okay," she said. "Do you have the bus guy tied to the crime scene somehow?"

"It was in the same part of the city," Rook said, feeling as he was losing the argument.

Bednarek turned back to her screen. "I'm gonna stick with weak. Now, I should get back to my car rental agency canvassing."

Not one to roll over, Rook held the printout of names in front of her. "I have a list of nine names. If you saw what this guy did to the Garcia woman, you'd do anything and everything to get him off the streets. It was horrible. Bite marks covering 90 percent of her body." Pulling out his phone, he said, "I have pictures if that helps you decide."

She held out her hand. "Give me the list."

Bednarek entered the names and reviewed the results. On the fourth one, she held up a finger. "Hold on."

Rook studied the screen while Bednarek read. "Michael Thomas Pavich, Milwaukee address. Twenty-six years old. Six feet six, 220 pounds, brown hair, blue eyes. No driver's license, but has a state-issued ID, expired. Police picked him up for lurking outside a woman's home a year ago. The charges were dropped. No reason given."

The picture showed an unkempt man with lots of hair and a neglected beard.

"Weak still?" Rook asked.

"Getting stronger by the minute," Bednarek said.

"Agreed. Let's get Milwaukee homicide on the phone. It might be enlightening." Rook jotted down Pavich's information.

"I'm on it," Bednarek said, looking up the Wisconsin city's police contact information. She dialed and after several minutes, they had Detective Alan Bell on speaker. Rook and Bednarek introduced themselves.

"What can I do for you, detectives?" he asked with mild interest in his gravelly voice. "I don't get many calls from the Twin Cities."

"We're working a case that appears to have ties to your city. Have you encountered murdered women with bite marks? A lot of bite marks?"

The line was silent while Rook waited for Bell's response. He exchanged glances with Bednarek.

"Who is this again?" Bell asked after a long moment's pause.

"Detectives Rooker and Bednarek with the Five Below major crimes task force in Minnesota."

"I'll call you back," Bell said. "Where are you working out of?"

"St. Paul police headquarters in downtown St. Paul," Bednarek answered. "The number is—"

Bell ended the call mid-sentence.

"That went well," Bednarek said. "I don't think he liked your task force name."

Shaking his head, Rook leaned back and put his feet up on Bednarek's desk. Hands clasped behind his head, he smiled. "*Our* task force name. He'll call back."

She looked at him, clearly not sharing his optimism.

"I would have hung up, too. When you're dealing with sensitive information over the phone, you don't want to start sharing without confirming your caller's identity. Bell definitely doesn't want to be quoted on the front page of the Milwaukee paper giving away important details of his case. So, you hang up and call the main department phone number and ask for us."

"Detective Bednarek, call on three-three," the overhead page announced.

"Right on schedule," Rook said, taking his feet off her desk.

"Sorry about that," Bell said when he was back on speaker. "I needed to be sure. You're asking about an active case and mentioning the one detail we've managed to keep under wraps. A particular grisly detail."

"No worries," Rook said. "So, tell me more about your case."

A pause, then, "Why don't you tell what you have there and what led you to call me here?"

Rook leaned toward the desk phone. "Fine. On Thursday, a 32-year-old hotel worker was found dead on her Minneapolis front porch. We believe she was killed between 5:30 and 6:00 p.m. the evening before. The distinguishing characteristic of her death were the bite marks found."

"Just a couple of them then?" Bell asked.

"Yo man, not even close. She had bites over 90 percent of her body."

"Interesting," Bell said.

"You might say that," Rook stated.

"Any witnesses?" There was a hopeful tone in his voice.

"There was, actually." Rook took a breath. "A neighborhood boy may have walked up to her door as it was happening. He panicked and ran home, not telling anyone until the next morning. He described a large man with a lot of hair."

"Yes, that's him." There was excitement in his voice. "So, the son of a bitch left our state."

"Sure looks that way. You're welcome to have him back."

Bell let out a dry chuckle. "Nah, you can keep him. Knowing Wisconsin, we'll have another serial killer soon enough."

Bednarek looked confused.

"My fellow detective doesn't follow you," Rook explained.

Bell cleared his throat. "It's nothing we're proud of, but Wisconsin has been home to some of the most notorious serial killers ever. You've heard of the cannibal Jeffrey Dahmer? That's us. How about Ed Gein, the inspiration for the Texas Chainsaw Massacre movie? Also us."

"And don't forget the Milwaukee Brewers," Rook added. "That's an embarrassment right there."

Bell broke out with a loud laugh. "The Twins aren't anything to write home about, either." After a few residual chuckles, Bell turned serious. "What I want to know was how you knew to call us here in Milwaukee?"

"The unsub was seen by another youth leaving the scene pulling a suitcase. The only thing that made any sense was that he'd walked there from the nearby Minneapolis bus terminal. It's a mile straight south from the crime scene. Video surveillance cameras there captured a man who fit the killer's description. A large man with bushy hair and beard pulling a suitcase who got off the Mega Bus from Milwaukee."

"No shit?"

"Yes, shit," Bednarek added. "And we have a name." There was fire in her eyes now.

"Don't leave me hanging here. What is it?" Bell now sounded excited.

Before Bednarek could speak, Rook jumped in. "It's your turn, Detective. Share what you've encountered with this killer. And then you'll get the name," he added.

Bell let loose with a few choice words before sighing.

"Fine. We've had five murders here. All in the fringe areas of Milwaukee, sort of industrial, sort of seedy, if you know what I mean. It's never downtown or in the suburbs. The victims were workers of the local sex trade and others who lived or worked in the area. All died from blood loss from numerous bites. Each subsequent murder has got more uncontrolled, more vicious. The last victim had her throat torn out. It's brutal and sadistic."

"Suspects?" Rook asked.

"Why are you doing this to me, man? You already got a name."

Rook pictured Detective Bell shaking his head in frustration. It made him smile.

Bell sighed. "Yeah, there were a few. People in the area caught on camera. Not a damned one panned out. None. But I'm convinced it's someone that lives in the immediate area. We talked to profilers at the FBI, and they told us it's likely someone within two miles or uses public transportation. They said it was unlikely the unsub had a running vehicle of their own."

"What else did they tell you?"

"That the unsub would have poor social skills, is likely Caucasian, under thirty years and has trouble holding down a job."

"That's half the people I went to high school with," Bednarek said.

Bell laughed. "Mine, too. But yeah, that's the problem with these profiles. It doesn't narrow down the population enough to lead you to a suspect, but after they're caught, you'll see that the suspect ticked most, if not all of the boxes, from the profile."

"Did any of your suspects tick off all the FBI boxes?" Rook asked.

There was a long pause before Bell answered.

"The name, Rooker. Just give me the damn name," Bell spat out.

"Michael Thomas Pavich."

There was a loud sound as if Detective Bell had slapped his desk. Rook suspected he'd done exactly that.

"Pavich. Yes, he lives with his mother in the right geographic area. He was my number one, was spotted on camera twice in the area, but it was never right when the murders happened. His mother vouched for him at the time of the killings. Said they regularly had late evening board game sessions at the kitchen table. She was so vehement about it that we had to move on." Bell paused in thought. "He was one of those basement gamer teenagers that never grew up when he became an adult. Zero idea how to talk to a real person. Completely awkward."

"Well, he's here in Minnesota, and now we've had an identical murder. I don't believe in coincidences. Do you, Detective Bell?"

"Not on your life." The phone jostled for a second, and Bell continued. "Have you tracked him to his lair yet?"

"No, we got his name, but we don't know where he's staying yet. We'll start canvassing the hotels and motels right away," Rook said.

"I'm on it," Bednarek added.

"Don't expect him to be at a 4-star hotel," Bell said. "They don't look to have much money. They live in a less-than-modest house in a less-than-modest neighborhood. But he'll almost certainly have checked in under his own name."

"Noted," Bednarek said. "Flea trap motels first."

"Damn, I'm excited," Bell said. "This is the first break we've had on this case. I'm headed out to talk to the mother. She needs to answer some questions. And she'll likely know where he's staying."

"Um, shouldn't we be worried that the mom will contact her son and he'll run?" Bednarek asked. She looked to Rook.

He shook his head. "That's a possibility, but it's better than him hunkering down and picking off victims here like stray cattle," Rook said.

"Without a shadow of a doubt. I'm going to get Pavich's location out of her, so be ready to roll. If she doesn't offer it up, I'm hauling her to the county lockup, so she can't reach him. She's an accessory to multiple homicides. She's not going anywhere."

They exchanged mobile numbers and ended the call. Rook looked at Bednarek with expectation.

"What?" she asked.

"Weak was the word you used, wasn't it?" He had a playful smile. "You said my hunch was weak. Care to update your analysis of my detecting?"

Bednarek nodded. "You are a strong detector, Rook. I underestimated your abilities. My apologies."

"Forgiven. Now let's get this rolling."

"Yes, detective," she said sweetly.

CHAPTER 18

Sunday

Since he'd been given his own keycard, Cade found his way to the basement computer lab. For as quiet as things were outside the door, it was positively humming with activity inside. Crocker was there along with nearly a dozen grad students. Working in pairs, they were spread around the room at computer workstations. Tubbs was nowhere to be seen. Crocker came over to meet Cade.

"I see you're keeping busy," Crocker said, putting a hand on Cade's shoulder. It was a fatherly gesture. "Heard about the latest killing. How are you holding up?"

"I'm tired and frustrated. We have to catch these guys. And soon."

Running a hand over his head, Crocker said, "Sorry, we haven't been able to give you anything yet. But we'll get there."

"No worries," Cade said. "A question that's been bothering me: Have either of the killers posted anything about their killings? In the past, it sounded as if they enjoyed bragging about these things."

Crocker shook his head. Cade's eyebrows rose.

"Well, has anyone on the site commented about our killings yet?"

Again, Crocker shook his head. Cade scratched his head.

"Really? I find that unusual. This site is their forum. Why stop posting now?" Cade shook his head. "So, what are they talking about instead?"

"We've been so focused on what they've previously posted, I don't know." Turning around, Crocker called, "Kenzie, pull up the current logs on the site, will you? I want to know when the most recent post was made. And what it was about."

"Sure thing, professor." In her mid to late twenties, Kenzie had light brown hair with blonde highlights and dressed better than the other female grad students. She seemed to have the attention of the room's male population. "Last posting was Thursday."

Cade exchanged glances with Crocker and moved over to Kenzie's workstation. "I'm Cade," he said.

"I remember," Kenzie replied evenly.

"So, there's been nothing for the last several days?"

Kenzie nodded.

"Isn't that unusual?"

Cycling through the site, Kenzie shrugged. "Maybe, but not unprecedented. There have been gaps here and there, some several days, some over a week. You have to remember these guys have a life outside of their work."

Cade studied her, ultimately deciding she was being facetious.

"I suppose they can't be online 24/7," Cade agreed. "But is there a way to alert me when a new post is added?"

"Sure thing, Detective Dawkins. If you give me your mobile number, I'll set up a repeater of sorts. It will automatically text you the latest posting. Will that work for you?"

He nodded. "I couldn't ask for anything more. Thank you." He jotted his number on the pad next to her as his cell phone buzzed. It was Rook.

"What's up?" he asked, stepping away. "Tell me something good."

"I have something on the second killer." Cade heard the excitement in Rook's voice.

"Really. Do tell."

"He's from Milwaukee and his name is Michael Thomas Pavich. I've confirmed with Milwaukee P.D. that he's been a person of interest in similar killings they've had there."

Cade walked out into the hall. "Wait, what? This is huge. Have you located him yet?"

Rook sighed. "Well, not yet. Bednarek is getting cops out to all the area motels and hotels. Milwaukee P.D. is headed for his home where he lives with his mother. She covered for him, so that's why Pavich never got past being a person of interest. The detective said he believes Ms. Pavich will be more forthcoming this time. He's got leverage he didn't have previously."

"Accessory to homicide is mighty big leverage," Cade agreed.

"Damn straight."

Cade paced in front of the door. "Anything I can do on my end to help?" he asked. "I'm at the computer lab."

"No, stay there. I'll let you know when we get a location and then you can join the arrest."

"Sounds good. And great work." Cade ended the call and went back inside. A grad student got up and gestured for Cade to sit next to Kenzie. She looked at him with steady eyes.

"Developments?" she asked.

"Possibly. We'll see," he replied.

"I have that repeater set up," Kenzie said. "You'll get a text of each new post as it's made. Anything else?"

Cade scratched his chin. "I was wondering if there's a way to find geographic tags in the site posts. It'd be helpful to know where they're posting from." He shrugged. "Sorry for my ignorance. I'm not the world's most computer literate individual."

Kenzie smiled. "Don't worry about it. I'm sure you're useful in your own way. But no, one of the features of the dark web is that it can only be accessed using software that renders user's IP addresses untraceable."

"Well, shit." Cade shook his head. He felt like he'd been doing that a lot lately. Things had to turn sooner or later.

"What about EXIF?" Courtney asked from the next station over.

"Oooo. That might work," Kenzie said.

Cade looked back and forth between the two computer science

grad students. "Humor me, guys. What's EXIF? In terms I can understand, please."

Kenzie held up a hand. "I got this. EXIF is data that accompanies photos, which often includes the time and date of the photo, as well as the make and model of the camera used. Pictures taken with a smartphone go a step further and include a precise geotag providing the exact location where the photo was taken. Courtney is suggesting that the photos uploaded to the site may still have the geo data attached. The posters may have forgotten—or didn't know—to delete this data."

Cade glanced from Kenzie to Courtney and back again. "Wait, they've been posting photos on the site? I hadn't realized they were doing that."

"Yeah," Courtney said. "Not everyone, but some have."

Cade slid to the front of his chair. "Does this mean you can check the photos for this geographic data? This could be huge."

Courtney nodded. "Of course, we can. It's not difficult."

"Not at all," Kenzie agreed. "One hand tied behind our backs."

Courtney giggled. "Kenzie likes bondage."

"I'll let you two sort things out." Cade turned away smiling, spotting a recently arrived Tubbs conferring with Crocker. The psychology professor looked upset and was doing that raising-your-voice-without-really-raising-it-louder-than-a-whisper thing while gesturing animatedly. Since that was the most interesting thing happening, Cade ambled over that way.

Tubbs stopped mid-sentence when he noticed Cade, who gestured for him to continue. "Don't let me stop you. I'm a curious guy by nature, so I wanted to eavesdrop on your conversation. It sounds interesting."

Tubbs appeared to want to say something and then thought better of it. And instead turned to Crocker, who for his part, shrugged.

Looking equal parts angry, frustrated, and I want to shout at someone, Tubbs took a deep breath and sighed. "We've had some grad students posting on social media about joining the hunt for the Twin Killers. Hashtag CatchingtheKillers. Even hashtag SmarterthanSerialKillers if you can believe it. This must stop."

Crocker shrugged. "I don't know, maybe it's been good advertising. That's how we've been able to get so much help. And this is how they communicate with each other."

Tubbs waved a finger in front of his friend. "No way. This isn't a good idea. Other people can read the posts, too. Homicidal kinds of people." He turned to Cade. "Okay, Detective. What do you think? Since we're at an impasse—which happens way more often than you may think—you make the call. Social or no social?"

Cade scratched his head, thinking he'd rather be somewhere else. "How do you gentlemen usually settle your previous impasses?"

Tubbs looked away. "Rock paper scissors," Crocker said.

"It seemed better to leave it to chance," Tubbs said. "Chance based on your choice and your opponent's choice."

"I see," Cade said, but not really seeing. Looking to Crocker, he continued, "My concern is these postings could put a target on the grad student helpers. These killers have a remarkable instinct for self-preservation. Let me ask you this: if the killers had a way to disrupt the investigation by taking an opponent's chess piece off the board, don't you think they'd make the move?"

Professor Crocker gave a nod. "That makes sense, tactically speaking." Addressing Tubbs, he said, "Okay, I'm with you on this. Let's talk to the troops."

"Hold on for a moment," Cade said before the men stepped away. "I'm concerned about something. Did the postings mention the Orbiting Cortex site? We don't want it out that we know about the site."

Tubbs shook his head. "No, sir. No mention of the site. Just that they're working on a project to help catch the Twin Cities' serial killers."

"Okay," Cade said. "But we should stop the postings before the site is accidentally mentioned. It's our secret weapon."

"It could be if it actually offers useable intelligence," Crocker said.

"We'll get there, old friend. Just keep swimming," Tubbs added with a wink.

Crocker grinned and said to Cade, "When Finding Nemo came out, he took to calling me Doryus Crocker because I can be a little absentminded at times."

"Got it, fish humor," Cade said.

"More like film humor, but yeah," Crocker said and addressed the students. "Gang, we need to set some expectations. Go ahead, professor."

Tubbs gave him a sideways glance but stepped up and addressed the group. "It was our mistake that when you signed the NDA when you came on board, we didn't specifically mention social media. But it never occurred to us that you might post about our work on social media." He glanced around the room. "Gang, it's called social for a reason. Anyone can read it. Serial killers are known to follow their exploits in the media. And, as Detective Dawkins pointed out, these killers have heightened survival instincts. Don't you think it makes tactical sense for them to hamper our investigation by removing the people who are trying to stop them?"

He paused, letting the words sink in.

"Is this really the chance you want to take? For some meaningless likes from strangers?"

Cade glanced around the room and based on the downcast eyes, the message was received by the posters.

Tubbs also glanced around the room. "So, no more posting anything regarding this working group. Capisce?"

Lots of nodding heads and murmurs. No one making eye contact.

"Looks like my work here is done," Cade said. "Let me know when you get the geographic data from the photos."

"We're on it," Crocker said. "Hopefully soon."

Cade's cell buzzed, and he waved to the professors and stepped out of the lab. It was Rook.

CHAPTER 19

Rook's voice had an edge of excitement to it. "Hey, man, it's me. I've got Milwaukee P.D. on the line. I'll conference you in."

There was a click, a buzz, and a silence. Then, "Detective, are you still there?" Bell's voice had a distant, tinny sound to it.

"Yo, man. I'm here and I've got Cade Dawkins, head of the task force, on the line. Cade, this is Detective Alan Bell with Milwaukee P.D."

"What did you find at the Pavich house?" Cade asked, skipping the introductions and getting to the point.

"Well," Bell began, drawing out the word. "Obviously, Michael Pavich wasn't at home. But don't worry, we looked thoroughly to be sure. He lives in the basement of the house, but it's more like an animal lives there, not a human being. He's obviously never used a trash can in his life. Leftover food sitting around his computer equipment, crusts of countless sandwiches and more chicken bones than you'd find at KFC on a holiday weekend. Even bottles of piss."

Bell paused for a moment. "Disgusting place. It was like an underground animal den. None of the overhead lights worked and the only lights came from the computer monitors and color cycling LEDs in his keyboard and hard drives. He had one of those padded chairs that gamers like; well-worn, like it was where he lives his life."

"Probably is," Cade agreed. "What did you get out of the mother?"

Bell blew out a breath.

"She gave me nothing. That woman is a piece of work. Same line of BS as before when I got there, going on about their close relationship and their nightly board game ritual. But then when I pressed her, she turned into something different."

"How so?"

"At first, she was all charm, flirty even. She'd get me looking one way and when I turned back, there'd be another button undone on her blouse. It happened twice. That's not how these interrogations go."

"Not ever."

"Nope." Rook shook his head.

There was jostling and Bell spoke. "You need to hear this."

The sound of a woman's voice came across. It was soft and almost lyrical in tone.

"I'm sure you help a lot of people, Detective Bell. I admire that in a man. What did you say your first name was again?"

A pause, then, "Alan. I'm Detective Alan Bell."

"Alan. I love that," she gushed like someone trying French silk pie for the first time. "It's such a virile name. If I had a stallion, I'd name him Alan."

Rook coughed.

"Ummm..." Cade said.

"Keep listening," Bell insisted.

Bell's recorded voice said, "Well, thank you. I'll be sure to pass on the compliment when I visit my mother at the care center. Now, Mrs. Pavich—"

"Why don't you call me Valerie?"

"Why don't I stick with Mrs. Pavich? When we spoke earlier you covered for your son. You said he was here with you playing board games."

"Yes, we were."

"You know there's not a single board game in this house? I looked."

There was silence.

"Mrs. Pavich. It's become apparent your son is responsible for the string of brutal killings in the area."

The change was immediate. "He threatened me," Pavich said. "Mikey said if I didn't cover for him, he'd rip my throat out." She sounded breathless and scared now, nothing like her earlier tone. "There was nothing I could do. Mikey is so large and powerful. I'm so incredibly thankful you're here, Alan."

"Detective Bell, please."

"I had to do what he asked. Mikey scared me, Detective. I've raised my son to do the right thing, but suddenly he was an animal. A rabid animal. It was terrifying."

The sniffling sounds were likely coming from Mrs. Pavich.

"Pay attention to this part, detectives," Bell said in real-time.

"That may be, Mrs. Pavich, but it doesn't explain you lying to me just now. You paid for your son to leave the state. You know he's far, far away and is no threat to you. Not now. Yet, you stuck to the board game story when I got here. And now you've gone into this scared, submissive woman routine. But I can see it in your eyes. You're not scared in the least. It's in the clenching of your jaw, the corded muscles in your neck. You're not terrified, you're angry." Bell paused. "Just say what's on your mind, Valerie."

The tension was palpable in the moment of silence.

"Say it!" Bell barked.

The voice that spoke changed from the lyrical and submissive one they'd heard earlier. Now, Mrs. Pavich's tone had an edge of venom. "You are so far over your head. My idiot son is a predator who will continue to do what he wants, killing who he wants. You don't have the brainpower or even the sack needed to find and stop him. You're nothing. I could take you out myself, and there'd be nothing you could do to save yourself. But my son is the killing machine, not me. He is the perfect instrument to rid the world of the sluts and sinners. He knows how good it feels to feed on their souls and bodies, yet knows no remorse or sorrow. He is powerful, yet stealthy. Savage, yet human. I couldn't be prouder."

Bell stopped the recording with an audible click.

"Do you see what I mean? A piece of ugly narcissistic shit." Bell paused. "Well, she's on her way to the lockup, charging her with five counts of accessory to murder. Her psycho ass won't be going anywhere soon."

"So, you got no idea where he's staying?" Rook asked.

"Sorry, no," Bell replied.

Cade rubbed his chin, thinking. "Detective, did she give any indication why she thought he was coming to the Twin Cities?"

"Again, sorry, but no."

"No worries. Can you describe Pavich's living area for me? Looking for any personal effects, things that show interests, relatives or friends. We have reason to believe he was motivated to come to Minneapolis because of a challenge issued on a website, but I doubt he'd have told his mother that."

Bell paused for a moment before answering. "Besides the stacks of comic books, there wasn't anything beyond his gaming setup. Pavich lived his life online, not in the real world. Certainly, there were no signs of relatives or of even friendships there."

"Okay, Detective. Appreciate your assistance. Let us know if you get anything from the mother."

"Will do. We bagged his hard drives, so maybe we'll get something. Sorry, there isn't more actionable intelligence. I'm doing my best here."

"I know you are, stallion," Cade said, ending the call as Bell let loose with a stronger than a PG-13 rebuttal.

Something tickled just below Cade's conscious thought as he walked down the dimly lit hallway. He didn't have a better word for it, but there was something he should be seeing. Whatever it was, it was elusive and lingering, waiting to be recognized and realized. Hopefully soon. He pushed the button to get out of the basement.

THE LIGHTS CAME UP and the camera operator pointed to Reynolds.

"I'm Reynolds Devries, and I'm joined by the head of the Five

Below major crimes task force, Cade Dawkins. With three murders now, the task force is more important than ever in stopping these killings."

She turned to Cade. "Thank you for agreeing to speak with me today. I know you're busy."

Cade looked at her—and not the camera as he'd been instructed—and nodded. "It's important the public knows what's happening."

"Can you tell us what has happened and what you know so far?" Reynolds looked radiant in front of the camera, her long blonde hair catching the light.

"We've had three murders, from what we believe are two different killers. The first and third were nearly identical in how the women were killed and how their bodies were found. The first was in Minneapolis, while the third was killed in a St. Paul motel. But the second killing was a completely different animal altogether. Unlike the other murders, no weapon was used, and the body was left where it was murdered. This was in the north side of Minneapolis."

Reynolds nodded solemnly. "Do you believe the second killing to be the work of a serial killer as well? Even though there's only been one murder that fits the killer's M.O.?"

Cade nodded. "Evidence is coming to light that this killer has committed similar murders previously in a different state. We're following up on that evidence as we speak."

Reynolds leaned forward. "Can you elaborate on the evidence? Or where it came from?"

"I'm sorry, not at this time. I don't want to show all the cards in my hand. But, I can share some things we've discovered about the first killer."

Reynolds looked intrigued. "Do tell, detective."

"I can do one better. Instead of telling, I can show you the killer."

Cade had not shared this part with Reynolds, and it showed on her face. Being a professional, her surprise quickly morphed into rapt interest. Cade opened a folder and pulled out an 8x10 blow-up of the killer's bare torso. Grace had done an excellent job of enhancing the video still to bring out the tattoos covering the killer's back. He held it up to Reynolds before turning it toward the camera.

"This is unusual," she said. "I've never seen anything like it. Where did you get the picture?"

"I'm not ready to share the picture's origin, but it's the first killer at the last crime scene. And you're right, we thought it was unusual as well. We've reached out to experts in multiple disciplines to decipher the strange hieroglyphics. They were all stumped. That was, until..."

He paused, wanting to build the tension. Reynolds shot him a look that said *get moving*.

"Surprisingly, it was an expert in Egyptian symbology that gave us our breakthrough," Cade lied. There hadn't been any breakthroughs with the strange writing, but no one else needed to know that. It didn't serve his plan. "Our expert said the markings were reminiscent of ones used for male fertility rituals."

"Really."

"Really. Only with one major difference. These were meant for male fertility. See this part right here near the lower spine?"

Cade pointed at the image.

"According to our renowned expert, this indicates the male is seeking intervention from Wadj Wer, the Egyptian fertility god." Cade flashed a quick smile. "And you know as well as I do—maybe better—that when a man needs fertility help, he's having issues."

"You mean he's..."

"Yes, our killer needs the little blue pill to get or maintain an—"

"I see," Reynolds said before Cade could finish the thought. "And this lack of..."

"His impotence has built up a rage, according to our profilers, that drives him to kill. He goes in search of women that would be otherwise unattainable to him. And because he can't have them, he kills them."

Cade paused and faced the camera, looking directly at it.

"It's difficult to understand the deviant mind of these killers. They don't think like you or I do. They have different backgrounds, different motivations. But I get angry when they take out their frustrations over their...shortcomings...on innocent victims. If you're such a man, come for me. But I don't think you will. You're the hyena circling the stronger animals of the herd, looking for the weakest one to pick off. Next, you'll be living off roadkill. It's sad. You're sad."

Cade shook his head and turned to Reynolds. "That's all I got."

"Thank you, Detective Dawkins. Good luck with your hunt. This is Reynolds Devries with the Five news team."

The camera lights winked out.

"I don't have to tell you how explosive that will be. Your words will be top of every broadcast around the nation." She paused, concern coloring her expression. "You put yourself in the killer's crosshairs, you know."

Cade nodded. He knew.

"I figured you knew, but I can still worry. You stepped into the cage of the world's most dangerous animal. And he's demonstrated a ferocious appetite."

Reynold's eyes had a watery quality that threatened to overflow, but she took a deep breath and pushed the emotion away. Always the consummate professional, Cade thought as he studied her. Always in control.

"I've got this," he told her. "It's all part of my plan," he said, steepling his fingers.

"You can use humor all you want, but this is deadly serious," Reynolds said.

"As am I," he said. "As am I."

Ari loved the freedom of being someone else. Normally being in crowds was difficult for the thirty-year-old, but not now, not here. No matter how odd you were, here you fit in. Blue hair, fine. Seven feet tall, also fine. A third eye, why not? Ari's long orange hair and tight blue bodysuit attracted a lot of male attention, and a fair amount of female attention as well. She smiled. All attention is good attention, and she was an equal opportunity player.

Of course, this all was a far cry from Ari's everyday life. In the buttoned-down world of the legal profession, unless you were a rainmaking trial attorney, you kept your head down and your nose to the grindstone. Her expected forty-five legal briefs per week wouldn't write themselves. So day after day, Ari sat in her sparsely decorated cube in a sea of sparsely decorated cubes at Barnett, D'Errico, Stride and Morgan. Three years in, she still giggled at the firm's initials. Wearing her conservative business attire and sensible heels, Ari was chained to her desk for ten hours each day of the week writing her briefs as she slowly died. She'd often try to picture what it must look like when her soul escaped from her body. Ari pictured a light pink mist (with paisleys!) dancing and swirling away as it rose—thankful to be away—to freedom.

Ari's legal briefs were nowhere near as dramatic.

But here, she could let her true colors show—as well as more than a hint of her dangerous curves. The bodysuit left almost nothing to the imagination as she pranced, danced, and twirled carefree through throngs of like-minded people.

As things often happen at these events, Ari recognized several potential suiters. She saw familiar faces—or to be more precise, a giant, an archer and a wood nymph—that reappeared more often than mere chance would allow. She's done this before and wasn't bothered that she couldn't see their faces or their eyes. She hoped one will make a move soon and ignite her repressed passion.

If anonymity was fire, spontaneity was gasoline.

As evening became twilight and then something darker, Ari's options coalesced down to two. The archer had dropped out of the race and the wood nymph and giant remained, both nearby. Weighing the pros and cons of each, seeing advantages at either end, Ari ultimately decided on the giant.

Lurking nearby, he loomed over the crowd as he surreptitiously gazed in her direction. Fortune favors the bold, and Ari hooked a finger at the man-mountain. There wasn't anything he could do to resist her siren song, and so he came.

Pushing past elves, aliens and countless superheroes, the giant came for her.

Ari was pleased.

Standing nearly seven feet tall with the full hair and beard of a Viking warrior, the man was broad in the chest. With arms that could hold her dangerously tight, and a mouth that could unravel her very soul, he was a specimen. Her love language was quite clearly physical touch.

Ari grabbed a finger of the giant's hand and led him through the crowd. Nothing about this was usual, yet here, nothing about it was unusual, either. The crowd thinned and then disappeared altogether as she brought him to a dimly lit corridor.

Fortune favors the prepared. Ari had scouted her environment throughout the day, noting the restroom off the beaten path, the lack of overhead lights that end in darkness at the woman's restroom.

She pulled the giant into the dark hallway and smiled. With a skintight bodysuit and a trailing giant, nothing was off the table in her immediate future.

Ari shivered in anticipation as she led the giant farther into the dark, her heart racing with each step.

CHAPTER 20

"Why the governor ever put such a minor character in charge of a major crimes task force is beyond me."

Barry Weiss stood on Minneapolis' iconic Stone Arch Bridge, the picturesque downtown skyline in the background. Wearing his trademark vest, this time a plaid one from Patagonia, Weiss glanced at his clipboard.

"Three gruesome murders in the Twin Cities and nothing to show for it. I've heard unprecedented grumbling in the law enforcement community that Cade Dawkins is the wrong man for the job. These grumblings aren't just from beat cops or the veterans of countless homicide investigations, but even Dawkin's own Minnesota State Patrol troopers. To a man, they all agree that the Twin Killers will continue their horrific crimes until Governor Ritter replaces Dawkins with someone competent."

Weiss took a step toward the camera.

"My wording is intentional. Notice I didn't say *more* competent, which would imply he was at all competent. Dawkins is not that in the least. Give us a warm-bodied meter maid and we'd have a better chance of stopping these madmen. The governor needs to make a change and soon."

He paused, nodded, and said, "I'm Barry Weiss, and this is the award-winning Barry Weiss Report."

Rook took a sip of his beer and turned to Cade. "That man is such an ass hat. He gives hats and asses a bad name." He tipped his bottle of Blue Moon to his partner. "Can he say those lies with complete impunity? You know he hasn't talked to a single cop. He's pulling all of this out of his butt. It should be called the Barry Ass Report."

Cade laughed and took a sip from his bottle. "Yeah, he can say what he wants. It's his prerogative."

Rook took a drink. "Karma's gonna get him someday."

Cade rolled his head side to side, feeling the tension in his neck. "If you say so."

Rook looked over at him, an eyebrow arched. "Wait, you don't believe in karma?"

Cade sighed. "I believe that karma sometimes needs a helping hand."

The news anchor was back on screen. "Coming up after the break, we'll tell you the story of a small parish with a dynamic new priest who's invigorated the community while becoming something of a media darling. But first, we have a super story to share." The news program on the television over the bar switched to a news reporter standing in the middle of a crowd, surrounded by costumed superheroes.

"I'm Alex MacCarthy, here at the Minneapolis Convention Center on the last day of the MegaCon, billed as the world's largest comics, sci-fi, horror, anime, and gaming event. In the midst of our tragic killings, I have to say, I've never felt safer. When a dozen superheroes surrounded you, there's nothing to fear. Can you imagine a safer place to be?"

The camera pulled away and swung around to show the convention's interior. Large and small, colorful and dark, costumes were everywhere. The camera panned back and zoomed in on the shield of a superhero. It was red and white circles with a white star in the blue center.

"Oh, shit," Cade said glancing at Rook. "That's the symbol on Pavich's shirt at the bus terminal. And Bell said there were stacks of comics at his house. He's at the MegaCon."

"You don't think he'd..." Rook said, already sliding off the stool.

"Yes, that's exactly what I think," Cade said, moving toward the door. "He's at the convention center stalking his prey. He's going to kill today."

"I'm driving," Rook said. "You drive like my mother, bless her heart."

Cade called out obstacles while Rook steered around them on the drive to the convention center. He also reached out to Bednarek and Thao, got them headed to Minneapolis as well. After that, he got Grace on the phone.

"Grace, we believe the second killer is at the MegaCon," Cade said. "Blue minivan."

"Blue minivan?" she sounded puzzled.

"Not you, I'm helping Rook drive."

"Like that's a good idea," Grace said. "I've ridden with you."

"Ouch."

Grace continued. "But, Cade, I'm at the MegaCon right now."

Cade shouldn't be surprised, but he was. Grace was one of those who made connections most people missed. She knew about the comics, the killer's gaming setup, and travel attire. She clearly was a step ahead of him, that is, unless it was a coincidence she was there. With Grace, it could go either way.

"I think he'll be attracted to the anonymity the costumes offer," she said. "No one is going to judge you when you're someone else."

Cade decided to file that away for now, while Grace continued.

"He'll be in costume. Most people are, but I'd stake my life that he's dressed as a warrior or a knight or a barbarian of some kind. He won't identify with a hero, so he's not going to dress like one."

"Got it. Any idea of the type he'll go after?" Cade asked.

"Someone normally unattainable to him. Someone who catches his eye and won't let go. He'll be like a child attracted to bright colors. I'd expect him to follow her around, his tongue hanging out the entire time."

"Okay, that helps," Cade said. "By the way, what are you wearing?"

A pause.

"Don't worry about me. Just get over here." Cade ended the call as the Minneapolis Convention Center came into view. Rook jumped the curb and came to a stop by the entrance. They raced for the door.

The Minneapolis Convention Center was a sprawling complex designed to simultaneously hold several large events or one ginormous one like the MegaCon. Cade had been there for an auto show and found it cavernous with its many rooms and multiple floors. Seeing the throngs of costume-wearing people everywhere, Cade stopped. The convention goers weren't confined to the exhibit area, they were everywhere. He counted three different Wonder Woman costumes, let alone every superhero, alien, fantasy, Vulcan, Klingon, Star Wars and monster movie character possible. It was overwhelming.

"We need to contain this somehow. There's just too much. Too many people, too much space, too many exits." Cade glanced around before his eyes landed on a security officer surrounded by a group of large minions. "There," he said, pointing to the security officer and headed that way.

"Nice costume," the man said as he looked at Cade. "Who are you supposed to be? A barista?"

Cade held up his badge rather than give the reply that came to mind. "I need you to get your supervisor here. Like now. It's an emergency."

"Sure, man. I got this." He turned to the minions. "Later, little dudes." Fumbling with his radio, he managed to get it unclipped and to his mouth.

"Yes, sergeant. It's me, Dylan."

Rook leaned in and offered a suggestion. "These radios work better when you push the talk button before you speak."

The guard stared at him, blinked once, twice, then lifted the radio again, this time keying the talk button. "Yes, this is Dylan. Looking for the sergeant."

"Go ahead, Dylan." There was a note of exasperation in his tone.

"I have police officers asking for you at my gate. They said it's urgent," he added.

"I'll be right there."

Dylan turned to Cade. "He'll be right here."

Cade gave him a thumbs up and leaned over to Rook. "Better living through chemistry, I'm guessing."

"I'd have to agree," Rook said. "I wonder what color the minions were that *he* saw?"

"Gentlemen, how can I help?" a uniformed mid-forties man asked. His bearing made him look former military. "I'm Sergeant Joaquin Izquierdo."

Cade gestured for the man to step away from the guard, Dylan. "We have a situation. We believe our homicide suspect is here stalking his next victim, most likely he's in costume."

Izquierdo's eyes narrowed. "I'm guessing you're talking about the killers that have been in the news. But do you have any idea how many people are here? There are thousands upon thousands here, and ninety-five percent of them are wearing costumes. Narrow it down for me." He folded his arms.

"I can do that," Cade said. "Our suspect is approximately six feet, six inches tall and weighs 220 pounds. He has a full head of dark hair and beard."

The security supervisor nodded. "That does narrow it down. What do you need from us?"

"I need your security staff to walk the place and call in the location of anyone that resembles our suspect's description. I'll walk with you to stay in radio contact, and my partner will stay with officer Dylan there. Sound good?"

"Yes, we can take halls B and C, your partner can take halls D and E. That keeps us efficient and able to respond quickly," Izquierdo said.

"Perfect, get them rolling," Cade said.

Izquierdo nodded and got on the radio, efficiently coordinating how and where the officers would deploy. Cade gave him a thumbs up when he finished and followed Izquierdo into the abyss.

One issue Cade saw right away was the lack of visibility. The exhibits were tall enough to restrict their sightlines. He wouldn't be able to simply look out across the sea of convention goers and spot the killer.

The first call came within a minute. Izquierdo led them through the B portion of the hall to a waiting security officer who in turn pointed to a huge man wearing a cape. He stood in the collectibles exhibit with his back to them.

"He's big alright," Izquierdo said. "Ginormous."

"I need to get around to his front, see his face," Cade said.

"That may take a while," Izquierdo said, holding his hands out wide.

Shaking his head, Cade stepped into the collectibles booth. It was all anime art and action figures and he stopped to pick up a plastic hero. The large man looked like a powerlifter and his 300-style gladiator costume helped that impression a lot. Cade wasn't sure handcuffs would fit around the man's massive wrists if it came to that. Moving closer to a bin of matted anime prints, Cade looked up to the man's face. He had the beard, but the shape of his head was all wrong. And his smile revealed a missing front tooth that the forensic team's body examination wouldn't have missed.

Cade looked to Izquierdo and shook his head. *Not our guy*. Truth be told, he was relieved. Cade was in good shape from playing soccer, but he'd be swatted aside by someone of the man's bulk. It'd be like stepping into the ring with the Rock or an elephant. His odds of surviving had to be close to zero—unless he could outsmart the giant or pull a thorn from his paw.

They headed back out into the throngs of elves, heroes and monsters, past movie memorabilia, gaming demonstrations, and comic collections. Another call came through and since it was in the D section, Rook took the call. Another minute, another, "Not our guy."

Cade took a call from Thao and directed her and Bednarek to walk the perimeters and check the restrooms. Next, he checked in with Grace.

"Anything?" he asked.

"Nothing yet, but I'm sure he's here."

Cade paused. "Is that what brought you here?"

When she didn't immediately answer, he continued. "Wait. You're not setting yourself up as bait, are you? Using your profile knowledge to draw him to you?"

Pause.

"Don't worry about me. Worry about yourself." Before Cade could formulate a suitable comeback, Grace ended the call. He stared at the phone before shaking it off.

Over the next hour, he and Rook responded to a dozen calls to verify the suspect. Who knew such a variety of enormous men went to comic cons? But none were close to the description.

Instead of the break coming over the radio, it came from a call. Detective Lorie Thao got to the point right away. "We've found a smear of blood. It's on an exit door. Sending you my location."

Summoning Rook, they followed the directions to an area outside the exhibits and found Thao and Bednarek waiting outside a dimly lit hallway.

"Down here," Thao said, leading the way. "I don't know why it's so dark down here."

"Must be a circuit issue," Izquierdo said. "Our staff should have caught this."

Thao switched on her flashlight and led them past the men's and women's restrooms. It got progressively darker the farther they went. They stopped at a pair of metal doors at the end of the hallway. She directed the light at the door's edge, right above the push bar. Examining the dark smear, it looked like blood. Recent blood.

"Where does this door lead?" he asked Izquierdo.

"The marshaling yard and loading docks."

"Okay, it's a large open space out there." Cade glanced at the others. "Ready?"

Weapons drawn, Rook, Bednarek and Thao nodded. Cade put his sleeve on the bar away from the blood and slowly opened the door.

"Hells no," Rook exclaimed.

"Eff me," Cade said quietly.

Bednarek wretched and ducked into the restroom.

On the ground outside the door was a woman's body. Inches from safety, this was where she died. And from the looks of it, it was a painful death. As before, bite marks covered her body, and the cause of death had to be her ripped-out throat. Blood splatters colored the pavement. Someone had torn the woman's blue costume to shreds.

"That's Mystique," Izquierdo said.

"You know her?" Cade asked, turning back to the security man.

"No, I mean she's wearing a Mystique costume," he explained. "Don't you ever go to the movies?"

"Holy shit," a familiar voice said from behind Cade. He turned to see a virtually identically costumed woman behind him. It took a moment to put the voice together with the lithe woman's blue bodysuit and orange hair.

"Grace?"

"Yes, it's me," she said, going to the woman. Grace knelt at her side and put a finger against the dead woman's cheek. "She's still warm. The blood splatter is still dark and hasn't begun drying around the edges. This is extremely recent. There's a good chance he's still here in the area." She gestured to the surrounding marshaling yard.

Turning to the officers, Cade gave directions. "Rook, go right. He might have gone to the fire station," he said, pointing to the brick building diagonally across the lot. "Lorie, go straight out and walk the lot. He may be hiding among the parked vehicles. I'll head left."

He turned to Grace. "Call this in and get squads rolling. We need to lock down the area."

"There's a security fence around the perimeter back here,"

Izquierdo said, gesturing in a half-circle. "The gates are there and there. But the fence won't stop anyone who's highly motivated to enter or leave. It's only a deterrent."

"It may slow him down, which is all we may need," Cade said. "Stay in contact and be careful. I'm not sure how human he is." Cade drew his Glock and headed out.

The hazy moon did little to illuminate the marshaling yard beyond the overhead lights. Using a two-handed grip on his weapon, Cade held it out and moved into the yard. The wind had picked up, and a flyer skidded across the pavement, the sound making his heart race. No matter how much you trained for all kinds of possible scenarios in law enforcement, nothing prepared you to stalk a serial killer. At night. In a deserted parking lot.

Moving down the side of the building, Cade scanned the area. He wanted to be the one that spotted the killer and not the other way around. Getting blindsided by Pavich could and probably would be deadly. So, that wasn't going to happen.

Cade's cell buzzed, and he took a glance to see who had messaged. It was an unknown number. He read the text.

I killed tonight.

Wait, what? But a sound to his right had him tucking the phone away and getting both hands back on the Glock. Across the pavement, near the fence was a small outbuilding, along with several containers and dumpsters. The sound had come from that direction. With his weapon leading the way, he crossed the lot.

A shoe scraped the pavement.

Pausing mid-step, he tried to determine where the noise originated. The sound had echoed across the marshaling yard, and it could have come from the outbuilding, container, or dumpster. He couldn't tell, and waited to hear it again, taking long, slow breaths to keep his heart rate down while he listened. Yet, no other sound followed. Cade decided that the container was the most likely spot and headed that way.

I killed tonight.

The wrongness of the text haunted him, and he stopped. How did this killer get his number? And why text him? Had Pavich killed because of him? Was he responsible for the deaths of all four women?

Numbly, Cade continued moving toward the container. The fear that he was responsible for the deaths of Kimberly Albright, Victoria Garcia, Veronica Valley and now the costumed woman had his heart racing.

He paused, wiping his forehead sweat on his sleeve. The Glock wavered in his hand, his muscles feeling both tight and shaky. His mind raced to an indisputable conclusion: Two killers came to Minnesota because of him. It had been a mistake going public with why he shot and killed the blonde killer, Marlin Sweetwater. It never occurred to him that there were others like Sweetwater out there. That there were serial killers who took an interest in the outcome. Killers who took it personally when he went in front of the cameras and glibly discussed ending one of their own.

I killed tonight.

The text should've read that Cade killed tonight. If it weren't for him, that woman would still be alive. She'd be enjoying the comic convention with her friends. The woman would've returned to the safety of her home with memories of a pleasant escape from reality.

He lowered the Glock without being consciously aware of it.

Sudden rumbling pulled him back from the brink. It wasn't from the clouds, and it took a moment to register what he saw and heard. The large blue dumpster parked by the container bore down on him, picking up speed as it got closer. He would be smashed against the fence by the marauding garbage container. His weapon was useless against the steel container, and he did the only thing he could do. He dove out of the way.

The unforgiving pavement arrived too soon, and Cade landed harder than he expected. His weapon was jarred loose by the impact and slid away. Everything felt slow motion as he laid on his side, his outstretched arm reaching vainly for the pistol that slid in the wrong direction. The dumpster continued until it hit the fence, which shook from the sizable impact.

It was impossible to get a breath. Flashback to when he'd fallen from a large dirt mound as a school kid. The panic he'd felt having the wind knocked out of him. The panic wasn't there this time, just the urgency to recover enough to get up and defend himself.

Pavich, dressed as a giant in calf-height boots and leather gauntlets on his massive forearms, and a leather onesie that no baby store ever sold, stepped out from behind the dumpster. From Cade's point of view on the pavement, Pavich looked even larger than the earlier gladiator, if that was possible. Air was getting back into his shocked lungs, and he rolled onto his stomach.

Cade got to his knees, taking stock of his situation. He was alive and functional. However, the Glock was a long way off. There was no help in sight and a massive serial killer stood ten feet away. Could be worse but could be a whole lot better.

The killer stood staring as Cade got to his feet. Once there, he rolled his head side to side, cracking his neck. Looking across the scant space between them, Cade nodded at the killer. Pavich's face still had blood smeared around his mouth and face, the killer hadn't bothered to wipe it off.

"Michael Thomas Pavich, you're under arrest."

For the briefest of moments, Pavich's eyes widened but then flicked to where Cade's weapon lay. His gaze returned to Cade, and he grinned.

"You're him. The lawman. Dawkins."

"Yes, yes, and yes," Cade replied. "Now, I need you to get on your knees and place your hands on your head. Before someone gets hurt."

Pavich found Cade's instructions funny. His laughter wasn't the typical reaction to arrest instructions.

Pointing a finger at the giant, Cade said, "This is your last warning."

Pavich growled as he took a step forward. The ten feet between them didn't feel nearly safe enough. "I'm going to bleed you," he growled.

Nine feet now.

"Don't bite off more than you can chew," Cade said, also taking a step forward.

Eight feet.

Pavich blinked. "I see what you did there." His hands clenched and unclenched and he took a step closer to Cade.

Seven feet.

"Does your mother know?" Cade asked, taking a step and folding his arms. Cade already knew that Mrs. Pavich was aware of her son's killings. But he'd learned from Grace that nothing can get in someone's head like a mother. "Does she know that her son is an animal? She'd be so proud."

Six feet.

Pavich sneered. "My mother. I wouldn't be the man I am today if it wasn't for her. Who do you think set me on the course I took? But I'm more than she ever expected. When she sees pictures of your bled out body, then she'll know." He took a step and then another, his hands rhythmically clenching and unclenching as his jaw muscles tightened and churned.

Five, then four feet.

Another step and the killer would be on him. If he got tied up by the man mountain, that would be it for Cade. He couldn't compete with the sheer strength of the killer. But he didn't have to.

The flick of Pavich's eyes and the shifting weight was enough of a tell to sidestep the lunge when it came. Had it connected, though, Cade would be the next victim.

Pavich made a low animal growl that raised goosebumps on Cade's arms. The killer's eyes burned into Cade. Even though it was sudden, the same two tells prefaced the lunge and Cade easily sidestepped this one as well.

The thing about most real-life fights is how quickly they end. Unlike in the movies, people get tired. Fighting is anaerobic, and muscles fatigue quickly. If you can hold off your opponent for a few moments, their fatigue gives you considerable advantage. Cade had picked up a few tricks when he was part of a club he couldn't talk about.

Pavich's eyes flicked to Cade's left side right as he shifted his weight to his right. The killer's savage swipe of his left paw slid by as Cade stepped to his right. The sound of Pavich's teeth snapping shut felt dangerously close.

Once again, they stood across from each other, the killer's eyes burning into Cade. Words were gone as he took in large gulps of air through his mouth. His hands continued their clenching, and he growled. It was a long, drawn-out primal sound that belonged in a forest or on the Scottish moors. At least the moon wasn't full.

The next lunge nearly caught him, only his last moment shift saving him. As it was, the killer knocked Cade off balance with his massive shoulder as the arm pushed past him. Again, the coming together of teeth made a loud clacking. If the teeth sank in...

Regaining his balance, Cade considered his options. He'd moved farther from his service weapon, but Pavich was a little too close. He hoped the killer wouldn't go for the gun. In law enforcement circles, getting shot with your own service weapon was pretty much at the head of the top ten worst rookie mistakes. It was followed by losing your handcuff key after letting your girlfriend restrain you and having to call a fellow officer to release you. Cade briefly considered making a strategic retreat, but the idea of running away would haunt him for decades to come. So, no.

While the two circled each other warily, Cade pulled his phone out, calling Rook. He put the call on speaker. Rook answered on the first ring.

"Hey, man," Rook said. "I got nothing. I've met up with Lorie and she's got nothing either. The big ugly must've split."

"He can hear you, Rook."

"Wait, what?" Rook sounded confused.

"He's right in front of me. Want to say hi?" Cade asked.

"Yo, Mikey. Let's take your giant ass in."

Pavich's eyes glowered, and he let loose a guttural growl and lunged. Cade avoided this one, but he knew even one slip would get him killed.

"I could use backup here. We're near the outbuilding at the back fence."

"Already on the way," Rook said.

Hate emanated from the killer as he stared at Cade. The drying blood smeared across his face adding to the eeriness. It didn't feel like there was much human left in him, but there had to be some.

"We've arrested your mother," Cade said in an even tone. "Milwaukee police have her locked up. There are things she needs to answer for." He took a step forward. "As do you."

His backup arrived, the others fanning out in a semi-circle around him. Weapons were aimed at Pavich's center mass, as they were taught. Sirens were in the air, becoming as omnipresent as cicadas in a southern state.

"Things will go better for you if you get on the ground," Cade suggested. "You don't have to die today."

Born of anger and frustration, a low growl rose from the hulking man. Rook glanced to Cade, as the sound grew louder by the second. This was unchartered territory.

Multiple squads raced across the lot, beelining toward the unusual standoff. Cade never took his eyes off Pavich, even as the arriving officers scrambled out of their vehicles, their shotguns and pistols adding to the arsenal directed at the killer.

Pavich's gaze never left Cade, that was until...

A flash of blue and orange came into Cade's peripheral vision. Grace, in her Mystique costume came to Cade's side. The giant's eyes were drawn to her.

"Don't even think about it," Cade barked. But Pavich was clearly thinking about it. It was as if his human side was pushed back, allowing what was underneath to rise to the surface. The transformation was unmistakable as he stared at Grace. Eyes narrowing, jaw tightening and his lips pulled back to reveal prominent canine teeth. His low guttural growl filled the air, causing Cade to shiver. The response was visceral and unstoppable, dating back to the earliest human encounters with predators of the night.

"Don't do it," he warned, but even as he said it, Cade recognized Pavich's tells again. A quick flick of the eyes and back to Grace as he shifted his weight. Wrapping an arm around Grace's waist, Cade pulled her from the path of the killer's lunge. They went down to the pavement, with Cade covering her.

The gunfire was deafening as both handguns and shotguns let hellfire loose on the charging killer.

And then there was silence.

"Oh, hells no."

Cade lifted his head and was shocked by the sight. Pavich was still on his feet, even though much of his face was gone, the shotguns having done what shotguns do well. And then, like a great Jack pine felled by a logger's saw, he fell. With nothing to break his fall, he crashed face first into the unforgiving pavement of the marshaling yard.

Pavich was dead before he left his feet.

CHAPTER 21

"Crocker, what the hell?"

As soon as he found a moment in the chaotic aftermath of Pavich's death, Cade called the university professor.

"I...I have no idea what happened. They said it was an accident, but I don't know." Crocker's usually smooth baritone could narrate nature documentaries, but his voice sounded ragged now.

Cade paused. There was something off here. It was great that Crocker was upset about the data breach that allowed Cade's number to get to Pavich, but he shouldn't be this worked up, should he?

"We might be talking about different things. I called because of the text I received tonight on my cell. It read simply, 'I killed tonight.' The message came from an unknown number, right after the second killer, Michael Thomas Pavich, killed a woman outside the MegaCon at the Minneapolis Convention Center."

"Oh, hell."

"Pavich is dead, but the only logical way he could have gotten my number was from you guys. I gave it to Courtney to set up a relay that would send new site postings to my cell. She said it was easy to forward them directly from the Orbiting Cortex site. Ask her."

The pause was deafening.

"Darius?"

"She died tonight. Courtney is dead."

Cade's stomach tightened. This wasn't the direction he expected the conversation to take. Not at all.

"Tell me what happened."

Crocker struggled to get his words out, and after several false starts, he spoke with a cracked voice.

"They found her on the street. It looks like she was hit by a car, a hit and run. She was on her bike. The bike was mangled, but she was worse."

"No driver, no witnesses?" Cade asked. He knew the answers, but still couldn't help himself from asking. Routine continues when the mind has shut down. He'd just been talking to Courtney. She'd come up with the idea to search the posted images for geotags that could help identify the killers.

Crocker sighed. "No, a delivery driver came across her body and called it in. She was dead when the officers arrived. Her roommate saw the commotion and came out. She identified her. For a big school, the U can be a small campus, and word traveled fast. It hit us hard down here."

"I'm speechless," Cade began. "In the midst of our serial killer hunt, life and tragedy continue to unfold. One random chance encounter with a bad driver and just like that... Things like this aren't supposed to happen to people you know."

"Obviously, I'll follow up to make sure her work continues. The geotagging data mining is relatively straightforward, and I'll get that rolling, as well as looking at the relay. I'll be in touch." Crocker ended the call, and Cade suspected the professor was having difficulty talking.

"Rook," Cade called, waving him over. He also had Grace join them. Walking them away from the law enforcement crowd, he shared the news about Courtney's death. Both shook their heads. You can't be in law enforcement and not be touched by death.

"Grace, can you follow up with the university police? This could have been a totally random thing, but man, the timing is messing with me. Sure as shit, coincidences happen, but I'm having trouble with this one. Go see if there's any evidence that might point in any other direction other than the car meets unfortunate cyclist story."

"Will do," Grace said as she headed out. "I don't know if they're going to take me seriously when I'm wearing this."

"They sure aren't going to ignore you," Cade said as Grace slipped out. He turned to Rook. "We need to go sit on Crocker until they extract the locations from the images. And I want to find out how Pavich got my number." They walked toward the entrance where Cade's truck sat.

"Wait, what? He called you? When?"

Cade walked him through receiving the text and showed it to him. "I gave my cell number to Courtney for what she called a simple relay that sends each new Orbiting Cortex post directly to my cell. I wouldn't have guessed it would've exposed my number."

"Um, boss," Rook said. "I have a bad thought. Are you sure the text came from Pavich?"

Cade stopped. "I didn't recognize the number. Who else could it have come from if it wasn't him?"

"We do have another killer in play," Rook replied. "As well as another dead body. One that's related to our case."

"You make a good point, college boy," Cade said. "There's one way to find out if it was Pavich. Let's go back and look at his phone."

They found the phone sticking out of Pavich's right boot, and Cade pried it loose with a pen. Using the dead man's finger to unlock the screen, he navigated to the messaging app and studied the list of conversations. The last text was over a week ago.

"Well, shit."

"Let's see that text you got," Rook said. "See what the number is."

Cade pulled his phone out and showed him the number. The area code was 612, a Minneapolis area code. Definitely not from Milwaukee. Then who?

One good way to find out: ask. Cade replied to the text: *Who is this?*

The reply was nearly instantaneous.

To paraphrase, the chill you're feeling
Ain't the weather. It's death approaching.

Another text appeared: *Death approaching.*

And another: *Approaching death.*

One after another, the texts flooded in on top of each other, all with the same last message. *Approaching death.*

Cade powered off his phone to make it stop. "Somebody programmed that. No way anyone was live-typing that."

"Worse than any telemarketer," Rook said. "We don't need your stinkin' extended warranty."

"Why they can send billionaires to space but not stop those calls is beyond me," Cade said. "Let's go see Crocker."

The mood was somber at the computer lab. People still worked, pushing through the feelings of pain and loss. Cade got it. Working in law enforcement was dangerous and sometimes tragedy struck. There are times when working was the only thing that could get you through. You needed to believe what you're doing was essential and could help save other lives.

Crocker waved them to a table, and the three huddled.

"Professor Tubbs is on his way, but let's talk." Crocker's eyes gave away the pain he must be feeling. "First, I couldn't find any way that your phone number was exposed on the Orbiting Cortex site. The relay was designed to forward the posts as they appeared on the site. The relay is not part of the actual site. Also, as an added precaution, our work is done behind a secure firewall."

"How secure?" Cade asked.

"Think 20-foot-tall steel-reinforced concrete wall with razor-sharp barbed wire on top, a moat, and a pack of hungry wolfhounds in front of it. And a dragon."

"Got it," Cade nodded. "It's secure."

"It's impenetrable," Crocker said. "And the other thing is, there hasn't been a post today or yesterday. So, there's no way the breach happened here.

Crocker's words had him frowning.

"Still no new posts?" he asked. "I'd expect the site to be a beehive of activity with two active killers answering the site's challenge."

"One killer now," Rook added.

"Gentlemen," Tubbs said as he took a seat next to Crocker. "Catch me up."

"There was concern that Detective Dawkins' number was released into the wild because of the new post relay Courtney set up. He received a text earlier."

Cade held up the phone for Tubbs to read the message. On the way over, Rook had blocked the number to stop the deluge of texts.

"But Courtney created a reader program that forwards each post as a text to Detective Dawkins. Her program is completely separate from the Orbiting Cortex site. And because we're monitoring the site from behind an ultra-secure firewall that Kenzie set up, there's no possible way his number was released. And as I pointed out, there haven't been any new posts that would have triggered the relay."

Tubbs nodded. "Thanks for making the explanation plain-speak. I appreciate it."

"Professor Tubbs," Cade said. "Maybe you can shed some light on what's bothering me. When you first told me about the Orbiting Cortex site, you said the participants got worked up when the Blonde Killer was caught. Doesn't it surprise you that now that two killers have answered the come to Minnesota challenge—posted on the very same site—and are now killing here, there's been zero comments? Why would they go dark now?"

Tubbs leaned back, stroking his chin, the picture of deep thought.

"This has been keeping me up at night as well. There are, of course, several explanations that come to mind."

"For instance?"

"For instance, since it was a challenge, perhaps the site posters are waiting to see who bests the detective. No offense, but their mindset is they are smarter and more capable than you, Detective Dawkins."

"And they can be wrong," Cade said. "On both counts."

"Underestimate their cunning at your own expense. These people live to kill, but they also kill to live. They are wired for this and need it to feel complete."

"Understood. I don't take them lightly." Cade folded his arms.

"Don't." Tubbs leaned forward, speaking earnestly. "I wrote my thesis on the abnormal psychology of the UK's most prolific serial killer, Harold Shipman. A doctor, he was convicted of killing 15 of his patients. However, a clinical audit estimated he may have been responsible for at least 236 total patient deaths. Shipman injected his patients with morphine to kill them and then altered his medical records to add symptoms the patients never had. In his care, over 500 patients died."

"Woah."

"Understandably, such a high death rate prompted concern from several colleagues. One colleague in particular, a local undertaker, noticed that many of the good doctor's patients exhibited similar poses in death. They were fully clothed and sitting up or reclining on a sofa or a settee, as they call it across the pond."

"That's crazy," Cade said. "That many patients died before people noticed?"

"Exactly my point," Tubbs said. "Shipman was cleared in an earlier investigation because his medical records covered him, and he was quite believable. Shipman had a domineering mother—no surprise—who installed in him a sense of superiority at an early age. Word was, he was never well-liked or had any close relationships because he carried that superiority with him throughout his life."

"And then he became a doctor," Cade said. "Don't doctors usually have a god complex as it is?"

Tubbs laughed. "I don't know if I'd go so far as to say usually, but it's not uncommon. When you're capable of saving lives, it can affect one's psyche."

"So, what made him go to the dark side, to go from healer to killer?" Rook asked.

"It may have been his mother," Tubbs said. "When Shipman was 17, he cared for her while she suffered from terminal lung cancer. He was fascinated by the effects and relief morphine brought her. How it eased her suffering. It's no coincidence then that he became a doctor and started injecting morphine into his elderly patients and watched them die."

"There has to be more to it than that," Rook said. "A normal person, even in the worst of circumstances, wouldn't make those choices."

"No, they wouldn't. But these killers are different to the extreme. Maybe it's their abnormally developed brain or crossed wires, but it's closer to one in a million who would tread down the dark path of a serial killer. That's what makes their abnormal psychology so fascinating." He lifted a tablet. "I have a favorite quote from an interview with a serial killer that goes a long way to illustrate how different they truly are. Let me read it for you. 'I had a compulsion that was irresistible. On the one hand, it was a hunger that was unquenchable, unsatisfiable, but on the other hand, it fed me. It made me feel complete. Up until recently, I've never experienced a feeling of guilt. I do feel regret. I do feel remorse. I do feel sorrow. These are feelings I've never experienced before. I have become what I think is a responsible citizen. I'm a good neighbor. I'm a good friend. I'm a good employee. I think I'm basically a decent human being if it wasn't for the fact that I was also a monster.'"

"He has a sense of being self-aware," Cade said. "He knows he's not normal, and yet he speaks so matter-of-factly about it."

Tubbs nodded. "Hence the appeal."

Cade turned to Crocker. "Where are you with the geotags?"

"I wrote the app to extract the tags and started it. I'm sure it's completed by now." He turned over his shoulder. "Miguel, is the tag capture completed yet?"

"Just finished. Printing the summary now." Miguel stood over a printer, making a hurry-up gesture with his hand. When the sheets popped out, he walked them over. Crocker mumbled thanks as he glanced at the data before spreading the sheets out on the conference table.

"Okay. Here's what we have. Images posted were taken in the Los Angeles, Charlotte, Milwaukee, Toronto, Richmond, Portland, and Phoenix areas. There's always the chance the images were simply used by the poster but taken by someone else. But we have multiple images from the cities I listed, so the correlation is high."

Cade glanced to Rook. "This could make a huge difference. We need to contact the local law enforcement in these areas to see if they've experienced killings with similar patterns. Obviously, focus on our remaining killer's pattern, with Pavich out of the picture now."

"I'm on it," Rook said. "Can I take this?" he asked Crocker, reaching for the pages.

"All yours, Detective."

"Maybe you pull in Bednarek or Thao to speed things up," Cade suggested.

"Will do, boss. I'll talk to Bednarek."

JARN WAS naked in his hotel room. He'd finished his yoga routine to calm his mind and the television news was on. Laying back on the bed, he watched the detective speaking with the Devries woman. She'd been his favorite of the local media and he'd considered going after her. She'd be fun, but he wasn't convinced she was attainable. He'd been by the station a few times, but the sprawling complex had security officers and a police presence that had to be because of the killings. He could wait until she left and follow her, but there were too many routes out of the station to easily latch onto her.

There were other intriguing targets, though.

Something the detective said made him sit up and pay attention.

Egyptian? Fertility? That made no sense, and it simply wasn't true. Hearing Dawkins question his manhood in front of the woman infuriated him. Even though he knew the detective was baiting him, he couldn't stop his rising anger. Seeing Devries, the corners of her mouth turning up as she suppressed a smile, made him furious.

He got off the bed and paced. Jarn knew he had to calm down. Of course, he was being provoked. The lawman had nothing, and was grasping at straws. He stopped and forced his clenched fists open. Breathe, in, out. The thing was, his mother had been a master provocateur too. She knew exactly which buttons to push. It used to make him so angry. His hands clenched again, thinking of her. His mother yelled at him for anything, humiliating him. It didn't take a rocket scientist to know she was responsible for his unusual activities, for lack of a better word.

His mother, the wicked witch of the southwest, had pushed him so far. She'd asked his friends if they wet the bed, too. She'd slap him if he interrupted her. She'd make him crawl like an animal if he spilled or dropped any food—for hours at a time. Of course, there were consequences. It was no wonder his friends dwindled away to none. It was no wonder he dreamed of violently attacking his mother, though he never could. It was no wonder he resented animals to such a degree that he began catching and torturing rabbits and the occasional squirrel.

The animals helped him cope. For a while.

But his mother would always find new ways to rob him of his confidence, honor and resiliency. He needed to act.

As it turned out, two of the world's most toxic mushrooms could be found in Arizona. False morels and death caps. He chose death caps simply based on liking the name. Just half of one is enough to kill an adult human, making it the deadliest mushroom on Earth. A little research led him to where they grew nearby. Carefully picking a few, he brought them home and kept them hidden in the back of the refrigerator for a week before deciding how best to use them. His mother was a voracious salad eater, which he was tasked with making for her nightly. At first, he mixed in a few tiny pieces. Over a week, he gradually added more. Her symptoms were minor in the beginning. Stomach pain and nausea, but as the amount grew, she suffered through worsening bouts of diarrhea and vomiting.

Of course, he tended to her, taking care of her every need. All the while enjoying each second of her suffering.

When she mentioned going to the doctor, Jarn backed off the mushrooms. He didn't want his poisoning discovered.

He discovered an interesting side effect as she was getting marginally better, was her hallucinations. His mother often stared into the distance, spacing out. She'd swing her fists at the empty air and rage against unseen entities. One night after nearly a month of daily mushroom dosing, she completely lost it. When the police arrived some ten minutes after he called them, they found her on the floor, fingernails ripped out, self-inflicted bite marks on her arms, broken blood vessels in her eyes and her voice mostly gone from her non-stop shrieking.

To this day, she was still locked up in a state psych institution. Jarn visited her from time to time whenever life got him down. It never failed to pick him up.

Jarn's hands relaxed as he pictured her with the what-the-hell-happened-to-my-life look she perpetually wore. Turning his attention back to the screen, he studied the blonde newscaster with an appraising eye. Anchoring the news alongside Barry Weiss, Ava Anderson was intriguing. She ticked most, if not all, of his favorite boxes. Beautiful in an athletic college girl sort of way, though she was likely a half-decade out of college. Her hazel eyes were striking, and when she smiled, it brightened everything around her—even the pompous dork in the vest. But, best of all, she was attainable.

He'd followed her for the last two nights, from the station's suburban Eden Prairie location to her one-story Minneapolis home. She lived on a quiet street near the lakes.

It bothered him watching the Barry Weiss Report as the buffoon tore down the lawman. It wasn't because Dawkins was being treated unfairly. It was plain to see that Weiss had been snubbed by the lawman, and this hatchet-job was his revenge. It also wasn't because of some begrudgingly respect between adversaries.

No, he couldn't wait to kill the detective.

Like many things, it came down to ego. Jarn wanted to best the best, and not someone the media ridiculed as incompetent. The situation put him in an awkward place. *It is what it is.* You played the cards you were dealt.

But now, instead of playing his 5, he would play his 9.

Jarn wanted a very public, very prominent victim to raise the stakes and gain notoriety. His original plan was to take the lawman's woman, but since she was the lone voice in Dawkin's corner, he couldn't take her off the board. But a nice compromise presented itself in Weiss' coworker.

Ava Anderson.

Her name screamed Scandinavian, which was a rarity in Jarn's hometown. The Latin women were beautiful and plentiful there, but there was something about the difference Anderson offered that appealed to him. Maybe it was a survival of the species' primal instinct thing, or simple boredom. Either way, the newscaster called to him.

Jarn couldn't help but smile. He'd have her soon.

CHAPTER 22

Tuesday

Lorie Thao answered with a cheery, "Hello, boss."

"What are you up to?" Cade asked, steering onto the entrance ramp without conscious thought of his destination. His truck knew where to go.

"Waiting for your call," she said with obvious sarcasm. "I have a life, you know."

"Don't worry, being a detective can fix that," he said. It was true that since crime didn't rest, neither did the people trying to hold back the horde at the gates. If the last week was any indication, sleep was not in the immediate forecast.

Cade brought her up to speed on the developments from the computer lab.

"Los Angeles, Charlotte, Milwaukee, Toronto, Richmond, Portland and Phoenix were the cities that were tagged in the image data."

"Should I be writing this down?"

Cade paused, gauging her tone.

"Of course, I'm writing this down," Thao said. "I'm Asian, I write everything down."

"Okay..." Cade hesitated.

"I'm overly caffeinated, I apologize. I get a little flippant when I've had more than two coffees or tea in a day."

"How many have you had?" He had to ask.

"Just two. Of each." Thao laughed. "In my defense, it's been a crazy day."

"That it has." Cade took the Cretin exit and took a right at the light. "Since we've established when the license plates were stolen, you can run flights from those seven cities that came into MSP. Actually, it's only six cities, as you can take Milwaukee off the list. We would have heard if there was another active killer there. That should give us a list of passengers that's more manageable than we had."

"On average, the airport has over 400 planes arriving every day. That's a lot of potential killers."

Cade's truck turned right on Marshall. "Yeah, but you exclude all women and children. And anyone 60 plus. Sort your database to exclude those factors."

Cade paused as Thao's silence became awkward. He turned left onto the quiet neighborhood street.

"You do have a database, don't you? I figured you must with all the flight information you've been gathering." He waited.

Thao laughed. "Of course, I have a database. I'm Asian, after all."

"I'm not sure what to say when you say things like that," Cade said. "I don't want to offend you."

"It's okay. It's just the caffeine talking again. Sometimes I like to make fun of the stereotypes."

"I get that."

"Like, you know why Asian kids don't believe in Santa?"

Cade shook his head at the absurdity of the conversation.

"It's because they make the toys." Thao laughed again.

"I was honestly afraid of what you were going to say." But he was smiling.

"But stereotypes aside, I never thought being a detective meant sinking into spreadsheet hell."

"Well..." Cade stopped in front of a white two-story with green trim and shutters. He turned off the truck. "Being a detective means you do a lot of things you'd never have guessed you'd be doing someday. The glamour is tarnished when you find yourself crawling through a sewer or sweating in a car for hours waiting to see if someone shows up. There's no 'It's not my job' here. Especially in a small task force."

"I get that, and I'm not complaining. Really. I enjoy being overly dramatic sometimes. It's who I am. You'll get used to it."

Cade laughed. "If you say so. Are you up to the spreadsheet task? Can you filter the list to get us a set of names that meet the unsub's demographics for each of the cities?"

She cleared her throat. "I was born for this."

"Stop. Just stop." But he was laughing as he walked up the sidewalk.

Reynolds didn't look surprised to see him at her door. She was comfortably dressed in a light blue long sleeve Adidas pullover and athletic shorts. Her long blonde hair was pulled back into a ponytail. She waved Cade in and he followed her into the living room. She sat and opened her laptop.

"I was doing my nightly competitive research. Have you been watching the news reports at all?" Her serious expression told him it wasn't going to be good. "It's not only Barry Weiss anymore. The other stations are turning on you. Frank and Amelia are pretty much neutral still, but that's it."

"It's all about ratings. I don't take that shit personally." He smiled sheepishly. "No offense. I know you do."

"You think?" She flashed her eyes at him, her jaw tight. "It's the yardstick that my profession is measured by. I may not be concerned about overnights, but the long-term numbers paint a picture of my future. I've worked my ass off to get where I am, and I intend to stay there until the network comes calling."

"What are you saying?" He studied her as Reynold's eyes looked at her hands. "Is there a problem here? Do we have a problem?"

Reynolds shook her head. "For a smart guy, you can be clueless. Look at this." She turned her laptop around and hit play.

The clip was from Eyewitness News, with anchor Bill Fischer, a longtime Twin Cities newscaster.

"Good evening, there's been breaking news in the hunt for the killers terrorizing our community. A shocking discovery of another murdered victim and a shootout outside the Minneapolis Convention Center has the state reeling. Killed in the shootout was a 26-year-old Milwaukee man, Michael Thomas Pavich. Police believe he was responsible for both the most recent murder and for the death of Minneapolis' Victoria Garcia. Here with your Eyewitness News report is investigative journalist, Skye Greeder."

The screen switched to the front of the Minneapolis Convention Center. A woman in her twenties in a pale blue blazer looked at the camera.

"The MegaCon, comics, sci-fi, horror, anime, and gaming premiere event, has been running at the Minneapolis Convention Center for the last four days. It has brought people together from all over the upper Midwest to celebrate their love of comics. One of the people who attended was thirty-year-old Arielle Summers. Tonight, police are disclosing that Summers was murdered at the event."

There were visuals of police cars and emergency vehicles shot from a distance.

"The killer, now identified as Michael Thomas Pavich of Milwaukee, was gunned down by police following the killing. Pavich is believed to be responsible for the recent murder of Victoria Rae Garcia, found in her Minneapolis home."

The reporter looked earnestly at the camera.

"Reporting at the scene, I'm Skye Greeder for Eyewitness News."

Anchor Bill Fischer was back on screen. "For more on this breaking story, we're going to the St. Paul Hotel in downtown where our own Faith McMahon caught up with Governor Winston Ritter at the Sanneh Foundation's annual Gala for Goals Fundraiser.

Wearing a tux, the governor stood by a stairway as the reporter held a microphone.

"Governor Ritter, with the news of a fourth victim in the murderous serial killer spree in the Twin Cities, do you have any comment?"

The question looked to catch him by surprise, but he recovered quickly. "My heart goes out to the victim's family and friends. Obviously, law enforcement and our major crimes task force are doing everything they can to bring these killers—these out-of-state killers—to justice."

The reporter glanced at the camera, before turning back to Ritter.

"You must not have heard the police are saying that the killer was shot dead in the convention center parking lot." McMahon looked to him for comment before adding, "Word is, he was unarmed and was shot nearly two dozen times."

Ritter visibly swallowed and his eyes narrowed.

"It wouldn't be prudent for me to comment on an active investigation."

McMahon looked like a car salesperson when a prospect said they wanted to see what other dealers had.

"Governor, there are numerous reports that members of law enforcement have expressed doubt that Cade Dawkins is competent to lead the task force. With him directing the hail of gunfire to kill an unarmed suspect, do you still stand by your appointment of Dawkins?"

Self-consciously adjusting his bow tie, Ritter smiled. There was no joy or humor in that smile, only malice.

"I will look at the facts of the situation before rendering judgment. If there were mistakes made or errors in judgment, Dawkins will be removed and charged to the full extent of the law. Minnesotans have high standards and deserve the best in our public officials. Which is why I'm running for governor again in the next election, but make no mistake about it, I will do what's best for our state. And that's my promise to you."

By the end of his ad hoc speech, Ritter was staring directly into the camera. Cade thought it was possible the governor was going to salute, but it didn't happen.

McMahon's eyes widened at the surprise home run she'd hit. There was a trace of a smile as she signed off.

"A new priest is ringing in change at this south Minneapolis parish," Fischer said, "And here with the story is—" Reynolds closed her laptop.

"Do you see what I mean? This is where the story is going. Where I need to go." She leaned forward. "Did you really direct them to kill Pavich? I mean, he deserved it, but that's pretty badass."

Cade stared at her, a half-dozen responses passing through his head. Yes, their suspect was technically unarmed, but at close to seven feet tall and with razor-sharp teeth that had killed two Minneapolis women, the man himself was a weapon. And Cade hadn't directed the officers to shoot. He'd been on the ground after pulling Grace to safety as the killer had attempted to maul her. But none of the responses needed to be said. His weariness had sapped the fight out of him. Realizing this would likely be his last time visiting Reynolds' home, he glanced around and stood up.

"I'll let myself out."

CHAPTER 23

Cade was accelerating onto 94 when his cell rang. When he looked at who was calling, he thought about not answering, but he had enough respect for the office to not be that petty.

"Hello, Governor."

"I heard that you got one of the killers off the street. Good job."

Cade cocked his head. Not the words he was expecting. Such was his tiredness that he had the governor repeat his words, thinking he'd misunderstood.

"I wanted to tell you that you did a nice job catching the killer after he attacked that woman at the comic convention."

Rubbing a hand over his cheek stubble, Cade shook his head. Ritter was lying to someone. Either to the reporter or to him. There's a reason some jokes have endured. Like, how do you know if a politician is lying? His lips are moving.

Ritter continued. "It's a tragedy about the woman, though. Now you just have to catch the other killer and we can put this all behind us."

"Before the election next year?"

"Well, of course," Ritter sputtered. "But also to keep the women safe. I'm not completely self-serving."

"A rare quality in a politician of your stature." Worried he'd gone too far, Cade waited for Ritter's reaction. Judging by the longish pause from the governor, he was debating the sincerity of the "compliment."

Deciding it best to get things moving, Cade continued. "So you called to let me know I was doing a great job, and I had your full support?"

"Essentially."

"I see," Cade said, but he didn't like what he was seeing. Not in the least. "I caught your appearance on Eyewitness News."

"You did? That's great. I'm happy to hear you're following your media coverage. That's the mark of a savvy operator."

At no point in his thirty-one years did Cade ever aspire to be known as a savvy operator. Ritter's compliment made him want to take a shower to wash the slime off, but it felt counterproductive to mention that just now. Instead, he deferred to a noncommittal, "Hmmm."

"Did you like what you saw?"

"Not exactly. What I saw was you on camera throwing me under the bus."

"Well..."

Cade didn't want to hear the doublespeak he knew was coming. "There's no other way to interpret it. When you threaten me by saying you'll have me removed and prosecuted, there's no room for your political wiggle."

Cade waited for a long pause.

"Fine," Ritter said. "I don't plan on replacing you, but in the political arena, things like these killings are massive firestorms that aren't easily forgotten. But when people hear me coming down on you, I'm remembered as being tough. Best of all, the focus is on you and the pressure is off me. A win-win."

"Usually when someone says win-win, it means both sides get a win. Not seeing my upside here."

"Cut the crap, Dawkins. Not everyone can win. Are you one of those who believe everyone deserves a participation medal? That's not what made this country the best country in the world. It's liberals like—"

Cade turned the volume down before he said what he was thinking. How people dealt with this kind of crap on a regular basis went beyond his understanding. He'd always bristled under authority, but throw in Ritter's unchecked ego and his uber weaselness and Cade's self-control went out the window. An incoming call was the thing that saved him.

"Sorry, governor. I'm getting a call from the medical examiner that I need to take. Catch you later." He ended the call before Ritter had a chance to say a word. Better that way. One more word and he would've lost it.

The call was from his Minnesota State Patrol supervisor Capt. Leah Rejene, not the medical examiner. Ritter wouldn't have liked it if he was interrupted by someone from his chain of command, hence the lie.

"Captain. Happy to hear from you."

Rejene laughed. "Really? You must be having a day."

"And then some. To top it off, I was on the phone with our governor when you called. Ritter can be such an..." He paused. "Put it this way, I was about to lose my shit. I owe you big time for saving me from myself."

"There's something about politics and power that draws in the assholes. Not everyone who rises up is one, but the correlation is strong."

Cade steered onto the exit for 35E north. "How do you do it? How do you not tell someone to go eff themselves when they are completely clueless, and it's obvious their commands are primarily for their own benefit?"

The laughter that echoed in his truck didn't help his mood any. But Rejene's words did. "My first sergeant taught me something that I use to this day. His tried-and-true technique was to smile and nod with each infuriatingly idiotic statement while thinking happy thoughts about the person's demonstrated shortcomings. Let me give you an example. Let's say your supervisor tells you it's better to stop a car with your siren than your emergency lights to save battery power. Just say to yourself that somewhere there's a village missing its idiot. Or when the governor says you need to wear a sport coat whenever you talk to the media, you think he's missing a few buttons on his remote control or he's a few fries short of a happy meal. Got it?"

"And that helps?"

"It's worked for me. Try it next time. But remember not to say what you're thinking out loud." She laughed again. "There is a distinction, though. If you are directed to do something that goes against what you know to be right, you need to politely state your case. I'm not abdicating common sense or ethics, only offering you a path to sanity and job retention. You still need to do the right thing."

"Understood."

"Good," Rejene said. "I was calling mainly to check in, see how you're holding up. Rob's been kind of slow lately, so if you need him for something, go ahead and reach out. The entire city is living and breathing your case, so not much else has been happening. I know he'd like to hear from you."

Cade swung into the lot and parked next to Grace's car. Of course she was back at work. "I'll give him a shout tomorrow. And boss, thanks for the mental health advice."

"My pleasure. Can't have you self-destructing before you catch the killer."

"Maybe not after, either," Cade said.

"You heard what I meant."

They were both laughing as he ended the call. The night air was cool on his skin as he headed for the entrance. There were several cars in the lot besides Grace's green Honda, but he was confident no one else spent as much time here as she did. Yet, he was glad she was here.

"Hey," Grace said when he walked into her BCA lab. "Quite the night."

Grace had ditched her Mystique costume and was back in her regular clothes, which were a plain white T and a skirt. No shoes in sight.

"It has been quite the night. And to top it off, the governor called and was his usual self, in other words, a real..."

"Ass hat?"

Cade grinned.

"Shit tard?"

Cade smiled.

"Wanker?"

Cade laughed.

"Plum tree shaker?"

Laughing harder, he said, "I haven't heard that one before. But I like the visual." Sitting next to Grace, he shook his head. "The man gives weasels a bad name. If he'd stick to governing and let me stick to detecting, life would be better."

"I hear you. So, I checked on Courtney's body. I didn't see anything that made me suspicious, but the pathologist said she'd do an autopsy-lite."

"That's a new one. What's that exactly?"

"She said it's not a full cut-the-body-open, weigh-the-organs kind of autopsy, but an exacting surface examination looking for all signs of trauma."

"That's all we need."

"My thoughts exactly."

They fell into a comfortable silence, Grace going through her notes, Cade going through emails. He looked up once and caught her looking at him. She quickly returned to her screen.

"Favorite comic book character?" she asked without looking up.

"It was Black Panther, but I have a new respect for Mystique now."

Grace smiled but kept her eyes on her screen.

"Favorite literary vampire?" she asked after a moment.

"The one in Sesame Street."

"He doesn't count."

"I can assure you that he does," Cade said with a grin. He got a light shoulder punch for his humor. Totally worth it. He went back to his emails, still smiling.

Another few moments of comfortable silence. And then.

"Are you ever going to kiss me?" Grace's voice sounded oddly matter-of-fact.

"I've been thinking about it."

Neither looked away from their screens for a moment or two.

"What's stopping you?"

Cade thought about it for a beat or three. "Reynolds and I are done. We broke up."

Grace stopped her scrolling.

"I don't want us to be a rebound thing," Cade said. "And my head is not in the right place to start something. Not now, not in the middle of this case. It's consuming me, and I barely get three hours of sleep a night. I'm not at my best. I've grown tired of people, reporters, politicians, television and anything yellow."

"You must really hate minions then."

"I do. With the passion of a puppy chasing his ball."

Grace nodded, stood and waved Cade to do the same. With hands on his knees, he pushed himself up. She beckoned him closer. He numbly took a step and was in her arms. They held each other, neither speaking, neither willing to move.

CHAPTER 24

"Are you ready for this?"

Bednarek leaned forward in her chair and nodded solemnly.

"It's your last chance to back out," Rook said earnestly. "I won't think any less of you if you do."

"No way, you're going down." Bednarek's eyes flashed, and she grinned. When Rook had proposed splitting the list of six cities to call, she'd suggested a prize for the one who struck gold first. After much negotiation, a steak dinner at Mancini's St. Paul steakhouse would be provided to the winner, with the loser picking up the tab.

"Let's do it then." He reached across the scratched and stained desk and fist-bumped Bednarek.

Rook's list was Los Angeles, Charlotte, and Toronto, while Kristen's list had Richmond, Portland and Phoenix. He decided to begin with Los Angeles and Hollywood Homicide. With so many precincts to choose from (21), Rook picked Hollywood based on one of his favorite literary detectives, Harry Bosch. Since Bosch had been with Robbery Homicide in Hollywood, it was as good as any place to begin. He found the front desk number and asked for a homicide detective, saying he was with a major crimes task force. Within a few seconds, a tired sounding voice answered.

"Jeffries, Hollywood."

"Detective, this is Terrance Rooker with the Five Below Major Crimes Task Force in Minnesota. We're—"

"Five-Oh?

"No, Five Below. Like the discount chain stores." Rook's soul hurt, but it was the fastest way to move this on.

"What nimrod came up with that name?"

"Above my pay grade. Anywho, we're working on a case involving serial murders here that may have ties to the Los Angeles area. Wondering what active cases you may have involving a serial killer using a knife. Our killer has used a specific knife, the Morakniv Companion. It's a hunting knife with a four-inch blade available at most outdoor stores and Amazon. So far, he's killed only women, leaving the blade behind, still in his victims. Does this sound at all familiar?"

"Hmmm," Detective Jeffries drew out. "It doesn't. The only active multiple murder case I'm aware of in our area is the beating and killing of homeless people. We've had five murders so far, spanning two years. The unsub burns his victims, though. No knife."

"Sounds ghastly."

"Just another day in Hollywood," Jeffries said. "Doesn't sound like your killer."

"No, it doesn't."

"Well then, good luck. Gotta run." And the call was disconnected.

Rook wrote out the notes from the call and glanced to Bednarek. She was wrapping up her call. When she hung up, she turned to Rook.

"Nope. Richmond has a killer that uses a wire to strangle the victims. All teenage boys."

"There's a lot of evil in our world."

She held his eyes and nodded. "That's why we're here."

Turning back to his list, Charlotte was next. He'd visited the North Carolina city twice and had stopped for numerous layovers but had never had any professional dealings there. Until now. As with Hollywood Homicide, Rook began by calling the front desk, identifying himself, and asking to speak with a homicide detective.

He was asked to leave a callback number and the on-call detective would be paged.

While he waited, he researched killings in the area. There had been a few over the last several decades. The return call came within a few minutes.

"This is Detective Harper Decorsey from Charlotte Homicide/ADW." Her voice was hoarse, like she'd been yelling at her kid's championship soccer game that lasted for two overtimes. She cleared her throat, but any improvement was marginal. "What can I help you with?"

This time he skipped the task force name and went directly to describing the killings he was looking for a match to.

"What made you call us?" She cleared her throat again. It sounded painful.

"Maybe you should switch to filtered cigarettes, Detective."

"Funny man. I'm getting over a cold."

"Good to know. But Charlotte came up because images tagged with your location were posted to a website our killer frequents. We're trying to narrow down his location."

Decorsey paused. Then, "I'm sure there's more to that story, but in the interests of time, let's proceed." She cleared her throat again. "We haven't had any non-gang-related stabbings in the Charlotte Mecklenburg area that haven't been solved. Not in the last several years."

"Okay, what about unsolved serial killings?"

"We have a killer of ten women locked up awaiting execution, and more recently, several sex workers were found shot to death, but that's all. Nothing that matches your M.O. remotely."

"Okay, then. Thanks for your time." Rook went to end the call, but Decorsey told him to hang on.

"Will you send me what you have on the images from Charlotte? It might help with our case."

She gave him her email address and thanked him before clearing her throat again.

Rook made his notes and glanced at Bednarek. She was in an animated discussion, and he returned to his list. One last city. Toronto.

The internet came up with a page for the Toronto homicide and a direct line. Easy.

"Hazelton." It was a man with a clipped voice.

Rook introduced himself and the reason for his call.

"Are you a reporter?"

Rook paused. "No, I'm from the major crimes task force in Minnesota, like I said. I'm not looking for details or sensitive information. Just corroboration."

"Are you from the Sun?"

"No man, I said I'm from—"

Click. Silence.

Rook set down the phone and rubbed his eyes. He counted to ten.

Bednarek was still on her call laughing with the much friendlier law enforcement professional on the other end. Life wasn't always fair.

Rook's mother didn't raise any quitters. She was tough on him and his two brothers. If you signed up for football and didn't like it, tough. You finished what you started. School sucked, and you wanted out? Tough. You opened your books and did what you had to. And if he survived his career misstep—as he liked to call it—he could survive the Canadian bacon homicide dick.

He picked up the phone and redialed Toronto homicide.

"Hazelton."

"Detective Hazelton?"

"Yes, this is Detective Hazelton."

This was going better.

"I'm Detective Rooker."

"You're from the Sun?"

Now it wasn't.

"No, man, I'm from the moon. I'm wearing—"

Click. Silence. Rook wanted to slam down the phone and swear like a circus roustabout. Instead, he stood up, walked to the vending machine and got himself a root beer. Everything was always better with root beer. He took a sip and forced himself to walk slowly back. No hurry. Kristen wrapped up her call, profusely thanking the person on the other end. She looked up and shook her head. They were both 0 for 2. Bednarek turned to her list to begin her third call.

Rook's mother didn't raise any fools either.

"Let's swap cities," Rook suggested. "I'll take Phoenix, you can have Toronto. It turns out I don't speak Canadian." He held out the slip of paper with his list.

The look he received said she didn't believe him, but whatever. She took the paper, as she flipped her hair. "I'm still going to win this."

Phoenix's Homicide Unit was primarily a daytime investigations unit with detectives available for call-out 24 hours a day. Rook made the call to get the ball rolling. He reached someone at the information desk for the Violent Crimes Bureau which housed the homicide unit. After explaining what he needed and giving his call back number, he sat back and waited.

Bednarek was on her call and laughing. Laughing? She must be on the phone with someone different. She had to be.

"No, no, it really happened. You wouldn't believe the look on her face." Bednarek giggled. "I know, I thought the same thing."

It went on like that, but Rook tuned it out while reading about the Phoenix police. Based on their website, Phoenix was in full recruiting mode. He thought about what made him consider law enforcement as his career. It wasn't the fast cars and handguns as he liked to joke. It'd started in fourth grade when he'd read a book on the secret service. Something about the cover captured his imagination when he first saw it. A man stood defiant against the tides of evil-doers in his trench coat and fedora. There were also vignettes of a hand holding an open badge case, a car chase, and a thwarted presidential assassination. How could he not love the book? After that, he read books on Scotland Yard, the FBI, and the Canadian

Mounties. Throw in Hardy Boys, and Encyclopedia Brown books, and his career path was decided.

The incoming call pulled him from his childhood remembrances. He answered and found himself on the line with a Detective Walczak.

"What can I do for you?" Walczak was gruff and to the point.

"We're working on a case involving serial murders here that may have ties to the Phoenix area. Our killer has used a specific knife, the Morakniv Companion, that he leaves behind—still in the victim. Wondering if you have any active cases that fit this M.O.?"

"Are there markings on the body?"

"There are, but we don't know what they mean."

"It's him," Walczak said. "The Jaguar."

"The Jaguar?"

"Someone came up with the name here, not sure who. It fits. Stealthy, cunning and intelligent, a cold-blooded killer. He's responsible for seven murders over the last four years, but I suspect there are more. Maybe a dozen more."

"Jesus. All women?"

"Yes, at least the seven women. There were a couple of men in the maybe category, but I can't say for certain if it was the Jaguar. They were stabbed earlier in the Jaguar's timeline, but there was no sign of a murder weapon at the scene. We've been focused on the seven women as we're sure it was him. They were marked with the same eerie writing."

"If it was me, I'd focus on the anomalies," Rook said. "There's often a personal reason for the killings, rather than it being a psycho following his urges."

"If it was you? Screw you and the horse you rode in on," Walczak spat. "Don't call me up and tell me my job. We've exhausted every potential lead and clue. Every damn one."

"Chill, man. I was thinking out loud," Rook said, wanting to placate the detective. "You know, this guy has killed way more than I would have guessed. He's quite good at keeping out of sight, too."

"The thing that got me about the murders is the victim selection," Walczak said. "The Jaguar doesn't select his victims from the fringes of society, women that walk with their heads down or place themselves in risky situations, meaning sex workers or drug users. No, he finds the women that should know better. Somehow, he lures these intelligent, tough, and successful women into killing situations. And he does it in public spaces and in front of cameras and still never gets identified."

Walczak paused. "Can you tell it's my most frustrating case?"

"Understandably."

"And now he's killing in your area? Minneapolis?"

Force of habit, Rook nodded, before adding, "And St. Paul."

"Damn. I don't envy you. We've been chasing him for years with nothing to show for it. There was this Italian soccer star that scored goals consistently for decades. The other team knew he was deadly and watched him closely, marking him carefully. He'd lull them into complacency with his half-hearted effort, and they'd get thinking that today wouldn't be his day. But then he'd strike, and the ball would be in the back of the net before the other team knew what happened. This killer is like that. Nothing happens for months, and then in a matter of days, we have two dead women days apart."

Rook paused after listening to the detective. "His first victim was exactly like you described. A beautiful and successful woman taken from a prominent suburban restaurant; however, his next victim was a sex worker."

"Really? That breaks his pattern." Walczak paused for a beat. "Tell me about the crime scene."

Rook walked him through the staging in the no-tell motel as well as the video documenting Valley's killing.

"That's unprecedented. We've never caught more than a passing glimpse of him in any surveillance footage we've found. I'd be interested in seeing it."

"I'll send you a Dropbox link." Rook sighed. It felt like the conversation was going nowhere. There was no usable information here. "Have you had any suspects?"

"Not a one."

"Have you drawn up a profile on him?" The FBI criminal profiling process was used to identify the perpetrator of a violent crime by identifying the personality and behavioral characteristics of the offender based upon an analysis of the crime committed. When Rook first became a detective, he'd learned about FBI profiling. Their instructor had stood in front of the group and asked, what if you could catch a criminal by learning and understanding his behavior patterns, even though you don't know him? Even guessing his age range, race, and even what he usually wears? Rook was understandably intrigued. As a black man, he knew profiling could be harmful when used based solely on race, religion or class. But used correctly, profiling offenders could offer insights into behaviors and likely demographics. Hopefully enough to catch the killer.

"We consulted with the local field office, who used the FBI profilers at Quantico. They said our unsub is likely a white man in his mid-thirties to mid-forties. He'd be white-collar, intelligent, likely a business owner or an independent employee as the killings occurred at all different times of the day. He'd dress well—likely expensive suits and shoes, have above-average social skills, is fit and takes care of his personal hygiene. His vehicle might be a high-end SUV or BMW sedan, likely black. His background would include an absent father, a domineering mother, and a history of killing small animals."

"So did you put all that into the computer and have it spit out a name for you?"

Walczak laughed. "Wouldn't that be nice? Unfortunately, it doesn't work that way. We need some suspects to use the profile to narrow them down."

"And you have none," Rook said.

"Screw you. It's not for the lack of trying. He's just unbelievably slippery."

"That's for sure. Maybe together, we can piece together enough to get a lead on him. I'll send you the clip and everything we have if you can do the same. I'd love to look at the crime scene details and background on all the victims."

Walczak hesitated. "I can do that. Do you want the seven confirmed cases only, or the suspected ones as well?"

"I trust your instincts. Send me the others as well."

They arranged the logistics of the data transfer and agreed to update the other with any insights or new developments.

"Catch this guy, okay?" Walczak ended the call without waiting for Rook's reply.

Rook jotted several notes and waited for Bednarek to finish her call. She caught his eye as she hung up. Bednarek shook her head and sighed. After a moment, she said, "Looks like we both struck out." Her displeasure was all over her face.

"No, it looks like I'm a better poker player than you are."

"Wait, what?" Her eyes widened. "You found him?"

Rook nodded, enjoying the moment.

"Tell me." Exasperation in her voice.

"After you tell me that I'm a better detective."

"No way. You took my city. And it was plain dumb luck. There was no actual detecting involved."

Rook laughed. "Okay, don't sweat it. But I did win the dinner."

"Fine. Now give."

Rook walked her through his conversation and the impending data transfer. "We can see if we get anything from the Arizona crime scenes. With a larger sample size, we're bound to come up with something, right?"

Bednarek nodded.

"There's the enthusiasm." Rook shook his head.

"No, it's more that he's remarkably good at killing," Bednarek said. "We're going to need a little luck on this one."

Rook nodded and added. "Maybe more than a little."

CHAPTER 25

Cade swung the truck into the parking lot. He'd arranged to meet Rob at the Caribou Coffee off 694, the same coffee shop they'd used as a base of operations for the Blonde Killer case. Rob's Malibu was backed into the space closest to the exit and he backed in next to him. People in law enforcement rarely parked nose in or sat anywhere with their back to the door. As he walked across the lot, his cell rang. It was Reynolds.

"Hey, we need to talk." She sounded unusually subdued.

Pausing at the door, Cade said, "I'm headed in to meet with Rob. Can I call you back when I'm done?"

There was a lengthy pause and then: "I've been offered a position with GMA." Good Morning America had been Reynold's dream since they first met. It was her call-up to the majors. Going to New York for a national morning show was the pinnacle for someone in broadcast journalism.

Cade opened the door for a woman but waited outside the entrance. "That's great, and well deserved. Congratulations."

"Thank you. I'll be staying here until the Twin Killer case is resolved. It made the most sense to stay for the biggest story of the year. It's been picked up nationally. I'll be making live reports on the story for the network until then. The producers said it would be the ideal way for the nation to get introduced to me." She paused. "This is a huge deal."

"As are you," Cade said. "I'm proud of you."

Another pause. "I'm not sure you understand. Now, more than ever, I need to focus on my career. So as fun as our relationship has been, it's time to end things. But, don't worry, we'll still see each other. It's important that you continue to come on the air with me. That access is vital to my successful introduction. Do you follow?"

Cade nodded. "Let me see. You want preferential treatment over the other news outlets, but we're done seeing each other because you need to focus on your career. And it's definitely over after you move to the network mothership. But you need me to help your career. Does that sound accurate enough?"

"You make me sound like a cold-hearted bitch."

"There may be a good reason..."

"Cade." Her voice cracked. He imagined her looking at him with eyes that could melt Hannibal Lecter's heart.

Rob waved at him from inside, gesturing to the second coffee cup sitting across the table. He decided he'd rather be inside with his friend drinking a delicious mocha than out here doing the awkward dance with his now ex-girlfriend.

"I should be going."

"Really?" Reynolds spat the word out like it was poisonous. "I suppose you're going to go talk to Barry Weiss now. After all we've been through."

He couldn't help but laugh at the absurdity of it. "Barry? No way, there must be better options than that poser."

He opened the door and stepped inside. "Take care, Reynolds." Cade ended the call.

Rob nodded as Cade joined him. "Got you your usual."

"Sweet."

Cade took a drink while Rob leaned back. "It's been quiet while you've been gone. But not just at the office, the streets have been unusually dead."

"Really?" Cade asked. "Don't tell me even the hayseed truckers have been lying low."

The hayseed truckers were a ragtag group of hillbillies from rural Wisconsin that hauled meth into the Twin Cities and brought back stolen cars. They'd been a nuisance for a half-dozen years now.

"They have. Not even a sniff of them."

"Well, I'll be. It's a miracle." Cade laughed.

"It's more likely they're staying away because of the increased police presence that the Twin Killers brought on," Rob said. "So, I haven't been doing much."

Rob took a drink and looked off in the distance.

Cade grinned. "Of course, you can help with our task force. I'd love to have you. You don't have to ask twice."

"Technically, I didn't ask."

"But you really did."

"I didn't."

"You did, but let's move on. Agree to disagree, and all that."

Rob shrugged and took a drink. "So, tell me where you're at."

Cade set his coffee next to his plate. "No doubt you've heard we've stopped the second killer. Which means it's down to one. But he's been remarkably adept at keeping his face from any cameras. He has an instinct to know where they are. After drugging his first victim in Edina and pushing her into the back seat, he held up his middle finger to the camera. But his hand was held directly in front of his face."

"Smart and smug. We really need to shoot him."

"Yes, we do. We did get him on video with the killing of the sex worker in Saint Paul. Let me send you the link, so you see for yourself what we're dealing with." Cade pulled out his phone. "It's the file labeled Midway. You can fast forward past the parts where nothing is happening."

Rob navigated to the file and started watching. "No sound?"

Cade shook his head. "Be thankful there isn't."

While Rob was watching, Cade's cell buzzed. It was Rook.

"Yo, boss. I got something."

That was music to Cade's ears, and his ears hadn't heard music for a while now.

"What do you have? Don't keep a guy waiting." Cade stepped away from the table. He wanted his full attention on Rook.

Rook sounded excited. "The killer is from Phoenix. I spoke with a detective there. He said they refer to him as the Jaguar. He's had seven confirmed kills, but they believe he may've been responsible for as many as a dozen more. This killer, the Jaguar, preys on women who are intelligent, tough, and successful. Not the usual easy-to-acquire victims."

"Are all 19 possible victims of the same type?" Cade asked.

"For the most part. He said that several of the possible victims include men."

"Really?"

"Really. They were earlier in the Jaguar's timeline, apparently. But the detective said they haven't been able to confirm it was our guy that killed them."

Cade paused as he thought. Then, "I'm most interested in the outliers. If he killed these men, it's likely he had different motivations than for the ones that fit into his pattern. That motivation may reveal more than the others do. What do you know about these male victims?"

"I have their names. The crime scene documents have been uploaded to Dropbox, but I haven't had the chance to look at them yet. I'm sending you the link now."

"Can you send the link to Grace at the BCA? I'd like her to look them over."

"Sure thing."

"One more thing. Can you head over to the university computer lab and meet with Crocker or Kenzie? Now that you discovered the killer's origin city, they can pull up all the postings he's made. See what he's posted recently. We need to find where he is now."

"Can do, boss."

"Let's get this guy before he kills again." Cade ended the call and returned to the table, waiting while Rob finished watching.

After a minute, Rob set down his phone and said nothing as he stared into the distance. Cade gave him his space. He'd been there.

After a long moment, Rob said, "Well, hell. That was seriously disturbing."

"Couldn't agree more. Any observations?"

"There's something seriously wrong with him. I know these pattern killers are wired differently than you and me, but everything about that was off the charts psycho. Who did he call just before he used the knife?"

"The victim's mother."

Rob didn't say anything for a moment. The only tell was the clenching of his jaw muscles. Cade knew his partner and recognized it for what it was. Rob was furious. "That's a level of cruelty I hadn't experienced before. I understand that he's not feeling our same emotions, or possibly any at all, but why does he want others to feel such depths of hurt and terror? What is he getting from it?"

Cade stared ahead, his face unreadable. "No idea. It's beyond my understanding. However he came to be, he's evil incarnate now. The devil himself could be no worse."

Rob leaned forward. "Funny you should say that. I noticed something with his tattoos. Did you get a good look at them?"

Cade slid a folder across the table.

Rob looked through the pictures in the folder, pausing at a blowup of the killer's bare torso.

"These tattoos are so intricate, with so many details woven in throughout. It looks like some language I don't recognize or some sort of ancient hieroglyphics."

"I never understood art," Rob said. "It doesn't have any discernable meaning."

"That's where you're wrong, old friend. All art has meaning," Cade said with a grin. "Though most of it means 'I'm horny and have religious trauma.' But we haven't been able to identify or decode any of the killer's symbols. Not a one." Cade folded his arms.

Rob pursed his lips and squinted as he stared at the image. Suddenly, he jumped and knocked over his coffee. "No way." Rob's eyes were wide.

Cade sat up. "What? Did you see something?"

Rob pushed the picture across the table. Cade picked it up and held it close. He didn't see anything he hadn't seen a dozen times already.

"I think you're looking too closely. Hold the picture out and squint a bit."

"I don't—"

"Just do it."

Cade held the picture at arm's length and scrunched up his eyes.

"See how parts have more weight than others?" Rob asked. "It goes down his spine and across his shoulders."

Cade's mouth opened. "It's a cross, the crucifix."

Rob shook his head, "Technically, it would need to have Jesus on the cross to be a crucifix, but yes it's a cross."

"I can't believe we didn't see it."

"You were looking too closely at the trees." Rob picked up his coffee and leaned back. He paused with the cup near his lips. "But we don't know the context. In other words, what it means to him, the killer. Only then would we have insights to what he's got going on in his head."

Cade picked up his cell. "I'm going to let Grace know what you discovered. Maybe she'll have an idea." He paused as he read through a text. "This is from Rook. He called while you were watching the video. He made the connection that the killer was from the Phoenix area. Apparently, he's responsible for at least seven kills, possibly a dozen more. They refer to him as the Jaguar there."

"Interesting. I never know who comes up with the nicknames for these killers."

Cade shrugged. "I think it's usually the media. They like to brand everything. Gives more weight to the story by making the unsub into a countercultural icon."

Rob smiled. "Countercultural icon? You sound like a college boy."

"I did go to some of my classes." He set his cell on the table between them. "Rook sent over the Phoenix files."

He paged through crime reports and crime scene photos. There were close-ups of the knives left on the scene. Another page detailed potential cases. Of the 11 named victims, two were men.

"Men too?"

Cade leaned forward. "I was intrigued by that. Any victim who doesn't fall into the killer's usual pattern may tell us more about him. I have to believe they were personal to him. Someone he knew."

Rob nodded. "That makes sense. Did Phoenix P.D. find anything unusual with them?"

"Not that I'm aware of. But Grace will be going over the files. Maybe she'll see something."

Rob stroked his chin absently. Cade let him think while he texted Grace about Rob's cross discovery. She replied right away, saying that she should have caught that.

"Those men," Rob said, before lapsing back into thought.

Cade mentioned the analogy of the forest and the trees, and said he'd missed it too.

"Have you pulled the flight information from incoming Phoenix flights? Looked at names of men that arrived shortly before the Jaguar started killing here?"

Cade nodded. "We have. I borrowed a couple of rookie detectives from St. Paul and got them working through the list. Last I heard, it was still close to 800 names after ruling out the women and obvious couples traveling together."

Rob held up a finger. "This may lead to nowhere, but why don't you see if these two anomalies, these men from your Phoenix file, are on that list? Anthony Scott Jarn and Patrick Sean Flandrick."

Cade tipped his coffee cup to his Patrol partner. "Brilliant idea. Our killer could be flying using identification from his victims."

Maybe it was the caffeine, but he was buzzing as he got back on the highway.

CHAPTER 26

Rook was surprised. The computer lab was empty. Well, almost. Someone was hunched over the last computer station in the back.

"Hello," he called tentatively, not wanting to startle anyone. "It's me, Detective Rooker."

"Hey, Rook." It was Kenzie, the grad student. She stood and stretched.

"I don't think I ever saw this place so empty."

She gave a weary smile as she rubbed her eyes. "They're all at a thing for Courtney. I probably should have gone too, but I wanted to be here. It seemed like the best way to honor her was to keep working on the Orbiting Cortex site. She wanted desperately to stop these guys."

"I get you. I'm dead tired and need a drink, yet here I am, too. Doing God's work." He sat on the edge of a table.

Kenzie gave him a look. "Is that what this is? It feels more like grunt work."

Rook laughed. "I guess that's how my father motivated me to do my chores. He'd say that we should delight in doing the little things, that if those things were important to God, they should be important to us. How else do you get a seven-year-old boy excited to take out the trash on a cold winter's night?"

Kenzie raised an eyebrow. "Did that really get you excited?"

Shaking his head and laughing, Rook said, "Well, no. But it gave me something to say as I ran to the cans in the dark. It could be a little scary out there at night."

Kenzie moved a little closer and stood across from him, her arms folded across her chest. "Do you really believe in God?"

"I do," Rook said. "I take it you don't."

Her pale blue eyes looked into the distance. "I can't say I've ever seen anything that would lead me to believe. Certainly, no actual proof."

Rook shrugged, wondering how the discussion had taken this left turn. "It's not really a matter of proof, is it? That's why they call it faith. It's more like a feeling."

"Explain." Kenzie held her rigid stance in front of him.

"I'm a detective, and in my profession, we don't often see the whole picture right away. Sometimes, it's only a glimpse of something. Maybe an observation here, maybe a disconnected observation there. But our brain can put disparate things together. That's where a hunch comes in. We get a gut feeling that something isn't right, or if these things add up, we'll have our proof. My belief is the same way. I can't point to one single thing as indisputable proof, but I know. I just know."

Kenzie shook her head. "I'm much more science-based. Nothing is real until it can be proven. Until then, life is a series of random events without meaning."

Rook laughed. "You must be a lot of fun at parties."

"I can tie a cherry stem into a knot with my tongue," she said with a twinkle in her eye.

"Good enough for me," he said with a grin. "Maybe we'll have to grab a drink together after all."

Smiling, Kenzie asked, "So what brought you into the dungeon this evening?"

"Our active killer, the one that started this whole thing, is from the Phoenix area where he's known as the Jaguar. He's killed at least seven women. Since you guys were able to pull the geolocation from uploaded images, what can you tell me about the user that's posted the images from Phoenix?"

Kenzie led him back to her computer station and gestured to a chair next to hers. She navigated through several pages before stopping. Lit by the screen's glow, her face looked cold, but beautiful at the same time.

"His username is Ghostface. He's posted 37 times over the last 36 months, so roughly once a month on average." She scanned through the data in front of her. "Of course, it's not that uniform. There'll be months without a post and then a cluster of posts when something apparently piqued his interest. For instance, he posted five times after Dawkins caught Marlin Sweetwater. That certainly caught his attention."

"What did he have to say about it? Maybe I can learn something so we can catch this killer too."

Clicking on a link, Kenzie read, "Dumb luck from a simpleton."

"Pardon me?" Rook asked.

"That's the message. His first response to the news. I'll keep reading the others." She scrolled. "Maybe not just luck, but someone with more going on intellectually would leave the detective chasing his own tail. I would not be stopped. My faith is my shield."

She looked up and read the next one. "Some interesting side plots happening in MSP."

"Hmmm," Rook said. "Not sure what that means."

"Another one," Kenzie said. "Sweetwater was onto something. The spotlight makes things...interesting."

Rook jotted down the post. Interesting.

"And finally," she said, "Achieving notoriety means living forever. Look at Gacy. He'll never go away. You can do it through sheer numbers and an enduring career, but don't you want to enjoy the adulation? There's another way. Striking fear into the sheep with audacious kills goes a long way, fortune favoring the bold and all that. It's how you get into the spotlight and the spotlight brings fame. But what about the person shining the light? That's another level, that's instant notoriety."

Rook stopped writing. The implications of the Ghostface posts were staggering.

Kenzie turned to him, the soft glow of her screen highlighting her eyes. "What do you suppose he meant? The person shining the light."

Rook scratched his head. "If I had to venture a guess, it sounds like he's referring to the media. They're the ones putting the killings into the public's attention."

Kenzie leaned forward. "It could also mean the detective. This is the person shedding light on the crimes done in the dark. And think about it, killing the person charged with stopping the murderer is bold. That's what Sweetwater wanted to do. There's no greater challenge."

"You may be right, but it comes down to the motivation driving the killer. Murdering the detective is the right call if they're looking to best the challenge. But if they're looking for fame, it might be killing a media celebrity. The question is, what's driving Ghostface?"

Kenzie put a hand on Rook's knee. "Your life could be in danger, you know. The killer could be looking at you right now. How do you work when you know danger awaits behind every curve?"

Rook regarded Kenzie, her gentle touch more than a little distracting. She wore a Gopher sweatshirt and jean shorts that showed off her legs. Rook was tired, but not that tired.

"I don't know, I focus on what I'm trying to accomplish and not worry about what may or may not happen."

Kenzie stood up and held out a hand. Rook accepted it and she pulled him up. "I could go for that drink you mentioned earlier. It's been a long day."

"There's a lot of bars near here," Rook said, "but I don't know which one to recommend."

Kenzie laughed. "I guess I'm not much of a college student. I don't know the bars here at all. But I'm new here. Moved to the Twin Cities for the graduate program."

"I didn't realize that. So, where should we go?"

Still holding his hand, Kenzie said, "I don't think I'm ready for crowds. Do you have a bottle of wine at your place?"

"I have two," Rook said.

"Sounds dangerous."

"Danger is my middle name."

"That's funny. It's mine too. Let me grab my bag," Kenzie said as she let go of his hand. It was still tingling.

The door clicked shut behind them as they headed down the darkened corridor.

CHAPTER 27

Jarn stood in front of the mirror, staring at his reflection. He hadn't yet gotten used to the look of his goatee. He'd had a beard for the last three years, but a change in cities meant a change in appearance. Coming here was intended to be short term, but there was something to be said for the change in climate Minnesota offered. You couldn't discount the relief the cooler weather brought, especially when you wore black every day.

He reached up and plucked off his collar.

Some may say the collar makes the priest, but Jarn believed otherwise. It was how you viewed the world and how you carried yourself. The love you showed and the caring you demonstrated to your community. The internal compass of the word colored your decisions day in and day out.

He unbuttoned his shirt and discarded it on the weathered wood floor as he stared at the man in front of him.

The bare-chested man who looked back had an internal compass too. But this compass was damaged. He knew that, but also accepted it as being beyond his control. Like much of life—like fast and slow, hot and cold, and of course, good and evil—there was a dichotomy running through his earthly existence. The embodiment of his love was on display in his work and not just on Sunday mornings. He ministered to his community with tenderness.

But on the other hand, he was compelled to kill. The desire could simmer for a while until it became all-consuming. And truth be told, he enjoyed the hunt.

He unbuckled and took down his pants, kicking them into the heap with his shirt and collar. It was time to become.

Ava Anderson came to mind and ultimately to his body. The blonde newscaster would be a tasty treat to enjoy. He found her intruding into his thoughts when he was living his other life, and that could be bad. Jarn had always been able to compartmentalize his two halves. Both sides respected the other's boundaries, allowing for peaceful coexistence. But when thoughts of prey intruded, he knew action was the only way to keep the animal inside at bay.

Ava Anderson, with her fresh face and athletic physique. Ava Anderson, with her beautiful eyes and blonde hair. Ava Anderson, submissively cowering at his feet. He picked up the Morakniv, enjoying the feel of the knife in his hand. The blade was razor-sharp and ready. He held out his left arm and drew the sharp edge across his forearm. It cut, but not deeply. He'd need both arms for what was to come. Right now, he just wanted the blood.

Using his fingers, he smeared the blood across the cut. He held the bloody fingers in front of his eyes for a moment, before smearing a blood trail across his chest. Repeating the action several times, he painted a symbol formed of blood on his chest. Jarn luxuriated in the power of the symbol and lost himself in an Ava Anderson-fueled fantasy while the blood dried.

It could have been hours or minutes, but when he came back, the blood had dried. It was time. Jarn tugged on a tight black pullover and matching black track pants, the urgency rushing him. Black socks, shoes and a drawstring bag, also black, with his tools for the evening. He looked at the man standing in front of him. A killer like no other stared back from the abyss.

He was ready.

CHAPTER 28

"I found him." Detective Thao sounded excited.

Cade sat up. "Wait, what?"

"I'd sorted the arrivals and car rentals based on the six cities you requested. Los Angeles, Charlotte, Milwaukee, Toronto, Richmond, Portland and Phoenix. And since then, you've had me focus on Phoenix. I narrowed the list to 228 potentials for the unsub that arrived in the specified time period. I had queried ViCAP to see if there were any matches."

The Violent Criminal Apprehension Program, or ViCAP, is a database designed by the FBI to help catch the nation's most violent offenders by linking together unsolved crimes.

Thao continued. "There were no matches, but I'm discovering not many departments use the system. It's not mandatory for them to enter their cases like it is in the Canadian version. Only something like 80 out of 100 of the largest police forces in our country use the database. Phoenix is one of the 20 that don't use ViCAP, as it turns out."

Cade was getting impatient. "But you said you found him."

"I did. It wasn't until I ran the names of the male victims that Phoenix sent over that I found him. It was earlier than we thought. Two weeks ago, an Anthony Jarn arrived on the Southwest flight from Phoenix. This Anthony Jarn, as it turns out, was murdered nearly three years ago. But apparently, he was feeling well enough to have rented a car." Cade heard the smile in her voice.

"If he arrived several weeks ago, what do you suppose he was doing all that time before his first kill?" she asked.

"Good question. Most likely getting the lay of the land. Serial killers are notoriously detailed planners—at least the organized ones. Keeps them from getting caught."

"Tell me about the rental."

Thao cleared her throat. "Using the Jarn ID, he'd rented a silver 2022 Chevy Cruze. The license plates were found on a Nissan Altima at the airport. Unfortunately, he looks to be switching license plates frequently. The Nissan plates, which were seen on the killer's car at the restaurant in Edina, were found on a vehicle that spends time at a park and ride in Maplewood. A trooper entered the plates from that car on a Civic she'd pulled over. That car had four lacrosse players driving home from a tournament, so clearly not our guy. We're looking for the Civic's plates, but so far, there's nothing."

"He's careful. It would surprise me if he hadn't already switched the plates several more times." Cade stood up and paced as he liked to do when he thought. It cleared his head and helped him be more creative.

"What about hotels? He had to stay somewhere. You don't come to a new city and not have a place. There's always the chance he forced his way into someone's home and is hiding there, but that doesn't feel right. We need to check the hotels."

"I may be new to this detective thing, but I'm not new to being thorough," Thao said. "Kristen and I have been calling all the hotels in the metro area. We started with the core area of the two downtowns and then moved our perimeter out into the suburbs. Anthony Jarn stayed one night at the InterContinental in downtown St. Paul. After that, we haven't been able to see where he's been."

"Well, shit."

"I know."

Cade took a step and paused. "What about the other male victim from Phoenix? Maybe he's that ID as well."

"Damn. I should have thought of that." There was a pause. "He was killed at his church. His name was Patrick Flandrick. A catholic priest."

"See what you can find under his name. There must have been a reason he was killed as well."

"Will do," she said. "What are you gonna do?"

"I'm going to the InterContinental. See what I can learn." Cade paused. "I appreciate the great work you two have done. Let me know if you come up with anything from the Flanders ID."

Overlooking the Mississippi River, the InterContinental was a luxury hotel that stood tall in contrast to the rundown Midway motel, site of the killer's last murder. Driving past the Xcel Energy Center, home of the Minnesota Wild, Cade went up Kellogg until he saw the hotel. One advantage of law enforcement was not having to look for a place to park. He drove right up to the valet and identified himself. The valet suggested he back up and leave it right there, promising to keep an eye on the truck.

Inside, the lobby counter was stacked several deep, and he headed for the concierge desk to avoid the wait. The woman glanced up and smiled.

"How can I help you?" Her nametag read Sherry Preister.

Cade sat at her table and slid his badge case across. "I'm looking to learn as much as I can about a recent guest here at the hotel. Room charges, video, like that."

"That's not my area, obviously. You really should be talking to our general manager. Let me have him come over." She picked up a small radio and spoke briefly. "He'll be right out."

"Thank you," Cade said and looked around for surveillance cameras. There were a few in view.

A round-faced man with designer glasses approached. He was dressed in an expensive charcoal suit with a gold manager nameplate on his breast pocket.

"How can I assist you?" he asked, his manner professional but friendly.

Cade showed his identification and said, "I'm looking for whatever information I can find on a recent guest of yours. His name is Anthony Jarn."

There seemed to be a wall that went up. The earlier friendliness had gone away. "I'm sorry, officer."

"Detective."

"As you may well imagine, within the hospitality industry, guest information is privileged. We do not share information about our guests, certainly without a signed warrant from a reputable judiciary official. And even then, I will need a waiver to come down from corporate before any—and I will stress—limited information can be released. My hands are tied." The general manager said this with the finality of someone answering the first question of a quiz game show.

Cade took a deep breath. It was his tried-and-true strategy to avoid saying the first unpleasant thing that came to mind when he dealt with assholes, the stubborn, or in this case, both.

"I get that your hands are tied. But his victim's hands were tied too. It made it easier when he used his knife on them. Your guest, Anthony Jarn, is a serial killer. He's responsible for the brutal deaths of up to 17 women in Arizona and now he's here. So far, he's murdered two Twin Cities' women." He looked at the concierge. "Most of his victims have been intelligent, professional women." Cade held up his phone as he scrolled through images of victims and their crime scenes. "Do you really want further deaths to be on you because your hands are tied?"

He leaned back, arms folded, waiting for the man's response.

The general manager held Cade's gaze and said nothing.

"Dale..." the concierge began.

He held up a hand. "Fine. But this lives and dies with you two. If word got out—."

"It won't," Cade said. "I'm only looking for something that can point toward his current location. He needs to be stopped."

Cade followed him to his office, a richly appointed space with a cherry wood desk and a vanity bookcase with a dozen framed photos of famous guests posing with the manager and staff. Cade recognized two of them.

Cade waited while the man navigated through the hotel's database. The manager confirmed Thao's earlier statement that Jarn had stayed just the one night. There were no additional room charges. Next, the general manager brought up the hotel's video feed from the check-in day.

"I'm surprised, pleasantly, that it's in color," Cade said.

"We've found that upgrading to color cameras in our higher traffic areas was worth the investment. It has made it far easier and faster to identify individuals among the horde."

"Got it." Cade stood over him as the video fast-forwarded to the right time.

"That should be him," the manager said, pointing to the screen as the video played at normal speed. A lone man pulling a suitcase and carrying a duffel over his shoulder walked up to the counter. He wore a baseball cap that hid his face from the lens. Not once did the suspect lift his gaze during the interaction between the front desk clerk and the killer. The camera caught nothing helpful.

"I'm guessing that wasn't terribly helpful," the manager said. "He never showed his face. Not once."

"This one is incredibly wary of showing his face to cameras. So, this doesn't surprise me." It didn't make him any less angry at the fact either.

"Let's go to the next day for checkout," the manager said as he pulled up more footage. Together, they watched the footage of the front desk. No one looking like their suspect appeared. "Not all our guests do a formal checkout. Some simply leave. Although guests are encouraged to drop off their room cards in the lobby box, many leave them in their rooms."

"Well then, this isn't going so well." Cade sighed. But he wasn't ever going to give up. "Wait, they still have to leave, don't they? Can you pull up a camera that shows your guests as they're leaving?"

The manager nodded. "I'm not sure how that will help, but I live to serve."

Cade gave him a sideways glance, but the manager's straight face convinced him to let it go.

As before, the video streamed by at an accelerated rate as people fast-marched across the screen. Then, Cade pointed.

"There. Can you bring it back a bit?"

"Of course."

The man who caught Cade's attention entered the screen. Pulling a suitcase, he also had a duffel slung over his shoulder.

"Look at the duffel bag. That's got to be our guy."

The manager sniffed. "Generally speaking, we are not a duffel sort of establishment. This could well be your suspect."

"Will you be so kind as to back it up and pause when there's a good view of him?"

"It would be my delight."

Cade shook his head and leaned forward as the manager froze the video. Although the unsub wasn't wearing a ball cap, his head was down. It appeared the man was looking at his feet as he walked, which meant there wasn't a view of his face. Again. The man wore a black suit with a black shirt underneath. No tie.

Cade looked at the manager. "I would be interested in hearing your observations about him. What do you notice?"

"Several of the many qualities that can make a hospitality professional stand out are their powers of observation and rapid assessment. I sincerely appreciate your recognition of the fact."

He zoomed in on the man's feet. "See the light reflecting off his shoes. That means they're likely leather that's been cared for. Polished. Notice the way the trousers' hem breaks ever-so-slightly on the shoe? His is a tailored suit."

Moving the focus higher, he paused in the man's mid-section. "Only the top button is used. He knows how to wear a suit. The gentleman's bag obscures his side here, but when you look at the opposite side, you see how it is pulled in here?"

"I do."

"That tells me this is not an off-the-rack suit from the Men's Wearhouse or JC Penney. It's an expensive suit. He's not wearing a tie, but that doesn't mean that much in today's more casual environment. It used to be de rigueur that ties were worn whenever a suit was worn, but that standard has relaxed. Myself, I prefer a tie to express my unique individuality."

Cade glanced at the man's plain blue tie.

"Anything else?" Cade asked, ready to leave. He moved toward the door.

"There is something else if you are interested." The manager held his gaze.

"I am extremely interested." Cade stepped back toward the desk.

"I went to a private university out east, and although it was run by the catholic diocese, we didn't have the stereotypical nuns with rulers. While most of the professors were lay, the school's leadership was nearly universally clergy." He pointed to the man's neck at something Cade hadn't noticed. "And that, my friend, is a clergy collar."

CADE'S HEAD SPUN. The second male victim in Phoenix was a catholic priest. Patrick Flandrick. He killed the priest to become a priest himself?

Didn't see that coming.

He picked up his cell and saw a message from Rook.

Met with Kenzie. Phoenix killer posted about getting notorious by killing the person shining the light on his deeds. Could mean you or the media. Subject to interpretation obviously. Getting some R&R. Later.

Cade decided to call Rook but got his voicemail. He left a message telling Rook it was urgent and to call him back ASAP.

Wanting a sounding board with this new information, he called a familiar number. Grace had always been helpful with her perspective and deep knowledge base. She answered on the first ring.

"Cade, I was just going to call you." She sounded breathless.

"That's what they always say."

"No, this is important." Grace sounded anxious. "Look, I just heard something, something you're not going to believe."

CHAPTER 29

"It wasn't a hit and run," Grace said.

Wait, what? Cade pulled over to the shoulder.

"I spoke to the coroner. Courtney had bruises from the car, but she was stabbed a dozen times. Cade, Courtney was murdered."

"Oh shit," he said as ramifications coursed through his head. "Was this the work of our first killer? It couldn't be the second. He was at the convention center stalking Mystique. It had to be the first killer."

"It doesn't feel right," Grace said. "Yes, he uses a knife, but this doesn't match his previous M.O."

"Maybe it was a crime of opportunity. He saw her and made a quick decision." Even as he said it, he knew it didn't feel right. This killer was methodical and didn't leave things to chance. He liked to take his time with his knife. Draw out the ordeal for the victim.

"No," Grace said with complete conviction.

"I agree," Cade said quickly. "I spoke too soon. This wasn't the work of the first unsub. This is something else, but I have no idea what. Coincidences happen, but not to the computer person who gave us the best ideas. She's the one who came up with the idea to look at geotags in the posted images. I have to believe she was targeted."

Cade paused. "One other thing. Professor Tubbs recently blew a gasket when he found out the grad students posted about helping with the investigation on social media. I'd told him they might be putting a target on their backs."

"It looks as if that might have been the case. Do you know if Courtney was posting, too?" Grace asked.

"I have no idea, really." Cade ran a hand through his hair. "We'll have to check now that we know she was murdered."

Both paused under the weight of the moment.

"So, why were you calling me?" Grace said after a moment. "Was it about the cross on the killer's back? Religion does play a large part in the life of many serial killers. Many come from strict or repressive religious backgrounds."

"That relates to why I called. But it's bigger than a strict upbringing with this one. Beyond the oddly formed cross tattooed across his back, our killer has taken it further. Way further."

"Really? Do tell."

Cade took a deep breath. "When we learned of his Phoenix origins, the detective there said they have confirmed seven of his kills."

"Yes, you sent over the case files."

"But there's a good chance he was responsible for many more, including two men."

"I saw that too."

"Good," Cade said. "Those two men are important. And by the way, I now consider them confirmed. Our killer used the ID of one of them, Anthony Jarn, to fly here and rent a car."

"Confirmed. And the other man?"

"You're extremely impatient. Has anyone ever told you that?" Cade asked.

"Fake news. But yeah, I've heard that."

"Anyway, he used the ID of the second man to reserve a room at the InterContinental hotel in St. Paul. The victim, Patrick Flandrick, was killed in his own church back in Phoenix."

"Interesting, but okay."

"This is where things go from interesting to pretty damn intriguing. We caught our unsub on hotel surveillance video as he left."

"Really? Did you get a look at his face this time?"

Cade paused. "Well, no. It's ingrained in him to avoid getting any camera face time. But, the interesting part was what he was wearing."

A pause. "You're going to make me ask, aren't you?"

"Yep."

"What was he wearing?"

"I'm glad you asked. The killer was wearing a black suit—with a clergy collar."

There was silence on the line.

"You didn't see that coming, did you?" Cade asked.

"Not at all. Holy hell, what is he up to?"

"You got me. It's a great cover, but it feels at odds with the smooth-talking ladies' man we witnessed when he charmed his first victim to leave with him."

"Agreed. You don't think of that sort of dynamic personality when it comes to members of the clergy." Grace paused. "There's something I feel we're missing here, but I can't for the life of me figure out."

Cade laughed. "I know you. It'll come. It always does."

"I appreciate your support. You always did look out for me."

"Someone has to," Cade said. "Can't leave you to your own devices."

"Whatever that means. Using devices wouldn't be my first choice."

Cade snorted. "That's not where I was going. At all."

They both laughed for a moment, then, "Anywho," Grace said. "What else do you know?"

"I got a text from Rook about what our killer has been posting. Let me read it to you. '*Met with Kenzie. Phoenix killer posted about getting notorious by killing the person shining the light on his deeds. Could mean you or the media. Subject to interpretation, obviously. Getting some R&R. Later.*'"

"Hmmm," Grace began. "Did he give you any more details on what he wrote? I'd love to read his exact wording."

"No, and he hasn't returned my call or texts. He must be exhausted."

"As we all are," Grace said. "That's the nature of these big cases. You grab onto them, trying to understand what's happening and who's involved. Before you know it, the case has grabbed you and will not let go. You not only have trouble sleeping, but you also don't want to sleep for fear of missing something. Food becomes an annoyance. Friends are forgotten, and even sex is an afterthought."

"A warm afterthought."

"Amen."

"I've heard that rest is a weapon," Cade said. "If you can carve out time to recharge, you'll function better, and you'll gain some advantage over your opponent. But like much in life, it's easier said than done. Hopefully, Rook will get back on grid soon with a better brain than my tired one."

"Hopefully," Grace agreed. "Let's go back to Rook's message. Beyond a killer's previous actions, the best predictor may well be his words. From the glimpse Rook left us, the unsub wants to gain notoriety. Certainly, mass shooters are often driven by their narcissistic traits to seek fame through their killing sprees. The same can be said of serial killers. It may fly in the face of the fact that keeping a low profile would extend their careers, but many killers have contacted the media and even originated their own moniker. So, we have our unsub posting to other killers, that he could better gain notoriety by killing the person who is shining the light on his deeds."

"Yeah, that's what Sweetwater was after by targeting me. It was the ultimate challenge." Cade still had those middle of the night, lying awake, thoughts about what happened and how much worse it could have been.

"I don't think this is the same. I haven't gotten the sense this killer is here just to best you. Sure, he came here because of the challenge from the site, but he hasn't reached out to you at all. I think, for him anyway, coming here offers a larger spotlight for him to work under.

And if I'm interpreting things correctly, that spotlight is the media's attention."

Cade's stomach churned at the realization her words offered.

"These killers want people to be terrified. It's like how Fox News works, getting more attention through sensationalism, which results in people being mad and afraid. That's what he wants, to spread fear and panic. And when you think about it, what better way to create a media sensation than to kill one of their own?"

CHAPTER 30

Jarn sat in the dark of the quiet suburban street. He'd been in the neighborhood many a time lately, even smiling and waving to the unsuspecting locals. A genuine smile always worked magic, though his collar certainly helped. It was a matter of trust. Misplaced, but that was on them.

Anderson's modest home was the second from the corner. There were lights on in the bedroom and a faint glow from the front room. He guessed her kitchen was nearby. And she was home.

But he stayed put, sitting in the quiet, waiting, watching. He wanted to absorb the neighborhood energy and flow, get the rhythm of things. See if there were furtive glances from the edges of curtains, a glow of a cigarette from a darkened room, or maybe a lack of dog walkers. Really, anything that didn't feel quite right. He wouldn't put it past the detective to have people staking out Anderson, let alone all the high-value media targets. You don't catch his breed of hunter without anticipating your opponent's strategy and being moves ahead in the game. And the detective had a strategic mind.

Jarn had played chess in middle school but gave up the game when it became apparent there was a complete lack of worthy opponents. After the first handful of games, he started winning. It wasn't long before he could beat anyone in the room in minutes. It was then he challenged the club teacher supervisor to play him. For some reason, even he no longer was willing to play after his third straight loss. The man wouldn't look him in the eye as he tried to pass him off to other students. So Jarn walked away.

One by one, lights blinked off in the neighboring houses. It would be time soon enough.

Then there was a car at the corner. It paused before turning onto her street. Jarn slid down, not wanting to have his movement noticed. He kept his eyes on the vehicle, just in case. If he had to make a move, he wanted to be ready. The car came alongside. It was a white SUV that looked like every other white SUV. It drove past him without slowing and was soon lost beyond the curve.

Patience was the key to survival. He would wait. A little longer.

EVERYTHING WAS BLURRY. Rook's head felt like it was the morning after a particularly rough night of drinking. The kind that even the slightest head movement caused an ache to the entire brain. Like that. Only worse by double. He closed his eyes.

Deciding his best strategy then would be not moving, he had time to think about what led him to this present moment. It was confusing, as he didn't actually remember going out drinking. Usually, times like that involved people, laughter, music, and drinks. None of that sounded familiar.

He furrowed his brow, which hurt, too. So, he unfurrowed and tried to recreate what led him to this condition. He'd been to the University of Minnesota lab. Yes, this was a positive step. He remembered talking with a graduate student. It was Kenzie. Yes, Kenzie, the one with the pale blue eyes. He liked her because she was different and more mature than most of the grad students. She was likely just five or so years younger than he was. It had been an emotional day, with the loss of...he struggled with her name. What had he been drinking?

But, yeah, someone had died.

They were both feeling the loss and had decided to have a drink together. Where did they go? Visions of driving and checking his rearview to see if she was still with him. And then being relieved to find two spots outside his place. On-street parking could be challenging in his neighborhood. They'd gone to his home.

So, was he in his own place? He briefly considered opening his eyes to check but abandoned the idea when a wave of nausea hit. There was a reason most people didn't drink like they were in college. The price was too large. Ahh, adulting.

He went back to recreating the evening. Kenzie and her haunting pale blue eyes. Walking to his door, wondering what surprises the evening might hold. Opening the door. Flipping on the lights, Kenzie's appreciation of his place. Listening to his recent vinyl purchase. De La Soul. Wine. The couch. Turning off some lights. Those pale blue eyes. Then...

That's where things got off track.

Try as he might, he couldn't go any farther. It was like a wall of darkness went up, and there was no way around it. He couldn't think of anything that might have happened beyond that. He even tried to furrow his brow. No joy.

He was going to have to open his eyes.

His left eye didn't feel the need to open for some reason, so he went with the right one. Still blurry, he wasn't sure what he was seeing. Maybe a change of view. He steeled himself to shift, knowing it wouldn't be easy. It wasn't.

It was impossible.

The why of the impossible intrigued him. There was a reason, he simply had to sort it out. If his brain was firing on all cylinders, he'd have a ready answer for sure. But as his mother often said, you worked with what ya got. He squeezed his right hand. That worked. Same for the left. His feet moved, toes wiggling in his boots. Right arm now. Nope. Left arm. Same thing. But why not?

He tried to bring his hand to scratch his nose. Not happening. It felt like his arm was stuck at his side. Both arms in fact. Like they were immobilized somehow. A flashback to those cartoons he'd watched endlessly as a child. The ones where the villain—Snidely Whiplash?—captured the hero, binding him up in an impossibly large spool of rope, leaving him on the railroad tracks in front of an oncoming locomotive.

He tested his arms again.

A feeling of panic raced through his very core. He was tied up.

CHAPTER 31

Ian was working the board at the station. Radio had significantly changed over the last decade. Even though some stations had their hosts drive into the station, the new norm was that they could call in from anywhere as long as they had a clear signal with a quality microphone. It was only fitting on a national program called Coast to Coast AM, that he could host from his home studio. It was also a tad ironic that he was nowhere near either coast.

The overnight show leaned heavily on conspiracy theories and the paranormal. The more outrageous the better. Got a story of a ghost dog caught on video? Bring it on. The Bible and extraterrestrials, most definitely. Killers that feed on blood, living in New York sewers? Hell yes. As crazy as it sounded, airing these kinds of stories had been a recipe for success with millions of avid listeners spread around the world, thanks to affiliate stations carrying the program as well as satellite radio and the internet.

As a frequent guest host, Ian thought the program was entertaining. The guests came across as impassioned believers. The listener call-ins added a level of unpredictability and kept the show's fans coming back day after day. It certainly wasn't dull.

The first segment had wrapped up, the guest talking about his abduction experiences. Ian let a little of his skepticism show, which had his guest getting worked up as he went on. It was great radio. It was a fine line as a host, you didn't want to accept everything as gospel, but you didn't want to call your guest a liar, either. Finding the balance was something Ian excelled at.

Keying the mic as the commercial concluded, Ian said, "Welcome back to the second hour of Coast to Coast AM. The nights are getting longer and the blood moon is full. Let's open up the lines and see what's on your mind. Clay, who do we have?"

His producer, and oft-foil, came on. "We have Adrian, who says he knows something about the serial killer plaguing the Twin Cities in Minnesota."

"Yo, Adrian. Thanks for calling. You may not know this, but I used to hail from St. Paul. I hosted a morning radio show there with my wife. Great area. What are you up to tonight?"

"Not much, just chillin' like a villain."

Ian continued. "I've been following the Twin Killers case, and it's been horrific for the people living through it. Even though one of the two has been caught, another is still out there. So, tell me, what do you know about this killer?"

The voice was low but firm when he spoke. "I know a few things about him. Things that aren't common knowledge."

As a host, Ian appreciated the teaser the caller was giving. It kept people listening.

"We'd love to hear about them. I know from the media accounts, the police are getting frustrated with their lack of progress."

"Yes, there hasn't been much they can do to stop him," he said. Ian thought the caller sounded oddly pleased with that. "The first thing I know about him is he listens to your show. Religiously."

"You mean, twice a year? On Christmas and Easter?"

"I mean he follows the show regularly whenever he can."

"Really?" Ian let his skepticism out a little.

"Really. And although the killer is from the southwest, he's enjoying the Minnesota climate. He's considering making it a permanent move."

"I may have to stop you there. There's really no way you could know this." Ian paused. "Unless..."

"Yes," the caller said forcefully. "Unless I am the killer."

Ian took a drink of his earl grey. This was an intriguing development.

In his experience, things could go one of two ways from here. The man will show himself to be a fraud and he'll laugh it off for the rest of the program. It'd happened before when some so-called witness to a saucer crash turned out to be some wag pulling a prank. The other way would be the man showing actual insider knowledge and broadcast history would be made. Either way, Ian was buckling up for the ride.

"Let's be frank with each other. Are you the other half of the Twin Killers?"

Ian swallowed and waited.

"While there were two of us, we were not equal halves. He was an animal."

There you have it, Ian thought. Instead, he said, "Just because you step on a cornflake, it doesn't make you a serial killer. The challenge we have here, on our program that strives to get to the truth of the matter, is that not everyone on here speaks honestly. I'm not calling you a liar, but I am doing my due diligence. Can you give me something that only the Twin Cities law enforcement would know? Maybe something about one of the crime scenes?"

The pause was pregnant with the expectation that the caller would end the call. Ian held his breath.

An instant message from his producer popped up and read, "Keep it moving."

Still Ian waited. This was the moment.

Then...

"The first victim had a number that would be significant to the detective, Dawkins."

"What do you mean when you say had a number?" Keep him talking.

"I wrote a number and circled it so it wouldn't be missed. Trust me, the significance of not only the number but how I wrote it, wouldn't be lost on him."

"Trust is a hard thing to come by, and it needs to be earned. Obviously, I can't confirm your statement at this time, but the fact you've shared it with me has helped. So, Adrian—which I assume is not your real name."

"It's not."

"And what else do you want to share with the Coast to Coast AM listeners?"

"I'm parked on a quiet suburban street. The neighborhood has gone to sleep, oblivious to what is to come. I am outside her house, and soon I'll make my entry."

Another instant message read, "Holy hell. Is this for real?"

Ian's goosebumps were telling him this was in fact real. He replied, "It feels like it."

The caller continued. "I've also done my due diligence and scouted her place thoroughly. There's no alarm system and no dogs to slow me down. Her doors are steel reinforced, and the locks are quality, but that doesn't mean anything when the window in her study is open. It'll take less than a minute to get inside. And then..."

He let the words hang there.

Ian wasn't even a little torn. Whether or not this was a legendary moment in the show, he had to do something. This man had to be stopped.

Ian picked up his cell. Who to call, though?

Ava Anderson pulled her Audi into the garage and hit the button to close the door. Once it was closed, she slid out of the car. Her Louboutins clacked on the clean concrete as she headed for the comfort of her home. Ava liked the sound her heels made. It reminded her of her mother. She smiled, thinking of her and her sister, just kids, listening to their mother's black pumps as they struck the wooden floors when she got home. Depending on the cadence of her clacking, they could usually determine just how mad they'd made her. Hard and fast, with almost no time between each step meant she was mad. Light clacks with long strides were comforting, reminding them of a joyful mama who loved them very much. Mom transcended from omnipresent caretaker to full-fledged woman in the world by the way she presented herself: hair always done just so, brightly painted fingernails, and patent leather heels.

Ava loved the feeling she got when she wore her heels. Confidence, power and femineity, all wrapped up in one glamorous package. There was no sound more riveting and sexier than the distinctive clicking sounds of stiletto heels as they echoed their presence on a hard floor. It was not difficult to notice the looks she received from both men and women when she strode into the room.

But the issue was, she thought as she sat on the entryway bench, you could only wear them for so long. She slid them off and rubbed her tired feet. In the world of television news, there wasn't a lot of time to be off one's feet. It was run here, run there, from one meeting to another, story meetings, production meetings, all day long. A proper soak in the tub would help with her sore feet. Right after a snack, and of course, a glass of wine.

She padded off to the kitchen while the night's broadcast ran through her head. You were only as good as your last show, and she'd felt off all evening. Her partner, Barry Weiss, had been grating on her lately. Sure, Barry had been in the business for a long time—some said too long—but he really was a pompous asshat. His superior attitude and grandstanding weakened the show's credibility. Her producer, Megan, told her to ride it out. She said his ornery mood was because he was constantly upstaged by Reynolds Devries with the Twin Killers story. But Ava knew better. Barry was always an asshat.

Pouring herself a glass of chenin blanc, Ava grabbed some fruit and sat at the island. The plus side to working with the man was getting a lot of plum stories that Barry thought were beneath a journalist of his stature. The thing she'd learned from the start was that there was no refusing work. You took what was given, did your absolute best and made it your own. It was a foundation you were building, and as time went on, you found your voice. Then, when you spoke at meetings, the producers listened to you and your ideas.

Ava knew her career was a journey, and any shortcuts she might be tempted with would only end up hurting her in the long run.

As attention-getting as the Twin Killers story has been, her work on the dynamic priest who was transforming his south Minneapolis parish was better journalism. Megan thought it was some of her best and said she would enter the piece in the Page One Awards for the best in Minnesota journalism. Possibly for a regional Emmy award, too.

The priest was intriguing, making her job a whole lot easier.

Topping off her glass, she clicked off the overhead lights, leaving on the one over the sink. She double-checked that she'd locked the garage door before heading for the sanctuary of her bathroom and her waiting tub. A girl couldn't be too careful these days. There were a lot of crazies out there.

CHAPTER 32

Cade felt things were coming to a conclusion. Maybe not a logical conclusion—this was law enforcement after all, but something different was in the air. He hoped it would mean the end of their killer. As if to punctuate that feeling, Crocker called and got directly to the point.

"You need to tune in to Coast to Coast AM now. The killer is on the radio."

"Really? Is it for sure him?" Cade asked as he searched for the program. "Anything I missed so far?"

"Yes, he mentioned the Five logo he wrote on the first victim's body. I don't think that was released to the public."

"No, it wasn't. Well, shit."

The killer's voice came on.

"...Once I'm inside her house, I can take my time. She's alone. There's no one there to complicate things."

"I need to stop you right there," another voice said, most likely the radio host. "I can't in good conscience let you continue. If you're contemplating a crime—"

"I am definitely contemplating a crime."

"Who is this woman you've clearly been stalking? You can tell me, I'm all the way in Kansas. I can't stop you."

That a boy, Cade smiled.

"Not so fast. You have listeners..."

"Are you kidding me? It's nearly two in the morning, no one is listening."

The killer laughed. It was not a pleasant sound. Think evil clown meets used car salesman. Only worse.

"I'll give you this. Her death will be news. Big news." He laughed again and was gone.

"We're going to break now, but if you're in the Twin Cities, lock your doors. It looks like it will be a long night. Our prayers are with you. And if you're in law enforcement, stop this maniac. He needs to be put down. Tonight."

The station went to a commercial, and Cade switched it off. He picked up the phone. "Crocker? Are you still with me?"

"I'm here," Crocker replied. He sounded dragged out. "This guy..." His words trailed off.

"I know."

Crocker cleared his throat after a moment. "I tried to reach Rook, but there's no reply. Does he make it a habit of going off-grid in the middle of big cases?"

"I don't believe so. This is our first time working together, but from what I've seen, he's all in. He doesn't seem to be here only for the paycheck."

Cade ran a hand thru his hair as a call clicked in. "I'm getting another call, but a thought. Last I knew, Rook left the computer lab and was going to get some rest. He said he was talking to Kenzie. Could you check with her, see if she knows anything?"

The call clicked again as Crocker said he would check with Kenzie. Cade switched over.

"Detective Dawkins, this is Russ Horstead from 911 dispatch. Calls are pouring in from all over about a radio show. Apparently, someone claiming to be the killer is on the air."

"It was him. I caught the end of it, and it was chilling."

"Hey, sorry, but there didn't seem to be anything actionable from what we've gathered. No names, no addresses, not even a general location of where he intends to strike. He said the woman's study had an unlocked window, but that doesn't help much either. He's a pompous wanker if you ask me." There are times Horstead's British accent came out, and this was one of those times.

"Can't argue with your assessment." Cade paused. "He did mention that her death would be news. Since my ex-girlfriend is the cities' most prominent news person," Cade began.

"Ex? Sorry to hear that, mate."

"It's fine. But could you send a car over to check on her and stay there until first light? There's a very real chance she's his target."

"I'm on it. I'll send two to be safer. Take care, mate."

Cade pulled up a contact, his finger poised, before setting the phone back down. He put the truck in gear and drove a hundred yards before swerving off the road.

"Damn it."

He picked up the phone and looked at Reynolds' contact. Relationships brought complications, both good and bad. He decided he had to make the call.

Her voice thick from sleep, Reynolds croaked out, "Hello?"

"Reynolds, it's me. The killer was just on the radio."

"Seriously? Radio is so dead."

"Reynolds, focus. He made a threat that sounds directed at a woman in the media, possibly at you."

"Possibly? Elaborate."

"He said his next victim would be news, big news." As he said it, Cade thought it sounded weak and regretted calling. But he was already in and couldn't turn around.

"Just to be safe, dispatch is sending a car or two to your neighborhood."

"I'll be fine, my outside lights are on, and the doors are bolted."

"Look, I'm only ten minutes away, I—"

"Cade." There was something in her voice that gave him pause. "I'm not alone. I didn't want to say it, but you gave me no choice. I'm sorry."

That was a left turn he hadn't expected.

"Understood." He didn't know what to say.

"What else do you know about the killer?" Reynolds asked.

Thankful for a change in conversation topics, Cade went with it.

"He was based in Arizona before he came here. He killed at least seven women there with possibly a dozen more victims. They called him the Jaguar there."

"That's funny."

"Not really funny."

"No, I mean funny as in a coincidence. There's another story that's captured the local media's attention. There's a priest who's transforming his south Minneapolis Parish. He's calling it his den, and his congregation is his pack. He's also from Arizona."

There's a moment in life when the Vegas slot machine's spinning numbers slow down, as the first seven comes to a stop, quickly followed by a second seven. And, as you're holding your breath, the third seven makes its appearance. And then as it clicks into place next to the others, everything makes sense.

Oh, shit.

"Wait. What can you tell me about him? I missed the story. I've been kind of busy."

"Not much really. I never covered the story myself. Ava Anderson, the newer anchor at the Fox affiliate, broke the story and the rest of us jumped on. When there's an interesting story with a different angle, you'll see it appear on all the stations. Ava got there first, but she also seemed to capture his attention more than the rest of us, and he opened up. There was chemistry there."

"How do you know that?" Cade wondered.

"Oh, we talk occasionally. Anyway, I believe she did three interviews with him."

"Do you remember his name?"

"Patrick something or other. Flanders or Flandrick, like that." She paused. "Why do you ask?"

Cade pumped a fist in the air and then took a breath and tried to keep the excitement out of his voice. "I was curious, as I haven't heard about him," Cade said. "A feel-good story would be a nice change of pace these days."

"Okay," Reynolds said, but her tone sounded like it was anything but okay. It didn't matter as long as he got her off the phone.

"Sorry to bother you." Cade ended the call, not waiting for her response.

Sorry, not sorry, as they say.

AFTER ROOK REALIZED he was tied up, the first thing that came to mind was concern for Kenzie. Was she okay, had she been attacked, and was she still alive?

He opened his mouth, or more accurately, tried to open it, but it was taped shut. As much as he loved it, there was also an evil side of duct tape use. He struggled against his bonds, which only brought on another wave of nausea. With his mouth taped shut, choking was a genuine possibility. He stopped struggling, but the restraints brought on a feeling of claustrophobia. He pushed back his rising panic and took in several steadying breaths through his nose. After a few minutes, a sense of equilibrium returned. One eye opened again, and he took in his surroundings.

Rook was at his place, in his living room. He was in a chair. Nothing was knocked over or out of place. There was no blood either, thankfully. No sign of Kenzie, though.

Rook turned as far as he could toward the kitchen, hoping to see the grad student. The effort brought on a fresh wave of nausea and Rook had to return his head to center and breathe through the wave. When things subsided after a difficult minute, he ever so slowly turned in the other direction. He was worried about Kenzie and needed to know.

There were legs on the couch, but that was as far as he could turn. He was sure it was her, though. Rook tried making noise to see if she heard. But the body remained still. There was no way to tell if she was tied up or dead.

It was then that he saw it.

A brutal-looking knife sat on the couch in front of her.

CHAPTER 33

Cade worked his phone while he steered toward the freeway. His first call was to the 911 response center and supervisor Russ Horstead.

"Russ, I need an address for an Ava Anderson. Can you pull the DMV database and get me her address?"

"Sure thing, buddy. Do you have her DoB?"

Cade ran a red light and shot down the ramp onto Highway 36, headed west. "Sorry, no. Read me the names you come up with. We can narrow it down."

"Hold on, I'm on it."

The east metro highway was as deserted as an office on the Friday after Thanksgiving. With no other vehicles in front of him, he pushed the pedal down, and the truck soared past 80.

Russ was back. "This isn't terrible. I have five Ava Andersons."

"I can work with that. She should be mid-twenties, with a limit of 35 years. She was described as being newer to the television station." He was approaching 90 miles per hour.

"You didn't tell me there would be math."

Cade did a quick calculation in his head and said, "She'd be born after 1987."

"That helps. There's two now."

"Okay, where do they live?" Cade steered onto 694 and gunned it.

"One's in Minneapolis, near Lake of the Isles and the other is in White Bear Lake."

"I'm right by White Bear. It's the next three exits." Cade paused.

"Can you pull up her license picture? Does she look like someone that would be on TV?"

Russ laughed. "No, she looks like my mum, to be honest."

"Okay, then. What about the other Ava?" He passed the first White Bear exit.

"Definitely not my mum."

"Okay, send me her address."

"I'm assuming this is regarding the Twin Killer. Should I notify Minneapolis P.D. to route some units over there as well?"

"Hold off, this is a hunch, but I don't want to spook him either if he's there. I'll be in touch as soon as I know something."

"Godspeed, buddy. Godspeed."

Cade tried his partner again, but it maddeningly went to voicemail again. This was bad timing to be enjoying a break off the grid.

Taking the exit onto 35E south, he brought his speed up on the straightaway. His cell pinged with Russ' text. A click brought the address into maps and told him he'd be getting back onto Highway 36 and heading west.

Next, he called Kristin. She answered on the second ring. "Where are you?" he asked.

"Downtown St. Paul. What's up?"

"The killer was just on a national radio show. He said he was outside a woman's house and was going to go in."

"Damn."

"I know. He said the woman's death would be news, big news. But get this, Rook had texted me earlier and said the killer had posted about getting notorious by killing the person shining the light on his deeds. I think he's going after a woman television anchor."

"What would you like me to do?"

Highway 36 had more traffic, but Cade had plenty of space to maneuver through without slowing. His speed was now over 100 miles per hour.

"I'm headed to Ava Anderson's from Fox, and Reynolds Devries from the Five is already covered. Get ahold of Lorie and figure out the other possible targets and get cars over there pronto. This guy is in play tonight, and he needs to be stopped."

"Will do, boss."

"Be careful."

"You too."

He passed the empty Rosedale shopping center and merged onto 35W south. The skyline of downtown Minneapolis lay before him. People in bed, people still up, some working, some partying. All oblivious to the killer in their midst.

One more person to call. Grace answered on the first ring.

"Where are we at?"

"Remember we caught the killer on video leaving the hotel dressed as a priest?"

"Yes..."

"Have you caught the news stories about the south Minneapolis priest that is transforming his congregation?"

"No way!" Grace shouted. "No effin' way. That's our guy? I knew I was missing something, but this? I figured religion was important to him, but to actually become a successful priest after killing the original one? Color me surprised."

"I know."

"So, we go to his church and pick up his sorry heathen ass."

"We can't wait that long. There's more you need to know," Cade said as he got to the 35W bridge that had collapsed in 2007.

Cade ran through the killer's radio appearance and the "big news" clue he'd given.

"This fits." Her voice rose in pitch as it did when she got excited about something. "We talked about him wanting to create a sensation by possibly killing someone from the media," Grace said. "It sounds like that's his play. You have an idea who he may be after?"

"A Fox reporter, Ava Anderson, first broke the priest story. She's been out to see him a few times since. Reynolds mentioned they had chemistry. It feels like our best option. And that's where I'm headed."

"What if you're wrong and it's someone else he's moving on?" Cade appreciated her willingness to challenge him.

"I thought of that too. I have Bednarek and Thao getting squads out to the other media possibilities."

"And Rook, he's backing you up?"

Cade was on 94 now with the ramp to Hennepin Avenue coming up. "Sadly, no. I haven't been able to reach him since he sent a text saying he was grabbing some R&R. My calls go to his voicemail."

"Should we be concerned?" Grace asked.

"That's a good question, but there's an immediate crisis, with someone's life in danger. We have to focus on stopping the killer."

"Send me the address, and I'll back you up."

An image of Grace with her leg opened up by the sickle blade of the Blonde Killer flashed in his head. But Grace was one of the most intelligent and resourceful law enforcement professionals he knew, and he couldn't refuse her help.

He read off the address from the maps app. "I'm less than five minutes away, and I won't wait for you. Just know I'll likely be inside when you arrive."

"I won't shoot you. Promise."

Cade barked out a laugh. "Get your ass moving then."

THE WATER WAS the perfect temp, and the tub was lined with candles. Her refilled wine glass was on the ledge next to her iPad. All she needed for such an ideal scenario would be a partner. But her dating life was on hold—and dating apps deleted—while she focused on her career. But was that healthy? It was her father, not surprisingly, that recently reminded her that life was about balance. He'd sent her a quote from a commencement speech made by Brian Dyson, the former CEO of Coca-Cola, in 1991.

"Imagine life as a game in which you are juggling some five balls in the air. You name them work, family, health, friends and spirit. And

you're keeping all of these in the air. You will soon understand that work is a rubber ball. If you drop it, it will bounce back. But the other four balls—family, health, friends and spirit—are made of glass. If you drop one of these, they will be irrevocably scuffed, marked, nicked, damaged or even shattered. They will never be the same. You must understand that and strive for balance in your life."

Easier said than done, but Ava had cried when she first read it, and kept it with her. She knew she needed to have a life outside of work. She certainly met a lot of interesting people along the way. Maybe something organic could spring from such an encounter. But in a man's world, her priority would always be her career.

Ava opened her robe and let it fall around her feet. Glancing at her reflection, Ava was happy with what she saw. Her hard work at the gym had been worth it. Sliding into the tub, she loved the warm embrace of the water as it enveloped her body. She picked up her glass, thinking this moment of self-care was taking care of two of those balls, health and spirit.

Ava picked up her iPad and navigated to the latest episode of her favorite true crime podcast. If she had one guilty pleasure, it was true crime. The more salacious, the better. Dead bodies found in trunks, awesome. Unexpected killers in the neighborhood, perfect. Murderous stalkers breaking into unsuspecting victims' homes in the dead of night, delightful. Bring it on.

The narrator began. "In 1978, Rodney Alcala won a date on the popular TV show, The Dating Game. What no one knew was that he was a prolific serial killer in the middle of a cross-country murder spree."

"Yes," Ava said, but then hit pause as she listened. Had she heard something?

After a moment, and not hearing anything else, she hit play again.

The narrator continued. "Leaving behind a trail of murdered women..."

CHAPTER 34

It was time. The killer slipped out of the car.

Even though the interior light was switched off to avoid attracting attention, he knew no one was left awake. The neighborhood continued its oblivious slumber as he crouched and gently pushed the door shut. He waited a minute to see if his activity created any interest, but no. The sheep slept.

Climbing the steep hill between houses, he moved efficiently and effortlessly. There was a gate in the woman's privacy fence that he pushed open. It swung silently, thanks to the WD-40 he'd sprayed on the hinges during his previous scouting visit. It was all about preparation. Minimize risk and have contingencies, should the unexpected arise. It was a routine that had kept him alive so far.

Flicking on his flashlight, the red beam lit his way. The red light allowed him to see in the dark without ruining his night vision. He'd found it on an astronomy website and knew it would be an essential element of his kill kit. Rounding the house to the back corner, the woman's study and unlocked window waited. For such a moment as this.

Crouching by the window, he knew there would be no going back. Climbing through someone's window was an indefensible move if someone saw him. It was like a burglar exiting the house carrying a big-screen television. Anyone observing would know instantly what was going on. He crouched, unmoving, for a full three minutes. He moderated his breathing while listening as far out as he could. Satisfied, he raised up and lifted the double-hung window.

Quiet for the first several inches, as when he tested it earlier, but the last several inches groaned in loud protest. The sound echoed in the stillness.

He froze but decided action would be the most prudent move and wriggled through the opening. If someone heard something, it would take a few moments to look out the right window. If they did, he'd already be safely out of sight inside.

Inside Ava Anderson's home.

He couldn't help but smile, thinking of what was to come.

Slipping off the bag, he pulled out the Morakniv Companion, sliding the blade from the sheath. The handle felt right in his hand. With this came power. He got to his feet and moved farther into her home. The stillness of the house reassured him as he placed one foot quietly and carefully in front of the other. Anderson would likely be in her bedroom, but he wanted to get the lay of the land first. A solitary light burned over the kitchen sink, a single dish by its side. The rest of the kitchen and dining area were remarkably free of clutter. Not even a piece of mail, gloves or keys anywhere to be seen. He respected her orderly world.

Moving around the corner, he opened the first door. It was her laundry room. A single basket lay on the counter, the items inside neatly folded, panties on top. He closed the door and unlocked the adjoining one. This was the garage. Her still-pinging SUV, parked at an angle, was the lone vehicle in the garage. The shelves were orderly, with labeled boxes. He pulled the door shut.

Moving down the hall, he peered into the bathroom. Simple elegance, with not a towel out of place. It looked ready for company.

A guest bedroom was across the hall, the bed made, dresser and nightstand free of clutter. A single book lay on the nightstand. Curiosity getting the better of him, he stepped in to read the title. *Creating Your Reality.* He dropped it on the bed, uninterested. He was in the business of manifesting his own reality. No self-help book was going to augment that.

Anderson's master bedroom was at the end of the hall. The door was ajar, and he pushed it open with his foot. With the door creaking open, he brought up the knife with the intent to pounce if needed. But, the room was empty.

An expansive walk-in closet was next to the bathroom. The door was half open, enough to see rows upon rows of expensive clothes and shelves of high heels. The woman didn't hurt for clothing options.

Light came from under the closed bathroom door, and there was the sound of someone talking. He pressed himself against the door, needing to know if Anderson was alone. One doesn't usually talk to themselves for such a long time. At least he didn't. Those kinds of people were crazy.

The irony wasn't lost on him. He knew the things he did, what he strove to become, set him apart from pretty much the entire human race. But embracing his humanness wasn't his goal. Jarn longed to ascend from his earthly existence to become more. Exactly what that "more" looked like was an unknown. He'd know when he got there. It was a journey of death and rebirth.

The voice sounded like a recording, like Anderson took her Netflix binging to the bathroom. To each their own. In the gaps between the talking, there was splashing. It sounded like Anderson was in the tub. After a moment of internal debate, he decided to wait for her to come to him. He'd have her soon enough.

WITH HIS GPS app telling him Ava Anderson's house was on the next block, Cade turned the corner and parked. He didn't want to come in hot and force the killer's hand. He was here to save Anderson, not incite violence against her.

One other vehicle was parked on the street, a silver Chevy Cruze. The killer drove a silver Chevy Cruze when he abducted the Albright woman in Edina. He was here. Cade knew it.

He placed a hand on the car's hood, feeling the cold metal underneath his hand. Either it was someone else's vehicle entirely or the killer had been here for a while. But to be safe, he pulled out his pocketknife and plunged it into the front tire's sidewall. He didn't want the killer to get far if he managed to slip away.

Turning the corner, Ava Anderson's one-story rambler was the second house from the corner. The street was quiet, dead quiet. That would quickly change when he called Russ back at the 911 dispatch center. But Cade wanted to confirm the killer was at Anderson's before calling in the cavalry. If his hunch was wrong, it wouldn't look good on the news.

To get to the rear of Anderson's home, you had to go through a wooden privacy fence, the kind you'd find guarding a backyard pool. He headed for the gate, slipping his weapon from its holster.

A nearby owl let his presence be known with its distinctive call. The moon was bright in the cloudless sky.

The latch was quiet, and Cade pushed his way through. There was indeed a backyard pool sitting covered. With his Glock leading the way, Cade moved farther around the house. Every shadow held a potential threat, with a killer waiting with a knife that Crocodile Dundee would be proud of. But there was no other way, and he kept moving. When Cade saw the open window, any remaining doubt vanished.

He was here.

The first call went to Grace. "He's here. There's an open window in the back of the house."

"Can you wait for me? I'm minutes away."

"Every minute could mean her life. I have to go in," Cade whispered.

"I get it. And I wouldn't have waited for you either. Just saying."

"Good. Now hurry."

He ended the call and then reached Russell.

"He's here at Anderson's. The rear window is open enough for a man to get through and a silver Chevy Cruze is parked around the corner. That's the vehicle he drove when he grabbed the first victim."

"I'll get squads rolling. We'll set up a perimeter and have SWAT do the entry."

"I'm going in. Every second counts. Remember, don't shoot me. Also, there's a BCA agent right behind me, Grace Fox, so tell them there are two officers on scene."

"Roger that."

Cade put away the phone and crawled up to the window ledge. Raising himself up, he peered through the opening. No one was in sight. It was some sort of home office with a desk and bookshelves lining the wall behind it. With eyes on the doorway into the house—where the threat would likely come from—Cade climbed into Ava Anderson's home. Moving slowly, as not to call attention to himself, he entered headfirst. Not willing to put away the Glock, Cade had to balance with one hand as he landed on the hardwood floor. He didn't exactly stick the landing, but at least it was relatively quiet.

He took a moment to catch his breath and listen. All was silent.

Moving through the doorway, he passed the kitchen and dining area. A light was left on over the kitchen sink. No sign of a struggle. Just the opposite, in fact, it looked like the house was ready for the realtor showing. Everything was perfectly placed.

He moved down the hall, his Glock sweeping in front of him, pausing at the laundry and guest rooms to clear them. Nothing.

Up ahead, toward the bedroom, a light was on. One foot in front of the other, he headed that way.

Expecting the worst, he stepped into the bedroom. Not only was the room empty, but the bed was also undisturbed. Anderson hadn't been to bed yet. Cade swept the room, past the walk-in closet, makeup mirror nook and bathroom. He moved toward the bathroom, where a light was on behind the closed door. A voice came from the room.

"Alcala may have killed as many as 130 victims before he was caught. Thankfully, he was caught and died in prison. Join us for our next episode—" The voice, most likely a narrator, was cut off. Cade recognized the name as a prolific killer from the seventies. Rodney

Alcala was smooth-talking, charming and deadly. Sounds familiar, he mused.

Then, everything that had been coming together, came together.

Some would call it a shitshow. Most everyone would later agree with this.

The door opened to the bathroom and Ava stepped out. Wearing nothing but the towel that she was tying, Ava paused when she realized she wasn't alone.

"Oh," was all she said and dropped the towel.

Not expecting this in any possible reality, Cade lowered his weapon, at a complete loss for words.

"BCA officer, freeze," Grace announced as she stepped out from the corner. Her weapon was pointed at Cade. Recognition flashed, and she lowered it, eyes flicking between him and the naked woman.

Still at a loss for words, Cade shrugged.

From the corner of his eye, a shadow in the walk-in closet became a man moving toward them. There was something in his hand.

"Gun!" Grace shouted.

Chaos ruled as gunfire erupted.

Cade dropped to the floor, pulling Anderson with him. The man fell back into the closet. Grace also dropped, falling back around the corner.

That's when a man, shirtless, but wearing black pants and shoes, stepped out from the makeup nook. Dried blood was smeared across his chest in some sort of symbol, and as he turned, a heavily tattooed back came into view. After surveying the room, he turned back to Cade and Anderson. From Cade's position on the ground, he looked seven feet tall. He had dark hair, a salt and peppered colored goatee, and a handsome face. The deadest eyes Cade had ever encountered stared into him. In the man's hand was a knife. It was the same knife used on Albright and Valley.

"It's you," Cade said.

"It is truly me," he said in a low voice. "And I looked, and behold a pale horse: and his name that sat on him was Death, and Hell followed with him."

"Patrick? Reverend Flandrick?" Anderson looked confused, seeing this man in her bedroom.

Where is it? Cade glanced around for his gun.

Kneeling, a smile grew on the killer's face as he brandished the knife in Anderson's face. "I am not the man you thought I was. You were deceived by my intelligence and cunning. I am so much more than what you saw. That I might fill them with horror so they would know that I am the lord."

"You have an enormous opinion of yourself," Anderson said. She looked him right in the eye. "You're nothing more than a deranged bedwetter with a room temperature IQ."

This was clearly a tactic that potential victims hadn't attempted with him previously. The killer lowered his knife and stared opened-mouthed at Anderson. Emboldened, she got up to her knees in her full naked glory and jabbed a finger at him.

"You really have no idea what's happening here, do you?"

No response.

"It's time women took back what has been stolen from us. Our confidence and fearlessness, our equality and equity. From here on out, we're rewriting our history."

Her words gave Cade the feeling her remarks were prepared, but he didn't know how that could be. Cade glanced between the two, curious where things were going.

"You're going to have to trust me," she told him. "I don't have the time or crayons to explain it to you."

Steel returned to the killer's face, and he snarled. Things happened fast after that.

The knife came up, slashing toward Anderson.

Kicking out, Cade connected with the killer's heel, dropping him hard onto his back.

Cade dove and landed on the man's chest as he grabbed onto the wrist that held the knife.

The killer strained to pull the knife toward Cade. He was stronger than he looked.

With a desperate move, he locked his teeth into the back of Cade's arm.

Cade grabbed two of the killer's fingers, bending them back until there was an audible crack.

With a roar, the killer took his mouth off Cade's arm. Suddenly free, Cade pistoned his elbow back, connecting with the side of the man's jaw.

Grace, standing over them, stuck the barrel of her service weapon in his mouth.

"Don't. You're done."

The arrival of the Minneapolis SWAT team took away whatever options he might have considered. The killer dropped his head to the floor with an audible thud. Cade rolled him over and cuffed him.

The three heavily armed SWAT officers looked around the group, no one knowing what to say. Cade turned to the very naked Ava Anderson.

"Aren't you cold?"

Grace broke out with a barking laugh before regaining control and paused. She pointed to the man they'd shot, still moaning on the closet floor. "Wait, who is that guy?"

Cade looked down at the man. No, he'd never seen him before shooting him. He'd remember someone so imposing. Cade looked back at Grace. "I don't have a clue."

Ava wouldn't meet his gaze.

"Ava. Who is this man?"

She didn't appear inclined to answer, content to study her nails.

As a pair of paramedics pushed into the already crowded room, Cade's phone buzzed.

"I have some news, but you're not going to like it." It was Crocker.

CHAPTER 35

"Hold on, Crocker," Cade said, walking out of the madness that was the crime scene. More and more officers entered the house, as well as another two teams of EMTs. He went back to the study and closed the door to hear the university professor over the commotion.

"It's a little crazy, but we got him. We got the killer."

"Thank God."

Cade sat back in the office chair with a sigh.

"Okay, what's your bad news? I think I can handle it."

There was a pause. "Kenzie switched the site to a proxy. That's why there haven't been any recent posts. She also had pulled the video clips, so we couldn't see the faces of the site members when they did their verifications."

This information had Cade sitting up. "I think you need to look at those video clips. Right now."

"What are you thinking?"

Cade stood up. "I think there has to be a reason why she did what she did. And I'm thinking about the fact that I can't reach Rook. He went to go see Kenzie at the lab last night. And now he's completely off-grid."

Moving fast now, Cade maneuvered around the heavy law enforcement presence in Anderson's house and ducked out the door.

"I'm headed for Rook's place. Call me after you look at those videos."

"Will do."

Emergency vehicles were everywhere. Minneapolis squads,

Hennepin County Sheriff, medical, firetrucks. Oh, and plenty of media. Ducking past all of them, Cade got to the corner and headed for his truck. There was an issue, though. He was blocked in. The vest-wearing reporter, Barry Weiss, leaned on the hood of Cade's truck.

"Not so fast. You're not going to duck me this time." Arms folded, Weiss wore a scowl on his face.

Cade felt his anger rising. "Now is not the time, Barry."

"I think otherwise." Weiss made no effort to move. "You owe me after your blatant favoritism with the Five. With the women of this market banding together, I need something."

The last thing he wanted was to help Weiss, but he also didn't want him to know about his concern about Rook. "Look, this has been a stressful situation for us all. There will be a major announcement and I'll grant you exclusive early access. That's all I can do right now."

Weiss looked both skeptical and hopeful. "Exclusive? On camera?"

Cade was frustrated with the delay. "Yes, yes."

He tried to push by Weiss.

"When?"

"Today, 6 pm."

"Make it 5."

"Fine. Now move your vehicle."

Weiss moved the station vehicle with a smug smile that burned Cade's insides. Ten seconds later, he was racing up Hennepin Avenue.

"I SEE YOU'RE AWAKE."

Rook jumped at the sound of Kenzie's voice. She was still out of his view, so he couldn't see if she was okay.

But then his world turned upside down in an instant.

Kenzie knelt in front of him. She held the knife.

"I can see you're confused. It might have been the drug I gave you. The dosage can be tricky, and I might have given you too much."

She toyed with the knife, running the flat side of the blade against her skin. It was an enormous knife, looking like the sort of knife that hunters could easily kill a grizzly with. He strained against his bonds, realizing how much trouble he was in.

"Are you uncomfortable? It is what it is, and you'll feel even more intense discomfort soon."

Her pale blue eyes studied him.

"You might have realized things are not as they seemed. Let's play a game of yes and no, shall we?" She didn't wait for a response. "No, I am not a grad student at the university. Yes, I came here because of the Orbiting Cortex challenge. Yes, Courtney was hit by a car. No, it wasn't random. She was too good at her field, and so I ran her down. And then stabbed her a few times. Just to be sure. I was concerned that she suspected I was not who I claimed to be."

Her eyes had a spark as she talked. Rook didn't like what he saw.

"No, she wasn't the first person I've killed. Yes, there will be more. It's an intriguing sensation to take someone's life."

Maybe it was the adrenaline, but Rook's brain was beginning to unfog. Running his situation through his head, he didn't like his odds. His arms and hands were bound to the chair, which was too sturdy to break. She'd tied him securely, leaving no room to exploit or wiggle free. He was gagged, so he couldn't call for help. His neighbors would be no help. Everyone kept to themselves here. Gagging also meant he couldn't reason with her, but as his momma always said, "There's no reasoning with crazy." The only possibility he could see was his lower legs weren't bound. He could kick her if she moved closer, even a few inches. But he wasn't sure what might happen after that. It might make her mad.

Angry and crazy wasn't his favorite combination.

"Here's what's going to happen. See this knife? It's a Karambit. Made in Indonesia, it was inspired by the claws of a tiger. Badass, isn't it? Ideal for close-quarters combat, the finger hole makes it difficult for opponents to disarm you. I've honed the blade to razor sharpness. It helps me relax." She smiled at her aside.

"Have you ever seen a fisherman scale a fish? You can imagine how much pain you'll feel as I remove your skin piece by piece. Not enough to have you bleed out, but enough to inflict maximum pain. Pain can be such a good way to clear one's head. Chases the cobwebs right out."

She ran a finger along the blade's edge, drawing a small drop of blood.

"Anywho, I've always wanted to castrate someone. Removing a man's testicle without anesthesia might be uncomfortable, to say the least. And when I'm done, I'm going to bring them home with me in an olive jar. How does that sound, Sparky?"

Rook swallowed hard.

"Let's get started."

CADE PICKED up the call as he took a hard turn.

"What did you find?"

Crocker said, "She's there. Kenzie was on the site's video clips. I'm working on compiling her posts, but it will take a few minutes."

"I don't have a few minutes. Rook's place is right around the corner. I have a bad feeling about things."

"Go with God," Crocker said and ended the call.

Rook's townhouse was a brick two-story on the corner of the four-unit complex. Set back on a hill, the townhouse overlooked a busy avenue. Rook's blacked-out Charger was parked out front. Seeing Rook's vehicle only made the feeling of dread grow. Feeling his time slipping away, Cade opted for the direct approach.

The Toyota truck jumped the curb at the corner and Cade drove down the sidewalk toward Rook's, the last unit. His front door was on the right, his bay window on the far-left side. His first thought was to dump the vehicle out front and make entry, but the feeling of dread had him. It was all-consuming. His field of vision narrowed, his heart raced, and every nerve ending was on fire. In his heart of hearts, Cade knew Rook was about to die.

He gunned it.

The FJ Cruiser, with its aggressive low-end torque and high clearance, was built for off-roading. Cade didn't see any other option and turned off the sidewalk and headed up the hill. Directly at Rook's fancy bay window.

"Ramming speed," he said for no particular reason.

The few rows of bricks below the window did nothing to deter the force of his truck. The wood and glass of the window gave up without even trying and he crashed through the new opening and stopped in Rook's living room.

Cade was out of the truck as soon as he got past his deployed airbag, his Glock sweeping the room. He'd seen an open-mouthed Kenzie dive out of the way as the collision launched debris across the room. She wasn't in sight at the moment. Rook was tied to a chair that was knocked on its side. His partner looked at him with wide eyes. Cade left him there as he moved farther into the house, searching for Kenzie.

There was a loud scream and a flash of metal as Kenzie burst out from behind the kitchen wall. Cade pulled back to narrowly avoid the killing strike, but the blade ripped through his thin jacket. His shoulder burned from where she scored him.

Even though Cade's service weapon was still in his hand, such was the viciousness of her attack that he hadn't been able to point it at her. With his shoulder injury, he wasn't even sure he'd be able to raise the pistol.

Her breathing was loud, rapid, and totally unnatural as she glared at him. Her hair hung over her eyes as she stared into him. It came out as a *he, he, he* sound. In her hand was a wickedly curved blade. She no longer resembled the trend-right, put-together grad student he'd met in the computer lab. Kenzie looked feral and ready to kill. Ready to pounce.

Cade shifted his position to move his injured side away from her as she came at him. The knife cut through the air catching the front of his jacket but missing him. Right away, she swung the blade in a backhand that narrowly missed.

He, he, he. Her eyes never left his.

She came at him again, a whirlwind of flashing blades. Kenzie wasn't tall, but her fury made up for it. The curved knife was deadly in close-up fighting, so Cade kept moving out of her reach. The trouble was, he was being backed into a corner. If she boxed him in, he was done.

The mind is a funny thing. It can take a situation that, from the observer's point of view, is moving at lightspeed and slow it down. He'd seen it with the greats of the soccer world. Sprinting at full speed with a defender at their side, watching a lofted ball coming diagonally over the top, adjusting their body to shoot it one-touch into the far corner of the net.

His mind saw a possibility. He'd have to get close to neutralize the knife. He knew his countermove was dangerous but also his last good option.

She came at him with a vicious slash, and he moved inside, his hip making contact with her midsection. At the same time, he grabbed onto her forearm and used her momentum to send her over his leg. She landed hard on the floor but kept hold of the knife.

Time froze.

She glared up at him and a snarl escaped from her twisted mouth.

She swung the knife.

It went deep into his calf.

In a moment of clarity, Cade knew he had one option before she was at him again with the knife.

Things slowed. He pictured being on the soccer field and the clock nearly run out. The goalie well out of position, and one hard kick from 35 yards would win the game. Cade wound up and kicked Kenzie in the forehead.

Her fight and consciousness evaporated instantly, her head lolled to the side and drool rolled down her cheek. But that was it for Cade, too, and he collapsed beside her. Her eyes were open inches from his, but he knew she was past the point of seeing him. Or attacking him again.

After breathing through the pain, he rolled over and crawled to Rook. The effort took everything he had. The partners looked at each other, exchanging glances as he summoned the energy to move again. After a moment, he reached over and pulled the tape from Rook's mouth.

"Hiya partner," Cade said.

"Yo, man. Look what you did to my place."

"Couldn't be helped. I'd do it again if I had to." Cade shivered, thinking about how close things had come.

"I appreciate the save, not sayin' anything different. But damn."

"Don't worry about it. You can stay at my place."

"I hope you keep it cleaner than your truck." Rook grinned. "That thing is an embarrassment."

"That thing saved your life," Cade said as he glanced at his truck. It was going to need a little TLC. "Looks like we're going to have to take your car."

"Think you can untie me first?" Rook asked. "This isn't exactly comfortable."

Cade tried to lift his right arm, but it wouldn't cooperate. "I don't believe I can. But I can dial 911."

"Make the call, man. Make the call." Rook said.

"911. What's your emergency?"

CHAPTER 36

Located adjacent to Rice Park, the St. Paul Hotel was the jewel of downtown St. Paul. Known for its old-world charm, European-inspired elegance, style, and sophistication, this was the place to go when you had something to celebrate. And even though he walked with a limp and had an arm in a sling, Cade felt like he had plenty to celebrate.

When Cade walked into the bar, he was greeted with applause. Rook, Grace, Kristen, and Lorie smothered him with hugs. Even though his shoulder made him wince, he didn't mind a bit.

"Have a seat, boss," Rook said as he pulled out a chair. "You look like you should be sitting down."

"Yeah, it might be a while before I play soccer again."

"Football is life," Kristen said enthusiastically.

Everyone turned to her.

"Sorry, it's from a show." She shrugged.

Rob and Capt. Rejene walked in and pulled up chairs to their growing table. "Thanks for the invite," Rob said. He nodded to Cade's shoulder. "Does it hurt?"

"Not as much as my calf, but all things being equal, I'm happy it wasn't worse," Cade said before ordering a Blue Moon from the server.

There were nods all around the table. They all knew officers who'd made the ultimate sacrifice.

Rejene introduced herself to everyone and said they did great work catching the second Twin Killer. "How did it go down? I'm curious how you knew where he might strike. There are all sorts of stories going around."

Cade nodded. "I can answer that. The killer, otherwise known as Anthony Jarn, Patrick Flandrick, and, as we found out, by his real name of Jeffrey Dobrunz, was from Arizona. Things broke when he called into a radio show. He said enough that we knew it had to be him and not some other whack job. He made a threat that sounded directed at a woman in the media. And Rook," he said, nodding to his smiling partner. "Learned that the killer was looking to gain notoriety by killing the person holding the spotlight. He said his killing would be news, big news. When I called Reynolds to warn her, she happened to mention a news story about a transplanted priest transforming his south Minneapolis Parish. He called it his den and his congregation his pack. And he recently moved here from Arizona." "There are no coincidences," Rejene said. "At least not like that."

Cade shook his head. "Not like that. Reynolds said that the story was really Ava Anderson's with Fox. When she mentioned Anderson and the priest having chemistry, my immediate hunch was Anderson would be his next target. But to be safe, I called Kristen," he said, nodding to her. "I wanted her and Lorie to cover the other media targets in possible danger. But my money was on Anderson. And as it turned out, I was right."

The server stopped to drop off their drinks. Cade held up his beer and said, "To great people and a successful outcome."

There was a chorus of cheers, and they all took a drink. After a moment, Cade continued.

"I entered her house the same way the killer did, through an unlocked window in her study. Anderson was in the bathroom when I got there. But as she stepped out, a man with a gun popped up in her closet. Grace, who I'd called to back me up, saw him at the same time. All three of us fired our weapons, but only the man was hit."

"Who was the guy with the gun?" Rob asked. "It doesn't sound like the killer."

Shaking his head, Cade said, "It was private security, hired by Anderson. Former special forces. He was shot twice, but he'll be fine."

"Wait a minute," Lorie said. "Marin Nelson had private security at her house, too."

Kristen nodded. "So did Natalie Dunn."

Cade looked at both detectives. "They had cameras set up too, didn't they?"

Both nodded. "How did you know? I didn't see them right away, but when I performed a security sweep, I found two cameras, one in her closet, one in her bedroom," Kristen said.

"Same," Lorie said.

Taking a drink, Cade leaned back. "Something felt off with Anderson. Okay, a few things. Her willingness to drop her towel. I mean, who does that in front of the police? Also, her speech to the killer. It felt oddly prepared. The other thing was, before going to Anderson's, I'd called Reynolds and offered to come check on her. She'd told me she wasn't alone.

Grace gave him a concerned look.

"But I know Reynolds. She doesn't open up easily, certainly not just a day or so after we broke up. That's not nearly enough time for her. So afterward, I called and pushed her a bit. She and the other female anchors got together because they believed one of them would be targeted by the killer."

Rejene nodded.

"But they didn't want to play victim. Instead, they thought they could take advantage of the spotlight it would bring. So, they hired a security firm that discreetly placed guards in each of their homes. Cameras were hidden. One point of entry was left unlocked. And a speech was written that each memorized."

Rejene scowled. "I don't know what to think about that. It's either remarkably cold and cynical or remarkably brilliant. Possibly both."

"Anyway, in the aftermath of the altercation with her security, the killer emerges with a knife. We get into it, and he bites my arm. Grace shoves her gun into his mouth and tells him to cut it out. Then Minneapolis SWAT shows up to haul off our now-handcuffed killer."

"Damn," Rob said.

Cade nodded. There was a moment of quiet.

"How'd you know that Rook was in trouble?" Rejene asked.

Leaning forward, Cade said, "It didn't feel right that he went off-grid, but events were moving so fast I couldn't do anything until we caught the killer. And then, right after Minneapolis P.D. showed up, Crocker called and said Kenzie had switched the OC site with an older version. She also had hidden the video clips members used to verify identities during login. I knew Rook had been with her right before he disappeared. I had a bad feeling about Rook and knew I had to get over there."

"Okay," Rook said. "I need to admit something. I was the one who brought her back to my place..."

"But you didn't know she was a killer hiding in plain sight," Kristen said. "How could you?"

Cade stroked his chin. "It's funny, Rook mentioned early on that someone was acting odd at the university computer lab, but I never realized who he was talking about.

"I was actually talking about Tubbs," Rook said with a half smile.

"Oh," Cade said. "I never noticed anything with him either."

Grace spoke up. "Sometimes people are just difficult to read. The tools and strategies we use to make sense of people aren't exactly reliable—especially people we don't know. And because we don't know how to talk to strangers, we often misinterpret them."

"But I knew you were in trouble," Cade said, looking at his partner. "The feeling kept getting stronger and stronger, so I took the direct route when I got to your place."

"You drove your truck through my window. Right into my living room." Rook shook his head. "But you did right, man. Thank you." He patted Cade's arm and looked away.

"Kenzie woke up in cuffs and was madder than a three-legged dog trying to bury a turd on a frozen pond."

Rejene choked on her beer. "Say what?"

"Kenzie was madder than a mosquito in a mannequin factory? Anyway, Kenzie thought she was too smart to get caught by me. Guess she got that wrong." Cade smiled.

"The media didn't think you were the right man to catch the killers, but they were wrong, too," Rob said. "Especially that vest guy."

"Barry Weiss." Cade shook his head.

"What an ass hat." Rejene folded her arms. "People like him make our job tougher than it needs to be."

"We've all had run-ins with self-serving news people," Rook said. "But Weiss is the absolute worst."

"Couldn't agree more," Cade said before taking a long pull from his Blue Moon. "Speaking of Mr. Weiss, I had another run-in with him as I was trying to leave to rescue you."

"Go on," Rook prompted.

"I wanted to shoot him, but that's frowned on."

"It's true," Rejene said. "There's so much paperwork."

"What did you do then?" Rook leaned forward.

Cade smiled. "I made him a deal. He got out of my way with the promise of a reward. I told him he'd have an exclusive with our big announcement. And that we'd do it on his camera."

"Wait. What announcement?" Rook looked at Lorie and Kristen. Both shrugged and looked back to Cade.

Cade laughed. "You'll have to hear it from our new task force spokesman."

"Wait, we have a spokesperson?" Lorie asked.

Cade took another luxuriously long drink and set the empty glass on the table. He made a show of checking his watch before standing up.

"And that announcement should be in a few minutes. The Barry

Weiss Report is staging that announcement in the lobby of this very hotel. Let's adjourn to the lobby to witness Barry getting his well-deserved reward."

"I have a feeling he won't be happy with this," Grace said, not looking particularly concerned.

"You should always trust your feelings," he told her. They came around the corner to find the television crew. Barry Weiss, wearing a Viking's-purple colored vest with a monogrammed BWR, was beaming as he awaited the broadcast.

Barry approached Cade, putting a hand on his shoulder. "Sorry if I was hard on you, but it's just business. Like they say, anything for a story. I know you'd do the same."

Cade knew he wouldn't ever stoop to the lows Weiss had exhibited, but now wasn't the time to tell him that. He simply nodded, and Weiss went back to his crew.

Rook leaned in and said, "You never answered the question. Who's our spokesman?"

"He'll tell you." Cade pointed to Barry, who stepped in front of the lights and camera. He held a microphone with BWR on a large nameplate. The guy with the camera held up three fingers. Barry rotated his head from side to side. Two fingers. He stuck out a tongue and made an odd bird-like retching sound. One finger. Barry closed his eyes.

On what would have been zero, his eyes popped open. He looked directly into the camera.

"This is Barry Weiss from the groundbreaking Barry Weiss Report. The Minnesota major crimes task force, Five Below, battled amazing odds and dire circumstances to stop not one, not two, but three serial killers. Led by Cade Dawkins from the Minnesota State Patrol, the task force included Terrance Rooker, from Minneapolis P.D. and Kristen Bednarek and Lorie Thao from the St. Paul police department. Grace Fox from the BCA also worked with the task force. I spoke with Governor Winston Ritter, who said, and I quote,

'Cade Dawkins has always had my support and is respected by his peers for his brilliance and professionalism.'"

Cade shook his head. "Always" felt like a strong word for the Governor's wishy-washy support.

"I have the feeling he's going to regret saying that," Rook said quietly.

"Me too," Lorie said.

"As longtime fans know, the Barry Weiss Report is the leader in delivering exclusive breaking news. The newly appointed communications director for Five Below has joined us today for a significant announcement. Ladies and gentlemen, Gordy Stensrude."

Rook looked at Cade wide-eyed. "You didn't. Your whack-job friend Gordy?"

Rob also looked surprised. "Did you really?"

Grinning, Cade nodded. "I did."

"This is you giving karma a helping hand, isn't it?" Rook asked. Cade didn't reply but simply smiled.

"This is getting interesting," Capt. Rejene said, failing to hide a growing grin.

Gordy sauntered his way out before pausing to bump fists with Cade. Gordy followed the bump with the exploding fist follow-up gesture.

He winked at Grace and stuck his tongue out at Rob. If Barry saw this, he didn't let on.

The two men stood shoulder to shoulder at an angle so they roughly faced each other. It was a study in contrast with Barry looking very Lands' End, ready for a camping trip or possibly a safari. Gordy was dressed in a dark suit with a red and white polka-dot tie. It didn't appear that he had tucked in his white shirt in the back. He completed the outfit with white Converse high-tops. It was an unusually understated ensemble for Gordy.

"He looks pretty good," Rook said, leaning in. "You bought him that suit, didn't you?"

"I did," Cade said with a grin. "I wanted him to make a good impression."

The two men shook hands. "Thank you for the honor of making your announcement live on the Barry Weiss Report."

"No problem, reporter dude," Gordy said. "Can I?" He stuck out his hand for the microphone.

The expression on Barry's face was priceless. He looked hurt and sad, like the first grader having to give his school lunch Twinkie to the mean fifth grader. But he handed it over.

"Hey," Rook said quietly in Cade's ear. "See that guy off to the left? The one headed for the exit?"

A man in a plaid shirt, jeans, and work boots walked across the lobby.

"See how he walks?" Rook said, clutching his arm. "Notice how his right foot turns inward and wobbles. I think that's the dude who got away that dark day."

"Well, go get him, then," Cade said. "Follow him and see what he's up to."

"Later, boss," Rook said with a smile as he slipped away.

In front of the cameras and the growing group of onlookers, Gordy took the microphone from Weiss. He briefly examined it before making a show of wiping it off under his arm.

Someone giggled behind him.

Gordy loudly cleared his throat and spoke into the microphone. "First of all, I'd like to thank Bradley Weiss here, our honorable Governor, and his excellence, the Pope."

Cade stepped back and whispered to Grace. "Want to get out of here?"

Grace shot a look toward the circus that was the Barry Weiss Report. She shrugged. "Sure. Nothing's happening here."

They snuck away and turned the corner away from the crowd. Gordy was saying something about the hidden danger of protein receptors in broadcast signals.

Cade reached out and held Grace's hand. "How are you feeling?" he asked.

Grace smiled. "Feeling blessed." She squeezed his hand.

"You know, for an avowed atheist, you don't talk like one."

"I'm an enigma," she said with a mischievous grin. "Deal with it."

Cade couldn't help but smile.

ACKNOWLEDGMENTS

There are times that characters write themselves—certainly making a writer's life easier. As is my tradition, I'm letting one of my characters speak for me. In this case, my colorful character Gordy Stensrude wanted to make the acknowledgments. Buckle up for the ride:

Hiya, Gordy here. First, a big congratulations on finishing this book. Now go post a review. Allan swears it's not an ego thing, but it's important in getting this book noticed and finding a wider audience. I'll wait here until you're back.

Thank you for that honest review. We're flattered. And if you know any movie producers, feel to drop our names. Now, on to the writer guy's thanks yous.

The idea for this book came as Allan was on the treadmill at the YMCA (thanks Y folks) and he said it gave him goosebumps. There's a rule in life that says if something gives you goosebumps, you have to write about it. Just ask R. L. Stine.

A shoutout to the people that work in the coffee shops he frequents. Without you and the caffeine you so wondrously deliver, this writer guy would still be on the first chapter. You rock.

A special thanks to Melonie and Bill Fischer, who graciously offered to share their home so Allan and his family wouldn't be homeless. No one wants that. And fun fact: they offered great background on computer systems and the dark web. Stuff that helped this book be better. Thanks, guys; he owes you big time.

Allan really wants to thank everyone at Immortal Works Press. This boutique (small) publisher puts out some amazing literary works. And this book. Specifically, Allan mentions his editor, John M. Olsen, for sticking with him for three books now. Staci Olsen for taking a chance on Allan in the first place, as well as her legendary layout skills. Creative Manager, Ashley Literski for her brilliant cover design. Chief Editor Holli Anderson for being a great chief. And

Publisher Jason King for sending over that multi-million-dollar contract in the first place. While he's fully aware that money can't buy happiness, Allan says he wouldn't mind being known as the melancholy guy who drives the red Lamborghini Diablo VT 6.0.

Allan's family is important to him and he wants you to know that novels don't just happen. Having a family of loved ones behind him is the secret to his success. Thank you, Jen, as well as Abbey, Andrew, Ben, Cade, Dan and Suzanna for supporting, caring and listening to his near-endless plot ideas. Also, thanks to his mother, Eleanor and brother, Mark. And Tucker, his Cavalier King Charles spaniel. A magnificent beast if there ever was one.

Other people he'd like to thank (honestly, this guy won't stop talking) include the coaching family and players of the St. Croix Soccer Club. Local bookstores near him such as Valley Booksellers in Stillwater and Lake Country Booksellers in White Bear Lake. Author John Sandford and his Prey series for motivating Allan to write in the first place. His fellow Immortal Works authors. Also, Ian Punnett, the Pope, M. Night Shyamalan, Stan Lee, Lynda Carter, Jeff Probst, the cast of Ted Lasso and the person who invented the turbocharger. (Some of these may have been mine.)

And the friends who inspired many of this book's characters. To paraphrase a common legal disclaimer: any resemblance to actual persons, living or dead, is meant to be a compliment. Love to you all.

Okay, he's done. Finally.

I have just one important thank you of my own: Thanks to all the UFOs that stop by to visit our little planet. It makes things a bit more interesting.

~Gordy (for Allan)

ABOUT THE AUTHOR

Author Allan Evans has been finding success of late. His debut novel, Abnormally Abbey, was published in 2020, and the follow-up, Class Clown, came out in 2022. Silent Night, a short story, was in the Haunted Yuletide anthology (2020) and a serial killer thriller, Killer Blonde (the first in this series), was published in 2021.

Son of famed Twin Cities jazz musician Doc Evans, Evans has written advertising and marketing for nearly two decades. A soccer coach, he can often be found on the field teaching kids about soccer and life. Evans lives in the Twin Cities.

Visit evanswriter.com to learn more.

This has been an
Immortal Production

Printed in the USA
CPSIA information can be obtained
at www.ICGtesting.com
LVHW041659230524
780932LV00008B/476